THE PRICE OF COMPASSION

THE GOLDEN CITY - BOOK FOUR

A.B. MICHAELS

THE PRICE OF COMPASSION
The Golden City *Book Four*

For permission requests, please write to:

Red Trumpet Press

P. O. Box 171162

Boise, ID 83716

Cover Design by Tara Mayberry

www.TeaberryCreative.com

ALSO BY A.B. MICHAELS

"The Golden City" historical series:

The Art of Love

The Depth of Beauty

The Promise

Josephine's Daughter (2019)

"Sinner's Grove" contemporary romantic suspense series:

Sinner's Grove

The Lair

The Jade Hunters (2019)

To those who make difficult, life-altering decisions and have the courage to take responsibility for them.

ACKNOWLEDGMENTS

Writing a novel is a big undertaking, but not a solitary one. Thank you to my dear friend Ted Daley, a retired surgical nurse, for talking me through the process of opening a human being, repairing the inside, and closing it again. Your diagrams look better than mine.

Thank you to friend and fantasy author Donna Cook for pointing out after an early read that there were two books in the draft, not one. You were spot on!

To my editor, Andrea Robinson, I truly appreciate your meticulous work in helping me shape my vision; I will never look at ellipses quite the same way again.

To Tara, your talent for creating such lovely, expressive book covers is matched only by your forbearance in dealing with my half-baked ideas. I'm privileged to be able to work with you.

And, as always, a great big sloppy kiss to Mike for

putting up with my repeated exclamations of "Dang, this is a good story!" and for giving me unlimited support. You mean everything to me.

HISTORICAL NOTE

The incident at the heart of *The Price of Compassion* can be found in the history books—but that doesn't mean it happened. In post-disaster hearings, a Red Cross worker testified that such an event occurred, but others refuted the allegations, and official reports from that era deny that any such tragedy took place. Of course, those were the same authorities who recorded an absurdly low death toll—a number that, while still unknown, is now estimated to have been roughly six times higher than those in power would have had the citizenry believe. So, one may believe or disbelieve what happened at the Mechanics' Pavilion that fateful day; I simply created a story based on what might have happened.

The Price of Compassion is populated by a number of historical figures who kindly became flesh-and-blood characters. William Halsted, William Muldoon, Donaldina Cameron, and Sofie Herzog did indeed exist, along with ancillary characters such as the founder of the Bank of Italy (you know it today as the Bank of America), the founders of Saint Francis Hospital, the members of Michigan's history-making 1894 football team, and a number of medical and military figures involved in the post-quake evacuation efforts.

Medical belief in neurasthenia was well established by the turn of the twentieth century and served as the "diagnosis du jour" for several famous individuals, including writers, artists, politicians, and titans of industry. While the concept of improperly using one's allotment of "nervous energy" seems far-fetched today (as do the bizarre devices invented to "cure" the syndrome), back then it was latched on to by many who desperately sought answers for their ailments, from skin rashes all the way through alcoholism and even insanity. William Muldoon's "Hygienic Institute of New York" was among the first destinations in the country designed to address these issues from a physical fitness perspective. Combined with rapid advances in medical science, it must have been a heady time for those who had heretofore been told to just live (or die) with whatever physical or emotional challenge they'd been dealt.

The period between the Civil War and World War I is considered the golden age of American railroads. Railway surgeons flourished during the latter part of that period, leading to innovations in workplace safety, company-sponsored healthcare, trauma medicine, and techniques for intensive care. By 1900, these specialists comprised up to ten percent of the country's physicians and had their own journal, *The Railway Surgeon*.

In depicting the historical aspects of *The Price of Compassion*, I remained true to the historical record as much as possible, deviating only when necessary to serve the story's needs. Any mistakes are naturally my own.

For a list of books consulted in writing this novel, please visit www.abmichaels.com.

CHAPTER ONE

February 1907

W*ould a sane man have done what I did?* Tom Justice pondered that question as he lay on his narrow cot in the Ingleside County Jail, waiting for the dim light of morning to illuminate his cell. The air wafting in from San Francisco Bay was icy and dank, and smelled of mold mixed with disinfectant and misery. Far down the hall he could hear the jangling of keys, a tease of freedom.

When he could see well enough, he held up his right hand, palm out, fingers extended. By now the topography was so familiar, he could have mapped it. Veins, tendons, joints. Ridges and valleys extending from his arm to long tanned digits, lightly sprinkled with hair. The nails still clean and blunt. He looked at his hand and wondered *What is it going to be today? What will you put me through?* For so long, he'd gotten the wrong answer, or been fooled by it.

He waited for the answer and there was...nothing.

For the fifth day in a row. Nothing.

He almost laughed at the irony of it.

He sat up on the cot, pushing the coarse, government-issue blanket aside. In the corner, a scarred and spindly table held a jug of water and a bowl. He splashed his face and dried it with the scrap of towel he'd been given, surveying his beard in the small, cracked mirror hanging on the wall. He hadn't bothered asking for a razor, not knowing if they'd even give him one. But he could have shaved himself, easily. After five days, the lack of tremor meant one of two things: either he was convinced, at last, of his innocence...or accepting, in the end, of his guilt. Which was it?

The jangling grew louder and the guard rapped on the bars lightly, as if it were a social call. Mr. Kirby was a big, red-faced Irishman with a walrus mustache and sky-blue eyes. He was known for "educating" troublesome inmates when the need arose, which made his sweet deference to Tom all the more surprising.

"Mornin', doc," he said, handing a plate of mush and cornbread through the slot in the cell door. "Got your steak and eggs, pipin' hot."

"Looks delicious, Mr. Kirby." With a faint smile, Tom took the plate and set it on the table. "How's the hanging business today?"

Mr. Kirby's mustache twitched; he didn't appreciate that sort of levity. "Don't you go putting ideas like that out there where they don't belong," he warned. "That's askin' for trouble." He put his beefy arms on the bars and leaned in, sharing a confidence. "You're to have a visitor today. A Mr. Perris. Some la-di-da barrister from London, they tell me." He didn't sound impressed.

"Didn't know I was being tried in Jolly Old England," Tom said.

The guard shook his head. "I don't get it neither, but there it is. The idea of you killin' your own flesh and blood just don't make sense, period. You ask me, the whole thing's a bunch of shite."

Two hours later, Jonathan Perris, Esquire, arrived. Tom put aside the issue of *The Lancet* he'd been reading and stood up to greet him. The attorney was just under six feet tall with russet hair and a medium build. His hazel eyes had a wary look about them. He dressed the part of an upper-crust Englishman, all buttoned-up and formal. No doubt he'd move easily in the city's highest social circles. But there was something else about him: he didn't look to the manor born. Tom sensed some grit beneath the polish. That was comforting, somehow; it seemed like an asset in the man's line of work.

Mr. Perris immediately addressed the oddity of his accent. "Obviously I am not your typical 'good old boy,'" he explained, his tone mildly derisive. "I told Miss Firestone that I may not be the right person to represent you, since I've only just passed your state's bar."

Amused, Tom nodded. "But she insisted you were exactly the person I needed, that no one else would do. Do I have it right?"

Perris's eyebrows shot up. "Precisely. It sounds like you know Miss Firestone very well." When Tom didn't answer, the man continued. "She said that although she was perfectly capable of hiring any number of high-profile attorneys, she feared that their connections, political and otherwise, might prejudice the outcome. Do you think she has a point?"

Ah, already he was probing. The poor sod was probably wondering what the hell he'd gotten himself into. Was he up to the task? "I think Miss Firestone is a very intelligent woman, and I am incredibly grateful that she and her family have offered to find me counsel. If she's chosen you it's because she believes in you, simple as that." He indicated that Perris take a seat on his cot while he took the lone rickety chair that Mr. Kirby had scrounged for him. "You will of course keep track of your hours so that I can reimburse you if and when I'm able."

"She said you'd say that," Perris murmured. He busied himself pulling out a notebook from his briefcase along with a fancy fountain pen. Then he looked up, his gaze direct and unwavering. "You should know that no matter who pays me, I will do my utmost to represent you, just as I've done for my own countrymen for the past ten years. Justice works the same way here as it does in England, you know: you are innocent until proven guilty." He paused. "As your defense counsel, I'm not obligated to ask you this question, but I'm going to anyway: In the aftermath of the earthquake and resulting fire last April eighteenth, did you commit the willful murder of which you have been accused?"

Tom knew that most defendants would deny the charge in their next breath, but he weighed his answer. "Some might say so," he said. "I've thought a lot about it, and at this point, I would have to say, in some regard, perhaps I did."

Perris's tone sharpened. "*Perhaps* you did? Come now, doctor. Either you did or you didn't."

Tom remained tranquil. "I suppose in most cases the answer would be clear-cut. And years ago I would have agreed with you that the answer *should* be so. But I have come to find that it's not always that simple."

Perris glanced around the confines of the cell and took a deep breath. The look he sent Tom was tinged with irritation. "I'm afraid that answer will be inadequate in a court of law, Dr. Justice. When this case comes to trial, you're going to face twelve thoughtful men who are more than willing to see the law carried out. If they believe you committed murder, they will see you hang for it. They need to be convinced beyond a reasonable doubt that you are innocent. Can you help me build a case that does that, sir?"

A sense of melancholy stole over Tom. Could he? "I certainly hope so," he said, "but I don't know for sure."

The attorney let out a discreet sigh. "Well then, there is most definitely work to be done." He opened his notebook and prepared to write. "I'll need a list of anybody who knows you and can vouch for your character. I'll also need to know anyone who might *not* be in your corner because you can rest assured the prosecution will talk to them. And more than anything, I must know how you got yourself into this bloody mess, so I can try to get you out of it. That means I need your story, from the beginning."

"That I believe I can do," Tom Justice said.

Jonathan headed down the steps of the Ingleside facility's main entrance, turning his collar up against the chill of the fog. In front of him stretched a wide, landscaped courtyard leading around to the car park. Spying an unoccupied bench next to a trio of aspens, he sat down to collect his thoughts before braving traffic in his new Franklin Laudalette. Why people drove on the wrong side of the street in America was beyond him.

As far as jails went, Ingleside wasn't bad at all; England put up with far worse, having no desire to update its dreary, centuries-old gaols with anything more than a few gas lamps and steel toilet seats. And Ingleside had survived the big quake, which was admirable in and of itself.

Nevertheless, it was not a place in which any sane person would choose to remain, if he or she could possibly help it.

The question was, would Tom Justice help himself?

During his time in London, Jonathan had dealt with clients of all stripes, good and bad. Thieves, reprobates, even killers—no matter how high the mountain of evidence against them, they'd always, *always* proclaimed their innocence. After a certain point in his career, Jonathan had learned how to ferret out the truth, and fairly quickly.

But not in this case. At least not yet.

Perhaps it was the doctor's appearance. Tom Justice stood comfortably over six feet, with longish dark hair and a healthy beard. Dressed in drab prison-issue garments, he'd looked rather like a muscle-bound laborer—not the type you'd expect to see performing surgical procedures requiring years of education and a fine hand. Yet he'd been reading a respected medical journal and taking notes, as if he were still in practice and wanted to learn the latest techniques. Outwardly he was unruffled, yet there seemed to be a current of turbulence beneath. Was he anxious and adept at hiding it, or truly serene? That is what perplexed Jonathan the most: he could not read the man.

But he had promised Katherine to represent him, and represent him he would.

"He is not guilty," she'd told Jonathan emphatically the day she'd hired him. She'd invited him to lunch and he'd been so happy to see her, until she explained what she needed and who she needed it for. Her feelings for Tom Justice were obvious, but her defense of him wasn't sufficient to prove his innocence. Indeed, she could offer no solid evidence to back her claim. Even though she'd been with Justice on that horrific day, she hadn't been present during the actual time of the murder.

If there even *was* a murder.

Jonathan pulled out his notebook again and

scanned the lengthy list of those who knew Tom Justice and could vouch for him. Then he reviewed the record of those who might be happy to see him hang. He'd been given carte blanche to collect depositions and whatever additional evidence he could find. Katherine had told him to spare no expense.

It was the intensity of her request that sobered him. He and Katherine had gotten to know each other over the past several months and he was beginning to think something closer might develop between them. If he succeeded in getting the doctor acquitted, he knew at his core that he would lose her completely. If he failed, he might gain her company, but not her heart. It was a damnable conundrum.

She believes in you, simple as that. Tom Justice had hit the nail on the proverbial head. Jonathan would do whatever it took to clear the man of the charges against him because a charming, beautiful, intelligent woman believed he could do it. Yes, it was that simple.

Once more he perused the list. Where to begin? Nebraska, it looked like. The cold-blooded killer that the prosecution would try to sell to the jury had started out as a simple farm boy.

Jonathan could build on that. He would have to.

CHAPTER TWO

"He was large for his age, and seemed older, somehow. Sometimes he'd look at me like he was trying to figure me out. It was a bit unnerving, if you want to know the truth."

—Mrs. Francis Hill, Neighbor

Sometimes the days that change your life forever play tricks on you. They disguise themselves as just another morning's worth of chores, or a carefree summer afternoon. Sometimes you don't even realize their power until years, maybe decades later, when you finally look back and say, "Ah. That's where it all started."

Thomas Aaron Justice saved his first life on a day like that. He lost a life that day, too. He was ten years old.

"The accident," as he referred to it for years afterward, involved his cousin Eli Porter, who was two years older and a city boy who had spent the previous summer with the Justice family on their farm a few hours west of North Platte, Nebraska. Their mothers were sisters and Trudy Porter was once again traveling halfway across the world to visit her husband, John, an officer in the U.S. Army. One good thing about the summer of 1883: there was no real fighting going on, at least overseas. You couldn't make the same claim about Tom and Eli.

"He doesn't like me," Tom complained to his mother when she told him his cousin would be returning for a second summer. "He's sweet as molasses around you and Pa, but when we're by ourselves, he always wants to be top dog, and he always gets mad when I beat him."

Meg Justice glanced at Tom while she skinned cellar potatoes at the worn but spotless kitchen table. Sunlight slanted through the window, a light breeze ruffling the blue dimity curtains. "You know why that is?"

He studied the peelings, picking at one of them, not wanting to say what he felt to be true. "Not sure," he mumbled.

"I think you know." She submerged a cut potato in a half-filled bowl of vinegar water. "You can say it. It's just us."

Tom looked up at her. She wasn't blond and dainty like Mrs. Hill, his friend Joshua's mom, or fat and gray-haired like the old Mason sisters. She was strong and solid and calm, and she had dark brown hair and eyes, just like Tom did. She waited for him to speak.

"I dunno. I reckon it's because he's kind of little, but he wants to be big and strong like his daddy."

His mother nodded. "So you think maybe you could let him win some of the time?"

Tom puzzled through that idea. "That doesn't make much sense. You and Pa always say it's easy to win when you cheat. But isn't that about the same thing? I mean, it's easy to lose when you cheat, too. Either way, the winner didn't really win fair and square, did he?"

"Sometimes there are other things to consider." She handed him a slice of raw potato. It crunched cold and clean, tasting like the earth it came from. "Just be nice to Eli," she said, "or as nice as you can. Because I know he misses his daddy very much."

Eli came two weeks later and things played out pretty much as Tom thought they would. Eli would challenge him over just about anything, from how fast they could milk a cow to how many berries they could pick in five minutes. Eli didn't care if they had an audience or not; he just wanted to win. And Tom, who lived and worked on the farm year-round, beat him at just about every task. His friend Bart Palmer even called Tom aside one afternoon to ask, "What's up with that pint-sized cousin of yours? Don't he know you're gonna whup him every time?"

Tom had shrugged it off. "He's got his reasons."

Late that summer, on the day in question, the sun was blazing after half a week of welcome rain. The sky was cobalt blue as far as a boy could see, the clouds all wiped away, and the farm's endless fields of deep-green corn waved their wispy blond tassels in the breeze.

But today, the corn field they ran through wasn't just a corn field. It was a jungle maze like the one Eli's pop said he'd fought in down in Colombia years before. Carrying their "army rations" and towels in flour sacks, they had to race through the wilds in order to outrun the jaguar and reach the river, because everybody knew big cats didn't like the water. Playing the jaguar was the dog Eli had brought with him: a scruffy white terrier named Sergeant who barked nonstop, as if he had to tell anybody who would listen about his good fortune. Bein' a city dog off his leash must have felt like heaven, but he sure was noisy about it.

"My daddy sent special money for me to get Sergeant," Eli boasted the day he arrived. "Too bad you don't have a dog."

He'd scored a direct hit. Tom had been asking his folks for a pet for a couple of years and tried again in early August when Bobbie Patterson's border collie had a litter of black and white puppies. But Tom's pa hadn't budged.

"Let's wait until your little brothers are old enough not to get knocked over and then we'll see," he'd said. "What with the babies and your Nana Ruth, your ma and me got enough goin' on right now."

Tom's grandma was recovering from a broken arm, and his brothers were barely out of diapers, so it was going to be a while.

"I'm gonna beat you this time," Eli yelled as he pumped his shorter legs to gain ground on Tom. "Bet you a bag of penny candy I will!"

Do it, then, Tom thought, irritated. He considered

slowing his pace, so his cousin could feel like the big dog. But no matter what his ma said, it didn't seem right to throw the race, because, well, he *was* faster. He easily picked up speed.

The North Platte was a wide, relatively shallow, and meandering river, even during spring run-off. A good part of the floodplain was planted in corn and wheat, but close to the water, cheatgrass and cattail lined much of the banks, presiding over marshy bogs. Tom, who knew the terrain well in all seasons, emerged from the corn field first, then veered to a solid path that ran between the soggy patches and led up a slight incline to a stand of cottonwoods, one of which was thick enough to handle a rope swing. Tom's dad had strung it up at the beginning of the summer, telling the boys, "You be sure to swing way out where it's deep enough, you hear? Your mamas won't be happy with me if you come back with cracked noggins on account of hittin' your heads in the shallows."

Eli caught up and they dropped their bundles to climb up to the branch that was just below the dangling rope. It reminded Tom of a gallows.

Having lost the race (again), Eli decided they'd see who could swing out the farthest.

"I'll bet you another bag I can swing out to that log sticking up in the middle, with the water swirling around it. I'll drop a rock straight down right on top of it. The first rock that stays there wins."

Eli swung and swung, but the rope didn't carry him far enough, and every stone he tossed ended up in the river. Tom could have told him it wasn't going to work, but figured Eli had to learn that for himself. He did, finally, and after a while he gave up and dropped into the water. Tom followed him into the river while Sergeant barked from the shoreline, scaring some whimbrels from the reeds who flapped away in distress.

They passed the afternoon that way, stopping to pull out their pocketknives and devour the biscuits and cheese and sweet, blood-red raspberries Tom's ma had packed for them. Letting the sun dry their bodies, they used the towels as pillows, lying with their feet almost in the water. They chattered for a while—or rather, Eli chattered and Tom half-listened, until they both dozed in the warm shade of the cottonwood. Sometime later, Tom woke up and sensed something different.

There was no sound.

He turned to his cousin. "Hey, you notice something?"

"Yeah. You woke me up."

"No, I mean there's no barking. Where's Sergeant?"

Eli sat up and looked around. "Sergeant!" he called out. "Here boy!"

Nothing.

"Maybe he went back home." Tom started to stuff the remains of their meal back into his sack. "He's probably waitin' for you."

Eli scrambled up. "He don't know the way. He's probably lookin' for birds. Sergeant!"

The boys began searching around the trees, calling every few seconds, but there was no response. Eli ran ahead, away from the cornfield and along the riverbank.

"You gotta watch out," Tom called. "There's soggy patches all along the water."

But Eli paid little heed, consumed as he was with finding his dog. Tom could hear how worried he was by the change in his voice. He was calling out, frantic now, pleading. "Sergeant! Come here, boy! Where are you?!"

For once Tom fell behind his cousin, enough that Eli was out of sight when Tom heard his shrill scream of "No! No!" along with a splash.

The shore along the river was filled with grass-choked wetlands that hid murky pools with no firm edge, smelling of rot and easy to fall into but not so simple to get out of, especially for a curly-haired dog with short legs and a tendency to panic.

When Tom found his cousin, Eli had already pushed the grasses aside and jumped in to reach Sergeant, who was floating in the middle of a large stagnant pond, several yards away from the path. The black water was deep, and Eli was paddling hard through the muck. Tears streaming down his face, he yelled "Help me! I think he's still alive! Help me get him!" But Sergeant looked to be already dead, and once Eli grabbed him, he just wasn't big enough to carry the dog's wet body and swim at the same time. He slipped beneath the surface once before fighting his way back to the top.

"He's gone," Tom cried. "You gotta let him go now!" He looked around frantically for a stick, or a branch, or anything he could hold out for Eli to grab onto, but he couldn't find anything strong enough. His cousin kept crying and kicking his legs, and Tom could tell he was getting tangled up beneath the water. A plan came to him, but he needed his cousin to cooperate for it to work.

"Eli. Eli." Tom tried his best to sound as sensible as his pa. "You gotta listen to me now. Are you listenin'? Are you listenin'?"

It took a long, long minute, but at last Eli sniffed and said, "Y-yes. I'm listening."

"Good. You see those grasses over to your right?" He pointed, and Eli half turned in that direction.

"I see 'em."

"I want you to work your way over and hold on to them, you hear me?" I'm gonna go get the rope, and—"

"No! Don't leave us! Just come in here and help me get Sergeant out, and—"

"I'm not gonna go in there. It's not safe. I'm gonna go and get the rope and pull you out. But you gotta hold on to those grasses and quit movin' around so much. Can you do that? I'll wait until you've got a firm hold on 'em."

Eli was breathing hard now, but he started to dog paddle his way slowly toward the grass. When he made it to the first tall clump, he reached out, but only with one hand because he still clutched his dog with the other.

"You gotta let go of Sergeant for a little while," Tom said in the same firm, clear voice. "He's not goin' anyplace. You hold on to that grass with both hands and you don't let go until I come back, okay?"

Eli sniffed and nodded, finally letting go of his sad package. When Tom could see he was clinging to the reeds with both hands, he hightailed it back to the tree with the swing, pulling out his pocket knife and shimmying up beyond the jumping branch and up to the hanging branch where the rope was tied. He sawed through it as quickly as he could, taking care to wrap his hand around it so he wouldn't lose it in the water when it dropped. Then he coiled it up and slung it over his shoulder, climbing back down and running back to the bog. Eli was shaking all over, barely clinging to the grasses. Sergeant had floated back out to the middle of the blackness.

"I'm gonna tie my end down and then throw the other to you," Tom said. He found an old tree root hidden by grass to use as an anchor, testing it for strength. He tried throwing the rope out to Eli, but it wasn't long enough, so he wrapped the other end around his wrist and waded into the mud and the slime himself, until he was within a few feet of him. The water was up to his neck and getting deeper when he stretched out his hand as far as he could. "Take it," he called. "Let go now and come to me. It's just a few feet."

But Eli hadn't given up on Sergeant and looked back to where the dog was floating, as if he might swim back to him.

"No," Tom said. "You leave Sergeant where he is. You need to come this way right now." He was surprised at how old he sounded. Like an old man.

Eli hesitated, but then, with one last look back, he left the safety of the swamp grass and paddled awkwardly through the muck to reach out and grasp Tom's hand. Slowly, together, they worked their way back to firm ground.

For several minutes they just lay there, most likely in shock. A gust of wind came up, rustling the grass like a dog might have. Tom looked over and saw that while Eli had stopped crying, he was still shivering, even more than before.

"We've got to get back home," Tom said. "We'll bring my pa back and he'll figure out a way to get Sergeant out of there."

But Eli shook his head. "We can't do that."

"Why not?" Tom was already up, coiling the rope again. "Don't worry, my pa will know what to do."

"No, we're not going to tell them." Eli was on his feet now, too, only he was pacing with a strange look in his eyes and a high-pitched edge to his voice. "I can't let them know about Sergeant." He grabbed Tom by the shoulders. "It was up to me to keep him safe and I didn't do it! What'll my daddy think when he hears that? What'll he *think?*"

He was making Tom nervous. "What are you talking about? We can't just go home and pretend nothing happened."

"We go home and we say, 'Where's Sergeant?' as if he'd up and run home ahead of us. And when he's not there, we look all around so it'll look like he's run away. That's all."

"I don't know. It just doesn't seem right."

Eli was breathing hard now. "Follow me," he ordered with such ferocity that Tom couldn't do anything but comply. They went back to the place where they'd left their sacks and Eli pulled out his knife. Before Tom could say a word, his cousin had sliced across his own palm. A bright red line appeared. "Now you," he said.

"What are you doing?"

"We need to swear a blood brother oath. Hold out your hand."

Tom thought his cousin was a little cracked, but Eli's desperation brought to mind what his mother had said, to try to be as nice to him as possible. But there was no way Tom was going to let Eli cut him with a knife. He took out his own blade and carefully cut his right palm until a faint trickle of blood emerged.

"That ain't deep enough," Eli said. "Go deeper."

He reached over and Tom jumped back, causing the knife to slide deep into his palm.

"Dammit!" Tom said as blood began to gush. He tried to press the wound tightly with the edge of the sack, but Eli pushed his hand away and mixed his blood with Tom's.

"Now we're blood brothers and we swear a blood oath that can't never be broken. We never tell what happened here today—what we did, what happened to Sergeant, none of it."

"Blood brothers." Tom tried the words on for size. It all happened so fast, he didn't know what he thought. But promises were important, and he felt honor-bound to keep this one.

It all transpired as Eli had predicted: They shoved the sliced rope swing under a bush and returned home, asking Tom's mother if she'd seen the dog. She hadn't, of course, so they spent all that evening and the next day pretending to look for him. Eli didn't seem to have much problem acting sad that his dog had disappeared.

"I guess he just got lost," Eli said on the third day, after Tom's pa had spent several hours driving them around in the farm wagon to search a wider area. Each yell of "Here Sergeant, here boy!" felt like a nail pounded into the coffin of Tom's good character. More than once he made up his mind to confess the whole sorry tale to his parents, only to second-guess his decision. He'd made a blood oath, and besides, he wondered what would happen if Eli's dad learned his son had failed to do his duty.

In a few days they would have taken a longer rope back to the bog and used it to haul Sergeant out of the water, except that Tom, although he didn't know it at the time, had begun a fight for his own life, or at the very least, a vital part of it.

CHAPTER THREE

"He knew an awful lot about aches and pains and the old ways of fixing you up. Helped me out a time or two. Said he learned it from his grandma."

— CLYDE SHUMWAY, PATRON OF BALTIMORE'S OLD HORSE SALOON

Nana Ruth liked to tell people she was a Nebraskan before there was even a Nebraska. She also liked to boast that America fought a war over her, after which she'd always chortle and say, "The Lord strike me dead if that ain't the goldarn truth." That was on account of her being born in 1812, the same year America went to war with England, which Tom found out later had nothing really to do with her. It was also the same year President Madison created the Missouri Territory, which had Nebraska in it. She had a real strong sense of her own importance, Nana Ruth did.

She was a Plains woman, all bony and pruney by the time Tom knew her, her face carved by the sun and wind. Even though Tom's pa had built her a room in what she always called "The Big House," she preferred to live in her own little sod house on the far edge of the farm. Paul Justice was Nana's youngest son, and Tom could tell his father was still a little bit afraid of her, so he let her have her way.

A while back she'd fallen and broken her arm while tending the garden next to her house. She probably would have gone along without telling anybody if Tom and his ma hadn't brought the babies over in the wagon to visit. When they saw that Nana Ruth was only using the one arm to fix some coffee, Tom's ma had said in her quiet way, "Ruth, looks like you broke a wing, so you're coming to stay with us until you're better. Otherwise you'll cause your son all kinds of worry that he doesn't need or deserve. So tell me what you want to bring because you're riding back with us today." And Tom's mom must have had some kind of power over her, because Nana Ruth didn't kick up a fuss; she just did as she was told.

Which meant she was front and center when Tom and Eli returned from the bog without Sergeant, and she was there when Tom's hand started to swell up and jagged red streaks started radiating from the deep cut on his palm like the tentacles of an octopus.

Tom tried his best to cover it up around the grown-ups. But the third morning after Sergeant's "disappearance," he was found out. While his mother was upstairs putting his brothers down for a nap, and Eli was outside keeping up the charade of looking for his dog, Nana Ruth shocked Tom by pointing to the hand he'd been keeping in his pocket and saying, "Let's take a look at that wound you been hidin'."

He stopped short. How could she know a thing like that?

"I weren't born yesterday, Tommy," she said, like she'd read his mind. She beckoned with her own good paw. "Out with it."

Tom slowly withdrew his hand, which by now was a swollen, ugly stump that hurt like a son of a bitch. For all her verbal bluster, Nana Ruth's hands were gentle when she turned his palm toward the light coming in from the kitchen window. Tom could hear Eli's faint, halfhearted calls for Sergeant out in the yard.

"I ain't going to ask you how you got this, because you wouldn't be hidin' it if you weren't ashamed. But you got some gathering here," she said, pointing to the pus under the surface, "and those lines mean your blood's got some poison in it." She walked him over to the sink and put his hand under the pump. "Now you take some of that cake soap and you wash the cut as best you can." She started opening cupboards. "I know your daddy has a snort once in a while. Where does he keep his spirits?"

Tom hesitated to admit he knew where his father kept the whiskey bottle, but in the end he figured Nana Ruth would keep a lid on that too. With one hand he pulled an empty fruit box over from the corner and stood on it, reaching behind the soffit of an upper cabinet to pull out the half-empty bottle of Old Overholt. He handed it to his grandmother and returned to gingerly cleaning the surface of his wound. She had found a clean, well-worn cotton dish rag and was tearing it into strips with her one good hand and surprisingly strong teeth. Putting the strips down, she took his hand again.

"Now, I won't lie, this is going to hurt like the dickens," she said, pouring a bit of the liquor over his cut.

He hissed as a tongue of fire swept over his hand.

"That ain't the half of it," she murmured, firmly squeezing the two sides of the cut so that the pus was forced out. It hurt so bad, Tom felt light-headed. He thought he might pass out.

"Sorry, son, we got to get the poison out." After she finished squeezing, she wiped all around the wound, poured a bit more of the whiskey inside of it, and reached for the honey jar on the table. Using the dipper, she poured a generous dollop over the cut, and then, motioning Tom to help, she wrapped the strips firmly around his palm.

"The sweet drowns out the poison," she told him, "kind of like the Good Lord drowns out the Devil."

She had just finished tying off the last strip when Tom's mother came into the room. "Finally got the pups to sleep," she said, wiping her hands on the apron she wore like a uniform. She looked at the two of them, smiling but quizzical. "What's going on, you two?" She noticed Tom's bandaged hand and frowned. "What happened?"

"Took out a sliver, that's all." Nana Ruth glanced at Tom. "Ain't that right, boy?"

Tom felt tears rushing up, along with a soul-abiding love for his grandma. He couldn't bear to look up. "Yes, ma'am, that's right."

"And Tom here offered to drive me over to my place, if that's all right with you," she added. "I need a few things."

Tom shot a glance at Nana Ruth, then chanced a peek at his mother. He realized with a spurt of panic that she had spied the bottle of whiskey on the table, and the step Tom had used to retrieve it. She made no comment, however, and casually put the bottle back in its supposed hiding place. "Sure, you two go on over. Just be back in plenty of time for supper."

As Tom and Nana Ruth made their way to the buckboard, Eli ran up. "Hey, where you goin'? Can I come?" He looked tired of playacting.

Tom was set to say yes, but Nana Ruth made her own decision with a clear "No, son, it's just me and Tom goin' this time."

Tom was quiet as he drove the horse, holding the reins gingerly. His hand throbbed, but so did his heart. He'd let another person in on the deception, even if it was just part of it and not the whole thing. He kept playing the events of that afternoon over and over in his mind, wondering if there could have been another outcome. Wondering if maybe Sergeant hadn't been dead and they could have saved him. Yet Nana Ruth didn't push or prod him to reveal what was gnawing at him. Part of him was relieved, but another part wished she would pull it out of him and he wouldn't have to keep it packed inside so tight.

Once they reached her little house, Nana Ruth wasted no time in explaining why they'd come. "We got to make sure that hand of yours don't fester. I got some medicines that'll help keep the poison from spreading."

By "medicines" she didn't mean the bottles of elixir or packets of powder that Doc Graham usually prescribed. She meant the rows of little jars and bottles lined up on a shelf by her kitchen sink; none of them were labeled.

As Tom stared at the containers, he wondered with a touch of trepidation if his grandma was actually a witch. Maybe she lived alone so she could practice magic. Maybe black magic.

"You think I'm gonna cast a spell on you?" she asked in that uncanny way she had of knowing what he was thinking.

He swallowed hard. "Uh, no, ma'am."

"Well, I wish I could, but we got to rely on Mother Nature to fix you up." Using her good arm to pull one jar down and then another, she took a pinch from each and mixed it with oil from yet another small bottle. This she handed to him. "Now you got to change your bandage every second day, and each time you do, you put some of this on your wound. Understand?"

At his nod, she turned again to her mysterious collection and pulled down a tall bottle that stunk to high heaven as soon as she opened it. After pouring some of the liquid into a spoon, she held it up to him. "Now, this won't win any blue ribbons at the state fair, but it'll help fight off any poison you got running through you. You got to take a spoonful of this every day until your cut heals over."

Tom instinctively held back. What if this was worse than the poison already inside him?

"Come on, I don't got all day. Be a man and take your medicine. Lord knows I gave some of this to your pa a time or two."

Tom closed his eyes and let Nana Ruth pour the strange elixir down his gullet. It burned all the way and he gagged. "That's horrible!" he cried.

"I know, but it works. I take it every day, rain or shine, just to keep my innards in good working order." To illustrate, she took a spoonful and swallowed it right down, neat as you please. Then she winked at him. "How else do you think I got to be so old?"

Laden with his oil, the sour-tasting medicine, and some clean rags for bandages, Tom and his grandma returned to the farmhouse.

"That must have been some sliver," Tom's pa remarked at dinner.

Tom and Nana Ruth exchanged glances, and Eli looked confused. "What sliver?" he asked.

Tom held up his hand, staring Eli down until he finally got the hint.

"Oh yeah, that one," Eli said.

That night, in the warm, dark cocoon of Tom's bedroom, Eli's voice cut the silence. "You told your grannie, didn't you?" He sounded disgusted.

"No I did not," Tom shot back. "She didn't ask any questions, so I didn't have to tell her no lies."

Neither spoke for several minutes, but Tom could tell by his breathing that Eli was still awake. Then Eli said, "I think my dad would shoot me if he knew what happened." His cousin's voice was small and unsure. "He's got a pistol and a rifle, you know."

Tom snorted, making his voice sound as certain as he could. "I don't believe that for a minute. You didn't do anything wrong."

"Maybe not," Eli said, "but I've been thinking... maybe *you* did."

A week after the accident, Eli announced after lunch that he was going down to the river. Knowing where he was headed, Tom set off with him without being asked. They made their way to the bog, but there was no trace of Sergeant. He had probably sunk, or maybe, Tom thought with a grimace, he'd been eaten by the critters who lived near the water.

Usually a talker, Eli didn't say a word. He didn't come out and accuse Tom, but he didn't have to; it was in his eyes, his demeanor, his attitude.

Even in the worst of situations, when each day seems like a never-ending civics lesson, time still plods on. The end of summer arrived at last and Eli's ma came back to get him.

Aunt Trudy looked happier than Tom had ever seen her. She was all aflutter because Eli's pop was returning from overseas, and her good news was like an injection of happiness for nearly everyone in the Justice house; it relegated the shadow of Sergeant's disappearance to that of a momentary cloud passing through a bright blue sky. "That's a shame," she said after hearing Eli's rendition of what happened. "He probably found another good family to stay with. Maybe we'll get you a new puppy once we're back home."

What Aunt Trudy really worried about, it seemed, was how Eli and Tom would cope with this being their last summer together. Now that Eli's father was going to serve stateside, she and Eli would visit him when Eli finished the next school year.

The day came for their departure, and Tom hung back, waiting for the blessed relief of no longer having to deal with Eli's silent censure.

"I don't know what's gotten into you two, but you'd best patch it up before he leaves," Tom's mother said to him in the kitchen that morning. Tom was a bit unnerved that she had seen the change in their relationship, so he tried to cover it up with a half-hearted "I'm just sorry to see him go, is all."

"Then let him know it. Give him a hug," she admonished. "Who knows, maybe next year you can travel back east to visit him."

That is never going to happen, Tom thought. *Not if I have anything to say about it.*

Tom's father was going to take Eli and his mother all the way to North Platte to catch the train east. When it came time to climb up on the wagon, Eli made a surprising move as if to hug Tom, but when he leaned in, he whispered, "I've thought it through. You could have saved both of us. But you didn't. You owe me."

Tom wrenched himself away. "Says you," he replied in a voice only Eli could hear. Then, in a manner totally unlike him, he added six words that he knew would slice through his cousin like the sharpest sword. "Wonder what your pa would say?"

The next time he saw Eli they were both grown men.

CHAPTER FOUR

*"That young man cared about book learning more than just
about anything else, including working on the farm.
Anything to do with the body, he wanted to know about. He
was like a sponge."*

—Dr. Andrew Graham, Family Physician

That summer with Eli did have a silver lining. It
sparked a new and unusual bond between Tom
and his grandmother. Nana Ruth eventually returned
to her little house, and when she did, Tom often visited
her, of his own accord, to learn more about the herbs
she grew and the remedies she made with them. Nana
Ruth called it their "garden time," which sounded innocent enough. But in truth she introduced Tom to a
world that to him seemed nearly magical.

The strange concoction Nana Ruth had insisted
Tom apply to his wound healed it remarkably well,

such that in a matter of days, the only sign that Tom had ever been injured was a small, puckered scar in the middle of his palm. He had recorded the process in a little notebook each night before he went to sleep. It seemed amazing, but simply accepting it as a miracle or an answered prayer wasn't enough. Instead, he was filled with questions. What exactly was pus and why had it formed around the cut? How did the honey keep more from forming? What were the red streaks and why did they disappear? If the herbs were responsible, how did they do it?

"You got more questions than a horse has flies," Nana Ruth told him during one of their morning sessions. "Sometimes you got to just listen to what I tell you, and then put the why's and the wherefores together in your head later on." She was showing him the tall green plant with pretty, horn-shaped flowers known as woolly foxglove. "Though I like the name 'Dead Men's Bells' better," she told him with a wink. "You give a man with a bad ticker some of this and there's a good chance you'll ring a bit more life out of him."

Tom had reached out to pull one of the flowers off and smell it, but Nana Ruth stayed his hand. "Mind yourself there, boy. In the wild, that's a poison and even touching it can cause you a world of hurt. I'll show you how to make a special tea from it later." She turned to a bush with small golden leaves. "Now this here bridewort—some call it 'meadowsweet'—can cure a sour stomach as well as a headache." She plucked some leaves, sniffed them, and handed the blossoms to

Tom. They smelled like marzipan. "In the olden days they used to spread these flowers on the floors of big old castles to cover up the stink. And they did that in the church too when a bride got married. That's how it got its name."

Nana Ruth was full of strange facts and funny stories like that, and Tom soaked them all up. He learned how fennel tea could "help your food keep movin' down the pipes" and how a brew made from hops was good for everything from lack of sleep to too many farts. When Tom giggled at that one, Nana Ruth smiled herself, but made her point: "You can tell if a man is sick by the gas he puts out, and sometimes, you can even tell what's ailin' him."

Using a stick she broke across her knee, she showed Tom how to set a bone. She pointed out the parts of the body that bled the most and how to stop too much blood from flowing. She told him about fevers and different ways you could get them to come down because "it ain't good for the body to be too hot for too long — scrambles your brain like eggs in a fryin' pan." She taught Tom that if you had the right knowledge, you could heal the sick, and even save lives. The idea of that burrowed right down into his soul.

Over the next four years, Tom slowly forgot about the incident with his cousin, pushing the memory to the back of his mind like an old pair of fancy shoes, long since outgrown and stuck in the back of a closet.

Tom got bigger and faster, and proved it on the athletic field. He'd always played baseball, but football had finally come to the small high schools in their part of the state, and he took to it like ice cream on apple pie. Long hours of tilling the soil, shucking corn, and mending fences had built up both his muscles and his stamina, and he used them to his advantage against the opposing team as he pushed to get the ball over the goal line.

He excelled at the game, even though it gave his parents fits to see him roughed up on the field. Nana Ruth, though, she whooped from the sidelines, his biggest fan. And when he'd show up at her house a day later, sporting the kinds of bruises he'd never show his mother, she knew just how to fix him up.

Yet his questions about *why* the healing happened stuck with him. Nana Ruth didn't have those answers, but Tom knew someone who might.

On an unusually warm Sunday afternoon in autumn, when the families of the congregation had gathered outside under a grove of old hackberry trees to share a midday supper, Tom gathered his courage and approached Doc Graham.

"Sir," he said, "I was wondering if I might borrow some of your medical books. That is, if you have any you can spare. I would take good care of them."

Slightly older than Tom's father, Andrew Graham was a portly man with a chest shaped like the cider barrels stacked in the Justices' barn. He had gone to college back east and always seemed to know the latest medical news and remedies. The man looked surprised at Tom's request. "How old are you, boy?"

"Nearly fifteen, sir."

"Well, you're a strapping young man; why aren't you spending your time helping your pa in the fields? A big farm like yours needs tending. Your pa can't do it all himself."

Tom winced at the question; it was already becoming an issue at home. He straightened his shoulders, tried to look affronted. "I help my pa plenty," he said. "I just got a lot of curiosity, that's all."

Doc Graham looked skeptical, so Tom grabbed a low-hanging hackberry branch and pulled off some seeds until he had a pile of the small, round drupes in his hand. He presented them to the physician. "You know anything about these?"

Doc Graham didn't bother to pick one up. He shrugged. "They're hackberries. They make a mess on the ground when they drop."

"Yes, sir, they do. But they're sweet and the Indians mash them up and use them for food. And they're also good for medicine."

The doctor frowned. "You don't say. And what do they supposedly cure?"

Tom felt his cheeks redden, and it wasn't from the sunshine. "My grandma says they help with a woman's time, and, um, they keep the bowels from jigglin' too much." He took one of the berries and bit into it. "They can also help when your head's poundin' or you're feeling poorly from the influenza."

Doc Graham nodded as if he took Tom's words

seriously and was considering trying the berries out on some of his own patients. But his response was flippant. "Sounds like your grandma's a font of wisdom when it comes to healing. If you believe her, why go elsewhere for your answers?"

Tom frowned. Did it have to be one or the other? Nana's way or the doc's way? No. What did the law say? It's important to get the truth, the *whole* truth. "I don't think it has to do with believing or not believing," he said finally. "My grandma tells me that hackberry drupes can help someone get well, but not how or why that happens. That's gotta be in those books you have, which is why I want to read them."

The doc's gaze was intense. "Why do you care so much?"

The memory of that long-ago summer day tapped Tom on the shoulder and he paused to pay it some mind. He recalled everything about it: the way the poor dog must have paddled around that bog in a frenzy before finally giving up...the way Eli had slipped beneath the surface...how it felt to bring him to safety...how Tom's hand had so mysteriously healed itself. He couldn't say why he cared so much, not just because of the oath he'd taken, but because the caring inside of him ran so deep, all the way down to his core, that the right words wouldn't come. He hid behind a shrug, but it must have been enough, because Doc Graham nodded and said, "You stop by my office the next time you're in town and I'll see what I can rustle up." And it felt like he'd given Tom a gift better than all the Christmas presents that had ever come before.

CHAPTER FIVE

"I don't know who was more torn up about saying goodbye, her son or her grandson. They both took it hard."

—THE REVEREND EDSELL CLARK, FIRST METHODIST
CHURCH OF NORTH PLATTE

The time comes when all the healing power in the world won't postpone your day of judgment. That's what Nana Ruth always said, and in the fall of Tom's senior year, that time came for her.

It happened over a period of months. Her skin, which had always been nut-brown, began to turn yellow like a maple leaf, dry and golden, dropping in the fall. The whites of her eyes turned yellow, too, giving her a strange, otherworldly look, and she developed a protruding stomach that at first glance would make a person wonder how a lady that old could be having a baby. She wasn't pregnant, of course, but had a growth inside, one that she'd probably known about for months before Doc Graham examined her at his office, telling her and the rest of the family that it was a tumor growing on her liver. He advised her to seek treatment in Omaha, St. Louis or even Chicago, where they might be able to do something for her, like remove the malignancy.

"I'm sorry I don't have better news for you, Ruth," he said. "But if you're going to do something, you'd best do it as soon as possible. These kinds of tumors are in a hurry."

Back at the farm, the family gathered in the front parlor as if they were guests in their own home. A rarely-used kerosene table lamp with a fancy blue ceramic shade cast the room in a muted glow. Nana Ruth sat on the horsehair sofa next to Tom's mother while Tom's father, agitated, paced back and forth, full of fanciful plans. "We could catch a train in North Platte, Ma, and be in Omaha in a matter of hours." He stopped in front of her. "Maybe they can get rid of the damn thing. You're strong. You'll bounce back."

Nana Ruth reached out with her knobby fingers and rubbed her grown son's hand like he was an upset child. "Lord a mercy," she said calmly. "They'd cut me open and take half my innards in the process. I can't be doin' that, Pauly. It's my time, and you got to accept that."

His father began to cry then, and once he started, there was no stopping the tears. Except for Eli, it was the only time Tom had ever seen such sadness pouring out of anybody. Seeing his father laid low like that was almost as bad as hearing the diagnosis. The only thing keeping Tom from wailing himself was knowing his grandma wouldn't approve. So he sat there, keeping it all inside.

During the final weeks of her life, Nana Ruth refused to be anything but herself. She refused to stay in bed or moan or rail at the world for giving her such a bad turn. Instead she continued to live in her little house and tend her garden, putting it to bed for the winter, accepting no concessions except to have Tom stay with her.

She asked that her other children, two more sons and a daughter, come to see her and pay their respects. "I'd rather they come now so we can say a proper goodbye," she said. "Them attending the funeral won't make a difference to me, now will it?"

So they came and filled the Big House, bringing their own children, some of whom had babies of their own: aunts and uncles and cousins, most of them much older than Tom and his brothers. Tom's mother cooked up a storm—all the foods that his grandma loved, like fried chicken and grits and cranberry rhubarb pie, even though she couldn't eat much anymore. Nana Ruth treated it like one big party. She told stories about her sons and daughter that made everybody laugh, and later, when it came time to say goodbye, there were plenty of tears, too, with Nana Ruth saying, "Now, now, don't you fret" a lot. When they left, there was nothing more to do but wait.

For as long as her energy held out, she continued to teach Tom about the old healing ways, fussing over potions and salves she'd forgotten and insisting he repeat her remedies to make sure he understood everything before writing them down in his notebook.

"I have been listening and writing all along, Nana," he said. "I understand."

One afternoon, toward the end, she made her way to the kitchen and showed him a particular jar she'd set apart from the others. Unmarked, it contained a small amount of dark liquid.

"You see this," she said. "I've told your ma and pa that after I've said my good byes to them, I want to spend a little quiet time with you, alone. And when we have said all there is to say, then I want you to put a teaspoon of that in my mouth, just like I did to you that time your hand needed healin'. You understand?"

Tom swallowed. He didn't like her talking like this. "Is it the same tonic you always take?"

Nana Ruth gave him a half-smile, her once-strong teeth now yellowed and beginning to decay. "Pretty much," she said. "You just do as I ask, all right?"

Tom nodded and that was the end of that conversation. They talked of other things—how he had been accepted at the University of Michigan on a football scholarship, how he would be the first in the family to go to college.

"Have you told your folks you don't want to study farmin'?"

Tom glanced at her in surprise. But then, she'd always known far more than he gave her credit for. "No. I've been trying to find a way, but I know it's going to kill pa."

She took Tom's hand. "You tell your pa I said, 'to each his own.' Tell him I said he took to farmin' right quick, and chances are one of the young' uns will, too. But you got to go your own way. You were meant to be a healer, son, no matter what happened with that old dog of Eli's."

A tremor shot through Tom's body. He'd never said anything about that to anyone—*ever*. How did she know?

"I got eyes and I got ears, Tommy. I saw that Eli had a cut along his palm, same as you. Could be a coincidence, could be a blood oath. You go out with the dog, but you don't come back with him. And all that half-hearted callin' on your cousin's part just didn't ring true. And why would you hide your wound? I figured somethin' happened and you didn't want to let it out... or maybe you just felt it wouldn't be right to share it."

"I-I made a promise," he said.

"And I admire you for feelin' honor-bound to keep it. But you've a right to change your mind about what's right and what's wrong in this world, or what's important and what's not. Some things may be worth keepin' bottled up inside, but if they begin gnawin' at you, then maybe you ought to reconsider what to do with 'em." She smiled and squeezed the hand she held. "Now you got yourself an opportunity to make things better. You can let your secret out—" and here she cackled "—because I won't be around to let it go no place else. No sir, it's safe with me."

It was as if she'd opened the Gates of Heaven, a one-time shot for sinners to step up and atone for their transgressions. Tom, to his horror, burst into tears before choking out the story of what had happened, and the choice he'd made, and how he'd never been sure if it had been the right one. Nana Ruth wrapped her fragile arms around him and held his big, strapping body next to hers. When he finished, she took a handkerchief from her pocket and handed it to him so he could dry his eyes.

"Of course you did the right thing," she said in her no-nonsense way. "There's gonna be times you don't have every lick of information, so you gotta act on what you do know and do your best. You save who you can save, you let the others go, and afterward, you say a little prayer hopin' things turned out the way God meant them to. That's just how it is. That's the way it works."

Nana Ruth left this world ten days later, and it happened just as she said it would. She took to her bed, in her own house, and got so weak she couldn't eat anything, and couldn't drink anything either, so they all took turns wetting her lips and letting her taste a little rag soaked in cider. Her eyes glistened with a kind of sharp, knowing purity. She was the most composed of anyone.

Tom's mother held the family together, making sure quiet prevailed and the younger boys didn't run roughshod over the household, which was already heavy with grief. She kept food on the table, but no one ate much, and Tom knew that she'd take care of whatever little things Nana Ruth had told her needed tending. Those two had always been a team that way.

Tom's father was a lost soul. Tom couldn't bear the thought of losing his own ma, and now he knew that feeling didn't go away, not even when you grew up and had your own children. He helped his pa with the chores that wouldn't wait, like the milking and feeding the animals, but when there was nothing else to do, his father would go to the small study at the back of the farmhouse kitchen. He wanted to be close, he said, but it was too difficult to sit and watch his mother "wither away." Nana Ruth bore him no ill will for doing that. "We all cope in our own way," she said. "Ain't no way better than another."

Tom took up the slack, reading to his grandmother from his borrowed medical books, listening to her labored breaths, pretending she was just sick and not getting ready to leave him forever.

All too quickly, the moment came when Nana Ruth let him know it was time to bring his parents over to see her. When they came into the room, she reached for their hands and held them for a moment, her way of saying goodbye. After a bit she sent them home again, crying and holding on to each other for support. A short time after they left, she motioned to Tom to bring her the tonic.

He took the bottle off the shelf and hesitated. It felt so small and light in his hand. He wondered again what was in it. But he had made a promise, so he held the syrup on a spoon while she shakily opened her sunken mouth, accepting the drizzle and working it down her throat with her puckered lips. Her eyes closed as she reached for Tom's hand and squeezed it one more time, her farewell to him. And then, after several minutes, her hand fell away and she was still.

He sat there for a moment, taking it in, stunned. Gazing about the room, he saw that everything in it—the bed where Nana Ruth lay, the soft down quilt that covered her, the well-worn Bible on her nightstand—everything was plain and simple and good. But it was so very quiet. A volcano, deep beneath his heart, began to rumble until finally, the love he had for that old woman, and the sorrow he felt at losing her, all came surging out of him in torrents of roaring, undulating anguish.

CHAPTER SIX

*"He took advantage of my daughter. No gettin' around that,
although he tried to weasel out of it."*

—Ezra Appleton, Neighbor

Nana Ruth once said the best way to get over
losin' someone was to "fill yer life with livin'."
"You got to git on with it," she told him. "You got to fill
every hour with what's good and right and makes you
happy 'til you're so tired you can't keep your eyes open
anymore. Then you got to wake up and do it all over
again. And one day you realize you can slow down and
not fall to pieces. That's when you know you're gonna
be fine."

Tom took her advice. Over the next several months,
he kept himself busy with sports, playing shortstop in
baseball and helping the team take first in the league
because of his quick hands. He tried his best not to

slack off in his classes just because he'd been accepted to university, but spring fever hit just the same, and he nearly flunked English composition after turning in a slapdash essay on the life and times of Andrew Jackson. He counted the days to graduation as if he were getting out of jail.

Tom's parents had come to terms with the direction of his studies, but that didn't mean he was too good to slop the pigs, plant the corn, or muck out the barn. Chores topped the list every morning and every night. But there was still time left over for Tom to sow some wild oats—and time enough for him to nearly ruin his life.

Her name was Alice Appleton, but the boys all called her "Red Delicious." She had bright red hair, sure, but somehow she'd escaped all the freckles that usually went along with it. Instead, her skin was creamy and not too brown from the strong Nebraska sun. Her face was pretty, with red lips that she helped along with cherry juice. The whole class knew it because several boys had confided that they could taste it on her.

But what made Ali Appleton truly delicious were the curves of her body. Her breasts were like melons, only soft like goose down pillows, and her buttocks were round and smooth and welcoming. That had also been reported.

Tom was no babe in the woods where girls were concerned. He'd been stealing kisses since he was four-teen, and by his senior year he no longer had to chase the girls because they'd begun chasing him. He'd heard through the grapevine (because there was always a grapevine) that his nickname in select circles was "The Handyman," because he was a guy who "gets the job done."

But there was a difference between that kind of fooling around and doing the deed, which Tom had yet to do...and which he wanted to do in the worst possible way.

The opportunity presented itself in late May. Every year the families in and around North Platte put on a spring fair to raise funds for new uniforms and sports equipment and chalk and all the other stuff that the school seemed to need every year. The logic of it had never made sense to Tom: why go to all the trouble to bake a pie, give it away, and then go out and pay money to eat somebody's else's pie? Why not just bake your own and eat it for nothing? He brought the subject up at supper one evening. They were finishing up a *hasenpfeffer* made from a hare that nine-year-old Jack had proudly shot. Tom didn't care for rabbit stew, which had put him out of sorts.

"Fairs like this let people pitch in for something that's bigger than they are," Tom's father explained. "Helps the community and gives us a chance to catch up with each other. Besides," he said with a wink toward Tom's mother, "how else am I gonna be able to test out Annie Hill's pie, to see if it's as good as your mother's?"

"I think your pie's the best pie in the whole wide world," Jack pronounced. "I like the apple best, but I like the peach, too, and the—"

"You just like pie, period," Henry, the middle brother, said. "You'd eat pie all day long if you could."

Jack seemed to consider that idea. "Well, would that be such a bad thing?"

Tom's mother chuckled and rose to clear the dishes, but Tom's father shot Tom a look that said, *You do it.*

Tom stood and said, "I'll get that, ma." He gathered the dinner plates five high, balanced precariously with the forks still between the layers. "I see your point, but it still seems like a lot of extra work."

Tom's mother took the stack, as he knew she would. "I'm sure you'll find *something* redeemable about the fair."

She didn't know how right—and how wrong—she was.

The fair was always held on a Saturday evening on the high school playing field, where tents were set up along one side of the mown grass to cover the tables laden with all those pies and cakes and cookies and jam. To help raise money, most of the mothers also donated non-edible doodads: a rag quilt, some table cloths decorated with cross-stitch, or baby bibs embroidered with the likes of "I love Grammie" and "Jesus Loves All the Little Children—Even Me." The men pitched in with birdhouses, signs, or scarecrows made of dried corn cobs and painted wood. Every year, old Mr. Kirkus carved a new batch of western meadowlarks out of hickory. People liked his chubby little birds with the yellow breasts.

Along the other side of the field were games of skill and luck. Miss Andrews, the art and physical education teacher, had her senior girls draw a large round cake-walk on the grass with whitewash. Land on the lucky number when the fiddling stopped and you'd win one of Mrs. Mueller's Sacher tortes. You could also fish for trinkets or toss pennies onto porcelain plates or try to shoot the feathers off the cast-iron Indian's head.

Like a pack of dogs, Tom and his buddies followed their noses to Miss Mason's chocolate chip bars, but only after they'd eaten the barbecued turkey legs sold by the men's auxiliary of the Methodist church. Then they moseyed over to play Cornhole, one of Tom's favorite games, mainly because he was so good at it. He was so good, in fact, that after ten straight minutes of watching him pitch the bag of corn kernels into the hole and rack up prizes (tin whistles and popcorn balls), Bart and Josh wandered off, no doubt in search of games where *they* could show off.

Tom continued on his own, going for a record, when he heard a soft, sweet voice in his ear. "You're pretty good at that." He turned around and saw Red Delicious herself, looking up at him with those pretty green eyes of hers. She was standing real close.

"I'm good at a lot of things," he said in the manner of all cocky eighteen-year-olds.

"So I've heard." Ali's tone sent out a message as boldly as the red on her lips. "Care to show me?"

Caught up short, he gazed at her face, expecting to

see a sassy girl who matched her worldly voice; instead he saw uncertainty, even shyness, maybe, mixed with a spark of intensity, as if she'd come with a purpose. Although her words and her face didn't quite match, he didn't stop to wonder why. *It's just her way*, he reasoned. *The way she plays the game.*

He shrugged, hoping it made him seem like a man who did this sort of thing every day, when inside he was bucking and churning, a thoroughbred straining to get on with the race. He boldly took her hand, but she did the leading, heading toward the side of the school-house, where no one could see them.

As soon as they turned the corner she leaped on him, grinding her mouth against his.

"Whoa, whoa," he said, taking her by the arms and gently setting her back a foot. "That's not the way I do things."

She was already breathing hard, and he had a niggling sense that it wasn't excitement firing her up, but fear, or maybe just nerves. "Well, how do you do things, then?" she asked, a bit peevish.

"Like this," he said, and proceeded to show her, moment by moment, what had earned him his reputation.

"Oh," she mustered when she came up for air. And when they finally broke apart she said, "I want more."

"I can give you more," Tom said, leaning in again.

But she stopped him, saying, "No. I want you bad." She went on tiptoe to better whisper in his ear. "Inside me."

Tom swallowed convulsively. *This is it.* He looked

around for someplace to take her, but Ali put her hand on his arm. "Not here. Down by the river. I got a blanket there."

He glanced back at the crowd, deciding he had time, then silently followed her across the far end of the field and down the hill to where an offshoot of the river flowed low enough around a sandy spit to make a nice little swimming beach. It was twilight and might be full-on dark by the time they finished. He wished he had a light with him, but he figured it was a small price to pay.

Ali led him right to a spot near the water and pulled a ratty old blanket from behind a bush. She spread it out and without saying a word, began to unbutton the tight-fitting jacket she'd been wearing. He'd noticed the buttons straining from the minute he'd seen her, imagined they were glad to finally let those luscious melons free. As she undid her shirtwaist, Tom could see her breasts spilling over her chemise. He couldn't help himself and reached for her, but she shooed his hand away. "Let's get on with it," she said in a shaky voice.

She lay down on the blanket and pulled her skirt up to her waist. "I got on open drawers," she said, "so you can get in easy." She hadn't even taken off her boots.

It was all happening so fast that Tom had to stop and think about what exactly was going on. It didn't feel right. Ali tried to drag him down on top of her but he resisted, pushing back onto his knees.

"Just a second," he said. "You're…this…why are you doing this?"

She rose up onto her elbows. "What do you mean?

Every boy in school wants me. You want me, don't you?"

"Well, yeah, but not like this."

"What's wrong?" Suddenly Ali Appleton did the worst thing in the world she could have done: she started to cry.

"Come on, now, don't do that. Don't cry."

Out of instinct, Tom pulled her into his arms and started soothing her, pushing her hair gently away from her face and whispering that he didn't mean to make her cry, that she was beautiful, that he really did like her. As he said those things, he began dropping little kisses on her eyelids and her cheeks, eventually reaching her mouth, where the kisses turned carnal and the dance officially began.

Tom pulled her breasts out of their confinement and began to suckle them, eliciting hisses and whimpers that he told himself were cries of passion even though he suspected they were something else. And when he saw her nipples, even in the waning light, he knew what was going on and still he stayed the course because he wanted to *do it*, for God's sake. He was only human, and it felt so good, and her body, in all its roundness, really was beautiful. The last thing he remembered before the brain below his belt took over was *don't worry, everything's fine.*

He did his best to make it all right for her, even though he figured it probably wouldn't be, and when he finished, after lasting as long as he possibly could, he saw that she was glad it was over. She would have no doubt liked it better had he been quick about it.

When his breathing slowed, he climbed off her, buttoned up his trousers and said, "That was nice."

"We'd better get back. They'll be wondering about us," was all she said.

He didn't think anyone had seen them leave the fairgrounds, but when they returned, he saw that Bart and Josh had spied them from across the field. His two buddies jogged toward them.

"No matter what everybody says, you were my first," Ali told Tom. "I'll swear to it."

Tom couldn't make out her face in the gloom, and he wanted to see her expression, to make sure she understood his question. "Why me?"

She did understand. "Because someday my pa will like you."

In that instant Tom saw the whole story, how she wanted it to play out, and how it would play out. "No," he said, guilt and shame taking residence inside him. "He won't."

Tom knew the next chapter was coming, he just didn't know when.

It played out ten days later, after ten days of whispers and gossip and rib-poking and demands for details— none of which Tom acknowledged or supplied.

On a Thursday evening, just as Tom and his family were finishing supper, there was a knock on the door. Standing on the front step was Ezra Appleton with

Alice in tow. Mr. Appleton, a grizzled widower who was already getting on in years, did not look happy. That didn't surprise Tom at all.

"I got something to say, Paul," he told Tom's father. "Something you ought to know about. It concerns your son and my daughter."

Tom's stomach took a sour turn. Just because he knew Judgment Day was coming hadn't made its arrival feel any better.

Tom's father, who sized up the situation real quick, asked Tom's mother to take Jack and Henry upstairs. She nodded and gathered the boys, but not before she shot Tom a look that said *I really hope this isn't what I think it is.* He wanted to tell her it was all right, but it wasn't, not really.

"Come on into the parlor and set yourselves down," Tom's father said. "You look like you've got something pressing real hard on your mind."

Alice followed her pa into the room and sat primly on one of the wooden chairs, her hands resting in her lap. So far she hadn't said a word, and Tom figured she wouldn't if she could help it.

"I'll get right down to it," Mr. Appleton said once the four of them were seated. "Your boy here knocked up my little girl and he's got to make it right by her."

"I see." There was silence for a moment, as Tom's father turned to Tom. "Is this true? Did you impregnate Alice?" He used the word like he was a scientist, like he was bound and determined not to let this be all about emotion.

Tom took a deep breath and exhaled as slowly as

he could. He wanted to let Alice know he was sorry for what he was about to do, but she was concentrating on her tightly clutched hands and didn't look at him.

"No sir," Tom said. "I did not."

That brought her eyes up. Surprised, she glared at him, then glanced at her father.

Ezra's face, which was reddish to begin with, turned crimson. "Are you telling me you never lay with my daughter?"

"No sir, I'm telling you I didn't get her with child."

"What, you poked her, but you didn't put your seed in her? What'd you do, pull out? Use something else? We all know those methods don't always work, don't we, Paul?"

Tom's father was obviously embarrassed by the turn of the conversation, and no doubt irritated with Tom for having brought the need for such a conversation into the house to begin with. He nodded but remained quiet.

"No, we didn't use any birth control method," Tom went on, "but it wouldn't have mattered even if we had."

"Wouldn't have mattered?" Ezra looked puzzled. "Are you telling me your seed's no good? You're confusing me, boy."

Tom spoke to Alice instead of directing his answer to her father. "Alice, how many times did you and I lie together? Be honest."

Ali hesitated, then mumbled, "One. Just one time."

"Once. And when was that?"

Alice looked up at him with a desperate anger. "The spring fair," she said.

Tom turned back to her father. "I am sorry, Mr. Appleton, but it would be nearly impossible for Alice to exhibit her current symptoms if the egg had been fertilized just ten days ago."

Ezra frowned; he seemed to have lost his footing. "What are you trying to say here?"

Tom sat up straighter. He was on solid ground and he knew it. "I couldn't have impregnated Alice, Mr. Appleton, because she was already pregnant. I know the signs because I read about them in one of Doc Graham's medical books. And I could see it with my own eyes. If Doc examines her, he'll tell you she's at least two or three months along." He turned to Alice again. "You know I'm right."

The look Ali Appleton sent Tom contained many reactions at once: surprise and anger, betrayal and uncertainty, but most of all, dread. And for the first time, Tom considered what might happen to her now that her plan had blown up in her face. He didn't like to pity people— he'd always thought it was an insult, as if they didn't have enough brains or guts to get their own selves out of whatever mess they were in—but in that instant, he pitied Alice Appleton.

Her father's next words clubbed Tom in the gut. "Let me get this straight. You knew my little girl was knocked up and probably feelin' right poorly about herself, and you went ahead and plowed her anyway, thinkin' you could get away with it because someone else got there first and planted their seed instead of you. Is that about the size of it?"

Tom didn't say a word. What could he say? He had no defense. The sordid truth of what he'd done sat upon him like a cement yoke.

"Yeah, I thought so." Bitter sarcasm colored Ezra's next words. "You got yourself quite an upstanding young man there, Paul. Yes siree." Then he rose and looked down at his daughter. "You tried to trap this sorry excuse for a man, which means the real culprit must be even worse. Or are you such a slut you don't even know who it is?"

"There's no call for that kind of language," Tom's father said.

Ezra scrubbed his face. "Yeah, well, you're the lucky one. You've only got boys who stick their wicks where they don't belong and get away with it. I got a girl who's stuck with the results. And that means *I'm* stuck." He turned back to Alice and grabbed her arm. "How many more were there?"

Alice was quietly crying now. She looked at Tom and then at her father. "Only one," she said in a small voice.

Ezra scoffed and turned to Tom. "You believe that?"

Tom gazed at Ali for a moment and took a leap of faith. "Yes, sir. I think maybe she's worried you won't like the father of her baby, so she hoped I might stand in for him."

Her father's voice was tight. "Who is it?"

Ali didn't answer right away, and there was no

getting around the look she gave him. It was one of fear, pure and simple.

He leaned into her. "Tell me," he bit out, the words cold and sharp.

"Rain Watkins," she mumbled.

"The half-breed?"

Ali straighten up for the first time since she'd entered the room. "Rain Watkins is a good boy and I love him."

It happened so fast, neither Tom nor his father had a chance to stop him. Ezra hauled off and cracked his daughter across her pretty face. She rocked back in the chair, her hand reaching out for balance and sending a little redware rooster tumbling to the floor. Tom's father was up in a flash, his arms shoving Ezra halfway across the room. "You pull something like that again and I'll mop the floor up with you."

"It's none of your damn business now." Ezra's chest was heaving. "Your boy's in the free and clear, but we got the shame of a lousy half-breed get to deal with, and a bastard one to boot." He turned to his daughter. "And we'll deal with it, all right."

Tom's father wasn't a talkative man, or a righteous one, or one who had ever looked for trouble, at least as far as Tom knew. But he stepped into Ezra Appleton's face and said the most amazing thing.

"Ezra, you're a decent human being down deep, and I hope you can reach that far and find the goodness in you to deal with your daughter in a caring way. Because if I hear that you have harmed one hair on her head, or her child's, or the head of the child's father, I will see that you pay dearly for your actions. You know I'm a man of my word."

Then he turned to Alice and said, "I'm sorry if you feel shame for what you did with Tom and I hope you can forgive him for his part in it. But if you ever have a fear of your pa and what he might do to you, if he ever harms you in any way, you come to us and we'll protect you. Do you understand?"

Alice looked at Tom's father, then at her own. Ezra was still mad, but seemed to be under control now.

"She won't be needin' you," Ezra said in disgust.

"If she does, she'll be welcome—and you'll be in trouble."

With a mulish look, Ezra took his daughter and left. Tom sat quietly on the chair, waiting for his father to speak. He knew it wasn't over.

"I guess you know how disappointed I am," his father finally said, his calm censure worse than any tirade. "I never thought a boy of mine would take advantage of someone in such a vulnerable place."

His words seared Tom's core like a white-hot poker. He felt his eyes prick with tears and took a gulp, not wanting to demean himself even further. After a moment, his father put his hands on his knees and stood up.

"You wait there," he said, and headed up the stairs.

After several agonizing moments, his father returned (not with his mother, thank God). He carried a small package which he handed to Tom. Tom opened it to find a prophylactic, what people were starting to call a "rubber" because it was made of rubber instead of animal skin.

"Wait," Tom said. "Isn't...isn't there a law against —"

"Whether there is or isn't doesn't matter. What matters is that you learn how to use it, and *use* it. God gave us the ability to procreate, but I also think He meant for us to take responsibility for what happens afterward. If you want to make a child and raise it up, then by all means do so. But if you don't, it's better to take control of the situation from the get go. Don't leave it to the woman to decide your fate, neither. Not everyone is as trustworthy as your ma, a lesson which I assume you just learned."

"Yes, sir," Tom said, fingering the package like it was a packet of rubies. "I don't expect I'll be needing it for quite some time, but I thank you all the same."

Tom's father quirked his lips, the first leavening of his demeanor since the Appletons had come to call. "Yes, well, we'll see about that, won't we?"

Alice Appleton graduated with Tom and the rest of their class, but left North Platte shortly thereafter. It turned out Rain Watkins had left town a few weeks before the spring fair, and nobody ever heard of either of them again. It was the kind of story that tested a person's outlook on life. Positive thinkers imagined the two lovebirds reuniting someplace else and living happily ever after; cynics figured one or both of them met an unkind fate.

Ezra Appleton never had to face the wrath of Paul Justice, but he suffered nonetheless: no one ever saw him with a cute little grandbaby, a little boy or girl who surely would have showered the old man with love.

As for Tom, it was another case of wondering, another instance of questioning the decisions he'd made. Only one thing came out of the affair for certain: he learned how to wear rubbers and he used them without fail.

CHAPTER SEVEN

"Tom was good at just about everything he put his mind to. He was a real winner, make no mistake. You just knew he wasn't going to stick around the farm like the rest of us."

—BART PALMER, CHILDHOOD FRIEND

It was a hell of a way to end his college football career.

In his senior year, on a cold and miserable afternoon two days after Thanksgiving, Tom put on his University of Michigan uniform —jersey, knickers, long socks, and leather shoes—and jogged onto the Detroit Athletic Club's field with his fellow Wolverines. The noise of four thousand raucous fans—not to mention a few jeers from Cornell sympathizers—greeted them.

"Damn. Ain't that somethin'." Jim Baird, the quarterback, shot Tom a grin as they stood on the field, waving to the screaming students and alumni who filled the stands. Normally the Wolverines played home games back in Ann Arbor, but everybody knew Regents Field wasn't nearly big enough for the crowd this game would generate, so they'd moved it to Detroit. As it was, the Athletic Club's facility had never held so many people—nearly ten times the capacity of Regents.

"Just as long as you deliver," Charles "Fatty" Smith said. "If you don't, they'll be coming after you when the game's over." Fatty was only five-foot-ten and weighed over two hundred and thirty pounds, but you couldn't ask for a better center.

"You do your job, I'll do mine, and together we'll make history," Jim shot back in that cocky way he had. Their job, with the help of Tom and the rest of the team, was to bring down Cornell's Big Red once and for all.

It was all about revenge. Cornell had bloodied them three weeks earlier in Ithaca, but this time, Jimmy's knee was healed well enough after the hit he took against Michigan Military, to be back as starting QB. It was time to show the Eastern powerhouse just who they were messing with.

Tom glanced up at the stands to see if he could spot his girl, Carina Villa, in her bright red cloak. Yes, there she was—slender and small with long, black hair and so pretty she could rev him up in nothing flat. He waved, but she was talking to his cousin Eli and didn't see him.

Eli. After ten years of no contact, Tom had received a letter out of the blue:

Remember me, old chap? I'm taking time off after earning my sheepskin from Rutgers. Exploring my options. Thought I'd come and see how the other half lives—ha ha! Actually, my ma said you were plowing through UM and that I ought to look you up. Are you open to a visit from your blood brother?

Reading the letter had unsettled Tom's gut worse than any exam. Cold as it seemed, he had no desire to resurrect their friendship. But Eli's father had been killed fighting the Indians a few years back, and that had to be tough on anybody. Good manners dictated he extend an invitation, and his cousin had readily taken him up on it.

Eli was full-grown now, but he'd not fared well in the height department. He was more than half a foot shorter than Tom and slight of build to boot. But he had thick, wavy blond hair, a pleasant face, and the same engaging manner he'd always had, at least when it came to people he wanted to impress.

This time around he was on his best behavior, fully understanding that Tom had little time to entertain him. ("I just busted out of that prison myself," he said. "I know what you're going through."). Surprisingly, he'd decided to extend his stay beyond a few weeks. He rented a room nearby and got a part-time job as a store clerk. And once he'd done that, he proceeded to make friends with Tom's circle—a circle that of course included Carina. Since the beginning of football season Eli had taken on the role of her escort; he and Carina had attended practically all of Tom's games together.

He knew he should be grateful for Eli's willingness to step in. Tom had met Carina through her brother Giovanni, a fellow Wolverine, and to this day Tom couldn't understand what she saw in him. Over the past two years she'd quietly put up with his long hours both in the classroom and on the field. She knew Tom's athletic scholarship paid for his schooling and that he couldn't give up either one of them. She'd never whined, never made him feel guilty. In that way she reminded him of his mother (which he quickly assured himself was the *only* similarity). He needed a woman with the kind of fortitude his mother possessed, and he'd opened his mind, just a little, to the possibility that maybe Carina and he could build something that lasted far past his graduation in the spring.

So it came as a surprise when, at the start of the fall term, she'd begun pouting now and again, albeit in the most feminine way, letting him know she felt he was neglecting her. The change in her attitude bothered him, but Eli's appearance had at least put a stop to her subtle complaints.

He looked up again to see Eli touching Carina's red-clad shoulder and pointing in Tom's direction. Once she saw him on the field she began waving wildly. He broke into a grin and waved right back. That pretty thing was his girl—his girl!—and he was going to play his heart out just for her. He waved once more, put his restless thoughts away, and concentrated on the matter at hand: beating the pants off Cornell.

"You got to go out there and show them who's boss," Coach McCauley admonished the team at halftime. "You're every bit as good as those East Coast snobs. No, I stand corrected. You're *better*. Now go out there and prove it."

That meant a lot coming from Coach, since he'd played for Princeton, one of those very snobs, just the year before. Today he was all Wolverine. Michigan was up by two, but that was only because Cornell had missed the conversion after their touchdown. That made it way too close for comfort, and no one in that locker room wanted to chalk up an eighth straight loss to Big Red.

The best opportunity to increase their lead came halfway through the second half. Jim called for a draw to the right, signaling Tom to hang back for a lateral pass on the left. "Don't you cross the line," he hissed in the huddle.

At the snap, Tom shot straight left. *Keep it straight,* he told himself. *Don't veer.* He barreled laterally, keeping the scrimmage line on his right side the whole way. He could hear the Cornell defender pounding behind him, right on his tail. Dammit. Keep going. Keep going.

Now *turn.* Tom looked over his left shoulder, stretched his arms out and captured the football, knowing with sickening certitude that he was about to be mowed down. A split second later he felt the weight of a two-hundred-pound tackle smash into the back of his head and heard the crack of a bone somewhere on his body. Pain sliced through him like a saber cut. "Gotta be worse than jumping in the North Platte River" ran through his brain. Just before he blacked out, he felt the ball slipping out of his hands.

By the time Tom regained consciousness, he'd been carted off the field and sent directly to a nearby hospital, where he now lay in a sterile-looking room with pale blue walls completely unadorned. He smelled disinfectant and felt queasy, no doubt because railroad spikes were being pounded into his skull (at least it felt that way). He searched his foggy memory for one of Nana Ruth's cure-alls, but came up empty-headed. Reaching back, he checked to see if the lump he knew he'd find was as big as he imagined it to be. It was.

"Don't touch," his longtime roommate Jimmy Wong warned him. "The nurse is unhappy to be working on a Saturday. Especially this Saturday. She told me to keep you from moving around too much, and if you disobeyed me, I would have to answer to her. She scares me."

Tom tilted his head back and smiled, which brought on a wave of sharp, nauseating pain. At that moment he also realized his left leg was in a cast. He squinted as he looked at his good friend. "So, who won?"

Jimmy pulled his chair closer. He barely fit in it. Tall for a Chinaman, he was also hefty, a Buddha statue come to life. The Wolverines could have used him on the line, but he had no interest in it. He'd come to the United States to learn all he could about Western science; there was no time for anything else. Tom was lucky Jimmy had even come to see the game.

"Between you and the defender, I would say you lost. But between Michigan and Cornell, despite your fumble, we squeaked by, twelve to four. Everybody is still celebrating—except Cornell, of course."

"Nice." Tom laid his head back down. Michigan had finally made it to the top tier. Too bad he hadn't been awake to see it happen.

Jimmy reached into the satchel he carried everywhere and took out several books along with a pair of professional journals. "I don't know how long you are going to be in here, but I have been meaning to show you an interesting article on some new findings by a Dr. Pavlov, who studies the secretions of dog saliva in response to certain stimuli. It fits in nicely with our study of the digestive system." He pulled out another periodical. "Also, this will interest you: it is a treatise on the use of valerian and passionflower for sleep disturbances. I thought you might want to compare it with your grandmother's notes."

Tom had to laugh, although it hurt like hell to do so. Studying was the absolute last thing he wanted to think about at the moment.

Just then, Carina rushed into the ward with Eli close behind. *Why is she rushing? The game has been over for a while.*

"Oh, how are you, Tom?" she cried, leaning over him and taking one of his hands in hers as she gazed at him intently. Her wide brown eyes looked almost comical up so close; usually he had his eyes shut when they were close enough to kiss. As always, she smelled delicious, like a cinnamon roll.

"I've been better," he said.

"Ha—that's the understatement of the year. How's it going, old man?" Eli sounded almost jovial. He'd come up to Tom's bedside, standing next to Tom's girl.

Tom glanced at Jimmy, who had quietly gotten up from the chair and moved to the side. He started to put the books back in his satchel, but Carina stopped him.

"Oh, don't leave on our account, Jimmy. We've got to run anyway to catch the train back to school."

"Jimmy probably has to get back, too," Tom said.

Jimmy shook his head. "No, I am staying with a cousin here in the city. So I can look after you for a few days."

Carina looked remarkably relieved. She leaned over to give Tom a peck on the cheek. "Well, then. Get better soon, Tommy," she whispered before turning to go.

"Don't worry—I'll take good care of her," Eli said as he ushered her out the door.

Jimmy and Tom were silent for a few minutes after they'd left. It was painfully clear what was going on and Tom appreciated the fact that Jimmy wasn't going to address it.

"Well then," Tom said.

Jimmy pulled his chair back up to the bed. "The deadline for applications to Johns Hopkins is in four weeks," he said.

Tom leaned back in the bed, trying to absorb what was unfolding in his personal life. "I can't afford it."

"I spoke to someone there about it. They have two scholarships set aside for deserving pupils. I am sure you can earn one of them. You are very bright...for a farm boy."

Tom mustered a half grin. "Farm Boy" was the moniker he'd been stuck with ever since he'd arrived in Ann Arbor three years before. At first he'd been sensitive about it, but hell, he did look like a farmer—or maybe a plow horse: long-suffering and strong. And yes, he had to admit that in many respects he was a plodder—sometimes it wasn't easy, but he always completed the task. It was only after they'd seen Tom on the football field that the stereotype broke down, but the label stuck and now he didn't care. Jimmy didn't seem to mind his own nickname either, which was "Panda."

"You going to apply?" Tom asked.

"Yes, most definitely. I have a better chance because my country is willing to pay full tuition." He grinned, lifting one of his massive thighs. "I think that will give me leg up, don't you think? So, you are with me?"

Tom ran a hand through his stiff, dirty hair. What would he give to be able to go to medical school? Reality reared its head. "I want to, but I'm not sure Carina would want to move to where I'd be going to school, if she's willing to put up with more years of this at all."

Jimmy's silence spoke volumes.

"I just don't know," Tom repeated.

Tom's roommate shrugged as he once again reached for a journal. "Promise me you'll apply at least."

"That I'll do."

"All right then. Let me read to you about this Dr. Woof Woof."

In time, Tom's headaches, as well as the knot on the back of his head, faded away. It took longer for his leg to heal, but by the new year he was able to bear weight on it again. He'd probably never run quite as fast, so it was a good thing the football season, and his athletic career, had ended.

What would he have done without Jimmy? The earnest young student Tom had been paired with as a freshman turned out to be the best friend a man could ever hope to have. Throughout their college years, Panda had been there for him, and he was there for him now. He helped Tom get to class, carted books to and from the library, and ran whatever errands Tom needed. Mrs. Cartwright, who managed their boarding house, did what she could, but it was Jimmy who brought meals up to their room, Jimmy who kept the place clean, and Jimmy who made sure Tom got the notes for any lectures he missed in their pre-med classes.

Much to Tom's surprise, Carina was there for him, too. She stopped by every day, sometimes bringing him still-warm bowls of her mother's homemade ravioli, or crunchy, buttery cannoli laden with sweet cream. She would sit next to him, holding his hand as she chatted about the latest news regarding their mutual friends. If a dance or an ice cream social or an impromptu snowball fight cropped up, she always offered to stay with him instead of joining the fun, although more often than not he insisted she go. Naturally, Eli was available to escort her, a more than willing substitute.

Yet on those rare occasions when they were alone together, she was as eager for Tom physically as she had been since the first time he'd kissed her. They'd yet to consummate their love, but they'd come damn close more times than Tom cared to admit. And, if he were honest, it was Carina who needed reining in as much as he. But his father's admonition stuck with him: *If you want to make a child and raise it up, do it. But if you don't, take control.*

He began to wonder about Carina, though, and with so much thinking time on his hands, the wonder slipped into a mild obsession. Why did Carina respond to him so readily yet act so happy to be with Eli all the time? Was she loose? He found himself imagining what Eli must feel when she spent time alone with Tom. It connected him to his cousin in a way he never would have imagined or wanted. Yet the link was there.

Fortunately, he could always count on his roommate to distract him. In addition to their regular coursework, Jimmy held Tom to his promise, insisting they study for the Johns Hopkins entrance exams. Unlike most other medical schools, which merely asked for a knowledge of English and a hefty tuition fee, this new institution set the bar considerably higher. It required a college degree, high grades, and decent scores on chemistry, physics, and biology examinations. Shortly before the deadline, Jimmy helped Tom hobble to the science building, where an assistant professor proctored the test. Jimmy mailed their application packets and they settled back to wait.

Tom didn't mention anything about it to Carina.

The response came in March, during midterm week of his final semester. He'd passed on joining his usual study group and walked back from campus by himself. Mrs. Cartwright heard him come in and stuck her head out of the kitchen. He could smell lamb stew cooking, one of his favorites. "You and Mr. Wong got some mail today."

Sure enough, there on the little table near the door were two simple white envelopes, each emblazoned with a blue-and-gold shield. *This is it*, he thought. He took his missive into the front parlor and sat down to calm his jitters. Then he opened the letter and read:

Dear Mr. Justice,

The Department of Admissions at Johns Hopkins University has reviewed your application and is pleased to inform you that you have been granted provisional acceptance to its medical school for the fall term of 1895. Please contact Mr. Joseph Cannon at your earliest

opportunity to discuss acceptance of this offer and the
financial details pertaining thereto.

Sincerely,

William H. Welch

Dr. William H. Welch

Dean of Admissions

Tom looked around the room, rubbed his bum leg out of habit, and then read the letter again. Nope. The wording hadn't changed. He'd made it. He was in. God have mercy. He was *in!*

It took all the willpower he had, and then some, not to rip Jimmy's letter open as well. There's no way they'd accept him and not Jimmy. No way. He laughed out loud to the empty room, his mind already plotting how they would pull this off. And he was still smiling when Jimmy walked in and he handed his roommate the second letter.

"We're going to Baltimore!" Tom crowed.

Jimmy's eyes grew wide and he quickly opened the envelope, but as he scanned the contents, Tom could tell it didn't contain the same news. A look came over his roommate's face: disappointment, sadness, acceptance, all rolled into one small smile.

"I think one of us is going to Baltimore," he said.

"Let me see that." Tom snatched the letter from him and read it quickly, a frown forming. "I don't get it. There's no way they could pick me over you. Your scores had to be higher than mine. I know your grades were."

"Not by much, and I believe you underestimate

yourself." Jimmy carefully set down his satchel. "Of course, it could also be your prowess on the playing field," he added with a grin.

"Oh hell," Tom said, too absorbed to even comment on Jimmy's gentle sarcasm. "What am I going to do?"

Jimmy raised his brows. "What do you mean? You're going to go, of course. And you are not going to worry about me. Because I too have news."

"What?"

"I was asked to report to the Admissions office this morning, and when I arrived, they told me I had been accepted at the medical school here. It is only a three-year program, but I will try to learn all I can. And I have the advantage in that I already know many of the professors. They must be willing to put up with me."

Tom frowned. "You never told me you had applied here."

"I knew you could not afford to attend this school, and I did not want to have it sitting out there between us."

Jimmy was right: The University of Michigan was not known for graduate scholarships. But Tom knew how much his friend had been hoping to attend Johns Hopkins—it really was unlike any medical school in the country.

Tom searched Jimmy's round, earnest face and saw no sign of envy or resentment, only kindness. The idea of leaving this big-hearted fellow brought a lump to Tom's throat; he tried to skirt past it with humor. "Well, we will have to share notes; that is the only way I'll make it through, you know."

Jimmy's face lit up as he clapped Tom's shoulder. "I would like that. Between the two of us we will learn all there is to know about healing."

Not too long after, Tom found himself hoping his first class would teach him how to heal matters of the heart.

CHAPTER EIGHT

*"I could have sworn they loved each other. But then he tells
me they're parting company, that she needs her freedom.
Surprised the hell out of me. I never understood what really
happened. Now I guess we never will."*

—Giovannie Villa, Football Teammate and
Brother of Carina Villa Porter

"Can we meet for coffee at The Hearth after your
class? I have something important I want to talk
to you about."

Tom had walked Carina to her English class and the
seriousness of her tone caused him to stop in his
tracks. "Of course. Want to give me a hint?" He smiled
uncertainly.

"No, it'll wait."

"All right, then." He pecked her on the cheek in
front of her lecture hall and headed to his own seminar

across the quadrangle. The sun was low in the sky; already shadows appeared.

It had been a week and he still hadn't told Carina about the letter from Johns Hopkins. He told himself it was a matter of finding the right time, but in truth he'd been waiting for something else—waiting for his girl to gather the courage she needed to tell him she'd fallen in love with his cousin. Now that she'd gotten up her nerve, did he have the strength to accept it?

It was impossible to concentrate on the evening's geography lecture. It didn't help that the topic was "The Physiography of Washtenaw County." Tom glanced at Jimmy, who sat next to him diligently taking notes. Panda was probably the only student at Michigan who wasn't suffering from some degree of spring fever. Tom lasted as long as he could, but a half hour before class ended, he leaned over and whispered, "I've got to be somewhere. I'll catch up with you later."

Jimmy sent him away with a distracted nod.

Outside, a murky twilight had overtaken the campus. The evening air stung as he inhaled, and pitiful heaps of sludge clung to the dark sides of buildings, the last vestiges of winter. The cold seeped through his sweater and sank even deeper into the heart of him. He flipped up the collar of his shirt, a meager protection, and hurried through the gloom.

He was losing Carina, and he had no one to blame but himself. He was the one who had put her low on his priority list. He was the one who had gladly let Eli take his place. How stupid was he? And the idea that she would feel terrible for what she was about to say and do—for what he had led her to do— made him feel like the worst sort of cad. And in that moment, he realized there was something he could do about it.

The Hearth was a favorite student haunt with well-worn red leather booths lining the back and side walls. It was dimly lit, and even the sawdust strewn on the floor couldn't tamp down the noise level of so many students letting loose. Somehow, that made private conversations easier. Carina waited for him in their favorite booth.

"You're early," she said.

"I couldn't wait. I have something to say to you, too." He slipped into the bench across from her. "Did you order?"

She nodded. "The usual." That would be an espresso for her and a beer for him. They made small talk while they waited; it was awkward, as if they were on a first date rather than a last.

The waitress brought the drinks and Carina took a small sip before setting the tiny cup down. "I know we haven't talked about what happens to us after graduation," she began, "but—"

Tom stopped her with a gentle hand on her arm. "Would you mind if I shared my news first?" he asked.

"No, go ahead." She seemed almost relieved to let him start.

Tom paused to get the words right. "I know we haven't talked next steps, and, well, there's a reason for that. I just found out I've been accepted at Johns Hopkins Medical School, and…and I don't think I will have time to give our relationship the effort it deserves.

So I think it's a good time for us to go our separate ways. You know, give you your freedom so you can find someone new." He offered a poor excuse for a smile. "It's all right, we can tell everybody that you decided to break it off."

He searched her face, hoping to find an expression of relief, even a well-masked one. Instead her eyes grew enormous and began to fill. He frowned, took her small hand in his. "I think it's the best thing, don't you?" he asked softly. "For both of us. In the long run, I mean."

She nodded, but he could tell she was still processing what had just happened. Unaccountably angry, he wanted to blurt out, "You see? You don't have to feel bad for leaving me—I'm giving you permission to do it!" He didn't say anything like that, of course, sensing he had stumbled into quicksand. He was sinking and there was nothing to hold onto. After a moment, all he could muster was, "I will always care for you, though. Always."

Tears flowing down her cheeks, Carina took the napkin that had sopped up some of the beer from Tom's glass and dabbed her eyes. She gave a little laugh. "I'm going to smell like a brewery." She looked at Tom for a moment and added, "Did you want to hear my news?"

Did he want to hear her announce her love for Eli? No, he sure as hell didn't, and why would she want to mention it now? Out of spite? No, that wasn't his Carina.

His Carina? No. Not anymore. "I don't need to, but if you have a need to tell me, go ahead."

At that she scowled, and something in her lovely face hardened. "Never mind, then," she told him. "It doesn't matter now."

They had little to say to each other after that. Tom walked her to her parents' house, then turned to make his way back to his room. He didn't notice the cold anymore; it was part of him now, as if his entire being had turned to ice.

That night Tom barely slept, finally nodding off near dawn. Consequently, it was mid-morning by the time he was awakened by a loud pounding on his and Jimmy's door. Sitting at his desk reading, Jimmy looked at Tom quizzically.

"What the hell?" Tom said, grabbing his trousers and pulling them on. "Who is it?"

"Eli. Let me in."

Tom opened the door and had no time to prepare for the fist that landed squarely in his face. He staggered back, covering his nose, which had already begun to bleed. "Jesus, Eli! What are you doing?"

Eli was pumped up. "That's for breaking her heart," he said, cocking his fist back to land another blow. "And this is for—"

Tom had the presence of mind and the reflexes to block Eli's next punch mid-swing. "Now wait just a goddamn minute," he said, yanking his cousin's arm away.

Jimmy positioned himself between Tom and Eli. "What is this about?" he asked.

"Tell him," Eli said, glaring at Tom. "Tell him how you casually announced to the girl who loves you beyond reason that you didn't have any more time for her. 'Sorry. So long.'" He turned to Jimmy then, a lawyer prosecuting a case. "And he didn't even want to hear what she'd done for him. All for him." Eli refocused on his cousin: "You're a heartless bastard. Always have been."

He'd thrown the words, a stiletto aimed for maximum damage.

Tom stepped back and spoke, his calm voice masking the rage inside. "I don't know what you're talking about. Yes, I broke up with Carina, but I did it for her own good." Hell if he was going to tell Eli why.

"Did you know she had talked to her cousin about you? He's got connections in real estate and banking. She knew you were worried about money, so she convinced him to get you a job right after graduation. She told him you were smart and honorable and the hardest worker she'd ever seen. That whoever hired you would never regret it. Boy, did she do a sales job on your sorry behalf. You would have had it made. And you thank her by booting her out the door."

Tom blinked. *What?* Had that been her news? Wait a minute. "No. I didn't know that. I didn't know any of that. I-I thought it was something else, so I didn't give her a chance to tell me."

Eli was starting to come down from his agitated state. He looked around the room as if he couldn't figure out how he got there. "God, I don't know what she sees in you. You don't deserve someone that wonderful. You fucking well don't."

It was Jimmy who put it all in perspective. "But Tom is not going to be a banker. He is going to be a doctor. Maybe it would be better for you to be the banker."

And just like that, the tumblers fell into place. Tom understood his cousin's predicament. To love a woman who doesn't love you back must be excruciating; Tom had only imagined it and it had caused him untold pain.

But what should he do? He could declare it all a misunderstanding and win Carina back; it sounded like she would welcome him if she knew the truth. But then her uncle's offer would come into play, and Jimmy was right on that score: Tom most definitely was not going to become a banker, no matter how much he loved Carina or she loved him. He was going to medical school, and that was going to take many more years and a lot more sacrifice. He couldn't ask that of her; he *wouldn't* ask it of her. Carina was meant to be with someone who loved her so much he would give up everything for her—even his own happiness.

Someone like Eli.

Tom paused, gathering courage. "Jimmy has it right," he finally said. "Whether I knew about the offer or not, the facts wouldn't be any different. We weren't meant to stay together." He looked directly at Eli. "She needs to be with someone who loves her like crazy. Who would do anything for her—even go into battle for her. She deserves nothing less."

They locked eyes until, at last, Eli seemed to receive the message. His cousin took in a breath and let it out slowly.

"She will need a good friend to be there for her while she mends," Tom said. "Maybe you can be that friend."

Eli nodded slowly. "Maybe I can."

After he left, Jimmy said in his wake, "You are no dog in a manger."

Still in a kind of shock, it took Tom a few minutes to realize he was still half dressed. He hadn't noticed the cold during the altercation with Eli, but now it took over, seeping back into his bones. Or maybe it was knowing what he had just given up. "What have I done?" he asked. He sat down on his bed, breathing shallowly, not wanting to inhale the despair.

Jimmy sat across from him. "This may not be an honorable question for me to ask of you, but I will ask it anyway. Do you love her?"

Tom answered without hesitation. "Of course. She's more than I could ever hope for." The emptiness inside of him seemed to be growing, a huge crater he could easily tumble into and never crawl out of.

"Then I would ask this of you. If you believe she would not be happy following you, do you love her enough to leave the path you are on?" Staring at his friend, Tom didn't know what to say, so he said nothing. And that, in essence, said everything.

CHAPTER NINE

Early March 1907

A *man is known by the company he keeps.*
Jonathan Perris knew from experience that the old English proverb nearly always rang true. With that in mind, he pondered the large circular chart he'd tacked to the wall of his third-floor office on Montgomery Street. It was a tool he called "The Tree Stump." Like a botanist who determines the age of a conifer by the number of rings extending from its center, so Jonathan hoped to know the real Tom Justice by getting to know the rings of relationships emanating from the core of his family. Over time the connections would all be added: childhood friends, schoolmates, professional colleagues, social relationships, even romantic liaisons (Jonathan frowned, knowing he may have to add Katherine to that ring). It was a terribly intrusive exercise—he shuddered at the

idea of someone composing such a stump about *him*—
nevertheless, it was necessary to understand clearly
just what type of man Tom Justice was, what relationships may have driven him to take another man's life (if
he in fact did), and who among the man's friends might
help persuade a jury that such a man couldn't possibly
have committed the crime (whether or not he did).

Next to the circular chart, Jonathan had posted a
long, horizontal timeline, one that accounted for the
moments leading up to, during, and immediately
following the alleged crime. The timeline would eventually show all of the major actors in what he irrever-
ently called "The Play." Each would be labeled with
their name, connection to Tom, and their whereabouts
during the event. Given the right motive, means or
opportunity, any one of them could turn out to be the
real culprit; it was just a matter of seeing them all on
the stage at once, and looking for a logical explanation
that put them there.

With those two visuals, the large blackboard which
he used for brainstorming, and his no longer tidy
conference table, Jonathan's office was beginning to
resemble a high-stakes war room. He couldn't claim to
be the field marshal, however; more like a traffic officer. Over the past several weeks, and with the help of
his secretary, Althea, he'd sent investigators and attorneys far and wide to collect the character witnesses
and testimony he hoped would paint a sympathetic
portrait of his client without drubbing the victim in the
process. Now the reports were starting to pile up.

Jonathan faced the two law clerks he'd hired to help

him build a case. They came highly recommended from rival law schools, a fact he rather liked, hoping a sense of competition would leave no line of inquiry unexplored.

"So," he said to the pair sitting before him. "I know it is early days, but what are your initial impressions?"

"I would say Tom's an onion with many layers. A man with heart, but ambitious, too. Sometimes those two are incompatible." Oliver Bean was a recent graduate of the University of California's Boalt Hall School of Law in Berkeley. Running a hand through his already-thinning blond hair, he flipped his pen onto the table and leaned back in his chair. True to his name, he was a beanpole, exceedingly tall with thin legs so long he had to point them away from the table in order to stretch out completely and not kick anyone.

"An onion," Cordelia Hammersmith said. "I'm sure we can convince the jury to acquit the good doctor on the grounds that he's a complex man with many so-called layers. Maybe he was busy cogitating when he accidentally pulled the trigger."

Miss Hammersmith was fresh out of San Francisco's Hastings School of Law, another University of California institution. She huffed as she straightened the files on her side of the table. In virtually every way she was the opposite of Bean: petite, dark-haired, quite obviously female, although any comments in reference to her gender would likely rain retribution down upon the poor speaker's head. She wasn't particularly skilled at hiding her disdain for ideas or people she disagreed with—she was much too honest. However, she was an exceptional logician. In their short time working together, she'd already proven her ability to put two and two together, combine it with seventeen other variables, and come up with a reasonable thesis based on the facts at hand. She was older, too—nearly thirty, he guessed—and he sometimes wondered if her prickly exterior could be attributed to some regrettable past experience.

"You're quite willing to denigrate Mr. Bean's analysis," Jonathan responded, his tone containing a hint of censure. "What, pray tell, is *your* take on Tom?" When it was just the three of them, Tom was "Tom"; to everybody else, including Tom himself, he was "Dr. Justice."

"Thus far, the depositions point by and large to a man used to having his way—and with women in particular. I'd say he's one of those 'love 'em and leave 'em' types, which doesn't bode well. Maybe it just didn't sit right with him that his college girlfriend left him, especially for a cousin that he admittedly did not like. Goes to motive."

Bean leaned forward. "Yes, but did she? Leave him, I mean? Sometimes there's both a public explanation and a private one. I'm not sure we know the full story yet as to who dropped whom.'"

"Well, she didn't seem to cry in her cups for very long—for which I give her high marks, by the way."

"I don't know. I think it was quite some time before she moved on, nearly two years before she began to see Eli Porter as anything other than a friend."

"By your standards that's long, maybe, but —"

As the two went at it, Jonathan wondered if both

Bean and The Hammer (as he already thought of Cordelia) were dealing with Dickensian-style ghosts of relationships past. That would never do.

He stayed the disagreement with his hand. "Those are each valid approaches, obviously open to conjecture at this point, but I hope you are both willing to change them as the facts warrant...*if* they warrant. It would be quite disheartening to learn that either of you let personal experiences cloud your judgment as to the true merits or flaws of this case. Whether he's guilty or innocent, Dr. Justice deserves the best possible defense we can provide."

Cordelia cocked her head. "Did you just call Oliver and my professional integrity into question? I think you did, but you did it in that understated English way of yours, so suppose I should let it go."

Jonathan heaved an inward sigh. American women could be so cheeky sometimes. He glanced at Bean, who was staring at Cordelia, aghast. At least *he* knew which battles to pick.

"I think you'd be wise to do that, Miss Hammer-smith," Jonathan said, "unless, of course you have someplace else you'd rather be."

He could see the instant in which she registered that she'd ventured slightly beyond the pale. She ran her hands down the sides of her small tweed jacket as if to check her uniform and fussed with her papers again. "Um, no. I'm fine right here...sir."

Jonathan turned briefly to his blackboard and suppressed a smile. That might be the only "sir" he'd get from The Hammer for quite some time. "All right, then. Mr. Bean, what have you got for us as it relates to the victim?"

Bean straightened in his chair. He really was a lanky fellow, even when seated. "We know that Elijah Eugene Porter was Tom's first cousin, that they weren't terribly close, as both men had a competitive streak."

"How novel," Jonathan observed dryly.

Bean ignored the comment and continued. "He came from a military family and by all accounts worshipped his father, tried in fact to emulate him by entering the service when he came of age, but the Army rejected him because he'd had rheumatic fever as a child. Supposedly the fever can cause heart damage that manifests later in life. None of the other branches would take him, either."

"That must have been heartbreaking," Cordelia said with surprising empathy, and paused before adding, "No pun intended."

Jonathan pursed his lips. "Continue, Mr. Bean."

"So, he barely makes it through Rutgers—not an exceptional student by any means, and there was some ruckus about possible plagiarism during his senior year before it was tamped down. He tries his hand at clerking for an export-import company whose owner had served with his father—who died fighting at Wounded Knee, by the way. But the job doesn't pan out and he just knocks around for a bit until his mother, Tom's Aunt Trudy, suggests he see what Tom's up to. His fortunes changed for the better after that."

"Considering where he ended up, that's a matter for debate," Cordelia said with a shrug.

"Quite," Jonathan said. "Keep at it, Mr. Bean; perhaps more details will emerge that shed light on their later relationship." He turned to Cordelia. "And what do you have for us, Miss Hammersmith?"

She stood on her side of the table, once more tugging on her uncooperative apparel.

"You're aware that shirtsleeves are acceptable when it's just us," Jonathan reminded her. "No need to remain so formal."

She gave him a perfunctory nod and began her report. "I've been grappling with Tom's career path. It's fraught with twists and turns. Frankly, he has me baffled."

"You, Miss Hammersmith? Baffled? I find that difficult to believe." Jonathan sent a faint smile in her direction

She didn't react to his chiding. "I know, but it's true. I think it's the strangest thing."

"What's the strangest thing?" Bean asked.

"Tom Justice had everything in the world going for him—I mean *everything*. He was on the way to the top. Yet he gave it all up. Why?"

Jonathan hadn't thought of Tom's life in that context, but Cordelia brought up an excellent point.

Why, indeed.

CHAPTER TEN

"The man was nothing short of brilliant with a scalpel."

—Dr. Kevin Huthchinson, Classmate at Johns Hopkins and Current Chief of Surgery, New York Hospital

"The patient is a forty-three-year-old Caucasian woman presenting symptoms of a growing tumor in the upper left breast. We will proceed to remove the breast, surrounding tissue, axillary lymph nodes, and pectoral muscles." Tom, now a second-year surgery resident, paused to let the secretary sitting in the first row of the operating amphitheater write down his running commentary. Although his mentor, Dr. William Halsted, stood by his side, it was Tom's first solo radical mastectomy, a procedure Dr. Halsted had pioneered twenty years earlier. Several medical students sat in the auditorium's higher rows to get a decent view of the proceedings.

Tom was the first of his class to perform the complicated operation. He was filled with a sense of controlled exhilaration, if such a thing were possible. Starting with the dissection of a frog so many years ago, on through biology, anatomy and physiology, and into the fundamentals of internal medicine and surgical procedures, Tom had sought the answers to all the questions of his boyhood. He was finally learning the "why" behind the art and science of healing; what's more, he was putting his knowledge to use. This was what Tom felt he was born to do, and now, at last, he was doing it.

The patient lay on Dr. Halsted's favorite operating table, which had been constructed from an old wood plank salvaged from a thirty-year-old army field hospital. Although the chief of surgery had advised against it ("Sometimes things go wrong, you know"), Tom had taken the time to meet the woman beforehand and explain the extensive procedure. He learned she was a seamstress who worked ten hours a day to help support her family. She was too poor to have an experienced practitioner operate on her, but Tom had assured her he was being guided by the most gifted surgeon in America. In fact, Dr. Halsted was a revolutionary when it came to training surgeons. Tom was damn lucky to have gotten into Johns Hopkins Medical School and later been selected for their new surgical residency program.

The woman's pretty face was now covered by a

large rubber mask through which another physician administered a mixture of ether and chloroform. Apart from her troublesome breast, her entire body was swathed in sterile sheets.

Tom took a moment to remind himself that Mrs. O'Brien was a live human being and not a cadaver or, worse yet, a surgical practice mannequin. Even if everything went right, she was going to have a tough recovery and might not be able to work as much as she had before. It was still better than the alternative, though. He'd seen patients in the last throes of cancer; it was heartbreaking.

"I will now make an incision above and surrounding the left nipple," Tom said.

Unlike some of his colleagues, he had no problem wearing the newly required rubber gloves; they covered the imperfections of his calloused hands and improved his dexterity. He needed every bit of that skill as he took the scalpel from the surgical nurse and sliced through the epidermis and then deep into the breast. Carefully unfolding the tissue to minimize blood loss, he worked his way to the tumor. It was the size of a walnut, but fortunately did not appear to be malignant.

"The mass is intact, approximately four centimeters in diameter, and appears benign."

"Strike that from the record, please," Dr. Halsted interjected. "Appearances can be deceiving. In cases such as these it is sufficient to limit your observation to size and shape."

Tom frowned at his mentor. Dr. Halsted stood a

few feet away with his hands clasped behind his surgical coat, unperturbed. Perhaps he hadn't seen what Tom had seen.

"It truly looks benign," Tom insisted, low enough that only Dr. Halsted could hear. "And even if it isn't, it appears encapsulated and therefore hasn't spread. Why can't I just remove it and sew her back up?"

Dr. Halsted stepped closer, his bald pate gleaming under the operating lights. He spoke quietly but passionately. "You are willing to tell this patient that you are one hundred percent sure she has no malignancy and that nothing will spread to the rest of her body? Truly?"

Tom looked down at the gaping wound he'd created. No, he couldn't say he was certain she had no cancer; that would be presumptuous. Yet his gut told him she would be all right, and much better off, if he simply removed the offensive mass and closed her up rather than remove so much of her. Unfortunately, if he announced his intention, he knew Dr. Halsted would ask him to step aside and would complete the operation himself. He took a breath and released it. "No, I can't say that."

Dr. Halsted nodded. "I didn't think so. Proceed, doctor."

During the next hour, Tom ably demonstrated his superior surgical skills. Following Dr. Halsted's protocol for performing a radical mastectomy, he removed the milk ducts, fatty tissue, nipple and areola, and all of the surrounding connective tissue. He excised the axillary lymph nodes under the woman's left arm and the pectoral muscles under her now missing breast. When he was finished, he deftly sliced away all excessive outer skin and carefully sutured the two sides closed, leaving a small opening for the post-operative drainage he knew would occur. From this point forward, the patient would possess only one breast; the other side of her chest would forever be unnaturally flat.

Dr. Halsted was known for his insistence on sterile technique; the proper control of bleeding; the gentle handling of living tissue; and the precise application of both dissection and wound closure. Tom Justice excelled in all of those procedures. But what he *wasn't* good at was telling a woman she might have just undergone a major, life-altering surgery that wasn't needed.

"She's facing a prolonged period of pain, if not a lifetime of it," he complained to Dr. Halsted in a private meeting after the surgery. The chief surgeon had an open-door policy, of which Tom now took full advantage. Dr. Halsted sat benignly at his meticulous antique desk while Tom paced. On the windowsill a small wooden planter contained bulbs just starting to sprout; the world-famous physician was renowned for his work with dahlias.

"She's a seamstress," Tom continued, "and the loss of her pectoral muscle might very well impact her ability to, I don't know, move the material through the machine or something. You know she'll probably suffer from edema because of the loss of those lymph nodes, not to mention numbness or weakness. What does she have to look forward to?"

"A much longer life, perhaps?" Dr. Halsted smiled faintly. "You admitted that you cannot categorically say she would be cancer-free without the mastectomy."

"But I can't categorically say that she had cancer, either. If she didn't, then she sacrificed an important part of her body for nothing!"

"Important? Come now, the woman was past child-bearing age, was she not?"

"Well, yes, but—"

"Then her need for one of her mammary glands is greatly diminished, wouldn't you say?"

Tom felt his anger rising. "A woman's breasts aren't just about producing milk," he said. "They are part and parcel of who she is."

Dr. Halsted looked at Tom. "Are you married, son?"

"No."

"On the verge?"

"No, sir."

"I daresay when you do reach that point in your life, you'll realize that it's far more important for a woman you care about to be alive than to be intact."

"All I'm saying, sir, is that we don't know if that procedure, with all of its consequences, was really necessary."

"Yes, it is one of the vagaries of our profession," Dr. Halsted admitted. The surgeon's hand quivered slightly. He reached inside the drawer of his desk and pulled out a small, dark bottle. "For my cough," he said, taking a sip.

It was common knowledge among the students that their revered professor was addicted to morphine and had been for years, although he still performed surgeries regularly. *Unnecessary ones,* Tom groused silently.

"Dr. Justice," Dr. Halsted said, "I'm sorry for countermanding you during the procedure, but you really did bring it on yourself."

Tom frowned. "How so?"

"It's simply that you went against my advice and got to know the woman behind the breast. It sounds rather cold, I know, but you must learn not to dwell on the individuality, or should I say the *humanity* of your patients. Your job is to focus on the technical challenges of each case and nothing more. Otherwise you will squander your talent—and it is considerable—in a morass of emotional entanglement. You have lives to save, sir. You can't afford to waste time on feelings."

Waste time on feelings? Hardly. Tom snorted as he left Dr. Halsted's office and headed toward the waterfront. Baltimore was usually gorgeous and temperate in May, but today an unexpected heat wave had descended, prompting everyone at the hospital to complain about "the spring that never sprung." He'd be covered in sweat by the time he reached The Horse. Good thing the clientele wouldn't notice.

Too many feelings had decidedly *not* been Tom's problem over the last several years. Since he'd arrived at Johns Hopkins in the fall of 1895, his life had consisted of school and work. Period. He'd missed Carina desperately at first, but over time, his feelings for her had faded to a slightly melancholic fondness.

There were times, especially when he found himself alone and staring at the bottom of a pint of Jack Daniels, that he'd wondered if he'd made the right decision. He had no doubt she would have been a lovely, loyal wife. And remembering how they'd been all over each other, he had no doubt that they would have satisfied each other on a physical level, too.

But even in his cups, Tom couldn't ignore the fact that Eli had been good for her. It had taken some time for his cousin to finagle his way into Carina's heart, but four years ago they'd gotten married, and according to his mother's latest letter, Carina was pregnant with their first child. If Tom longed for anything, it was a connection like that. Despite his decision not to become a farmer, his family had still been there for him, and instinctively he wanted to re-create that. But it hadn't happened yet, and most likely wasn't going to —at least not for a while.

It's not that he'd been a monk. Not at all. Thanks to a few fun-loving nurses and some ladies he'd met through work, he'd tasted the sins of the flesh many times. His hands, which had served him so well on the farm, the football field, and the operating room, served him equally well with women. He quickly learned how to give them exactly what they desired, and they in turn gave him what he needed, as often as he wanted it. But never did he leave the responsibility for potential consequences in their hands.

Only one woman, a fellow medical student and study partner named Cassie Fischer, had tempted him to pursue something beyond physical gratification. She was smart and pretty, and she was driven, like him. They'd progressed only as far as goodnight kisses when she accepted an internship working with Dr. Walter Reed in Cuba. That was a year ago, and she hadn't returned. He'd gotten a letter telling him how satisfying she found the work and her hopes that perhaps someday he might come for a visit, but her tone was certainly not of the "I can't live without you" variety. So died the almost-relationship he'd been hoping would end his solitary lifestyle.

It didn't help that Panda was happily married and a father already. Jimmy Wong had breezed through the University of Michigan's three-year medical program and fulfilled his promise to treat his countrymen back in San Francisco's Chinatown. He'd been working there for a while now, even set up a clinic and at one point had gone back to Canton to marry the woman his parents had picked out fifteen years earlier. Jimmy sent a photograph of them on their wedding day. There he was, all two hundred and forty pounds of him bursting with pride and standing next to Jinghua, who, with a sweet face and a serious expression, looked about twelve and barely came up to his massive shoulders. As mismatched as they looked, they were undoubtedly connecting on some level, because she'd already borne him two adorable little girls and was quickening with a third child.

It seemed like everybody was procreating these

days except Tom, and he had the box of rubbers to prove it.

Tom's scholarship to Johns Hopkins covered everything except beer, travel money, and the aforementioned prophylactics, so he'd found a job as a bartender at an old pub in Fell's Point called The Horse You Came in On. That part of town had served as Baltimore's port for over a century, and still kept its maritime flavor with a large number of bars and various dens of iniquity. Aside from being the oldest saloon in town, The Horse was known for being the last drinking establishment Edgar Allen Poe visited before his mysterious death in 1849. His ghost was renowned for showing up to make the chandeliers sway and the cash registers clang at odd times. Tom had yet to meet him.

"Hey Doc, you're just in time." Sally Merritt, the bar manager, untied her apron and tossed it to Tom. She was a fixture at The Horse, having worked there for thirty-five years. A lifetime of lager had left her with a red nose and a rounded belly, both of which she displayed with pride. She also sported a frothy bouquet of hennaed hair and a red tattoo on her left forearm depicting a voluptuous-looking seraph using two of its wings to cover its own nakedness. Script just below the angel's image read, "Prepare to be Amazed." "I assume you mean by God and not by what's under those wings," Tom had commented one evening as they were cleaning up, and Sally had let out a hoot.

"Makes you wonder, don't it? I say keep 'em guessing."

"Where you headed tonight?" Tom asked now, seeing that she was a bit more made-up than usual.

"Well, you sure as hell don't want me, so I had to look elsewhere. I got me a date with a handsome sailor man." She winked as she fluffed her hair.

Tom stepped behind the long, carved mahogany bar to set it up the way he liked it. "Whoever he is, he doesn't deserve you."

"You can read that both ways, you scalawag," she said, waving jauntily as she left the saloon.

Business was slow for the first hour of his shift; after that it started to pick up with a mix of dock workers, Johns Hopkins students, and neighborhood regulars. The Horse drew an eclectic, but always thirsty crowd.

A group of first-year residents came in. Tom recognized some of them from the operating theater's viewing seats earlier in the day.

The leader of the pack, a tall, earnest-looking fellow —Kevin Somebody—sat down heavily on a barstool, pulled some bills from his wallet, and slapped them on the bar. "A round of Arrow Premium for my buddies here," he ordered with a magnanimous sweep of his hand. "I'm celebrating. Just won a first-year surgery fellowship."

"Congratulations," Tom said. "Yours is on the house." He poured the drafts and lined them up on the bar. The students took them and raised an impromptu toast to their benefactor, sloshing some beer on the counter.

The grandstander leaned forward as Tom moved to clean it up. "Dr. Justice, that was some great slice 'n dice today. You were cool as a cucumber. Really carved her up good."

Tom winced at the imagery. "Thanks…I guess."

"So when do you get yours?"

Tom stopped wiping the counter. "When do I get my what?"

"Your chief assistant job."

"Ah, I'm not sure—"

"Not sure, my ass," Kevin Somebody said. He looked around to make sure they weren't overheard. "Pardon my French, but the word is that Professor Halsted considers you his heir apparent. You think he would have given you first crack at his most famous procedure if he didn't?"

"Well—"

"Listen, I've heard rumblings. They say once he taps you for Third Year Chief Assistant, you can practically sew 'House Surgeon' on your lab coat. You got it in the bag, man."

Tom quirked his lips as he resumed his cleaning routine. "You're pretty confident. Remind me to look you up when it comes time to buy some stock."

Kevin Somebody laughed and raised his glass. "That's a good one."

As Tom worked his way down the counter taking orders, the notion of Chief Assistant stuck in his mind.

There was no use dancing around it—he wanted it. Badly. He'd earn a small salary, which would come in handy. But more important, it was a major step up in the surgery department's pecking order. Kevin Somebody had it right: from there, it was usually a short hop to House Surgeon. And whoever made House Surgeon under the world-famous William Halsted could write his own ticket in the medical profession.

At the far end of the bar, one of the regulars, Clyde, was nursing a beer that Sally had poured before she left. He was smoking a cigarette and winced after taking a drag.

"Hey Clyde," Tom said lightly, drying his hands with a towel. "You do that little test I told you about last week?"

"Yeah, I did. Swallowed the lemon juice just like you said. Hurt like the dickens. Burned like hell. So thanks a lot."

Tom put his hands on the bar in front of Clyde. "No, that's a *good* thing. It confirms you've got way too much stomach acid. You may even have an ulcer. That's probably what's been giving you grief."

Clyde looked at Tom with bloodshot eyes. "Well, whatever it is, it ain't gettin' any better. Milk don't help, water don't help—" he held up his glass "—and this don't help, neither. But eventually it dulls the pain." He plunked the glass back down on the bar. "But too much of this swill gives me a headache, so the wife gives me those new aspirin pills she bought and the headache goes away but the belly kicks in again. It's the shits, and that's probably what I'll get next." He shook his head, obviously disgusted with the state of his health.

You a readin' man, Clyde?" Tom asked.

Clyde frowned. "I can, if that's what you're askin'. Why?"

"I got something I want you to look at. It's short and sweet." Someone had left a stack of flyers about an upcoming pro wrestling match at the end of the bar. Tom turned one of them over, took out a pencil, and began making a list. "Look," he explained as he wrote. "You do what I tell you on this list and I guarantee your gut will start feeling better." He finished writing and handed the note to Clyde, who read it aloud:

"'No smoking, no milk, no aspirin, no oranges...eat smaller meals more often...drink fresh-squeezed cabbage juice as much as possible...and drink a lot of water when pain persists.'" The man looked up at Tom, skepticism written all over his face. "At least you didn't say 'No sex or booze.'"

Tom grinned. "The point is to cure you, not kill you."

Clyde got up from his stool, plunked down the cost of the beer and stuck the ad hoc prescription in his jacket pocket. "I'll tip you later once I see how it works."

Tom cleared away the empty glass. "It'll work, all right. But you have to follow that plan. I'll check with your wife in a few weeks, see how you're doing."

Clyde dismissed Tom with a wave of his hand. "See ya, doc."

He'll probably do about half of what's on that list, Tom

thought as he filled more drink orders. But anything was better than nothing. What was it Nana Ruth used to say? *You do what you can do and leave the rest to work itself out.* He smiled ruefully, imagining his grandma's take on his current situation:

"Once you've done your best, you can't do much more about making chief assistant," she'd say. *"But you sure as hell can help a man with acid churning in his gut. Who's to say what's more important?"*

CHAPTER ELEVEN

"He didn't pre-judge the heathens like so many whites do. He had an open mind about them from the start."

—DONALDINA CAMERON, DIRECTOR, PRESBYTERIAN MISSION HOUSE OF SAN FRANCISCO

During college and part of medical school, Tom had been able to make it home for the holidays, but for the past three years, he'd pretty much worked year-round. He spent so much time at the hospital, in fact, that he and his fellow surgeons-in-training were nicknamed "residents." But Dr. Halsted believed in taking time off to rejuvenate before the all-important third year, so he gave his students a month off at the beginning of the summer. Tom decided a trip back to Nebraska was in order, followed by a visit to Jimmy Wong in San Francisco. Jimmy had hinted he wanted to talk to Tom about "something special."

Tom was set to take the three p.m. train when Dr. Halsted sent word to Tom's lodgings that he'd like to meet with him. Could he come to Dr. Halsted's office at one o'clock? Mindful of the tight schedule, Tom finished packing and brought his bag along so that after the meeting he could head straight to the station.

It was a mild day—the heat spell had broken—and the Johns Hopkins campus was quiet, with just a few stragglers remaining. Most of the undergraduates had already gone home for the summer, although Tom knew from experience that the med students were probably still working their asses off.

He found his mentor standing at the window, gazing out at the quadrangle that formed the geographic center of the university. It was one of the few times Tom had seen the man looking so relaxed. He knocked lightly on the open door and Dr. Halsted glanced at him. "Looks like you're all set to travel. Where's your home, son?"

"Nebraska, sir. I'm heading out to see my family before continuing on to San Francisco."

"What's out there? Not a girlfriend, I trust, since you told me you weren't involved with anyone."

"No, sir. My good friend Dr. Wong runs a clinic in the city. In Chinatown."

"Ah, a Chinaman, is he?"

Tom found himself bristling at the implication, as if being a "Chinaman" somehow put Jimmy in some kind of "exotic pet" category. "He was born in China. But he graduated from the University of Michigan with a degree in biology and then went on to study Western medicine there as well. He was an excellent student, and—"

"And yet he wasn't admitted to Johns Hopkins."

"No, he wasn't."

"I assume he applied?" Dr. Halsted raised his eyebrows in query.

As much as he wanted to lie and place Jimmy in a better light, Tom couldn't, and settled for a curt nod.

"Then he wasn't good enough to get in here, was he?"

Tom bristled even more. "Sir, I'm sure you didn't ask me here to grill me about my dear friend. So, if you don't mind, I'll—"

Dr. Halsted then sat down at his desk and beckoned Tom to sit as well. "I apologize. My wife chastises me for the artless way in which I often express myself. I was merely trying to make a point."

"What point is that, sir?"

The master surgeon fiddled with a pencil, holding it as if it were a small scalpel. His hand was beginning its usual slight palsy. Any minute now he would probably reach for his "cough medicine."

"I want you to be aware of how exceptional you are," Dr. Halsted said. "Because you are, you know. Your surgical skills are already far beyond your training, which means you're a natural...as I am." He looked Tom in the eye and smiled. "And that kind of talent doesn't come along every day."

Where was this going? "Thank you, sir. I appreciate the vote of confidence." Tom began to stand but sat down again when he realized the man had more to say.

Dr. Halsted pulled out a letter from the drawer of his desk and slid it over for Tom to read. "Yes, I do have confidence—and I'm willing to back it up with something concrete. I'm offering you the position of Third-Year Chief Assistant."

Stunned, Tom took a moment to gather his thoughts. Yes, he'd wanted it, but he hadn't presumed he'd get it. He owed Kevin Somebody a drink.

"Well? "Dr. Halsted asked. "What do you think?"

Tom felt a grin spread from one side of his face to the other. "I think I'll take it. Thank you, sir. I can't tell you what this means to me."

Dr. Halsted rose from his chair and extended his hand. "You deserve it, son. Now go on and enjoy these next few weeks. I'll expect you back and ready to work by the last week of June. There's a lot we have to cover before the First Years join us."

Tom returned the handshake. "Thank you again, Dr. Halsted. You won't regret putting your faith in me."

"I sincerely hope not. Now I think you've got a train to catch."

Tom's head was full of plans as he hurried out of the office. At last he could say goodbye to the depressing rooming house where he'd boarded for the past several years. With his new salary, he could maybe afford a two-bedroom place, or even a small house.

He made it to the station with ten minutes to spare and settled back to enjoy the sensation of complete and utter satisfaction, smiling at nothing in particular. If he could bottle such a feeling, he'd become a rich man overnight, for who wouldn't want to feel like this whenever they wished it?

Several weeks later, he longed for a swig from that imaginary bottle.

The three little girls waiting for their health examination looked identical, but upon closer inspection, Tom saw that they ranged in age from six or seven years old to possibly twelve. They stood huddled together in the outer room of the Chinatown Free Clinic, bone-thin and wearing pale blue dresses with puffy sleeves and little white collars, their hair cut in what one of Tom's lady friends might have called a "mighty severe hack job." Jimmy, known to his patients as Dr. Wong, stood by patiently while his wife, Jinghua, who was only slightly larger than the girls, chattered to them in Cantonese.

"She's telling them that there's nothing to be afraid of," Donaldina Cameron explained to Tom as they observed the scene from the front of the room. "She says her husband is just a big old panda bear who would never hurt them." At the end of Jinghua's assurance, the little girls looked at one another and giggled nervously. Jimmy smiled, then gestured for the first girl to join him and Jinghua in the examination room. They closed the door, and Miss Cameron spoke quietly to the remaining two, asking them to sit on the bench and wait their turn.

Tom had met Miss Cameron shortly after arriving

in San Francisco; she ran the Presbyterian Mission House and was one of the few non-Chinese who lived in Chinatown. Jimmy had been anxious for Tom to know he wasn't the only "barbarian" in the neighborhood.

By Tom's estimation, Miss Cameron was in her midthirties. She was pretty, though she took great pains to hide it behind a severe hairstyle and funereal clothing. According to Jimmy, she was married to her work, and although she could be a bit cantankerous, she was a true friend to the Chinese immigrant community, especially its children.

"Why are there so many orphans?" Tom asked as they waited for the exams to take place. "Jimmy—Dr. Wong—said there are far more men than women here. Are there not enough mothers to go around?"

"You could say that." Miss Cameron glanced at the girls sitting on the bench. "These two girls were brought over illegally as *mui tsai*—essentially slaves— and they have bravely chosen to leave their masters. Little Fai Jin was given to me by her mother, who is a prostitute here in Chinatown. She said that her clients were starting to look too closely at her daughter, and she wanted her to remain clean and pure. Dr. Wong is checking now to see if the mother was too late."

Tom couldn't hide his revulsion. "That's despicable."

"Indeed, which is why we fight for the body and soul of every child we can."

Miss Cameron smiled serenely, and Tom envied the absolute conviction with which she pursued her noble mission. She reminded him faintly of Cassie Fischer, who was no doubt living her own dream of helping others in the wilds of Cuba. He didn't think he was capable of such single-minded devotion.

Later that evening, Jimmy and Tom relaxed with a drink in the parlor of the apartment above the clinic. Jimmy and Jinghua had lived there until their second child was born, at which point his small but vocal wife insisted they move to a larger home. Now the apartment was a convenient space in which to care for their little girls whenever Jinghua helped her husband at the clinic. It was also the perfect guest quarters for Tom with its soft, silk-covered bed, efficient kitchen, and large reading chair in which Tom now sat.

"I am honored you took the time to come and visit me, Farm Boy." Sitting across from him, Jimmy leaned forward and tapped his glass of *baijiu* with Tom's. "Especially since you are such an important surgeon now."

"You're full of it, my friend." Tom took a sip of the vodka-like drink. It tasted faintly of plums—plums soaked in moonshine. "I told you, it's just a year-long teaching position."

"We both know it is much more than that. Our alma mater is acceptable, but Johns Hopkins is still far superior to everyone else in terms of the curriculum and the quality of its graduates. If they choose you for such a role, it is because you are truly exceptional." He paused and grinned. "Or unbelievably lucky."

"Aren't they one and the same?" Tom looked at his hands. "For some reason I'm pretty good with these. How's that any different than having brown hair or blue eyes? It is what it is." He pointed to Jimmy. "But you. I'd say you're the lucky one. Those children of yours are cute as can be, and Jinghua seems like she really dotes on you. And hell, you didn't even have to go to the trouble of finding her."

Jimmy leaned back and patted his stomach. "I cannot argue with you there. My parents were wise to select such a perfect match. I am fortunate that love bloomed where the seed was planted so long ago." He leaned forward, a new earnestness in his voice. "But I was joking with you. It is not mere luck that brought you the position you have been given. You have worked very hard to be where you are. I only wish you were not quite so good at what you do."

Tom laughed. "What?"

"All right, I am being half-serious now. Do you remember I said I wanted to talk to you about something special? Well, I had hoped that you would consider coming to work with me. Your skills are desperately needed here, and I am not simply talking about your surgical prowess, although that is part of it." He gestured around the room. "My people live in a ghetto in the midst of a magnificent city. A Golden City. They are feared and ridiculed by the ruling class. We need people who can traverse both worlds, who know us well enough to see that we pose no threat, that we only want to contribute to the wealth of this modern nation. And we need people—people like you —who can communicate that to those in power."

Tom was both surprised and impressed by Jimmy's fervor. Panda's energy had always been reserved for studies; everything else he had taken in stride. It was obvious his old friend now had a mission that meant a lot to him. But still. "What about Donaldina Cameron? You certainly couldn't find a better champion than her."

"Yes, yes, on balance she is a benefit to our community. But her help comes with a price. She requires conversion to the Christian faith for her brand of salvation. I am not opposed to your religion, but I do not care for the force-feeding of it."

"I don't blame you there, but I don't see what I bring to the table, other than the same skills you can recruit elsewhere."

Jimmy didn't respond right away. Instead he asked a question of his own. "Tell me something. Who was the last patient you treated and what did you prescribe?"

Tom pictured the various bodies he'd worked on, both alive and dead. By the time he saw most of the live ones, they were out cold and covered in sterile sheeting. He could describe what their body cavities looked like, but that was the extent of it.

Then Clyde came to mind. "A regular customer at the bar I work at," he offered. "He probably has an ulcer, so I gave him a list of dos and don'ts."

"You didn't tell him he needs some fancy medicine that he no doubt couldn't afford, did you?"

Tom smiled. "Not unless they're selling bottled cabbage water these days."

Jimmy leaned back in his chair again, apparently satisfied by Tom's answer. "My countrymen revere the old ways—and our old ways stretch much farther back than yours. Strange as it sounds, I have found that showing respect for the past is the key to convincing my people to embrace the future. I remember your stories of your grandmother, and the notebooks you filled with her wisdom. I think in your heart you understand that reverence for tradition, which is why the people here will come to trust you with their lives."

Tom snorted. "You sound like a salesman who doesn't bother asking the customer whether or not they want the plow, just which size plow they want." He took another drink. "My life is back east right now, Jimmy. And not to be too crass about it, but how would you propose to pay me, or any doctor, to come here? In fact, how *do* you get paid? In chickens?"

Tom meant it as a joke, but Jimmy nodded without a trace of irony. "Yes, sometimes. But money is not really the issue. The Chinese Consolidated Benevolent Association, which we call the Six Companies, looks out for the people of Chinatown. They, along with some charitable groups, support my clinic. And we have admitting privileges at St. Mary's Hospital. The clinic meets a vital need here in our community, and the right people know that."

Tom shook his head and finished off his drink. "I am flattered by your confidence in me, but as I said, my life is back in Baltimore."

"As you said." Jimmy heaved a sigh and polished off his own drink. "I will leave you to your slumber, Farm Boy. Tomorrow I hope to show you more of this great city, and this community that I have come to love so well. I will show you first-hand what my clinic is all about."

"Fair enough. I look forward to it."

It was midnight and Tom lay awake listening to the muted sounds of the street below. A horse clip-clopped slowly by wearing a bell that jingled lightly. The sound merged with that of two men speaking—Cantonese, no doubt. They seemed to be haggling over something, but not too seriously, since one of them laughed. They walked on and it was silent only for a moment before more male voices could be heard farther up the street.

Midnight in Chinatown was far different than midnight on the farm, different still than midnight on duty at the hospital. North Platte, Baltimore, San Francisco. He ruminated on the vagaries of his life and wondered how luck fit into it all.

Because of some hereditary fluke and yes, some hard work, he was poised to succeed beyond his wildest imaginings in a profession he loved. Yet the deep satisfaction he'd felt the day he learned about the chief assistant position hadn't lasted long. Why was that?

On the way West he'd gotten off at North Platte, where his brothers Henry and Jack had picked him up to take him home to see the folks. It seemed like forever since he'd seen them, and he was shocked: the boys had sprouted up like corn in July. Both were brawny and eager to razz him, squeezing his biceps and declaring he'd gone soft back in Baltimore.

"We'll see about that," he'd shot back good-naturedly. "I'll wrestle either one of you, or both at the same time, if need be."

When they pulled up to the farmhouse and he saw his mother running toward the buckboard, her so-familiar apron flapping wildly, he just about broke down. God, how he had missed them all! His father hung back, as he usually did. Tom stuck out his hand, but his father grabbed him into a bear hug and said softly, "We're so proud of you, son." Tom fought tears over that, too.

After a day of helping his siblings clean the plows and prep for hay cutting (his brothers griped that Tom had conveniently timed his visit to miss spring planting), he offered to help his mother wash the supper dishes. He joined her at the sink, where he towered over the woman who had brought him into the world. The light caught her aging features, and Tom was reminded of the quiet strength that infused her.

They worked in silence for several minutes before Tom asked the same question he'd asked for the past several years. "What do you hear from Aunt Trudy?"

They both knew that was his mother's cue to fill him in on the latest with his cousin. "She tells me Eli and Carina had a little boy. They named him Eli John, after Eli, of course, and Eli's father."

"And all went well with the pregnancy? The little guy's all right?"

"Carina sailed through it and the baby's doing fine."

His mother paused and looked at Tom. "Trudy loves Carina very much. She says the girl was meant to be a mother and she expects she'll be a grandma many times over. It's a very good thing. My sister needs something else to think about besides being alone."

"I know. I'm happy for them. Really." And he was. But the intangible ache he felt whenever he thought of Carina never quite disappeared. It was a strange sensation to know he might very well have traveled down that road with her. Who was to say he would have been any less happy?

All in all, Tom's visit was therapeutic, full of gossip and stories and laughing a lot with his brothers. He took his fill of barbecue and apple pie and camaraderie and unconditional love. And when he said goodbye again, it was with thinly disguised desperation, a sense that whatever he was heading toward couldn't ever be half as good as what he felt in that moment. Yet he wasn't meant to linger, and he knew that, too.

Spending time with his own family, and then with Jimmy's, only brought it all home: despite his professional achievements, Tom's life wasn't in balance. Would it ever be? And if it wasn't, would that be enough? Could he live with half a life?

"God, you sound like the guest of honor at your own pity party," Tom muttered in the dark and now quiet guestroom. "Next you'll be taking out a Lonely Hearts Club ad." Disgusted, he turned over and punched his pillow in an attempt to get some sleep. He remembered one of Nana Ruth's oft-repeated admonitions: *You got to make choices in life, and once you make 'em, you got to live with 'em. There's nothing else to be done about it.*

The decisions he'd made so far had led him to a very good place; it was just plain petty to complain that his life wasn't as perfect as others' seemed to be. Something else Nana Ruth used to say: *When you're climbin' a ladder with somebody else, only two things you got to worry about: not steppin' on toes and not fallin' off.*

That sounded about right. He couldn't worry about how everybody else was doing on their ladders; he just needed to focus on getting to the next rung of his.

CHAPTER TWELVE

"He good man, but he too skinny."

—Mrs. Liang Chunhua, Manager, Chinatown Free
Clinic

Tom, who had agreed to help Jimmy while he was in San Francisco, was roused out of his bed promptly at seven the next morning.

"It is time for you to rise and shine, Dr. Justice." Jimmy called up the stairs, a smile in his voice. "And please to come down looking decent, because my assistant is already on duty."

Mrs. Liang was a tidy Chinese matron in her early fifties who possessed an ungodly amount of energy. After traditional Chinese treatments had failed to cure her husband of gout, Jimmy said, he'd stepped in and prescribed a regimen that alleviated most of the man's pain, thus converting Mrs. Liang to the miracle of

Western medicine. Because she and her husband knew practically everyone in Chinatown, she began to talk up "The Amazing Dr. Wong." (Jimmy related this with a roll of his eyes.) Patients began showing up to the clinic in droves—so many, in fact, that Jimmy hired the lady to help keep order. The arrangement worked to everyone's satisfaction, since it enabled Jinghua to spend more time with their children and only required her to step in on Mrs. Liang's days off.

The woman was organized, efficient, productive, and vocal. She made sure Jimmy had the supplies he needed, served as an impromptu nurse when called upon, and most important, kept track of appointments and payment for services rendered. It was thanks to Mrs. Liang (with back up from Jinghua) that Jimmy earned anything at all; with his kind and easygoing nature, he would have given his services away for free and then fretted about not being able to pay his bills. With Mrs. Liang at the helm, even though the painted storefront window read "Chinatown Free Clinic—Pay What You Can," everyone paid *something*, even if it was one of those chickens Tom had kidded Jimmy about.

Over the course of the morning, with Tom observing (and often assisting), the "Amazing Dr. Wong" dealt with two broken bones, one dislocated shoulder, a case of insomnia, a gallstone attack, one stomach ache (the patient was four and had eaten an entire basket of cherries), a case of poison ivy, and an older man with hemorrhoids. Speaking in Cantonese, Jimmy introduced Tom to one and all as his professional colleague, describing his friend, or so he said, as "an award-winning surgeon from a very famous medical school in Baltimore."

"My stature rises when I show that I am associated with someone as accomplished as you," Jimmy exclaimed with a grin. "I am taking shameless advantage of our friendship."

Two other patients had needed minor surgery, and while Tom itched to perform the simple procedures himself, he knew it was best for Jimmy to refer the cases to St. Mary's, the nearest Western hospital. Rincon Hill was a little over a mile away.

"They do not always take my patients," Jimmy explained as he filled out the appropriate referral form. "I do not know if it is the patients or the referring physician they find objectionable. But I keep trying."

"Why don't you just do the procedures yourself, then?"

Jimmy smiled ruefully. "I think I have lost my touch with a scalpel, although I am not sure I ever had much of one to begin with."

Jinghua brought the men a quick lunch of fried pork and rice, and the afternoon, with even more patients, flew by. Mrs. Liang had kept her distance from Tom at first, but gradually warmed to him. By quitting time she was mother-henning him like her own flesh and blood, pantomiming what she wanted him to do as she kept up a nonstop monologue in her native tongue. She finally patted him on the shoulder, wagged her finger at him, and left for the day.

"She likes you," Jimmy told him, "but she says you

need to put more meat on your bones and cut your hair."

"Well, you can tell Mrs. Liang I appreciate her concern and will endeavor to heed her advice."

"Of course," Jimmy said. "That's what we all say to her."

The two men fell into a companionable silence as they straightened up the two examination rooms. Both had been taught the wisdom of Listerism and took care to wipe down the counters and soak the examination instruments in a carbolic acid solution. Tom had brought Jimmy several pairs of modern examination gloves specially designed by Dr. Halsted and while Tom carelessly tossed his in the trash, Jimmy peeled his off carefully so that he'd be able to use them again. It struck Tom how very different—and more primitive—conditions were here than back in Baltimore. It reminded him of a sensitive topic he'd been wondering about.

"What's the real story about the so-called 'China-town plague'?" he asked. "When I told my colleagues I was coming to visit you, they all shook their heads and said they'd pray for me. And half of them don't even go to church."

Jimmy's face tightened. "It concerns me. It is not a widespread problem, but the few cases of it have occurred in this part of the city. The governor of the state has tried to keep the story small, but it has grown big enough that doctors from your federal government are now involved. They know that it has something to do with the rats, and I am sad to say that Chinatown has very many rats."

"What are they doing about it?"

His friend continued to clean off the counter, frustration evident in the forceful strokes he made across the already-pristine surface. "They have thrown a very big book at it. They tried a quarantine of our community, but that didn't work. They tried to force vaccinations upon every Chinatown resident, and that didn't work either. Now they are starting to hunt the rodents in our neighborhoods, and some in the city—those who really do not like us— want to destroy every building in order to kill the creatures. They want to move Chinatown out of the city altogether."

Tom scoffed. "That sounds like using a sledgehammer to kill a flea. I can't see that happening, can you?"

"It is not entirely impossible." Jimmy had moved to the small sink by the door and now carefully rinsed his gloves before washing his hands and arms. "My people are vilified by many, and this may provide the perfect excuse to eradicate us along with the rodents."

"Have you seen any evidence of the plague here at the clinic? I mean, how do you deal with it?"

"Taking action is difficult, to say the least. We have had no one come directly to us, but the few times we have learned about a patient, we have been able to isolate him and manage his symptoms to the extent we can. Bubonic plague is nearly always a death sentence, but morphine can lessen the agony. Yet we are hampered even there."

"Why?"

The look Jimmy sent Tom was bleak. "Residents are so afraid of the government that when a citizen becomes ill, he often hides, and if he dies, his relatives dispose of his body secretly."

Tom nodded. "And if you don't know about it, you can't disinfect his surroundings to make sure it doesn't spread."

"Precisely. But do you know what is even worse? When patients come down with a malady that may mimic the plague, such as an acute rash or a very bad case of pneumonia, they often think they have caught it and they refuse to seek treatment. Sometimes they die of something that could have been cured. I tell you, it is the most troubling aspect of my work here."

Tom lightly tapped his friend on the back. "Sounds like you could use some help in all sorts of ways. Don't worry. You'll find someone."

Jimmy sent Tom a ghost of a smile. "Every day I pray that you are right."

They both knew it was a platitude, but what else could Tom say? It was a hell of a predicament to be in.

After an awkward silence, Jimmy lightened the mood. "Come along, my friend. I must put some meat on your bones so that you will have the energy to face Mrs. Liang tomorrow. She won't let up, you know."

Tom ran his hands through his too-long hair and grinned. "Maybe you can recommend a good barber while you're at it."

"Oh, that would be Jinghua," Jimmy said. "She has been anxious to get her hands on you." He grinned at

Tom's stunned expression. "She thinks only Chinese look good with long hair, that barbarians like you need all the help that short hair can bring you."

"I am hers to command," Tom said.

The next three days unfolded much like the first. Tom and Jimmy worked in tandem, seeing dozens of patients, forging a comfortable rhythm. Each night Tom would fall into bed, pleased with what he'd done, happy to sleep, wake up, and do it all again. He no longer ruminated about luck and the time passed quickly.

On the fifth day, Tom was awakened as usual by Jimmy, but this time he knocked on the door rather than called from downstairs. Nearly dressed, Tom greeted him with a smile, ready to chastise him for being so formal. The stricken look on his friend's face stopped him cold.

"What is it? What's wrong? Is it Jinghua? The girls?"

Jimmy shook his head. "May I come in?"

"Of course. Can I get you something? Some coffee?" He gestured for Jimmy to sit. "A drink, maybe?"

Jimmy shook his head again, beginning to pace across the small parlor.

"Come on, man, let me in. Sit down and spill it."

Jimmy stopped and looked Tom in the eye. "I said the other day that I was taking shameless advantage of our friendship. I am afraid I must continue to do that."

"What do you mean?"

"Late last night Jinghua and I received word that my father is very ill. He has had some heart issues and this time he is not expected to live beyond the end of the month."

As Jimmy's voice broke, Tom grasped him by the shoulder. "I am so very sorry. How can I help?"

"I have been seeking steamship passage for myself, Jinghua and the little ones since early this morning and have found only one ship willing to take us. It is with a new company, Pacific Global Shipping, and they are happy to give us passage at a price I can afford. The only problem is, the ship sails tonight."

Tom stared at his friend, knowing what Jimmy had to ask, and understanding how difficult it was for him to ask it. So Tom beat him to it. "I take it you want me to stay and work at the clinic for as long as I can?"

Jimmy wore the same expression he'd had when Tom had gotten into Johns Hopkins and Jimmy hadn't. Tom saw the disappointment...and the resignation.

"I know you have to leave in a few days. I know that your life is back east. I only ask that you see as many patients as you can and then close the clinic for me when it is time for you to go."

Tom frowned. "Close the clinic? You must have someone who can step in while you're gone."

"Tom, you may have been first choice in my heart as someone to help me, but in fact, you are the latest in a long line of polite refusals I have received. I have been searching for several months, in fact, to no avail. If I am not here, the clinic has no one and must shut its doors."

He shook his head. "Mrs. Liang is good at many things, but she does not have a medical degree."

"What about St. Mary's? Surely, they'll help out. Miss Cameron can take the girls there at least."

Jimmy slowly shook his head. "She does not want to deal with papists in any way."

"That's ridiculous."

"But a reality, nonetheless. I have heard that in a few years a group of well-respected physicians will open a modern hospital on the outskirts of our community. But until then, we do not have many options."

Tom reached out to console his friend. "Dammit, Jimmy. Of course I'll see your patients as long as I am here. You square it away with Mrs. Liang and then do what you need to do to get your family ready to go."

Jimmy's broad shoulders slumped, whether from relief or utter despondency, Tom couldn't tell. "Thank you," he said.

"It's no more than you would do for me. Now go. I'll finish getting ready and be down shortly." Jimmy was halfway out the door when Tom realized just what he was about to undertake. "Ah, Jimmy? I think I'm going to need an interpreter, and pronto. Maybe Miss Cameron can recommend somebody?"

"I will send Mrs. Liang to ask her straightaway," he said.

Tom spent nearly two hours dealing with both patients and the stress of communicating using nothing but pantomime and body language, but by mid-morning Miss Cameron had come through. Almost as large as Jimmy, Lee Pritchett had the look of a nearly bald mongrel, with round dark eyes, a pronounced cleft chin, and a thick, drooping, reddish-colored mustache that would have been right at home in the Highlands of Scotland. Mr. Pritchett didn't seem fazed by Tom's curious regard.

"My ma was one of the original hundred men's wives," he said jovially. And my pa was a miner whose seed must have been stronger than most." He tapped his chin. "You should see his."

Tom felt his face redden; he usually showed better manners than to stare at someone.

Lee smiled. "Don't you fret, doc. I'm an oddity, but I won't bite. I just got off a construction site and I need work. So if you're willin', I'm ready and able. I speak Cantonese and I can do any heavy lifting you might need, too."

Tom recovered quickly and stuck out his hand. "I'll have to figure out how to pay you, but for the time being, you're hired, Mr. Pritchett."

"Call me Lee. Everybody does."

"Lee it is." Heaving an inward sigh of relief, Tom gestured to Mrs. Liang. "Tell her I'm ready for the next patient, would you?"

Lee addressed Mrs. Liang in Cantonese, eliciting a wall-to-wall smile from her. Then she nodded at Tom, her look saying, *All right then, let's stop lollygagging and get to work.*

Even with Lee's help, it was a long, long day. After the last patient had left and Tom had cleaned and locked up, he headed over to Jimmy and Jinghua's home on Jackson Street to help them transport their baggage to the wharf. There the USS *China Sea* was taking on passengers for a nine p.m. departure. Tom boarded with them to find their stateroom and deposit their bags. He hugged Jinghua and their little girls goodbye before returning to the deck with Jimmy, who handed Tom a stack of papers.

"I have written a letter of introduction that you must take to Cheung Ti Chu at the Six Companies," he explained. "He will make sure that you have all the supplies you need as well as compensation for Mrs. Liang and Mr. Pritchett and yourself."

That didn't sit well. "I don't need anything for myself, Jimmy."

"I knew you would say that, but you have worked very hard and you are helping me tremendously. It is the least I can do."

He didn't want to waste time arguing. "So, how long do you think you'll be gone?"

"I wish I knew," Jimmy said. "The trip will take us at least three weeks, and by then, Jinghua will be too far along in her pregnancy for us to travel again. After the baby is born we will have to wait some time before returning."

"And the clinic?"

"It will stay closed until the Six Companies can find a replacement physician. Perhaps they will be more fortunate in their search than I."

The ship blew its whistle signaling *All ashore that's going ashore* and Tom's emotions threatened to swamp him. He and Jimmy may have been separated by a continent, but at least it had been the same continent!

The gentle giant he had come to love was leaving, and who knew when he would see his friend again?

Unlike most men, white or Chinese, Jimmy had no problem showing his deep love for Tom, nor his grief at having to leave. He embraced Tom fully, tears flowing down his large round cheeks.

"You are most honorable friend," he said. "I owe you—"

"You owe me nothing," Tom said gruffly, returning the hug. "You helped me so many times, I can't ..." He stopped because he didn't have the words to express how much this man meant to him. Tears fell onto his cheeks and he wiped them away with swift, angry strokes. He absolutely did not like saying goodbye—not to his family, nor to his closest friend. Not for reasons like this.

The whistle blew again and Jimmy stepped away. "Oh, I forgot." He pointed to the other papers he'd handed Tom. "There is a supply list and my address in Canton and some other things. When we arrive, I will write to you, care of the clinic, and have Mrs. Liang forward it to wherever you are going to be. Please be sure to give her your new address when you get it."

"I will," Tom said, turning to leave. Afraid he'd make a fool of himself if he stayed any longer, he trotted down the gangway and jumped onto the dock. He must have been the last to leave the ship because a dock worker soon pulled on a giant lever that raised the gangway, separating it from the ship. The worker then untethered the last line wrapped around the bollard on the wharf. Ever so slowly, the ship began to back away from its moorings.

"I will miss you, Farm Boy," Jimmy called to him.

"You take care, Jimmy!"

A final blast of the whistle and the USS *China Sea* began to steam its way to Canton.

CHAPTER THIRTEEN

"Tom Justice was more than just a roommate. If I could pick someone to be my brother, I would pick him. I have never met a finer man, either white or Chinese."

—Wong Jing Sau, Physician

The rest of the week and the next vanished, as time does when there are too many activities to fill it. The day of Tom's departure arrived and he woke early, tidying up the apartment, wondering idly who would live there next. He had agreed to keep the clinic open until noon, which would give him plenty of time to pack the last of his things and make his four o'clock train.

Lee and Mrs. Liang were waiting for him downstairs, as was a line of patients. They had evidently been told this would be their last chance to see a

Western doctor for quite some time. Tom worked as quickly as he could, treating minor ailments, following up on patients he'd seen earlier with Jimmy, writing down prescriptions and recommendations—much as he had with his ad hoc patients at The Horse back in Baltimore. Lee would have to transcribe those notes, since none of his patients spoke or read a lick of English.

Despite his efforts, the line didn't seem to be getting any shorter, and Tom worried that he'd have to turn patients away. That went against everything in his nature, so he picked up the pace.

Just before noon, a commotion outside the clinic caused the remaining patients to start talking all at once. Tom walked over to the large storefront window to see that a wagon had pulled up in front. A thickset, middle-aged white man was lifting a slender young Chinese woman into his arms in order to bring her inside; badly beaten, she appeared to be unconscious. Right behind her was Donaldina Cameron, fit to be tied and demonstrating why she was known by some in Chinatown as "The Angry Angel."

"We need your help, Dr. Tom. Lai Waa has been beaten by her procurer. She's not breathing very well."

"Of course. Bring her into room one." The man carrying Lai Waa looked to Miss Cameron for guidance and she gestured for him to follow Tom into the room. He laid the woman on the examination table while Tom washed his hands, and when Tom turned back around he noticed the missionary touch the man on his sleeve to get his attention. When he turned to face her, she used sign language, which must have instructed the man to take his leave.

"Wilbur is one of my most devoted volunteers," she said after he left. "Thank goodness he was there when we needed him."

Tom had already begun his examination. The patient suffered from multiple contusions and lacerations, and one of her wrists had been broken. Her blood pressure was low, and when he palpitated her ribs, she moaned, even in her unconscious state. "Who would do such a thing, and why?" he asked, tamping down the rage he felt toward someone who would treat another human being, especially a woman, so horribly. The irony wasn't lost on him that he wanted to kill the person who would do such a heinous thing.

"Lai Waa—she's the mother of little Fai Jin, do you remember? She just wanted to see her daughter, so she stopped working long enough to come down to the mission. Her so-called 'protector' did not want her off the street that long, so he thought to teach her a lesson. If there is a silver lining here, it is that perhaps now Lai Waa will join her little girl, accept the Lord, and leave her filthy life behind once and for all."

Accept the Lord. Jimmy was right about the price Donaldina expected her rescued girls to pay. It couldn't be as high as the one she'd just paid for remaining a prostitute, though, could it? Well, it wasn't for him to judge, only to help the poor woman. He checked her chest cavity with his stethoscope; it did not sound good.

"I'm afraid she has a broken wrist and a few

cracked, if not broken ribs," he explained. "But the more critical issue is that I'm almost certain her spleen has ruptured and it's causing some internal bleeding."

"The poor thing," Miss Cameron murmured. She looked up at Tom. "What can you do for her?"

"I would suggest she see a surgeon to have her spleen removed and to see if any other organs are damaged."

"Can you do it?" the missionary asked.

"Well, yes, but—"

"Then do it," Miss Cameron said without hesitation. "What can I do to help?"

Tom hesitated. The one thing he needed above all else was time, and Miss Cameron couldn't help with that. He pulled out his pocket watch. Perhaps if he began now, he could finish in an hour. It was a simple enough procedure. "Afterward you must have her admitted to St. Mary's. She has to be watched in a sterile environment over the next several days."

Sucking a lemon would have produced the same scowl appearing on Miss Cameron's face. "All right. I will try. Now let's get to work."

Mrs. Liang had been trained in the application of chloroform and Tom conscripted her to serve as the anesthetist. Surprisingly, Miss Cameron herself proved to be a perfectly capable surgical nurse, more than willing to scrub beforehand and don both surgical gloves and a sterile gown. The Angry Angel didn't flinch at the sight of a scalpel cutting into human flesh, the flow of blood, or the exposure of internal organs.

She remained calm throughout, and Tom began to see the woman's incredible strength.

He made an incision below Lai Waa's left breast and worked his way beneath the rib cage. The capsule surrounding Lai Waa's spleen had indeed been split, and part of the organ itself was damaged beyond repair. After separating the ruined pulp from the pancreas and tying off its blood supply, he removed it and suctioned out the excess blood that had pooled in the abdominal cavity. Finally, he examined the other organs, found no other major issues, and closed the incision. Throughout the procedure, Lai Waa showed obvious discomfort, but thankfully did not regain full consciousness.

When he finished the procedure, he stepped back and took a deep breath. All that he had learned, all of his training, had paid off; if things went well post-operatively, he could count Lai Waa as a success. He may have even saved her life. Now *that* feeling should be bottled.

He checked his watch: two thirty. That was cutting it close; even if he left right now, he'd just barely have enough time to get to the station. But he had to try.

"Remember what I said," he admonished Miss Cameron. "She needs to be kept in a very clean environment." He pulled off his gloves and gown and hurriedly left the makeshift operating room. Miss Cameron was right behind him.

"*Sing gung!*" she called out, smiling and raising her fist in the air.

The waiting room of the clinic, still filled with patients, erupted into cheers and applause. Someone began chanting "Dr. Tom! Dr. Tom!"

Tom looked back at Miss Cameron. "What did you tell them?"

"I merely said that you are every bit as wonderful as Dr. Wong and that they are very lucky to have you."

Tom frowned. "All that in two words?"

Miss Cameron tried to hold back a smile but failed. "Perhaps that wasn't quite a literal translation. Nevertheless, it's true."

"But you know I have to leave," he said, sounding almost desperate.

"Do you?" she said. "What more do you want, sir? What more do you need?"

Tom surveyed the sea of expectant faces. Young, old, male, female. They didn't look the same to him anymore; now he could tell them apart. There was Ah Cho sitting with his wife and scowling, even though she was patting his hand. He was suffering from a debilitating case of arthritis, and while Tom had prescribed some clearly unappreciated dietary restrictions, he hoped the ointment of black cohosh and feverfew had helped. Li Na, a servant, had burned her arm badly when she spilled a pot of boiling water on it; she was having the dressing changed today. The list went on, but they all had one thing in common: they all needed help.

He bartered with himself. *I can cable Dr. Halsted and tell him an emergency has come up. Maybe he'll give me some more time here. Maybe Jimmy will come back sooner and I can return to the surgical program before too long. Maybe...*

He glanced at his watch one more time and made his decision. "Where is the nearest telegraph office?"

CHAPTER FOURTEEN

Late March 1907

Jonathan was already seated when Cordelia Hammersmith entered his office holding a wooden box just over a foot high.

"Mr. Bean sent word he's going to be a few minutes late," she said. "He's waiting to hear from a witness, I believe." She set the box down in front of the large blackboard and stepped upon it. Without even looking at him, she murmured, "Don't say a word."

I wouldn't dare, Jonathan thought, willing his lips not to twitch.

She began by writing "Tom's Women" across the top of the board, which she could now reach. She then began to list several names.

Jonathan shifted uncomfortably in his seat. He knew this aspect of his client's life had to be examined, but he was not looking forward to it. Was he ready for what The Hammer had uncovered?

"I'm not sure—"

Oliver Bean swept into the room, rapidly removing his coat and hanging it on the hall tree before straightening his tie and finger-combing his wispy hair, all while struggling to handle a stack of folders. "Sorry. So sorry," he said. "I've been having a devil of a time nailing certain witnesses down." He placed his files on the table and sat in his customary chair. Cordelia had finished writing her list, which ended with the name "Katherine Firestone."

Jonathan grimaced. Oliver had only postponed the inevitable. "Proceed, Miss Hammersmith."

She nodded and remained standing on the box, choosing to ignore the image she presented of a little girl trying to be a grown-up. Jonathan made a mental note to lower the board for their next meeting. Then again, perhaps she preferred lording it over the men in the room. Should he ask her and risk having his head bitten off?

"Our assumption has been from the beginning that if the prosecution is correct, Tom Justice killed Eli Porter because the victim had eclipsed him and was living the life that Tom wanted, a life he felt that Eli had stolen from him. Our best defense under those circumstances would be that it was a case of voluntary manslaughter. Tom had a momentary break with reason and, overcome with emotion, meted out his own brand of ill-conceived justice. The prosecution will try to assert that Tom had a long-standing hatred of Eli, indicating aforethought malice and warranting the murder charge. We would argue that Tom had no way of knowing that Eli would end up in the Mechanics' Pavilion and that fact would abrogate their line of reasoning." Cordelia tapped on the names and looked back at her colleagues. "However, I think the prosecution's approach on this is, quite frankly, a bunch of hogwash."

Jonathan glanced at Oliver, who looked both surprised and pleased. It seemed his two clerks were about to agree on something. "What have you learned, Miss Hammersmith?"

"I heeded your advice, Mr. Perris, and tried to examine the evidence with an open mind. Having looked at the testimony from all these women, I have come to certain conclusions about our client."

"And those are?"

"First off, by all accounts he is an exceedingly attractive man, despite his relatively disheveled appearance at the moment."

Well, *that* was irritating. "You think so, do you?"

Cordelia nodded, oblivious to his tone. "Oh yes, a woman would have to be either dead or a follower of Sappho not to notice. I was able to talk to half a dozen women who admitted, some openly, and some under the condition of anonymity, that they'd had 'relations' with him. They signaled a keen satisfaction with his performance and none admitted to feeling as though he had given them—"

My God, we don't need bloody chapter and verse, Jonathan thought.

"—short shrift." Oblivious to the salaciousness of her report, she pointed to Katherine's name. "The last woman, Miss Firestone, did not admit to such a relationship, but I would stake my reputation on the fact that she had at least considered it, and is in fact closer to our client than any of the others. And that includes the one woman I could not interview, of course— Carina Porter."

Jonathan drummed his fingers lightly on the table. As he suspected, the bond between Katherine and Tom was stronger than he'd hoped.

"Your point is that he was not in fact suffering from unrequited love," Oliver said, following her train of thought. "That he had a healthy, uh, romantic life, and had moved well beyond Mrs. Porter."

Cordelia smiled. "Yes. I think we can easily present Dr. Justice as a typical American male who enjoyed women—without dipping into excess—but who had finally, shall we say, met his perceived 'soul mate.'" At this point she looked directly at Jonathan; the expression on her face held empathy. "The prosecution will try to portray our client as a man holding on to the past in twisted ways, but they are wrong. Sometimes we like to think that our first love was our truest love, or that the person we've decided is our true love can't possibly be the true love of anyone else. Sad to say, that just isn't true."

Jonathan found himself staring at Cordelia, sensing that somehow she'd intruded upon his innermost thoughts. He didn't appreciate it.

"Interesting," he said blandly. "Mr. Bean, what do

you have for us?" He noticed the flash of anger in The Hammer's countenance, which she quickly banked; she obviously did not like her work or theories being dismissed.

Bean seemed to rise in his chair, even though he remained seated. "First let me say that I quite agree with Miss Hammersmith's logic, although there is always a soft spot, as you say, for the first person who manages to capture your heart." He flipped open the top folder on his stack. "My investigation has traversed along more prosaic paths, yielding mixed results. During the past several years of his career, Dr. Justice has shown himself to be a more than competent professional. Those who have worked for him, and those who have been treated by him, invariably praise his work."

"I sense a 'however,'" Jonathan said.

Oliver shrugged. "Our client isn't always willing to follow the rules or the dictates of society. Certain decisions have put him at odds with those in positions of authority. He also has connections to individuals that, if brought up by the prosecution, will reflect badly on him."

"What kind of individuals?" Cordelia asked.

"The worst, I'm afraid," Oliver said. "The kind who kill."

CHAPTER FIFTEEN

"I was disappointed, to be sure. He had the makings of an exemplary surgeon. Even today I would offer him a position."

—Dr. William Halsted, Chief of Surgery, Johns Hopkins Medical School

Tom hefted his bag up to the overhead compartment of the second-class rail car of the Overland Limited and made himself as comfortable as possible given the seats weren't built for men his size. He knew from experience that sleep would be hard to come by.

Across the aisle sat a man and wife and their two young sons. The father, offering Tom some pickles they'd brought, said they were going to Kansas City "to see the wife's kinfolk." His wife, a plain, prim-looking woman, smiled briefly before reaching over and stopping her two sons from mock fist fighting in their seats. The boys looked like they had a bit of the devil in them. Tom met the father's eye and chuckled; they'd both been those boys at some point in their lives. But how would these two scamps drive their parents crazy on this particular trip? He noticed a slingshot sticking out of the older boy's back pocket. *Let's hope he's going to shoot targets out the window and not the other passengers.* The mother looked capable of giving her boys what for if they didn't toe the line.

Since 1900, Tom had made it home every November. Now, three years later, it still took more than three days to reach North Platte.

"You see family like before. Have good time. But come back. Go to work." Mrs. Liang's English was improving, but still limited. Nevertheless, she always got her point across. He'd been damn lucky to have her stay on along with Lee Pritchett. Between the three of them, the Chinatown Free Clinic was thriving.

He'd missed Johns Hopkins terribly at first. The only indication of Dr. Halsted's disappointment had been his clipped tone, but it was enough to send Tom into periodic moods of regret.

And yet, the challenge of tending real people's problems made up for much of his disappointment; it certainly fulfilled his Nana Ruth's prediction that he was meant to heal others. He used a combination of modern medical techniques along with his grandmother's natural remedies to great effect; in the process he was also learning the benefits of traditional Chinese medicine. Jimmy had been right: his ability to incorporate the old ways made his patients far more willing to try something new.

He even got to practice surgery more than he'd expected. Many routine procedures were handled on-site, but for more complicated cases, he'd been given both admitting and surgical privileges at St. Mary's. They'd also hired him to work a shift or two at the hospital each week, which helped his cash flow immensely. Although he did not personally care for the hospital's administrator (the man seemed more interested in garnering publicity than saving lives), Tom fit in well with the medical staff. They seemed to trust him more than they had Jimmy, no doubt because he was white. On the other hand, while ninety percent of Tom's patients were Chinese, they seemed to accept *him*, a "barbarian," just fine. He didn't like to dwell on the imbalance of such attitudes; instead he focused on what really mattered, which was helping his patients, whoever they happened to be, get better.

The worst disappointment of his tenure in Chinatown was learning that Jimmy would not be returning, at least for the foreseeable future. Panda had made it home in time to say good bye to his father, but as the only son in the immediate family, it had fallen upon him to assume the duties of the patriarch.

"I am hoping one of my cousins can step in and take over," he'd written three months after his father's passing. "But he is still young and must learn how to care for the family's holdings." Jimmy had gone on to praise Jenghua for blessing him with a healthy, hefty son. "She tells me she is only giving me three more children," he wrote. "I can be happy with that."

Six children. And Tom was having problems meeting a woman with whom he'd like to have even one. Through friends and co-workers at the hospital, he'd met a few ladies to whom he was attracted. One, a buxom widow in her late thirties named Adeline, let him know early on she was interested in a "close but discreet" relationship, but nothing more. "Being shackled once was enough for me," she'd said. They'd gotten together enough times to satisfy each other's physical needs, but that was as far as it went.

He wasn't sure he'd ever meet someone who would make him think, as he had with Carina, that there could be something more.

The balance in his life remained out of reach.

They'd passed Sacramento and were beginning the long ascent over the Sierra Nevada. The young boys had no doubt gone in search of adventure. Their father, who'd been trying to get some shut-eye, was prodded by his wife, who shooed him in the direction the boys had taken.

The rumbling, rocking motion of the train had almost put Tom under when the two kids came noisily back into the car, shoving each other and followed by their exasperated parent. He showed his wife the slingshot he'd confiscated and she tut-tutted, insisting the boys sit directly across from her, where she could watch them. It was going to be a long three days.

Needing something besides pickles to tide him over until dinner, Tom worked his way back to the lounge car, where a steward manned a snack cart. He was contemplating a ham sandwich when he felt a tug on his sleeve. A teenage girl he'd gotten to know from the mission surprised him with an enthusiastic smile.

"Dr. Tom! Fancy meeting you here. Or should I say..." She dropped her voice. "How delightful to see you again in such unusual circumstances." She giggled, her tone back to normal. "That is what my teachers at the Weems Academy would consider the proper greeting. It's the silliest thing, isn't it? But it's so good to see you! This is my first trip on a train. We are going to a wedding. Are you traveling to New York, too?"

The speaker was Mandy Culpepper, who worked at the Presbyterian Mission House after school. She'd been introduced to him as the mission's "historian," and Tom understood that to mean that, among other things, she and the interpreter Fung Hai went throughout Chinatown, looking for young women whom Miss Cameron could rescue.

"No, just as far as North Platte to see my folks," Tom said. "They have a farm a few hours away from the station."

Mandy took his hand. "Well, come with me, you must meet my guardian."

Tom followed the girl through the second-class cars and into the first-class section of the train. When they reached the middle of the second car she slid the door open to a spacious parlor where a young man and woman were seated.

"Look who I found!" Mandy cried.

The man, wearing a benign but confused expression, glanced at the woman and stood. He looked well-to-do, and the woman...

The woman was flat-out gorgeous. She was tall and trim but had outstanding curves beneath her elegant blue outfit. Her face was striking, with clearly defined cheekbones, flawless skin, and full, pink lips. And her hair... her hair was a shimmering color of gold, piled softly on top of her head.

God, I hope they are brother and sister.

Tom continued to stare at her until he felt someone nudge him. It was Mandy. He looked over to see the man's hand extended.

"Will Firestone," he said. "You're obviously a friend of Mandy's."

"Oh. Oh, I'm terribly sorry." They shook hands. "Tom Justice at your service." He immediately turned back to the woman. "And you are?"

"Katherine Firestone. I'm Mandy's guardian. Will's sister."

Thank you, God.

She waited a moment, returning his gaze before holding out her hand. He took it and held it. It felt incredibly silky against his rough palm and he had to force himself not to stroke it. She slowly removed herself from him.

"Silly me," Mandy said. "I just realized you all don't know each other. Dr. Tom works with the mission and helps the girls. He sees patients at the hospital, too. Everybody loves him."

Tom felt his face heating up. "That's hardly the case, Mandy, but I thank you for the compliment." He turned his attention back to Miss Firestone. "I understand you are all traveling to New York to attend a wedding."

The beauty looked up at him with incredible blue eyes and spoke in a voice he imagined she reserved for servants—civil, but nowhere near warm. "Yes, on Thanksgiving Day. And what about you, Mr. Justice?"

Odd. She'd either not heard Mandy say he was a doctor, or else she was deliberately downplaying his title. Which was it?

"Oh, I'm traveling back for the holidays as well. My family has a farm near North Platte. I'll have a long buckboard ride once I get off the train."

"Ah. How…quaint."

Her tone was dismissive, as though he were a clumsy rube. She may as well have called him "Farm Boy." Once again Tom felt his face flush. So, she was one of those society snobs. What a shame. He would have politely excused himself then and there except that Mandy took that moment to boldly call her guardian on her rudeness.

"My teachers at the Weems Academy tell me that the word 'quaint' means 'old-fashioned' or 'out of date.' It is something you say when you don't like something but are too polite to tell the truth. You didn't mean it like that, did you, Miss Kit?"

At that moment, Tom wanted the earth to swallow

him whole, and by the look on Miss Firestone's face, she did, too. They spoke at the same time, trying to cover up the social blunder, then lapsed into an awkward silence. After gazing at both of them, Mandy announced that she was going back to Tom's rail car because she'd seen some popcorn for sale or some such nonsense. She picked up a courtesy blanket and said he'd be more comfortable with it.

"That's not necessary," Tom said in a tight voice. The last thing he needed was Miss Firestone thinking he was a charity case.

Her brother waved a hand. "Best to let Mandy do what she's going to do; otherwise she'll find another way."

Tom couldn't leave fast enough. He hadn't felt so out of place since his first year of college, and he damn well wasn't going to suffer through that again, no matter how lovely the lady happened to be.

But oh, she was so very lovely.

CHAPTER SIXTEEN

*"At one point Dr. Justice was a real catch. I don't know why
one of the young debs didn't snatch him up."*

—DR. GARRETT SAMUELSON, PHYSICIAN, ST. MARY'S
HOSPITAL

Back from his Thanksgiving visit, Tom endeavored
to put Katherine Firestone out of his mind and
concentrate on more important matters, like the
continued health of his patients. The fact that he
wanted the woman more than anyone he'd met in years
didn't mean a hill of beans. It wasn't going to happen.

What concerned him now had nothing to do with
beautiful women and everything to do with rats.

Jimmy had been right: there was no denying the
presence of the plague. Over the past year, federal
health inspectors, led by Rupert Blue, had pulled out all
the stops to eradicate it, and by all accounts they were

gaining the upper hand. In terms of sheer numbers, the cases were low, a couple hundred at most. It was no longer front-page news.

But now and again, like a lone thief who sneaks in the back door to steal a family's valuables, the disease would strike—a prostitute, a factory worker, a cigar maker, a child. No one was immune.

Tom's patients were skittish of anything that had to do with the authorities, especially when it came to their health. So he let them know, through Mrs. Liang, that if they came down with something they thought it might be "the sickness," they could trust him to do whatever he could for them without getting the government involved. By making that pact, he hoped to bring more sick residents out of the shadows. So far it had worked, and while he'd dealt with lots of bronchitis, influenza, and mysterious rashes, he hadn't had to report any new cases of the Black Death.

The possibility of infection did remain, however. Worried about sending her historian and interpreter into Chinatown without protection, Donaldina Cameron had made an appointment earlier in the year to see Tom at the clinic. Behind closed doors she'd asked him to inoculate both Mandy and Fung Hai with the Haffkine vaccine, the same vaccine that had sent terror into the hearts of the Chinese immigrants back when the plague first arrived.

Tom had refused. "The vaccine doesn't work that well," he'd told her, "at least not well enough to justify all the negative side effects."

They'd settled on giving Mandy and Fung Hai small

doses of the Yersin antiserum, the drug used by all the federal health inspectors who dealt with the disease.

"Some people have bad reactions to it," he'd warned her, "so you need to let Mandy's guardian know what's going on in case she gets sick."

Donaldina had assured him she'd take care of it.

Now that he knew who Mandy's guardian was, he wondered if Donaldina had ever followed through on that promise. Perhaps Miss Firestone knew all about it and that's why she'd snubbed him, to show her dislike of the steps he'd taken without her permission. Or maybe he reminded her of someone she didn't care for. Maybe—

Enough. Tom vigorously shook his head. Katherine Firestone was hereby officially banned from his thoughts forever.

He saw her again three weeks later.

St. Mary's Hospital, where Tom was now employed part-time, held an annual charity ball for their children's ward. Tom wasn't thrilled about going, but he figured he should show support for his new employer and their cause. Fortunately, he had a tuxedo for the event; at least he wouldn't be mistaken for a "farm boy."

When he agreed to attend, however, he didn't realize he'd be part of the ball's main fundraising attraction.

"Come on, man," Dr. Samuelson urged after Tom's initial refusal. "We announce your bona fides to the crowd, so it's good promotion for the hospital. You get to know some of the movers and shakers in town, which is good for your career. And it helps the children, for Chrissakes! You can handle one afternoon with a simpering miss, can't you?"

With no reasonable comeback, Tom now stood with four other young professional men on a dais at the front of the packed ballroom. A four-course dinner had just been served; they were the "palate cleanser" before dessert.

The setting was opulent, a *Nutcracker*-inspired fairyland with waiters running around dressed as toy soldiers and life-sized mice to incite giggles from the ladies in the crowd. Several candle-laden Christmas trees were scattered throughout. One was decorated with nothing but crystal ornaments, another trimmed entirely in gold. The most slyly ostentatious of them all, however, was a ten-foot noble fir covered with homemade cut-outs and "Dear Santa" letters from the hospital's pint-sized patients, each stating a first name, diagnosis ("bone cancer," "consumption," "quinsy") and a plea for Santa to help little Johnnie or Carrie get better. It was a shameful play on emotion…and it was working. Tom noticed more than one couple conferring as they read the letters, the wife taking time now and again to sniff discreetly into a handkerchief.

Tom's cohorts on the dais seemed oblivious to such goings-on, preening and flirting with the young women who would soon be voting for them with hundred-dollar tickets, like they were slaves on an auction block. *I'm being raffled off,* he thought, mortified. If they asked to examine his teeth, he wouldn't be responsible for his actions.

"And our last bachelor is also our newest. Meet Dr. Thomas Justice, who hails from Nebraska's corn country. He's a graduate of the University of Michigan, where he attended on a full athletic scholarship and helped the Wolverines to their first-ever victory against Cornell's Big Red back in '94, which I'm sure many of you in this room remember."

Several of the men attending the ball cheered and raised their wine glasses in salute.

"He earned his medical degree from Johns Hopkins University Medical School, now considered the most prestigious institution of its kind in the country, and was a surgical resident under the world-famous Dr. William Halsted. Ladies and gentlemen, we are most fortunate to have one of the nation's most up-and-coming surgeons working on our staff today."

Dr. Samuelson couldn't have laid it on thicker with a trowel. He'd conveniently left out the fact that Tom worked full-time for the Chinatown Free Clinic. That would have gone over real well, no doubt.

Tom tried not to feel self-conscious as the debutantes filed past, some with their mothers, tittering and exchanging pleasantries with him. He did his best to appear interested in what they had to say, and happy to be on display. He could tell that most of the men and women were comfortable with the ritual, clearly having done it many times before. Thankfully, more than a few of the young women put at least one of their tickets in his basket, out of curiosity, perhaps, or sympathy.

The ladies' perusal of the bachelors had almost ended when Katherine Firestone walked up to him, several tickets in hand. She was dressed in an emerald-green gown that showed off her pale shoulders and hinted at the perfectly rounded breasts beneath the fabric. Her hair was swept up again, only this time it had tiny pearls woven into it. She radiated not just confidence, but an awareness that she was the envy of most of the women in the room, and she wore that allure with pride. He thought of the lemon chiffon cake his mother had once made for a church social and warned him not to touch because it was meant for others. Knowing it was forbidden had triggered an insatiable desire in him, which later he'd laughed about because he'd never even tasted lemon chiffon cake. He was not laughing now.

"Well, now you know," Katherine Firestone said to him, as if they were finishing a conversation they'd had before.

He frowned. "Know what?"

"How the other half lives." She glanced at his cloth-ing. "If you must know, I find it surprising you have such suitable clothing. You don't strike me as the type who has spent much time hobnobbing with ..." She gestured around the room to make her point.

Tom sent her the faintest of smiles. "With cultured, civilized people, you mean? You're right. I was actually given this suit in trade."

The look of boredom was replaced by a raised eyebrow. "In trade? For what?"

"A tailor in Chinatown has a little boy who'd fallen from a balcony." He leaned forward. "The floor had rotted through. Broke his leg and an arm, lacerations—a mess, really. We were able to set the bones and get the boy cleaned up. His father was grateful, but didn't have any money, so he made me this." Tom plucked his lapel. "We were both happy with the outcome."

Miss Firestone's expressions were subtle, but he read them all the same. He saw the moment she realized how small she'd sounded, and the moment she opted to brazen it out.

"Perhaps. Let's hope the boy doesn't walk with a limp, then we'll know for sure, won't we?"

Impugning his medical skills did not sit well. "Miss Firestone, may I ask you something?"

She was busy smoothing down her dress but looked up at his request. "Certainly."

"Is it men in general you don't like or just me in particular?"

For a moment her facade broke and he glimpsed a hint of vulnerability. Then it passed like a wisp of smoke and was gone, replaced by a bland expression and a flat tone of voice.

"I don't know you, *Doctor* Justice. Why would I care about you one way or the other?" He watched her return to her seat. On the way, she dropped four tickets in the basket of the bachelor next to Tom—a man she hadn't even deigned to look at.

"I know if I asked Miss Kit, she would ask her mother if you could come to Christmas and it would be all right," Mandy said two days before the holiday. She had stopped by the clinic to get a dose of the antiserum and to practice giving shots. She'd become quite adept at injecting water into the hides of unsuspecting oranges.

That's pretty much the last place I'd want to be, Tom thought. But he admired the wide-eyed optimism of Katherine Firestone's ward even if he didn't share it. "Thank you for thinking of me, Mandy, but I'll be working. You sound pretty excited about going, however."

"Oh, I am. It will be the first time meeting Miss Kit's mother and father. They were very kind to invite me."

"It seems only natural, since Katherine—Miss Firestone—is your guardian."

Mandy squirted the air bubble out of the syringe like he'd taught her and paused to consider the orange, as if there were a particular part of the rind that would absorb liquid less painfully than another. "Yes, but Mrs. Firestone was forced into it—if she had her druthers I would not be here and Miss Kit would still be living at home."

"How do you know that?"

Mandy looked up at him. She had a most arresting face—beautiful, really, for one so young, but odd, too. Her eyes, with their unusual curve, held a strange kind of power.

"I feel things about people, you know? Like Miss

Kit. She has so much love inside, but she is afraid to show it on the outside. I don't know why exactly, but I do know she is afraid of turning into her mother." She tipped the bottle of saline solution to refill the syringe. "I wish the two of you could become friends. I think she admires you, and I think maybe you admire her, too, at least the way she looks. And you are both lonely."

She hadn't looked up while she said the last part, which was good, because her words left Tom speechless. He had an excuse for his loneliness, but Miss Firestone? Hardly. He couldn't help but ask, "What makes you think Miss Firestone admires me? We didn't exactly hit it off, as you recall."

She patted the now waterlogged orange as if it were a patient that needed comforting. "She asks about you. And the clinic. At first she was upset that I wanted to work at the mission, but now I think she would like to do something good, the way you do, instead of worrying so much about things she knows don't really matter."

"Maybe she could help Miss Cameron," he said.

Mandy let out a chuckle. "I think going to church on Sunday is about the extent of Miss Kit's *religiosity*. Now that is a ten-dollar word if ever there was one! I think Miss Rodham—she's my English instructor at the Weems Academy—would be proud of me."

Tom gave Mandy a brief hug. "I think Miss Firestone is pretty proud of you, too."

"She is, although she is careful not to get too close, not even to me. She is like a prickly pear. On the outside she has spiny thorns, but on the inside, she is sweet and juicy. I know you would find that to be true if you got to know her."

Mandy had no idea of her words' connotation, but her description of Katherine Firestone stayed with him long after she left. *Sweet and juicy.* My God.

The end of 1903 came and went, and a new year brought with it more work and a sense that perhaps Tom would never find exactly what he was looking for, at least in his personal life. The result of the charity raffle was indeed an afternoon with a simpering miss, and one that he had no intention of repeating. He continued to see the buxom and jovial widow Adeline on occasion to satisfy his physical needs, but Katherine Firestone kept intruding on his thoughts, becoming his forbidden lemon cake. He saw her once in January, at a social event that Miss Cameron had dragged him to, and they'd exchanged brief but civil greetings. He'd begun to think that maybe, possibly, Mandy was on to something. Perhaps in time he would be able to explore beneath Katherine's spiny thorns.

The events of February thirteenth, however, dashed those hopes completely.

CHAPTER SEVENTEEN

"Back when plague in Chinatown, he know more than he tell government. He sneaky, that one."

—Shing Tao, Traditional Chinese Doctor

Tom opened the clinic as usual on Saturday morning, and had already dealt with a broken toe and a case of tonsillitis when Fung Hai, Mandy's interpreter, burst into the front waiting area. He spoke to Mrs. Liang in rapid-fire Cantonese and she began to chatter back, no doubt telling him to calm down. Making out the words "Dr. Tom" and "right away," Tom quickly finished washing his hands and asked Fung Hai what was troubling him.

"Is secret," the young man said. "Only for your ears."

Once the door to the exam room was shut, Fung spilled his story. Apparently Katherine's brother, Will Firestone, had spent the night with Tam Shee Low, the headmistress of the Chinatown School for Needle Arts. The two of them, along with Tam Shee Low's little girl, were suffering from "the sickness." Mandy wanted Dr. Tom to bring the antiserum right away.

The plague has finally hit home, Tom thought as he closed the clinic and packed his bag with supplies. *It's not just a disease of the "heathen Chinee" any more.*

He brought Lee Pritchett, his jack of all trades, along to help. Dressed in protective clothing, Tom and Lee drove the clinic's wagon to the school and ran to the upstairs apartment where Tam Shee and her daughter lived. By the time they arrived, however, the little girl, Sai Fon, was dead.

After administering the antiserum to the adults, Tom examined the mother. She exhibited all the signs of the advancing disease—fever, chills, abdominal pain, and, most tellingly, swollen lymph nodes in her neck and armpits. She was in shock, clutching the limp body of her child as tears streamed down her mottled face, her suffering beyond anyone's ability to console her. He would have to remove the poor child's body, but first he had to establish a quarantine.

Mandy, of all people, volunteered to remain sequestered with the patients and nurse them back to health. The building had already been exposed, she reasoned; why go anywhere else? And because she had been taking the antiserum for some time, she was uniquely qualified to stay and care for them. But she was so young for such a difficult task.

"I don't like it," Tom said to her. "It's too…irregular."

In her oddly adult fashion, Mandy pointed out that

Will Firestone came from a very powerful family and would be crucified by the public if they knew he had gotten the plague from someone they'd assume was a whore—which Tam Shee most definitely wasn't, Mandy assured him. Not only would such a scandal crush Tom's parents, but the whole affair would put Chinatown in a very bad light. Did he really want that to happen?

I can't fault her logic, Tom thought, and part of him couldn't help but add Katherine to the mix. She would be vilified by association if word got out.

"All right," he said. "I'll get you supplies, but you must let me know through Fung Hai if there's anything else you need, including more help."

She nodded. "But would you please tell Miss Kit what is going on? She needs to know."

Keeping the incident under wraps meant keeping Sai Fon's body from the authorities. But first he had to convince the devastated mother to let go of her. Like so many other Chinese immigrants, she was petrified of meddling Western doctors. Lee explained that she was protecting her child's soul; she didn't want Sai Fon's body cut open for fear of losing that soul forever. Using Lee to help him translate the more difficult concepts, Tom promised the woman he would not let the authorities perform an autopsy of her little girl, and damned if he wouldn't do everything possible to keep that promise. But in the end, he did lie to her. In the gentlest tone he could muster, he told Tam Shee that he would bring Sai Fon back to her.

She continued to waver, so Will Firestone leaned

over and spoke fervently to her, stroking the young mother's sweat-soaked hair. She obviously trusted him. After much hesitation, she slowly handed the body over to Tom. God, he would never forget the look she gave him: frightened, not for herself, but for her daughter's eternal life, beseeching him to keep his word.

I will not let you down, he vowed silently. He wrapped the little girl in a clean blanket and handed her to Lee, who took her downstairs to await instructions. He then turned his attention to the two sick adults. Tam Shee was in dire straits, but Will Firestone didn't look much better.

"Are you sure you can do this?" he asked Mandy.

"Without a doubt," she said. "Now go."

Lee proved to be worth more than his weight in gold, which was considerable, given how large the man was. Once he had placed Sai Fon's body in the back of the clinic wagon, they returned to the clinic so that Tom could pick up the supplies Mandy needed. Lee assured Tom that he would take Sai Fon to a Chinese undertaker he knew who would place the child's body in a "safe" place, securely wrapped and free from contamination. "She don't deserve to be poked and prodded by the government men," he said. Tom couldn't agree more.

After Lee left, Tom packed his medical bag and took a cab to Will Firestone's stylish residence on Russian

Hill. A beefy, pugilistic type answered the door and ushered Tom into the mansion's imposing entry hall. Its walls were beautifully paneled and the parquet floor featured an intricate floral medallion in the center. *What a lot of fuss for a space most people merely walk through*, he thought.

Then Miss Firestone appeared, looking every bit as graceful as the room she inhabited. Today she was dressed in an ivory-colored shirtwaist and a soft-looking, pale lavender skirt. His attraction to her irritated him; this was no time for such nonsense.

It was apparent that she knew he wasn't making a social call. She didn't mince words. "What is wrong?"

"I must speak with you privately," Tom said, glancing at the fighter standing guard by the door.

"You may speak in front of Fleming. He is Will's majordomo and is practically a member of the family."

Tom ran a hand through his hair. Sharing news like this was the absolute hardest part of his job. "Your brother—"

In a flash her eyes grew wide; her hand flew to her mouth. "I knew it. What has happened to him?"

"You brother is very sick, and Mandy is taking care of him. She wanted you to know that she would be tending him and not to worry. You won't be able to see him, but—"

"Dr. Justice, you must be insane if you think you can tell me something like that and not have me go to him," she said, giving a nod to Fleming, who promptly left the room.

"I'm sorry, but it's not safe." He took a consoling

step toward her, but she backed away, as if by avoiding him she could avoid the truth.

"Fleming!" she called in a voice tinged with frenzy.

The man hurried back into the entry hall carrying Katherine's coat and his own. They acted as if Tom didn't exist.

"You need to tell me where he is," she commanded.

"Actually, I don't." Tom, irked at her presumptuousness, watched her eyes spark with rage. "He is most likely contagious. But out of respect for Mandy I will ride with you so that you can talk with her and see for yourself what is going on."

Katherine glared at him, a test of wills. Did she think he would cave to her demands? She soon learned the folly of that but didn't capitulate completely; her attitude remained brusque.

"Very well," she said imperiously. "If you must tag along, I suggest we leave immediately, if not sooner. Fleming will drive us."

Tom sat next to Katherine in the back of her carriage as they rode to Chinatown. The maroon leather seats were soft and under different circumstances it might have been an immensely pleasurable ride. Now, however, the tension precluded any semblance of comfort, physical or otherwise.

He kept a neutral expression, offering no more details about her brother's plight. Whether it was pride that kept her from grilling him or something else, he was glad she remained silent.

After several minutes, she called to the front of the conveyance. "Fleming, can't you go any faster?"

Fleming turned slightly and called back over his shoulder. "Not in this traffic, miss."

"Take Vallejo down to Grant rather than Union," Tom said, leaning forward. "Less congestion that way."

"Right you are, sir," Fleming said.

Tom glanced at Katherine, who was staring out the window. She raised a hand gingerly toward her cheek but changed course and smoothed her skirt instead. She was trying very hard not to appear rattled but was failing miserably at it.

Suddenly she gasped and turned to him. "You said my brother is contagious and he's in Chinatown. Are you saying he might have…this…this plague they're talking about?"

Tom stopped her jittery hand with his large, warm one. "The symptoms point in that direction, yes."

She stared at his hand covering hers before slowly withdrawing it. Refusing to look at him, she said, "Well, that is unacceptable. We will simply have to do something to fix it."

"Look at me," he said in a quiet voice. When she refused, he reiterated the command, taking his hand and gently turning her chin toward him. "We are doing all that can be done, given the circumstances. There is nothing more you can add, which is why your visit will be brief."

He'd thought to offer her solace, but his words had the opposite effect.

"We'll see about that," she pronounced to the air in front of her.

There was no point in arguing, so he simply looked out his window until they arrived at the school. He was not looking forward to what came next.

Once they entered the little shop on the ground floor, Tom turned to Fleming. "For your protection I ask that you stay downstairs, sir. Miss Firestone will only be a few moments."

Fleming looked to Katherine for guidance. Tom could tell he was intensely loyal to Will and by extension to her. If she asked him to follow her, he probably would, and that could be a problem. Fortunately, it didn't come to that.

"It's all right, Fleming," she said, looking defiantly at Tom. "I'll be down to give you directions before you leave."

When they reached the apartment, Katherine forged ahead. "This...this *quack* here says that I cannot stay and take care of my own brother," she announced to Mandy, who was just stepping out of the bedroom; behind her, both Will and Tam Shee were huddled under blankets on the bed. "Which is ridiculous," Katherine continued. "How is Will doing?" She attempted to go around Mandy and enter the room, but Tom stopped her with an arm across her waist. She tried to break his hold, but he held her firm. Under any other circumstance their embrace would have filled him with pleasure, but not this one.

"Please!" she begged.

"No," he said. "You are not going in there."

"Will is sleeping now," Mandy said. "Come to the front room and talk to me, Miss Kit."

Reluctantly, Katherine followed her. They spoke quietly and Tom imagined Mandy was using the same logic with her guardian that she had on Tom.

"But why you?" Katherine cried, her voice rising loud enough for Tom to hear.

"Because I am perfect for the job." Mandy's voice was matter-of-fact. Lowering her voice again, she continued to talk, and Tom couldn't help but admire the girl's poise. At one point, Katherine whispered something that made Mandy shake her head slightly before she wrapped her slender arms around Katherine's shoulders and whispered something back.

Tom hated to intervene, but the longer Katherine stayed in the room, the more agitated he felt. He wanted her away from the danger. "I want to show you what I've brought in terms of supplies," he said to Mandy.

Katherine seemed at last to accept the situation; her focus now turned to her ward. "Are you sure you can do this, Mandy? We can't lose him...or you. We simply can't."

Mandy assured her she'd do her best. With one last look, Katherine grudgingly followed Tom down the stairs, where Fleming and Fung Hai waited.

"We'll know if he's going to pull through in a day or so," Tom said, trying to inject as much confidence as possible into his words. "As soon as Mandy gets word to me I'll pass the message on to you."

Katherine busied herself pulling on her traveling gloves. She looked up at him, her eyes a reflection of barely banked rage. "I will never forgive you for this," she said coldly. "You have put Mandy, me, all of us in an untenable position."

His eyes caught hers and held them. "I didn't bring the plague, Miss Firestone, and I didn't give it to your brother. Whatever you may think of me, this is the best way to handle the situation for all concerned. Even you."

She looked at him a moment longer, eyes flickering. A slight retreat, perhaps? "Good day, doctor."

Tom watched Fleming escort Katherine back to the landau; her retreating figure was a study in pride and forbearance. As the carriage door snapped shut, so did Tom's hopes that he could do anything to raise her low opinion of him. While his instinct was to give her comfort, he feared that was the last thing Katherine Firestone would ever want from him.

Some things, he supposed, were just not meant to be. With a nod to the interpreter who waited patiently below, Tom went back up the stairs to see what else Mandy might need. At least he could help *her*.

CHAPTER EIGHTEEN

"The man your legal system accuses of murder is incapable of committing such a crime. However, I can list several members of your government who have been involved in much worse. Shall I name names?"

—TANG LIN, BUSINESSMAN AND COMMUNITY
ORGANIZER FOR NEW CHINATOWN

The days, the weeks, the months rolled on. It was 1905 and Tom Justice filled his time with work at the clinic and St. Mary's, punctuated by the occasional milestone—a staff member's birthday, a family holiday, a life-saving surgery, which buoyed him, or the loss of a patient, which brought him low.

Katherine ("Miss Firestone" when they crossed paths, but now, in his mind, always "Katherine") was lucky to still have her brother. While the young Chinese mother had not made it through, Will Firestone had cheated death. Mandy had pulled him through the worst of it, earning Tom's respect for her bravery and compassion. The man she saved must have been adversely affected by it all, however, because several weeks after he recovered, Will Firestone took off for parts unknown.

'Parts unknown.' It had a nice ring to it.

In the meantime, the plague had finally petered out. Rupert Blue's all-out offensive against the diseased rats had kept the simmering tragedy from exploding into a massive one. After the federally mandated clean-up program, Chinatown did look better, and that was bringing more whites into the enclave, which was good for business. The leaders of the Six Companies had so far thwarted efforts to move the immigrants out of the city center; things were looking up on that front as well.

Tom stayed fit by walking and exercising whenever possible. The city's hills challenged his legs and his stamina, and the boys down at Winkler's Gym got to know him as "Big Doc." He didn't need muscles, but he lifted weights to keep them so that he could give his brothers a run for their money on the rare occasions they got together. He missed them more than he would ever admit.

The widow Adeline appreciated his efforts to stay in shape, at least. A firecracker of a redhead with curves to spare, she was more than happy to provide Tom with unfettered physical release whenever he needed it, and he reciprocated. He tried not to fantasize about the woman whose body he would have preferred to lie with. Somehow that seemed disrespectful. There were times, though, when he weakened, and imagined Katherine beneath him, taking him willingly into her body.

Jenghua was carrying baby number five—her "penultimate," according to Jimmy. The letters from Canton arrived like clockwork every other month, full of news about the family and Jimmy's responsibilities now that he was the patriarch. In his spare time he'd begun seeing patients using Western-style medical techniques, happy to be helping bring his people into the twentieth century. Although Jimmy never spelled it out, it was evident he wouldn't be returning to San Francisco. The possibility of sharing a practice with his good friend faded, not without a tinge of melancholy.

Tom did have a new assistant, however, if only a temporary one. A young doctor by the name of Anson Cotter had signed on for a year-long internship at St. Mary's, and part of his duties entailed working several shifts at the Chinatown Free Clinic. While the hospital was renowned for working with the poor, its policy was that certain "types" of poor were better served in their own neighborhoods. Now the board could brag that both Tom and Anson were part of their "neighborhood outreach" program.

Anson was from a wealthy East Coast family and wanted to see the West before putting down roots. Tom had to admit he showed promise, but he was a cocky son of a bitch, and he talked way too much. Tom felt old and staid by comparison.

"You really like working with the Chinee?" Cotter

asked during his first week. They were having lunch on the small porch in front of the clinic. Anson had brought out two beers from the clinic's icebox. "Liquid diet," he joked. He didn't offer Tom a bottle.

"I do like it," Tom said, annoyed by Cotter's inference.

The day was warm by San Francisco standards and Tom rolled up his sleeves so that he could feel more of the sun before pulling out the pork buns and dried fish that Mrs. Liang had brought in that morning. She was making amends by bringing his favorite snack after a tirade she'd had the day before—in front of a dozen patients, no less—about "Those no-good coolies no pay what they owe!" Tom appreciated her devotion to the clinic's solvency, but her bedside manner needed work.

As usual, Sacramento Street was full of commercial activity. His neighbor Li Zheng drove by, his horse wearing a tiara of chrysanthemums. Li had been at the produce market all morning and his wagon was full of fall fruits and vegetables for the local grocers. Li waved to Tom and then to Shing Tao, the acupuncturist who ran a clinic next door. Shing was sweeping his porch and took a moment to glare at Tom and Anson. He was not happy with what he perceived to be "barbarian interlopers"—at least according to Mrs. Liang.

Tom glanced at Anson, saw that he had no food, and shared what he had. Anson sniffed the dried mackerel and grimaced. "How can they eat this stuff? The smell alone will knock you over. Then again, they probably don't even notice, given how bad *they* smell." He wrapped up his uneaten portion and looked at Tom. "They're not exactly civilized, are they?"

"You'd be amazed," Tom said. He wondered if Anson had ever taken a course in world history. Doubtful.

The young doc didn't pick up on Tom's sarcasm and was already on to another topic. "I'll tell you what, though, this city has the prettiest white nurses I've ever seen. A new crop of students just showed up at St. Mary's for orientation. I hear one of them is a rich society miss just slumming it." He grinned. "Kind of like me."

Tom paused in the act of eating his fish. *So she's in her practicums now.*

The most surprising event of the past year had been Katherine's announcement to her family (certainly not to him) that she was going to nursing school. It seemed she'd made the decision just after her brother's brush with the plague, and Tom had to believe it stemmed from his refusal to let her help. If only she hadn't decided to loathe Tom as part of her resolve. The idea of Katherine and this young ass getting together bothered him considerably.

"You're rather young to be thinking of getting serious with someone, aren't you?" he asked.

"Whoa—who said anything about getting serious? I just like the ladies. And if they know how to look classy and still have a good time, so much the better." He took a swig of his second beer. "What about you? You don't go for the slant-eyed she-devils, do you?" He nudged

Tom lightly. "I'm not judging, mind you. In fact, I hear—"

Tom couldn't manage a dignified response, so he merely wadded up his empty food bag and stood up. He checked his pocket watch and announced, "Time to get back to work. I've got a one o'clock appointment."

That wasn't exactly true; he saw patients as they came in, but he'd had enough of Anson Cotter for one day. He shut himself up in the examination room that also served as his office.

So Katherine would soon be working in a hospital. His hospital.

All right. So what? He didn't pull that many shifts, and most of them were at night. Even if they passed in the hall, the chances of her working under him were slim to none.

But if she did, what then?

Shit. What then?

The dreaded scenario presented itself a few weeks later. A gas explosion at an old apartment building on Rincon Hill brought several dozen patients into St. Mary's at once, and the foyer was overflowing with the wounded and their relatives. The frenzied chatter was pierced with sharp cries and pitiful moans; the scent of blood overwhelmed the usual smell of disinfectant.

Tom had just finished a splenectomy on a teenage boy when he heard a panic-laced voice rise above the others. He walked out to see what was going on.

"Nate—is he all right?" A distraught woman dressed in a soiled, factory-issue apron had latched on to Katherine, whom he hadn't even known was on duty. She looked different somehow, and it wasn't just the uniform. Before Katherine could respond, the woman wailed, "He's just fifteen. He's—" She looked around the crowded room. "—he's not here. He's not here!"

One of the St. Mary's staff nurses hurried up and grasped the woman's shoulders firmly. "Calm down, ma'am. Are you his mother? He's in surgery with Dr. Justice right now. Best place he could be. Don't you worry." She spied Tom, waved him over. "Oh, look, here he is now."

"Mrs. Spellman," Tom said, extending his hand. "I'm Dr. Justice. We just finished a procedure on Nathan."

"Yes, yes, that's my baby," she said, her hair askew, her face ravaged by emotion. "How is he? Is he—"

"Your son's fine, ma'am. He's quite lucky. His shoulder was dislocated and his spleen ruptured, but we were able to repair the damage." He gave the woman a warm smile. "My guess is that boy of yours is a handful, so you'd better rest up because he's going to be right as rain in about a month or so."

The woman let out a cry of relief and wrapped her arms around Tom, which was awkward because she barely came up to his shoulder. He returned the hug as best he could and patted her gently on the back. Katherine, he noticed, was watching him.

He pointed the boy's mother toward the head nurse and walked up to Katherine. "It's the eyeglasses," he said, looking her over almost clinically. "I've never seen you in them." He cocked his head. "Or the uniform. But it suits you. Congratulations, Nurse Firestone."

"I-I didn't know you worked here," she stammered.

"I have attending privileges here and pull some—"

At that moment the doors of the hospital flew open and a group of Chinese highbinders poured in carrying a door upon which a man lay. A splint had been applied to his right leg, but it was still a nasty wound, the broken femur sticking out from the skin at an odd angle. From across the room, the man looked to be delirious with pain.

"Where Dr. Tom?" one of the litter bearers ground out.

Abner Huff, the hospital administrator, scurried up to the men. Tom had never cared for the man, and the next several minutes demonstrated why.

"Look here, you can't barge into a hospital like this! You need to stick to your part of town. You've got a clinic there."

One of the thugs, bigger than the rest, towered over Huff. "We have clinic, but no Dr. Tom. They say he working here. They say he the best body-cutter."

Tom walked quickly over to the patient, pulling a pair of rubber gloves from his pocket and donning them on the way. He said something in Cantonese to the man who'd spoken.

"Tang Lin say I speak English so barbarians understand," he responded. He say tell you he take walk and fall off roof."

Tang Lin? Yes, it was indeed the leader of the Hip Yee Tong. Tom had seen him once or twice, but tonight he looked completely different: haggard and vulnerable, rather than dangerous.

"A walk. Right." He gestured to the splint and spoke again in Cantonese.

The man nodded. "Lee say fixing it too hard for him and you the only man for this job."

Tom probed the perimeter of the wound and Tang Lin didn't flinch. There was only one reason for that. "What's he taken for the pain?"

"A bowlful only. Just to get him here. It wear off soon."

"All right. He'll obviously need surgery to clean and set the leg—and that's if we can even save it."

"Well, you are not doing that here." Huff swept his arm across the room. "We have actual patients here who need attention. We can't—"

Tom looked around the room as well. "We've already dealt with the worst of this group. I don't see anyone whose injuries are as severe as this man's." A surgical assistant had come out to the foyer to see what the ruckus was about. Tom got his attention. "Dale, set up OR number two for an orthopedic re-setting, would you?"

Abner Huff clearly didn't want to come across as nasty to the public, so he lowered his voice and gritted out his next words. "That Chinaman and his thugs do not belong here among decent people. I'm giving you ten minutes to lop that limb off and then they can carry him right back out."

Incredulous, Tom's response was low and hard. "Abner, it's hard enough for any of us to get through life with all limbs intact, so I'm going to do all I can to save this man's leg. And that sure as hell is going to take me longer than ten fucking minutes." He turned to the men who'd brought Tang Lin in and spoke once more in their language. They followed his direction and moved toward the operating room.

His authority questioned, the administrator blocked their path. "Just a minute, now—"

A woman with a reporter's notebook in hand was headed their way, obviously smelling a story. Katherine must have sensed it, too, because she immediately put her hand on the administrator's arm and said, "Mr. Huff, may I speak with you privately? I think there's something you should know."

Tom glanced at her but she ignored him as well as an officious-looking nurse who was likely her supervisor. The older woman looked anything but happy.

Katherine walked Mr. Huff down the hall to where they couldn't be overheard. Tom watched as she clearly beguiled the bureaucrat, keeping her hand on his arm the whole time before finishing her spiel with a demure smile.

Abner Huff nodded slightly and strode back to the main foyer. The tong leader's henchmen had already taken Tang into the room and were now milling about. Judging by facial expressions and body language, the remaining patients were none too happy about it; luckily the waiting room had thinned out.

Tom met the OR assistant at the door and asked him to have Huff assign a surgical nurse.

Dale nodded. "The Chinaman says only one."

Tom glanced at the large thug who had brought Tang Lin in; he was now standing guard outside the OR door. "Well, make it a good one, then."

The operating room was a small, pristine amphitheater whose viewing gallery was empty. Tom and Dale were scrubbing for surgery when Katherine entered the room. After a slight hesitation she began to wash up as well.

"They picked you?" He winced at the way it sounded, glad that his face was covered with a surgical mask.

"I volunteered."

"Ah." He raised his eyebrows in inquiry. "Would you prefer to assist me or to administer the ether?"

She paused before answering. "I-I must admit, I've never done either in practice."

Ah, so that was it—the Chinaman wasn't worth wasting an experienced nurse's time. He admired her courage, and there was no time like the present for her to learn, although anesthesia was out of the question.

He turned to the assistant. "Dale, if you'll do the honors with the happy gas, please?" Dale nodded and took his place at Tang Lin's head. "The guard dog said the patient's had one bowl of opium. I think we're all right to proceed, but monitor his vitals."

While Dale placed the mask over Tang Lin's face, Tom put on a pair of surgical gloves and handed another to Katherine. Then he leaned in and spoke so that only she could hear. "I'll just ask for the instrument and you hand it to me the way you were taught, all right? Don't worry if you aren't sure. I'll let you know which one I need."

She nodded stiffly, and Tom smiled. Oh, she most definitely did not like having to depend on favors from him.

"We have no audience today," he said, "but for both of your edification, I'll explain the procedure as we go along. How are we doing, Dale?"

"He's out, doc. Heartbeat steady."

"Good. Sponge, please?"

In a calm, sure voice, Tom demonstrated what he did best, blending his knowledge of the body and its intricacies with a pair of highly trained hands. After carefully cleaning the wound, he cut away the ragged, necrotic skin surrounding the break, then examined the muscles, tendons, and ligaments impacted by the fracture.

"The femoral artery is in good shape," he reported, "but the *vastus lateralis* has been compromised and will have to be repaired. And it's a vertical break, which is trickier to screw in place, but we will do our best."

Confidently, methodically, Tom reconstructed the inside of Tang Lin's thigh. As he did so, he indulged in quiet conversation, asking what Katherine had told Abner Huff.

"I simply told him that Tang Lin was an important person known to the upper reaches of government and that it would look bad if he were turned away."

Tom nodded at that characterization. "I suppose Tang Lin and the tongs are very influential in city politics, just not in the way you implied."

He glanced at Katherine and noticed her frown; she obviously didn't enjoy being corrected.

"I also told him that it would look better for him if he let *you* take responsibility for Tang Lin's survival," she said firmly. "If something should go wrong, then it will be on your head and not his."

"Thank you for the vote of confidence." Tom's tone was just short of sarcastic.

"He let you operate; that's the main thing."

"You're right, Nurse Firestone. That is the main thing." Tom now worked quietly, asking for a retractor or clamp as needed, eventually calling for needle and sutures. When he finished with the internal repair, he asked Katherine to take hold of Tang Lin's injured leg and pull firmly when he told her to. The bone needed to be re-aligned.

Dale winced. "I sure as hell wouldn't want to be awake for that."

"You and me both," Tom said. "Now, nurse, I need you to maintain your grip while I insert the supporting screw into the medullary cavity. And Dale, keep him completely under because the slightest movement will weaken the connection."

Tom used leverage to screw Tang Lin's bones together. "The human body is amazing, but at its core, it is a machine," he mused. "Much of surgery is simply tinkering with that machine to get it to work properly."

"Hey, you get tired of this, you can always work on cars." Dale capped his joke with a grin. "Lord knows that's an up-and-coming field."

Tom chuckled. "I'll keep that in mind," he said as he began to close the wound, which stretched for a good eight inches along Tang Lin's thigh.

"Will you have enough skin flap to cover it? It's awfully wide." Katherine sounded dubious.

"It's borderline," Tom admitted. "I'm going to give it a go because it'll be difficult enough for him to keep the leg immobile without worrying about another wound from a skin graft. But he may require some grafting down the road if it pulls too tight."

"What about his ability to walk?" she asked.

Tang Lin lay peacefully on the table. *Enjoy the rest while you can*, Tom thought. "There'll be some impairment because of the muscle loss, but he'll have a hell of a better time hoofing it than if we had done what Mr. Huff suggested and just lopped it off."

"I'm sure Tang Lin will be very grateful...not to mention generous. Who knows how this might help you."

Tom sent Katherine a look of disgust. "Are you implying something here? Because I can assure you I would have done the same thing no matter who was lying on this table."

Katherine glanced at Dale, who looked as though

he'd rather be anywhere other than where he was. She turned back to Tom. "I-I didn't mean to suggest—"

"Forget it." Tom was all business now. "In situations like this it doesn't matter who the parties are, does it? One does what one has to do."

His tone must have irked her, because she shot back, "Sometimes there's more to it."

"No, there isn't," he said, and left it at that.

Two steps forward, one step back, Tom thought later that evening. *I shouldn't have barked at her. But Goddammit it, she doesn't even know me. How can she think I'd care about someone's bank account when they're on the operating table?*

Tang Lin had come through the surgery without complication. He was, however, half mummified by a thick plaster cast that encased his entire leg both above and below the injury site. The wound itself was swathed in bandages surrounded by a stiff, muslin-covered removable cage.

Just before heading back to the clinic, Tom stopped in to see the tong leader. Awake now, the man was more than pleased to hear he'd walk again. "I do not have to run a race," he reasoned. "I am content to walk in the garden. And for that, I am in your debt."

"You owe me nothing," Tom said, more sharply than he intended. "Your recovery is in your hands, now. You keep that leg as still as possible, and whatever you do, don't let it get dirty. At this point in the healing process we lose more legs to infection than anything else."

"I'll keep that in mind. Now, how long can I stay here before your delightful hospital director kicks me out?"

Tom relaxed at that remark. Despite his occupation —which Tom assumed kept Tang walking in more alleys than gardens—Tang Lin was intelligent and personable. In another place and time they might have become friends. "How long do you want to stay?" he asked.

"A day or two would be most appreciated. I would like to regain a bit of strength before attempting the many stairs of my home."

"Let's make it three," Tom said. "If they try to kick you out earlier, let me know. And come to the clinic in a week so we can change the dressing." He turned to leave, but Tang Lin stopped him.

"Did Katherine Firestone assist you in fixing my leg?"

"She did."

He sighed. "No doubt she drew the short straw."

"No, she volunteered. More than that, she was instrumental in getting you the surgery to begin with. Mr. Huff was ready to have me lop off your leg and kick you out the door, but she intervened."

Tang Lin took a moment to digest that information. "She is quite a remarkable woman, isn't she?"

His wistful tone caused Tom to look up. "She's a good nurse. Do you know her?"

"I have met her only one time before, under... unusual circumstances. But she is someone you never forget."

Tom locked eyes with his patient. I struck him that Tang Lin was a capable-looking man. And he obviously possessed a man's needs and desires. Could Katherine be attracted to him? Is that why she'd volunteered? The thought that society would never sanction such a match gave Tom guilty solace, but not for long. If Katherine Firestone wanted someone, he doubted she'd let anyone—or any societal dictate—stand in her way. And if she didn't, well, wasn't he living proof that she could be just as hell-bent in her antipathy?

And just like that, the intense pleasure he'd felt when she'd first entered the operating room drifted away, replaced by the familiar, but no less dreary ache of missed opportunity.

CHAPTER NINETEEN

*"When it comes to family, you take the bad with the good.
That's what my grandma said, anyway, may she rest
in peace."*

—Henry Justice, Brother of the Defendant

After the roast turkey, the cornbread dressing, the mashed potatoes...after the green bean casserole and the syrup-kissed yams and the rolls laden with butter, Tom and his brothers sat in rockers on the wide front porch of their parents' farmhouse and watched the sun dip low while another Thanksgiving supper settled in their too-full stomachs.

Joining them this year was Cousin Eli, Carina, and their four-year-old son, Eli John. The air was crisp and the gold-tinged light caught the edge of Carina's white apron as she and her little boy stood at the bottom of the porch feeding pieces of carrot to Nicodemus, the plow horse. The boy held his hand flat and giggled as Old Nick nuzzled his palm with big, rubbery lips.

"You got yourself a real nice missus, Eli." Tom's youngest brother Jack took a pull of cider as he pointed to Carina. "Pretty as a picture and gave you a healthy boy. You are one lucky son of a bitch."

Eli grinned. "I am. No disputing that." He turned to Tom. "So, when are you going to settle down, cousin? You're the next in line, you know. After me, of course."

Tom, who had turned thirty-two a few months earlier, gazed at Carina while another woman—a tall, confident siren with honey-colored hair who wanted nothing to do with him—filled his thoughts.

After Tang Lin's surgery, he'd tangled horns again with Abner Huff, submitting his resignation from St. Mary's in exchange for the gang leader's extended stay. He'd run into Katherine just one time since the surgery, walking near Union Square with her mother. They were laden with shopping bags from City of Paris and I. Magnin.

"Maintaining one's status as belle of the ball is quite the challenge," she'd quipped with an air of gaiety. He assumed she affected it for her mother's sake; the Katherine he knew through colleagues like Anson Cotter was a tireless professional—the polar opposite of a spoiled society deb.

He might have mentioned something to that effect if she hadn't introduced Tom as if she barely knew him, as if he were just one of the many doctors she'd worked with. As if he were nothing to her.

"Tom?" Eli was looking at him intently.

Tom blinked the memory away. "I keep pretty busy," he said. "Not too much time for that nonsense."

"Folderol." Eli was back to pontificating; he waved his hand dismissively. "I can see we'll have to take you in hand. Once we get to Frisco, Carina and I will put our minds to fixing you up. Mark my words."

Tom's other brother Henry snickered. "You sure you want to head west? Look what it's done to poor Tommy here."

It wasn't really a question. They all knew Eli and his family were moving to San Francisco, taking the train back with Tom, in fact. Carina's cousin, Amadeo Giannini, had offered Eli a job in the bank he'd opened the year before—a small enterprise with a grand title: The Bank of Italy. The company prided itself on offering low-interest loans to everyday people, not just the top tier of San Francisco society.

When he'd first heard of their plans, Tom's gut churned. Given their history, his instincts told him not to spend too much time with Eli and his family, even though he knew that Eli and Carina would bend over backwards to reassure him he had no cause for concern. It would be a point of pride with Eli, in fact: *I am so confident that Carina belongs to me and not you, that I am willing to put the two of you together to prove it.* Tom shuddered at the prospect.

He knew he had to show some level of enthusiasm, so he settled for, "I think you'll like the city. It's a hell of a place. Lots to see and do."

Henry sniffed. "How would you know, brother?

Last time I visited I couldn't get you out of that clinic to save your life."

"Yeah, it was pretty busy. I wanted to get away, but—"

"Ah, stuff it. You're *always* busy." Henry turned as if to confide in Eli but pointed at Tom. "Old Dr. Tom here thinks Chinatown's gonna fall apart without him. He even lives above the clinic! I'll pay twenty dollars to anyone who gets him to think about anything besides bein' a doctor."

Tom snorted. "As if you've got twenty dollars to spare."

"I've got plenty of time to earn it while you spin your wheels trying to save the Chinee—who don't even want your medicine, by the way."

"Some do," Tom murmured. He leaned back in the chair and closed his eyes. "More than you'd think."

Tom's mother came out then to tell everyone to come inside for pumpkin pie and elderberry wine. Carina herded her little boy up the stairs and inside to wash his hands. As the men dutifully followed, Eli clapped his hand on Tom's shoulder.

"Consensus seems to be that you need a change, cousin." Eli's voice brimmed with confidence. "Carina and I are just the ones to make it happen."

Eli couldn't have known how right he was.

CHAPTER TWENTY

"He stared at my breasts too much."

—Miss Priscilla Winters, Employee of Eli Porter
who met Tom Justice

Despite his ongoing conflict with Katherine Firestone, Tom felt positive as 1906 began to unfold. His agreement to quit St. Mary's in exchange for Tang Lin's extended convalescence had actually worked to Tom's advantage. After word got out that he'd left the hospital's employ, he'd been immediately contacted by Dr. Walter Coffey, a well-known surgeon and one of the founders of the newly opened Saint Francis Hospital on Leavenworth Street, an address much closer to the Chinatown Free Clinic. Promoting it as "the most up-to-date modern hospital west of Chicago," Dr. Coffey sang its virtues while offering

Tom nearly twice what he'd been paid for the same number of shifts at St. Mary's.

It didn't hurt matters that within the rarified atmosphere of highly trained surgeons, Dr. Coffey and William Halsted knew each other very well. Halsted had obviously put in a good word, which meant his former mentor hadn't held a grudge over Tom's rejection of the Johns Hopkins opportunity years before. It led Tom to wonder yet again if he'd made the right decision to stay in San Francisco. Did the possibility exist, even now, of going back? It seemed far-fetched, but...

The other source of satisfaction was personal. During the Chinese New Year parade, Anson had been covering the clinic when none other than Mandy Culpepper was brought in. Someone had thrown rocks at the girls marching to represent the Presbyterian Mission House, and Mandy had gotten caught in the melee. Anson had treated the girl's head wound and couldn't stop raving about her.

"She's absolutely exquisite," he rhapsodized to Tom the next day. "Have you ever met her?"

At first Tom was confused. "Are you sure you got the name right? Mandy Culpepper? She's just a kid."

"If you think that girl's just a kid, you need your eyes examined, old man. She's got all the right womanly parts, believe me. Damn, would I like to get to know her better. Much better, if you know what I mean."

Tom's respect for Anson, which had not been that high for some time, slipped even further. The young man was now bordering on loathsome. "I'd tread lightly there if I were you," Tom cautioned. "She's protected by a very powerful family."

"The Firestones, I know. I've worked a few shifts with the daughter, who used to be Mandy's guardian. She's a looker, too, and I thought maybe I'd give her a whirl, but frankly, she's a bit intimidating. She doesn't take guff from any of the doctors over there. I think some of them are even a bit afraid of her. That Mandy, though...*man alive.* And she'll turn eighteen in just a few months, so who knows where it could lead?"

It's going to lead nowhere. That young girl is way too good for the likes of you.

The description of Katherine was another matter entirely. It kept him smiling for the rest of the day.

"And so when people ask me what a 'prissy winter' is, I tell them it's a season when you wear too many clothes!" Miss Priscilla Ann Winter—"Prissy" to her friends—laughed at her own feeble joke, displaying a straight set of teeth marred by an excessively gummy smile. Eli laughed along with her, nudging Tom to do likewise. He rallied with a chuckle, as did Carina, who made up the foursome at their dining room table. Prissy (because as of this soiree, they were, by her own declaration, "friends") was a teller at the Bank of Italy, where Eli was the assistant manager. He'd invited Miss Winter to their home on Linden Street for the express purpose, it turned out, of introducing her to Tom.

They were finishing up the last of a delicious Italian pot roast Carina had instructed their cook to prepare. It was one of Tom's favorites, and she'd made it for him many times during their college years together. He just barely stopped himself from saying, "Almost as good as yours."

Prissy continued to dominate the conversation. She was a San Francisco native and took great delight in pointing out the dos and don'ts of life in the city. Eli lapped it up. Carina merely smiled and nodded at the appropriate time.

Tom sat quietly, half listening. His mind wandered to the state of Prissy's breasts, which were unusually large in relation to the rest of her slim, boyish body. Her bustline was of such proportions, in fact, that he was sure she could balance a teacup and saucer on it with room to spare. Carrying those honeydews around everywhere had to be a strain on her musculature, like walking around with a ten-pound weight strapped to her chest day in and day out. Such a contrast to the poor woman he'd operated on more than five years earlier. Which was better, too much or none at all?

He wondered if Prissy would ever consider breast reduction surgery. It was a relatively new phenomenon, to be sure. Only in the past few decades had surgeons thought in terms of reconstructing the breast rather than simply removing it. New techniques had been developed for recreating the nipple as well as achieving a natural curve to the remaining breast tissue. And just recently he'd read an article about using the same procedures for purely aesthetic reasons, rather than to correct the result of cancer removal or other disease. Prissy would be a perfect candidate for—

"What's your thought about it?" Eli asked.

Tom was on the verge of saying, "I would highly recommend you try the surgery," until he realized the question was about an entirely different topic. "I'm sorry, I was preoccupied. My thoughts about what?"

Eli gave him a look that implied Tom must have been staring at Prissy's breasts, because he sniggered. "The plague, man. Prissy here says it was a tempest in a teapot, a non-story. What's your opinion? You dealt with it a while back, remember?"

He remembered, all right. Denying Katherine's impassioned plea to help her brother survive the killing bacteria. Carrying out the ravaged bodies of the young Chinese mother and her beautiful little girl. Those memories weren't likely to fade anytime soon. To those who experienced the horror of it, it was anything but a "non-story." "Yes, I did have some experience with it because of my work in Chinatown. We are just fortunate the federal medical officers were able to contain it."

"So is it gone completely, then?" Carina asked.

"Yes, of course," Prissy said.

"No," Tom said at the same time. "It may never be. But at least it's under control. I don't think most residents have to worry about it, so you can cross that one off your list."

He smiled at Carina as he said it. They'd often joked about her penchant for writing everything down.

At that moment, the housekeeper, who had stayed

late to babysit Eli John, entered the dining room and murmured that their boy was ready for bed. Eli got up, but Carina stopped him.

"Eli, darling, I wonder if you'd mind if I took Tom up to see him...about that...that matter we talked about."

She obviously didn't want to elaborate in front of Prissy. Eli looked concerned for a moment but sat down again. "Of course," he said. "I'll keep Prissy company while you two do the honors." He looked at Tom. "Just don't let Eli John wrap you around his finger," he warned good-naturedly. "He'll wrangle another story or two, and before you know it, an hour has passed."

Carina preceded Tom up the stairs. He noticed the sway of her hips, which seemed slightly larger than they had years ago. Childbearing changed a woman's body, he knew. The change looked good on her.

They went into Eli John's bedroom, which was filled with the paraphernalia of happy little boys: painted tin soldiers, a wooden sword, a model of a sailing ship. The little man himself was already asleep, curled up in his bed—a buccaneer catching forty winks before his next adventure.

They watched him for a moment before Carina said softly, "I'm sorry about the set-up tonight. I hadn't met her before, so I wasn't able to give Eli my opinion. He means well, but he tries too hard...and he's not very patient."

Tom gazed at her. "What would you have told him?"

"I would have said you are perfectly capable of finding a woman who suits you."

"Possibly," he said, "but I don't know about keeping her."

Their eyes met and the silence that followed was charged with the import of his words. At that moment, Tom couldn't have said whether or not he'd made the right decision to let her go. But it no longer mattered, did it?

He moved past the moment. "You mentioned you wanted to ask me something about little Eli?"

"Oh. Yes. Here, take a look." she leaned over the bed and gently pushed down the child's pajama bottoms. He was wearing a diaper, which Carina seemed embarrassed about. "He makes it through most nights. It's just once in a while, he—"

"It's all right," Tom assured her. Perfectly normal."

"What about this?" she said, pointing to a dark, oval-shaped mark on the inside of Eli's upper thigh. "I don't know. It's a bit different, and…well…"

Tom looked at the mark, and the memories of all they'd shared emotionally and physically came flooding back to him. He looked at her helplessly, and she at him, tears pooling.

"There's no need to worry," he said with a huskiness he couldn't mask. "It's just a mark proving he's your son."

She nodded, took a quiet breath, and let it out. As she pulled her son's bottoms back up she said, almost to herself, "I should have waited. I should have been more patient."

Tom knew she wasn't talking about showing him the mark. He wiped a tear from her cheek. "What about me?" he asked. "I could have—"

She touched his arm to stop his excuse. "No. Looking back, I think I was in too much of a hurry myself. Just like Eli."

"He *is* just like me, isn't he?" Eli's voice intruded from the hallway. "The spitting image." He walked up to Carina and put his arm around her as the three of them watched the sleeping boy. He glanced at his wife. "You're crying."

"Just happy is all," she said, wiping her tears. "Tom says there's nothing to worry about—just a birthmark."

Eli gave Carina a squeeze. "I told you that." He smiled at Tom. "She never listens to me. Has to hear it from an *expert*."

Tom nodded in response to the dig. There wasn't much else he could say.

But Eli could. "Of course, your crying at the drop of a hat has another explanation." He patted Carina's stomach. "We were going to wait a bit before sharing the news, but since you're a *professional*, you could probably already tell. My lovely Carina is increasing again."

CHAPTER TWENTY-ONE

Early April 1907

There were gaps in the investigation. Gaps in the "who"—not every ring in the tree stump of Tom's life had been filled out.

Gaps in the "how"—there was no murder weapon, only the bullet from a Colt single action revolver (ironically nicknamed "The Peacemaker") that had been extracted from the victim's brain. And when Jonathan, frustrated during one of their jail cell interviews, had asked his client point blank if he'd fired the shot, Tom had just said, cryptically, "I may as well have."

And there were gaps in the "why" as well. What could possibly have prompted Tom Justice to willfully take another man's life? Especially that of a cousin, whom he'd known since they were children?

The depositions that had come in were not enough, so Jonathan set out to gather clarification, particularly as it concerned the man who had accused Tom of the crime and set this entire case in motion.

Even a year after the tragedy, traveling about the city of San Francisco was a lesson in humility, a reminder of man's inconsequentiality when Mother Nature decided a change was in order, or that God (as some believed) felt a lesson needed to be taught.

The signs of re-building were everywhere, the pace of reconstruction as brisk as the air that habitually blew in from the bay. Hundreds of lots had been cleared of debris, causing the death of countless horses through overwork. As new foundations began to rise, bricklayers and day laborers were in high demand. Streetcars were running again, commerce was bustling, and San Franciscans seemed ready to forge ahead.

Yet for all that, the scope of the disaster was so vast that one could barely comprehend it, even when staring at its consequences.

City Hall was a fitting symbol of just how violently change had come to San Francisco. Covering a vast triangle of land at Market and Eighth streets, it had taken twenty-five years to build, and had basked in the glory of being the largest municipal complex west of the Mississippi. A three-hundred-foot dome atop the impressive structure advertised that San Francisco had arrived on the world stage, a "Golden City" eager to dominate the west. Unfortunately, the structure's brick, stone, and steel had been compromised by decades of cronyism and greed. Touted as a model of earthquake resistance, the entire structure had crumbled like a sandcastle at high tide, reminding Jonathan of the

Acropolis of Athens. Reports were surfacing of kick-backs and shortcuts, of shoddy building materials and sub-par workmanship. Lawsuits were being filed at an astonishing rate. As a result, the once-resplendent symbol of a city on the rise was now the poster child for its corruption.

City Hall was only the beginning. Jonathan scanned the landscape from the hansom cab taking him to his appointment in the Sunset District. Street after street had been flattened, first by tremors, then by inferno. Thousands of buildings still resembled junk heaps, their foundations having liquified beneath them. Entire neighborhoods were nothing more than burned-out carcasses, unsettling mementos of man's folly in thinking he could stop the spreading fire by using explosives to start another.

Hundreds of thousands were rendered homeless in a single day. Most of the tents were gone now, but many of the hastily built government cottages remained, providing shelter for those who still had no other place to go.

As for the injured and the dead, no one knew the true numbers. Many had been killed by tumbling bricks and lumber, still others trapped, their cries unheeded until it was too late. In Chinatown, where Tom Justice had practiced medicine, so much destruction had occurred that neither the inhabitants nor the city officials had dared conduct a survey.

In a perverse way, Jonathan was disappointed not to have been in the city during the event. Already a stranger in a strange land, he could at least have shared the camaraderie of those who still asked each other "Where were you when the earthquake struck?" over spirits or a pint. But he was an outsider in that regard, too, having arrived too late to be part of history, however ignominious it might be.

Located south of Golden Gate Park, the Sunset District had fared relatively well during the calamity, mainly because it was less populated than the downtown area. Jonathan had the driver stop at Number Six Judah Street, paid his fare, and knocked on the door. Upon seeing his credentials, the landlady gladly showed him to the rooms of Dr. Anson Cotter, the man with whom he'd set the appointment.

Dr. Cotter bade him enter. The young physician, an air of privilege swirling about him, was busy packing his traveling case, and for an instant Jonathan harbored the hope that the prosecution's star witness was leaving town. It was not what it seemed, however—a fact that Cotter was all too happy to point out.

"I know it's awfully suspicious, me leaving like this. 'Ooh, is the true villain escaping in plain sight?'"

Jonathan had to smile. "It had crossed my mind."

Cotter responded with a much colder smile of his own. "Sorry to disappoint, but I'm simply traveling back to Harvard to begin my surgical residency. They extended my internship so that I could help in the aftermath, but I've finally been released from my civic duty. Would a murderer have stuck around to aid the victims?" He gave Jonathan a knowing look. "I hardly think so. But I've assured the authorities that I'll be back for the trial." His movements turned jerky. "I wouldn't miss it."

"I appreciate your taking a few moments to clarify some things," Jonathan said, adding a bit of polish to his already clipped British accent. He could tell from his first interview with Cotter that the young man bought into the fallacy that somehow those with an "upper-crust" manner of speaking were more worthy of respect than mere Americans, even if they represented the opposition. Cotter's willingness to see Jonathan was also a sign of the doctor's firm belief in Tom's guilt and his own innocence (dammit), suggesting no fear of being trapped into an admission or dissuaded from his testimony. "I merely wanted to get clear in my mind what happened the evening you met my client and his cousin in late March of last year."

Cotter gestured for Jonathan to take a seat but continued to pack as he talked. "And his cousin's wife, poor soul."

Jonathan pulled out his notebook. "Tell me again how it came about."

"It was a Friday night and I was having drinks at The Cliff House with some co-workers from St. Mary's. Not sure whether I mentioned this before, but Tom wasn't much for that kind of thing, even before he moved to Saint Francis, at least that I saw. So I was surprised to see him walk in with this very good-looking couple—although both were much shorter than Tom. He seemed like a hulk next to them."

"What happened next?"

He paused in the act of folding a shirt. "Well, I could

see that all Tom was going to do was nod at me, so I stepped up and introduced myself."

"May I ask why you inserted yourself after Tom had indicated that he did not want further interaction with you?"

Cotter's jaw firmed up. "He was always like that. Almost from the beginning, he seemed to have a bee in his bonnet about me. I think he was jealous, frankly. I'd gone out with a female friend of his. He didn't have designs on her—or so he said—but he sure as hell didn't like the idea of me courting her. Warned me off her, in fact." He scowled at an apparent memory.

"Would this have been Amanda Culpepper Firestone, by any chance?"

"You know her?" Cotter looked surprised. "She's a fine-looking piece, wouldn't you say? I know I'm going to go to my grave thinking she's the one who got away. In any event, Tom didn't take to the idea of the two of us, acting like I was inferior to her, which, I can assure you I most certainly am not. My pedigree is no doubt as long as yours."

If you only knew, Jonathan thought.

Cotter continued to pack. "He was just as irritated when I set my sights on another woman he knew, one I know he wanted for himself. What a self-righteous prick—and he's got a violent side, let me tell you. Anyway, it rubbed me the wrong way, and I suppose I wanted to annoy him, just a little. Not very admirable, I know, but there it is."

Jonathan had heard from Katherine about Anson Cotter's pursuit of both Amanda *and* her. Admirable it certainly was not. No wonder Tom couldn't stand the sight of him.

"But the evening turned out to be pleasant," he prompted. "At least for you."

"Yes, it was. Eli Porter was a charming fellow, albeit a tad garrulous after a few drinks. He was one of those hail-fellow-well-met sort of chaps. He invited me to join them for dinner, and over the course of the meal I learned all about their relationship, how Carina used to be Tom's girl and how Eli, in his words, 'stole her heart away.' He said it with a wink, of course, as if it were all in good fun, but Tom wasn't laughing, I can tell you that much. In fact, it seemed as if he was holding in some anger. Eli's wife was somewhat embarrassed by it all. She kept trying to shush her husband and shift the conversation. Finally she got him to start talking about his work at the bank, which launched him into a bragging session, may he rest in peace."

"What was he bragging about?"

"Oh, this and that. His promotion to assistant manager, although, let's face it, who's ever heard of the Bank of Italy? Then there was the larger house they were going to move into at the end of April. He even took his wife's hand to show us the new ring he'd bought. It was rather gauche, but he was proud of it, just like he was proud of the fact that he had a son and another child on the way."

"So, you'd say that Tom appeared to be unhappy during this interaction?"

"Most definitely. He and Mrs. Porter glanced at each other a few times, as if, I don't know, apologizing to each other or something. Finally, after dinner, but before dessert was served, Tom got up and said he was on call and had to leave. I never checked up on it, since by that time we worked at different hospitals, but my guess is he was lying. He just wanted to get the hell out of there. It's obvious he's a poor sport, at least when it comes to women."

Jonathan paused before asking, "Did it occur to you, Dr. Cotter, that perhaps Tom knew that his cousin could be, well, talkative, and a bit of a braggart, especially when drinking, and that he hoped to spare you the experience?"

Cotter frowned.

Of course you hadn't considered it, Jonathan thought. *People like you always see matters filtered through your own fragile egos. Whatever transpires is always about someone slighting you.*

"I hadn't thought of it in those terms," Cotter admitted.

Jonathan suspected Tom's reluctance to include Cotter likely stemmed from his knowledge of both men. No doubt he would have preferred to spend the evening alone with Mrs. Porter—something that society would not have allowed. For a moment, Katherine entered his thoughts; if she were to marry Tom, he would be banned from spending time with her alone as well. A wave of dejection rolled over him and he had to force himself to return to the matter at hand.

"One more thing, Dr. Cotter. You stated during our earlier interview that during the time you spent with the Porters, Eli showed beyond a shadow of a doubt that he was left-handed. Are you quite certain of that observation?"

"Yes. Most definitely. He used his left hand for drinking, cutting his meat—in the European style, you know, without switching his fork—even gesturing. At one point, when speaking of his gun collection, he pretended to sight along his left hand. There is no doubt in my mind about that."

"And you're absolutely certain that you aren't basing your recollection on seeing him that day at the Pavilion?"

Cotter paused for a moment, then smiled and wagged his finger at Jonathan. "You've been told I walked toward the critical care section shortly after Tom did. And you're right. I did. But if anyone testifies that I went beyond the curtain, they'd be lying, and you know it." He extended his arms in a gesture of supplication. "As I said, I stayed. Your man didn't."

"I cannot dispute that, I'm afraid." Jonathan took his leave shortly thereafter, thanking Cotter profusely for talking with him, even though he hadn't been legally required to do so.

"Why wouldn't I? I have nothing to hide." His tone hardened. "And I want to see justice served."

As he waited on the street to hail another carriage, Jonathan mentally reviewed the interview. Thanks to Cotter's testimony, including his identification of Tom at the Pavilion, the prosecution would paint the picture of a jealous ex-suitor, cringing every time Eli Porter brought up his good fortune in comparison to Tom's barren life. With Cordelia's research on Tom's romantic liaisons, Jonathan felt confident he could counter that perception.

He could also muddy the water by emphasizing those critical moments when Cotter was not accounted for—moments that coincided with the time the murder took place. But why would Cotter have committed the crime? Without a motive, his location during the time of the killing would not seem as suspect as Tom's.

More important to Jonathan's case was knowing he couldn't refute the fact that the lethal bullet had entered Eli Porter's head from the right side. A left-handed person wouldn't shoot himself from the right side. He could not, therefore, argue a case for suicide.

There had to be another explanation for the tragic event that occurred—something other than the idea that Tom had snapped and killed the man.

CHAPTER TWENTY-TWO

"Rudest man I ever met, bar none."

—Jeremiah Dunkley, Medical Device Salesman

M rs. Liang was fit to be tied. "I tell him leave but he no leave," she fumed to Tom as he washed up after seeing his last patient of the morning. She had stormed into the examination room as soon as Lau Bo Jing left and shut the door firmly so that others presumably couldn't hear her tirade, except that her voice may as well have had a megaphone attached, it was so loud and strident.

"Calm down, Mrs. Liang," Tom admonished in softly spoken Cantonese. "Who and what are you talking about?"

She pointed at the door. "That salesman. That Mr. Dunkee. He come around two, three times, I tell him no. We no want. But he come back now and say he not leave until he talk to you. He say it have to do with man parts." She huffed. "Man parts. I no think he has any man parts."

Tom wiped his hands while suppressing a smile. "That I don't know about, but I'll get rid of him for you."

The intruder in question was sitting in the waiting room, a small leather suitcase by his side. He was a wiry man, barely taller than Mrs. Liang, and wore a blue pinstriped suit. The hair he had left was brown and valiant, but was situated like a pelted skirt around the back of his head. A pencil-thin mustache adorned his upper lip. Upon seeing Tom he rose and extended his hand.

"Jeremiah Dunkley at your service," he said. "You can call me Jerry."

"Do you need some help, Mr. Dunkley? Because we are quite busy here."

The salesman looked around smugly at the empty waiting room—always in that state during the noon hour because Mrs. Liang shooed everyone out for lunch. "Well sir, it don't look that busy to me. However, I am here to fix all that."

"Mr. Dunkley, I—"

"No, no. Don't thank me yet. Wait until I show you how you can double, triple, no, I mean *quadruple* your business. Ten minutes of your time, sir. Just ten minutes and then I'll let you shower me with gratitude —and don't forget to call me Jerry."

With a final indignant glare, Mrs. Liang left for her own midday meal while Tom mentally counted to ten.

Men like Dunkley had to earn a living, too, he told himself. They had families, they had mouths to feed. Hopefully "Jerry" got paid per demonstration and not per sale. "All right, Jerry. Ten minutes. But then I really must let you go." He ushered the man into the first exam room.

The next ten minutes—which stretched to twenty— would have been entertaining, had Tom not been increasingly horrified by what the man was peddling.

"We all know the scourge of neurasthenia that's sweeping the country," Jerry began. "I'm sure you're treating patients left, right and center for it—even if they are of the yellow race— because this disease don't care who you are. White, yellow, young, old, male, female, rich, poor—but mainly rich, if you get my drift. Am I right, sir?" He started to count off on his fingers. "You got your headaches, your skin rashes, your nervous twitches, your dyspepsia, your sciatica…your problems down *there*, if you know what I mean." He winked. "No matter who you are, it leaves you flat and flaccid, drained and debilitated, weak and worn out."

Continuing his patter, Jerry removed several odd contraptions from his suitcase and laid them out on the examination table. "But help is on the way." He picked up what looked like a red wool cummerbund with copper and other metal discs attached. The discs were connected to each other by a thin wire, one strand of which dangled below the belt and ended in a small noose.

"It's a good thing you're a medical man," Jerry continued, "otherwise I'd have to spend hours and hours talking to you about the many wonderful effects of electrical stimulation on all parts of the body. But no doubt you're aware of the enormous transmogrification properties inherent to the Voltaic Galvanic Principle." He presented the belt to Tom. "Now this here is Doctor Bell's Premium Voltaic Health Belt. Only eighteen dollars—easily worth two weeks of a working man's pay, as you'll see. Once it's soaked with the doctor's proprietary battery accelerator"—he handed Tom a small bottle—"your patient merely wraps the belt around his waist so the gentle current can reinvigorate all of his ailing internal organs, leading to relief of the kidney, bladder, liver, heart, lungs, and stomach, to name just a few."

Tom's eyebrows were in danger of taking flight. "You don't say." He pointed to the hanging loop. It couldn't be what he thought it was. "What does that thing do?"

"Ah," Jerry said with a knowing air. "I can see where your mind is headed, doctor, and you are perfectly right. An overwhelming number of neurasthenic cases can be laid at the foot, or should I say the *hand*, of excessive manual stimulation, leading to the depletion of productive—and virile—nervous energy. Any related pathologies, such as impotency or general lack of manly vigor, can be immediately cured with the simple insertion of the weakened organ into the stimulating loop, and —"

Tom held up his hand. "I get the picture." He took the stopper out of the bottle of "accelerator" and sniffed it. "This smells like capsicum."

"Well, that is one of the proprietary ingredients, yes sir."

It took Tom a moment to put it all together. "You basically have men wrap themselves in pepper oil so when they start to sweat, it burns like crazy. That's the buzz they get. There's no electrical current involved here at all."

Jerry sniffed with disdain. He began to carefully fold his "health belt" and put it away. "I don't know what you're implying, sir."

"I'm not implying anything. I'm telling you flat out that what you're selling is complete flummery." Tom glanced at the inside of the salesman's case and saw several bottles. He picked one up and read the label. "'Dr. Hardee's Florentine Liniment—apply liberally to affected area for instant relief and remedy. Good for combatting hair loss, stomach troubles, rheumatism, sprains, bruises, wounds, bee stings, chilblains, ear aches, sore throats, cramps, blood and liver complaints, bronchial infections, and insect, frost and snake bites.'" He looked at Jerry. "What do you charge for this?"

Jerry smiled. "Your cost, sir is minimal—thirty-five cents per bottle wholesale. You can easily get two dollars per bottle retail."

Tom stuck the bottle in his pocket. "I think I'll keep this."

"Certainly. Certainly." He finished packing his case and looked back at Tom with an oily grin, no doubt thinking he'd salvaged a sale from a near miss. "Just let me know how many dozen bottles you would like to order, sir, and I shall be happy to oblige."

Tom walked him through the empty waiting room and to the front door. "Mr. Dunkley, I'm going to keep your bottle and show it to every one of my patients— just before I warn them that under no circumstances should they *ever* purchase anything that looks even remotely like your quack patent medicine. And I'm going to ask my orderly—who is about twice your size, by the way— to kindly remove you from the premises the next time you set foot inside this clinic."

Dunkley puffed up, an offended pigeon. "Well, you don't have to be rude about it. Good day to you, sir." He nearly slammed the door on the way out.

Tom was still chuckling over Dunkley's explanation of "excessive manual stimulation" when the door opened and Fung Hai entered the clinic. He carried a small sack.

"I saw Mrs. Liang down the street and she asked me to deliver this," he said. "I think it is your lunch."

Tom peeked inside. Sure enough, his office manager had procured some pieces of fried chicken, a wedge of cheese, and an apple—not her favorite food, but his. She must have felt bad leaving him in the clutches of Jerry Dunkley. "Thank you, Hai."

"I have other special news," he added.

"Spill it." The young man frowned and Tom added, "It means, 'Tell me.'"

Fung Hai grinned. "Ah. Do you mean like, 'Spit it out'? Well, Miss Cameron told me to tell you that we have all been invited to wish Miss Mandy a happy eighteenth birthday, only she is not to know about it."

"A surprise party, huh?"

"Yes, at The Grove. We are to travel there on the Saturday after next and jump out all at once to wish her well."

"That sounds grand," Tom said. "Thanks for letting me know." He held up the bag. "And thanks for delivering this."

After Fung Hai left, Tom sat at his desk with his feet up and contemplated the party invitation while he ate his lunch.

A party.

A party where Katherine, Mandy's former guardian, would most definitely be.

The coward in him wanted to pass; it would be easy to plead too much work and avoid having to deal with the woman and the way she made him feel.

But another side of him argued the opposite. Mandy had grown from a charming girl into an exceptional young woman. He truly wanted to help celebrate her entry into adulthood. Besides which, he'd heard wonderful things about The Grove. It'd be a perfect opportunity to check the place out. And Mandy had a lot of friends. Who knows, the party could be so big that he might not even cross paths with Katherine Firestone at all.

Then again, he might.

And that possibility intrigued him more than anything.

The trip to the artists' retreat known as The Grove was

an adventure in and of itself. To get there, one had to cross San Francisco Bay and travel up the coast, just past a village on Creation Bay called Little Eden. Millionaire August Wolff had purchased the land as a getaway several years earlier, but after falling in love with the artist Lia Starling, he'd turned it into a camp in the redwoods where selected artists could spend a year, gratis, practicing their chosen medium. When Katherine entered her nursing program in 1904, Mandy had moved to The Grove to be the personal assistant to Lia Starling Wolff.

Early on a Saturday morning thick with fog, Tom caught a ride with his neighbor, Pang Wei, who took men down to the Ferry Building each day to work the docks. Donaldina Cameron was there waiting to board the ferry for Sausalito, along with several of her young charges. She was joined by Wu Jade, the director of the re-opened Chinatown School of Needle Arts, as well as Fung Hai, who was now Wu Jade's husband. Even Cheung Ti Chu, the chairman of the Six Companies, was along for the ride. Katherine was not among them, but Anson Cotter was.

"Hello, old man." Cotter was no longer deferential, now that they worked at different hospitals. "You wangled an invitation too, did you?"

Tom found it difficult to spend time with the cocky young intern and sought an escape as soon as he could.

The ferry ride took about an hour. Once across the bay, they purchased tickets on the North Shore Railroad, and at Point Reyes, they disembarked and loaded onto wagons that the Wolffs had provided to take them the rest of the way. Gus met them, explaining that Lia was in charge of distracting Mandy until they could surprise her at the appointed time.

Dispersed throughout the retreat, the guests doubled up with resident artists, where they found time to relax from their journey and dress for the party. Other friends arrived in a second wave.

Although they wouldn't be free to fully explore the grounds until the party began, Tom was already enthralled by the setting. To a farm boy from Nebraska, the combination of magnificent redwoods, towering cliffs, and a roiling sea was like an adventure novel come to life. He wanted to test his stamina on the rolling hills they'd passed; he wanted to sleep under the stars. *I need to get out more often*, he thought ruefully. *There's more to life than the Chinatown Free Clinic.*

Around the cocktail hour, Tom and the others were instructed to meet in the library and remain silent. Donaldina and Cheung Ti Chu had their hands full keeping their young charges quiet; a lot of tittering was met with whispered shushes. Tom, wearing his tux for the event, stood next to Cotter, who had already started drinking. Moments before the big reveal, Katherine swept into the room along with her brother, Will. She was dressed like a goddess in a rose-colored evening gown. Ignoring Tom completely, she sidled up to Anson to await the guest of honor. The lights were dimmed.

"You look good enough to eat," Cotter murmured to Katherine, loud enough for Tom to hear.

"Should I be on the menu?" she responded. Despite

the darkened room, Tom could see the inviting smile she sent the young doc.

It's going to be a long night, Tom thought with disgust.

"A toast to Miss Amanda Marie Culpepper, talented writer, reporter, model, artist's assistant, and all around charming young woman."

August Wolff lifted his glass of champagne and the rest of the three dozen or so guests followed suit, calling out "Here! Here!" and "To Mandy!" Tom had never seen his young friend look happier; she glowed.

The look on her face was in sharp contrast to Tom's inner turmoil. For the past two hours he'd been watching Katherine fawn over Cotter to the extent that the young man was practically salivating. But what man wouldn't when a woman as beguiling as Katherine turned her considerable charms on him?

Every so often she'd send a glance Tom's way, as if to confirm that her behavior was having the desired effect. She knew damn well that Tom wanted her—had known it since the day they met—and she was making it painfully clear that it wasn't going to happen.

Which is why he was shocked as hell at what transpired at the end of the evening.

They had all enjoyed a homespun meal of chicken and dumplings—Mandy's favorite— and afterward socialized in a large but comfortably furnished gathering room. Mandy was helping some girls rehearse for an upcoming mission fundraiser—ostensibly they were going to recreate actual paintings on stage in a performance known as *tableaux vivants*. Some guests offered suggestions while others chatted amongst themselves in small groups.

Anson Cotter had soaked up Katherine's attention —and the Wolffs' finest scotch—all evening long, only excusing himself after dinner to "get some air." On Cotter's way out, Tom noticed him whisper something to Mandy, who then accompanied him. When he returned a short time later, he looked slightly disheveled, and more than slightly angry. He tried to mask it by sloppily attempting to reclaim Katherine's focus, but she seemed to have tired of the game. To keep from staring at her, Tom struck up a conversation with Donaldina.

Later in the evening, after the opening of presents and a slice of birthday cake so delicious it reminded him of the North Platte spring fair, he saw August Wolff stop by the table Katherine was sharing with Cotter and murmur something to her. She rose and said, "No, I'll be fine, thank you." She said goodnight to Mandy, who asked if she wanted an escort to her cabin.

"I've already asked Dr. Justice to walk with me," Katherine replied. "We have business to discuss."

Cotter had wrapped his arm around her waist, but she removed it and walked purposefully over to Tom. Tapping him on the shoulder, she said, "I'm ready to go now, if you don't mind. You were going to walk me to my cottage, remember?"

He must have looked shocked because she raised her eyebrows in entreaty.

Seeing Cotter behind her, he quickly realized her predicament. "Certainly," he said.

Anson wasn't ready to give up. "I'll walk her," he insisted, swaying a bit.

Katherine turned around and pushed Cotter gently away. "Thank you, Anson, but I'll take it from here. I think you need to go back to your room, drink a lot of water, and sleep it off. If that doesn't work, call a doctor." She turned back to Tom. "Shall we?"

Tom extended his arm and she took it. He leaned in to whisper. "I have no idea where we're going."

"Follow me," she said confidently. As they headed down the stairs of the back porch, she picked up one of the gas lanterns that had been made available for night walks throughout the retreat. Tom took it from her and trimmed the wick to stop the flickering. The light fell on only a few feet of the path; everything else was lost in shadows, lending an intimacy to their stroll.

Once they had moved beyond hearing range of the house guests, Katherine turned to Tom. "I guess you'd like to know why I commandeered you."

"I assume you didn't want to be alone with Anson. He fancies you."

She huffed. "No, he fancies himself. And I can handle him. No, I wanted to...to talk with you about something that's been bothering me. It's about a certain man. You might even be acquainted with him."

"Really?"

"Yes, well, I met him on a train a couple of years ago."

Tom couldn't help but smile. "Ah. Almost two and a half, actually."

"Almost two and a half years ago. And, well, we got off on the wrong foot—because of my sharp tongue, I'm afraid. And then we've had some...disagreements... but I still can't seem to get him out of my mind. I've tried ignoring him, being rude to him—"

"Torturing him?"

She smiled. "That, too. I'm especially good at that. But nothing has worked. So I realized I need to change tactics. I need to ..." She paused. "I need to forgive him."

They walked a bit farther, saying nothing. Crickets were conversing in the night; a twig snapped and branches rustled somewhere nearby. It was a forest and they were the intruders.

"Do you think you can? Forgive him, that is?"

"I'm not sure yet, but I thought a good first step would be to get to know him." She stopped and looked up at Tom. "To get to know you. And maybe that would help."

They started walking again and Tom sensed something unfurling inside of himself. He kept his voice low and tinged with humor, not wanting the moment to sink with weightiness. "Well, let's see, you already know I'm a rube, a yokel from a farm in Nebraska who wouldn't know a tuxedo from a pair of overalls."

"I am sorry about that. You flustered me and I tend to use words as weapons."

Keep it light. Keep it light. "I've noticed you're talented in that regard. Well then, what else? You know I went to college, played football, attended medical school."

"Yes, I'm sure you received quite a few tickets the night of the fundraiser." He could hear the smile in her voice.

"I did, no thanks to you. And I met one Beatrice Marshall, who let me take her out for coffee while she went on and on about her real swain, a certain Will Firestone."

"Oh, poor Bea," Katherine murmured.

"Why do you say that?"

"Because despite our mother's best efforts, Will isn't going to marry her. In fact, if my hunch is right, you already know the girl he's interested in."

"I do?"

"Yes. It's Mandy."

"Mandy? But she's too—"

"As of today, she's no longer a girl, and very much a woman, one whom I suspect loves my brother right back." She glanced at Tom. "So, what about you? Why aren't you with someone?"

"What makes you think I'm not?"

Katherine stopped moving. "Oh. Well. I stand corrected."

She started to remove her arm from his, but he stopped her. "No, you were right the first time. I have... friends, but not that kind of relationship."

"Not ever?"

He hesitated. "In college. But I wasn't sure, and I was heading off to medical school. It didn't seem right at the time and, well, she married my cousin, actually. They have a young son and are expecting another child."

"Is she happy?"

Tom paused again. Was Carina truly happy? "I think so. I know *he* is. He always had a competitive streak, you see. What better contest to win?"

"Maybe you let him win."

Tom let a small chuckle escape.

"That amuses you?"

"No, you just reminded me of something my mother told me a long time ago. Maybe you're right." He waited a moment or two before adding, "What about you?"

They rounded a corner and came upon the cottage where Katherine was spending the night. A miniature version of the main house, it looked straight out of a fairy tale. Someone had lit the lamp that hung near the front door, enveloping the porch in a soft glow.

Katherine turned and gazed at him softly. "I think we've done enough soul-bearing for one night, don't you?" She started to open the door, but Tom put his hand on hers. He could feel her trepidation as she looked up at him.

"Would you mind if I checked inside before you enter? We *are* in the woods, and that could mean big bad wolves, you know." He said it casually but would insist if necessary. She stepped to the side and waved him in.

After a few moments he came back out. "All clear."

"I would hope so."

Tom sent her an amused look. "You don't like relying on anybody else, do you?"

She primly smoothed her skirt. "I suppose not. I

don't like feeling helpless. But I suppose you already knew that."

The memory of her anger over being denied access to her deathly ill brother re-surfaced. Could she really forgive him? He moved closer and murmured, "It's nice to talk about it, though. I hope we can get beyond it."

She appeared somewhat flustered and compensated by stepping back and extending her hand. "Thank you for walking me to my door, and for letting me get to know you so that I can…change my tactics."

Tom took her smaller hand in his large one and their eyes met. The current between them was strong, steady, inescapable. Something you cannot see but only had to feel to know it's there. He had never experienced such a strong connection before, not even with Carina.

Katherine began to pull her hand away, but Tom held her, pulled her even closer to him, until their bodies touched.

He was lost. "I have a new tactic too," he whispered, and lifted her chin with his other hand to kiss her lightly. His lips left hers for a second or two, and when he saw that her eyes were closed, he descended again with more purpose. She let him into her mouth. Willingly.

He regained his wits first, stepping back slowly, as if she were a feral creature that would scratch if he riled her.

"You must lock your door when I leave," he ordered.

She responded with humor. "Why? Are you afraid those big bad wolves might get me?"

"Yes," he said with no trace of levity. "Especially the ones with two legs. The ones who want to devour you in every possible way. Goodnight."

Katherine closed the door, and only when she slid the bolt in place did he head back down the steps and into the night.

There was no denying it, the woman fascinated him—her strength, her pride, her willingness to work hard and change her life rather than merely complain about it. She was a beautiful woman, yes, but there was so much more to her, and so much more he hoped to learn.

He had almost reached the cottage he'd been assigned when Cotter stepped from the shadows.

"You've got some damn nerve," Cotter said. He'd sobered up some, because his words were no longer slurred.

Tom did not want to deal with this bounder. "Anson, it's late—"

"First you warn me off Mandy, then you think you can move in on Katherine Firestone? Do you honestly think a fine piece like her would be interested in the likes of you?" He scrubbed his ravaged looking face; the downside of drinking a fifth of whiskey, even the finest whiskey, was obvious.

"I've got no beef with you," Tom said, and turned to go.

But Cotter wasn't finished. He shoved Tom

awkwardly. "Yeah, well, I got a beef with you. From now on, you keep your goddamn judgments to yourself, and you don't horn in on another man's action."

Tom felt his tether snap, and he pushed Cotter so hard that the man almost fell. "You're lucky I've got nearly ten years' worth of common sense on you. Because if I didn't, I'd be tempted to demonstrate the ill effects of a head bashing. Like the lady said, Anson, go sleep it off."

"Fuck you," Cotter said, but with less heat. Evidently he was smart enough to realize it wasn't his night. He headed down the path and Tom heard him mutter, "Ah, you're all a bunch of rubes," the insult fading with him into the darkness.

CHAPTER TWENTY-THREE

*"He seemed like a man who was quick to judge—he assumed
the worst of us and we hadn't done nothin' wrong."*

—Corporal Amos Fielding, Encountered Tom
Justice the Night Before the Quake

It was warm for April, and at nearly midnight, it
was also quiet at Saint Francis Hospital, where
Tom and Martin, the orderly, were finishing up the
swing shift. A waning crescent moon probably
accounted for the relatively few hospital admissions.
Census was low, patients were sleeping, and Tom had
sent Nurse Wilson home early because her son had
chicken pox. The two men were in the midst of a
routine inventory check when they heard a commotion
at the front entrance.

Two young soldiers stood outside, waiting to be let
in. One of them, the tall one, had a body slung over his

shoulder—a Chinese man by the look of his long black braid. The Chinaman looked like he'd been beaten up.

Tom held the door open for the two men. "What's happened here?"

The grunt let his human baggage slide slowly down, taking care to keep the fellow from crumpling all the way to the floor. He peered at Tom's lab coat. "Dr. Justice, I'm Corporal Benjamin Tilson, First Battalion, Twenty-Second Infantry Regiment." He pointed to his friend, a short, scrappy-looking fellow. "This is Corporal Amos Fielding. We came upon this poor sod in an alleyway and figured he could use some help."

Sure you did. "May I ask what you two were doing in the alley?"

The short guy, Amos, got huffy. "I'm not sure I like what you're implyin', doc. We was walkin' by and heard a scuffle. The men who did this scattered like rats and we brought the guy in to get some doctorin'. End of story."

Somehow that didn't feel like all there was to it. But hell, at least they'd brought the poor man in. "Let's take a look," he said. He gestured to Martin. "Would you kindly take the patient to the first examination room?" As Martin did so, Tom turned back to the soldiers. "Thank you both for stepping up. The Chinese don't have many white friends in this town. Where can I reach you if we need more information?"

"Fort McDowell, sir," Corporal Tilson said. "And thank you for helping him." He shook Tom's hand.

Nice young man, Tom thought. *I hope all the troops are like him.*

The two soldiers turned to go, but Tilson hesitated. "Ah, sir? One more thing."

"Yes?"

"You, uh, might get a couple more patients this evening. It wouldn't be a good idea for them to know you're taking care of the Chinaman."

I knew it. Tom looked pointedly at Amos. "End of story, huh?"

Shortie merely shrugged. What could he say?

"Thanks for your *service*, gentlemen." Tom didn't bother hiding his sarcasm. Why were so many arguments settled with fists? "I think it's best you head on back to your post now."

It was almost comical the way they both blurted "Yes *sir*" and beat a hasty retreat.

Martin had already begun cleaning up the young man's injuries when Tom came into the room. An examination revealed several cracked ribs, a broken thumb, a number of lacerations, and a concussion. It could have been worse. The poor fellow probably worked outside of Chinatown and was trying to get back to the enclave before dark. Jesus, what was wrong with people? He was curious to see how much damage the two soldiers had inflicted on the thugs who'd attacked the man, and kept waiting to hear another knock on the hospital's front door. But no one else came by and Tom had to assume they'd either self-medicated or gone elsewhere. That was probably for the best.

At twelve thirty the night shift came on and Tom said good bye to Martin before heading back to his apartment above the clinic. He noted wryly that he had no qualms whatsoever about being a white man walking in Chinatown after dark. The double standard was disgraceful.

When he opened his apartment, he noticed a letter had been slipped under the door. Mrs. Liang being efficient again, no doubt. The return address was Johns Hopkins University Medical School. Curious, he opened it to find a letter from Dr. Halsted in response to the thank-you note Tom had sent him after being accepted to the staff at Saint Francis.

> *I am glad you accepted the assignment, which I expect for the time being will make great use of your exceptional skills. To that end, I have a proposition for you that I'd like to discuss when I visit San Francisco the last week in April. Please inform as to whether a meeting may be arranged.*
>
> *Sincerely,*
> *William Halsted, M.D.*

Tom stared at the letter. After all this time, was there a chance he could restart his surgical career? The fact that Dr. Halsted had recommended him for the hospital position was flattering enough, but to want to talk to him about a future opportunity? Really? It was nothing short of miraculous.

He couldn't help it; his mind jumped ahead. Would it entail moving back to Baltimore? Could he do that? Did he want to do that? Who would run the clinic? Would it be in better hands with a Chinese physician?

Would Jimmy ever consider returning? Could someone else be recruited by the Six Companies?

Possibilities bombarded him, and into the maelstrom came thoughts of Katherine. For so long she had seemed elusive and unattainable, nothing more than a pipe dream. But their walk in The Grove had been instructive. Of the many things he'd learned about her, perhaps the most important was the fact that she felt the same pull he did. It was undeniable; she just didn't know what to do with it. He knew what *he* would do with it, but that was going to take some time. How could that happen if he were to leave?

My God, he hadn't even had the meeting with Dr. Halsted. Didn't have a clue what the man had in mind. Talk about the cart before the horse.

Tom poured himself a whiskey and stretched out on his bed. *First gather the facts. Then make a decision.* In the meantime, it was enough just to contemplate the lovely things he and Katherine might do together the next time they met.

It turned out they would meet the very next day. But there was nothing lovely about it.

CHAPTER TWENTY-FOUR

*"He kill my Bo San without a second thought. Who can do
such a thing?"*

—LI ZHENG, CHINATOWN NEIGHBOR

Somewhere a horse was screaming.

Half asleep, Tom didn't catch on to what was
happening, why the bed was sliding, why the walls
were groaning. He wasn't dreaming, was he? He sat up
in the pre-dawn gloom, trying to get his bearings, and
found he could barely hold on to the shifting frame.

He could hear his apothecary jars breaking downstairs and recognized the metallic crash of his instrument tray on the tiled floor. A cart—his examination
table?—seemed to be rolling back and forth, slamming
into the cabinets, like a bully venting his rage against
the room. Fully awake now, he understood.

Outside his window, whose glass had broken, Tom heard the continuing shrieks of a horse in agony.

As soon as the shaking stopped, he pulled on his trousers, shirt, and shoes, making his way down the stairs to the rooms below. As he'd imagined, they were in shambles. He stepped through the debris to the front door, but the door had twisted in the upheaval and could not be opened. Tom grabbed a towel from the linen shelf, wrapped it around his arm and broke out the glass in the large, cracked storefront window. Shards painted with "Chinatown Free Clinic" and "Pay What You Can" fell to the pavement outside. Stepping over the sill, he saw the full extent of the calamity.

The bully had raged against the world.

On either side of him, Tom's neighbors were filing out of their respective boarding houses, calling to each other in rapid Cantonese. *Are you all right? How is old Mr. Chin, did anyone check on him? What is happening?* Li Zheng, who lived three doors down, was standing by his horse, trying to console the panicked beast, but making the situation worse with his own keening cry. Li had been on his way to the farmer's market on California Street—his daily trek to buy produce to resell to Chinatown's neighborhood grocers. Except this morning, apparently, as they pulled away from the curb by the livery stable, the street itself had split in half and shifted, opening up a chasm just wide enough to swallow the back legs of the horse into a deep crevice. Still attached to the wagon by its traces and flailing for solid ground that didn't exist, the horse was being slowly stretched to death and was calling for help the only way it knew how. The animal could not be pulled out, so there was only one way to help it.

"We need a gun! *Coeng!*" Tom called out. "Please, we have to—"

"No! No! Bo San, she my precious morning!" Li cried, even though it was plain as day his beloved companion was doomed. One man, sizing up the situation, ran back into his room and came out a minute later brandishing a .38-caliber Colt revolver. He stopped at the sight of Li's hysteria and looked at Tom. It was obvious he didn't want to cause his countryman any more grief.

"Give it to me," Tom said, extending his hand. He took the man's handgun, checked to see that it was loaded, and approached the horse. Li went to stop him, but several clear-headed neighbors held the man at bay.

"Here now, easy girl," Tom crooned. The horse's wild eyes locked on his, beseeching him, it seemed, to do what he needed to do. Tom took the bridle firmly in his hand and tried to steady the horse's head as much as he could. He aimed the revolver between the animal's eyes and kept his hand locked. He wanted the first shot to be the last one.

It was.

At peace now, Li's Precious Morning stopped straining, and the weight of the horse's body caused it to slide all the way down into the gaping wound of the street. Someone stepped up to cut the traces and save the wagon. Moments later an aftershock lent a coda to the surreal tableau as the pavement buckled once more and closed over Bo San. Silence reigned for several seconds before Li's anguished cry split the air again.

There was no time to mourn the loss of a beloved horse when the rest of the world was close to falling into the same hellish pit. "Find out who is hurt and bring them to me!" Tom called out in Cantonese to the shocked crowd, then ran back to the clinic, realizing as he did so that he wouldn't be able to treat anyone inside the destroyed building. As he climbed back through the broken window, another aftershock caused him to slip and cut his hand, close to where he'd sliced it open as a kid. Luckily this time it wasn't deep. He quickly washed and wrapped it, then began to collect as many first-aid supplies as he could. Into a crate he tossed bandages, splints, packets of needles, thread, hydrogen peroxide, iodine, alcohol. He broke the glass to his drug cabinet, removed the cocaine, morphine, chloroform, and ether bottles, and carefully wedged them into his medical bag along with his surgical kit. He thought briefly about trying to maneuver a gurney outside; as long as the street didn't open up again, it would be a hell of a lot safer than being indoors.

He found a mallet and pounded on the door frame. After several whacks it straightened out enough that he could force the door open—just in time to see Martin, the orderly from Saint Francis Hospital, running toward him.

"They need you at the hospital right away," Martin said, his bulky frame heaving. "They told me to get you to bring whatever supplies you got, plus a change of clothes. You're going to be there a while."

"What about the people here?" Tom said. "I can't just leave—"

"All sorts of people are streaming in," Martin said. "Tell them to come to Saint Francis. They'll get treatment there."

Tom surveyed the remains of his clinic; there was no way he could be of any use there. He ran to his neighbor Wu Chang and told him to spread the word that the Chinese would be treated at the hospital—Tom would make sure of it.

With Martin's help, he transferred the supplies he'd gathered into two strong pillow cases; after stuffing an extra shirt and underwear into his medical bag, they headed to Leavenworth Street, looking like runaways setting off for the ends of the earth.

And maybe the earth was ending. It sure looked that way. The wooden buildings of Chinatown, which had appeared almost pretty after Dr. Blue's anti-plague beautification program, were now nearly all damaged in some way, as if the city fathers had made good on their threats to bulldoze the entire neighborhood. Like Tom, the residents had begun to pull out whatever valuable possessions they owned. For some, the piles were pitifully small. A young man dusted off his bowler hat, hefted a sack of tangerines over his shoulder, and started walking with nothing else but a small flute in his hand. An old woman without teeth clucked to her prize bird as she carried its cage. The people were walking toward higher ground as if a flood were on its way, but instead of rain, the air was murky, filled with the noxious odor of burst pipes, exposed sewers, and seeping gas.

How presumptuous we are, Tom thought as he surveyed the destruction. As if mankind could bend this planet to its will, build structure after structure—some of them ten stories high!—cover what's left with cement, and tame it all into submission under the banner of "progress." Forces below the surface were always at play, forces that humanity never even thought about, because people were so caught up in their flimsy little lives.

Today, though—today the earth had a bellyache and belched. We are nothing more than ants scurrying about trying to find a way to save ourselves and those we care about.

Katherine. Where was she? He knew she lived on Green Street. Did her little house survive? Did she? He shook his head. Worrying about her would drive him insane, and he couldn't afford that.

He thought of Mrs. Liang and Lee Pritchett and his cousin Eli and Carina and the lusty widow Adeline, and mentally took them to safety; he thought of his parents and brothers and Jimmy and his family, and thanked God they were nowhere near this nightmare.

By the time they reached the hospital, Tom had cleared enough of his mind to concentrate on the matter at hand: helping the dozens of patients who had already shown up to be treated. He thought he'd be spending quite a few days at Saint Francis, and wished he'd packed more shirts.

He was wrong.

CHAPTER TWENTY-FIVE

"I'd never seen anything like it, even on the battlefield. And I hope I never do again."

—SERGEANT STEVEN BRIGGS, QUARTERMASTER

The waiting room of Saint Francis Hospital was already overcrowded by the time Tom and Martin arrived. Both men immediately stepped in to help with triage, working quickly to assess and treat the wounded. Because of his quick and accurate suturing skills, Tom took the lion's share of cuts and lacerations. Before long he was no longer seeing his patients as individuals; they'd become a constantly moving assembly line of bloody arms, legs and scalps. His right hand began to cramp and he forced himself to slow his pace.

They'd been at it for a little over two hours when Dr. Coffey, the head of the hospital, announced that

Saint Francis would have to be evacuated. His voice wobbled as he explained that his beloved facility was directly in the path of the fire.

Fire.

When the quake struck that morning, ripping up streets and tearing down buildings ("God's temper tantrum," someone called it), fire was the last thing on everybody's mind—at least those who'd made it through the first wave. Steering clear of the after-shocks, watching for falling bricks and broken electrical wires, those were the big concerns.

But the temblor turned out to be just the opening act. Countless ruptured gas lines clashed with broken chimneys, and sparked by a careless match, led to blaze after blaze. Some were small enough to be snuffed out, but others quickly thundered out of control.

They'd learned through reliable sources that the city's fire chief had been critically injured during the quake and was out of commission. The acting chief didn't have as much experience and was relying on the Army to help stop the flames from spreading. But with virtually all the water lines broken, there wasn't much they could do to stop the onslaught besides using sand, the occasional water boat (if the fire was close enough to the docks), and explosives. The latter would destroy the structures in front of the advancing fire and thus, in theory, deprive the flames of the fuel they needed to survive.

So far, nothing was working, and Saint Francis Hospital was next in line to sacrifice itself to the fire gods.

Silver linings are sometimes hard to come by, but Tom looked for them anyway. At least the hospital's low occupancy from the night before meant fewer bed-bound patients to move. Another plus: thanks to the Army, there were enough vehicles to evacuate everyone who had come to Saint Francis and take them to...

...The *Mechanics Pavilion?* Tom had to laugh. That was about as far from a suitable hospital setting as it got. It was nothing more than a giant barn, for God's sake!

Martin was of a more practical mind. "At least it'll be big enough," he said as they loaded a dozen seriously injured patients into wagons and headed down Hyde Street. "How bad can it be?"

"Welcome to Hell."

Sergeant Steven Briggs, the quartermaster in charge of directing traffic at the Pavilion, didn't mince words.

They'd arrived at a madhouse—a mecca for the doomed. Hundreds of quake victims from all over the city were streaming into the temporary hospital, dwarfing the relative few transported from Saint Francis. They came in wagons and carriages and carts and automobiles, carried on stretchers and doors, on shutters and planks of wood, even on the backs of men—anything that would bear the weight of the burned, the crushed, and the maimed.

There was no distinction between male and female,

young and old, rich or poor, not even between those who had merely brushed against death and those who were staring it in the face. They had all come, along with those who loved them, to be fixed by Tom and whoever else could help them.

Despite its vaulted ceiling, the Pavilion's air was thick with the cloying stench of rusty blood, heavily chlorinated disinfectant, and unwashed bodies.

And the sounds. Hundreds of voices, each in the throes of their own personal nightmares. Undisciplined. Discordant. Matched by the insistent hum of hundreds more patients who murmured to others or themselves, staring with disbelief around the hall as if they had been abducted in the middle of dinner and dropped on an alien planet.

It wasn't the crying that got to Tom. Or the shouting. Or even the moaning. Those, at least, were sounds of life. It was the gasping, the rattling sound of air fighting its way through the lungs. The quietly panicked refrain of "Hold on now, Donny. Hold on. We're getting you help, son." And worst of all, the silence of those who were now beyond needing their voices ever again. Tom had never been in the middle of a war, but he wondered if there had ever been a massacre as gut-wrenching as the scene before him.

His heart began to trip at the sheer magnitude of it all. How could he make any sort of difference when there were so many—too many—who needed help?

Tom glanced to his left and saw a colleague walking toward him. Dr. Tillman worked at the emergency hospital in the basement of City Hall. "Till," he said, happy to see someone he knew. "How's it over your way?"

The young surgeon shook his head. "City Hall's gone. Our patients were the first to come over." He looked around at the chaos. "Glad you're here, Tom. We can use another surgeon and a dozen more like you. Let me show you what we've got."

Till pointed as they walked. "Triage there, Orthopedics to the right, Burns in the center, Critical Care along the back, Morgue to the left of that." He'd just started explaining the lay of the land when he was called away, leaving Tom to get oriented on his own.

He headed to the critical care section first. It had been cordoned off with a long rope, strung from one side of the hall to the other and hung with an assortment of sheets and blankets to provide an ersatz barrier. Even under these circumstances, someone had had the decency to insist that those who might be dying should go about it with some degree of privacy. Apart from a few from murmured voices, it was strangely quiet behind the curtain.

He moved closer, but a soldier stopped him. He wore a bland expression. "Special authorization required here, sorry."

"I'm a doctor," Tom said.

"I have my orders, sir."

One of the privacy panels was swept aside as two litter bearers, neither of whom looked old enough to shave, carried a linen-draped body between them. They turned to their right, no doubt headed for the morgue that Till had pointed out. Tom followed them.

It too was shielded by a series of curtains. One of the soldiers struggled to grasp the drape nearest him while holding on to his side of the litter, and Tom stepped up to help him. He almost gasped when he saw what lay behind the barrier.

Bodies were everywhere.

Everywhere.

As if a bomb had gone off in the midst of a crowd. As if a madman had decreed the end of a race.

His first instinct was to turn away from the horror of it; he was a healer, and the sight made everything inside of him scream *failure*. But he forced himself to move closer and take it all in, to give the dead what little respect he could by at least acknowledging them.

He could tell the story of what had gone on in the Pavilion by the way the bodies were laid out. At the floor level, individuals had been carefully wrapped in sheets and arranged neatly in two lines of bundled cadavers, as if they'd arrived at a funeral parlor and were awaiting preparation for burial. From what he could see, they were of all sizes, no doubt comprised of men, women and children.

But more bodies had come, and they were laid on top of the first layer. About halfway through, it looked like the soldiers had either run out of sheets or the time needed to encase the entire person. Even then, they sought to show respect by using baby blankets, of all things, to wrap around the heads of the victims. Did they use blue for boys and pink for girls? Did it matter at that point?

The litter bearers were up to the third layer now,

and there were no coverings left to provide a final dignity. Tom's gut twisted as he saw what was on their stretcher: two young girls with their arms wrapped around each other—sisters, it looked like. The fresh-faced soldiers were struggling to keep their emotions in check at what had to be the most difficult duty of their young military careers. Worse, Tom thought, than facing enemy fire: at least in those circumstances they had a fighting chance—the story wasn't already over.

As he watched the pile grow, it dawned on Tom that something wasn't quite right with what was happening. Something about the frequency, something...he was beginning to reason it out when Till ran up to him.

"Ghastly, isn't it?" he said. "Sad to say, these might be the lucky ones. Come, I'll show you what we need."

Focus. One patient at a time. Nana Ruth's words ran through Tom's head: *You save who you can save, and you let the others go. Always.* "Where do I scrub up?" he asked.

"I'll be back in fifteen," Tom said to the doctor replacing him as he pulled off his surgical mask. He grabbed a small towel and began wiping the sweat off his neck as he walked down the line of operating tables. For the past hour he'd been cutting, stitching, and repairing human bodies at an ungodly pace. Till was right: he and every other doc needed the break to let their hands relax and to get rehydrated; otherwise they weren't going to be able to keep it up. And by the looks of the crowds of wounded filling the Pavilion, it wasn't slowing down anytime soon.

Halfway to the exit of the ad hoc operating theater he felt a prickling sensation and glanced up.

Although Katherine was wearing a mask as she assisted another surgeon, he knew her immediately. Her beautiful eyes held his, and he couldn't help but smile in response. In that moment, the knot that had been painfully stuck inside him since that morning began to dissolve.

She was safe.

"Doctor, can you help me over here?" a stern-looking nurse called out to him. Reluctantly he turned from Katherine and followed the woman, whose name was Elkins, to a row of beds in which patients lay in various states of injury or recovery. One of them, a man who looked to be in his early twenties, was thrashing about. Nurse Elkins tried to restrain him. "There, there, now. You're going to be all right. Just stay calm."

Tom realized it was the same young soldier who had brought the beaten-up Chinaman to the hospital the night before. He checked the patient chart. Ben Tilson. That's right. The notes said another soldier had found him next to a dead looter earlier that morning and brought him in. He'd been coshed in the head. Tom put his arm on Ben's to help quiet him down. Within a moment or two the young man's eyes began to clear.

"Dr. Justice," he croaked.

Tom smiled. "I see your memory's intact...and that you still can't resist getting into a bit of trouble."

Ben tried to raise his head but fell back again with a grimace. "There was a man," he said. "I didn't shoot him."

"No you didn't, but someone else did, and they must have knocked you out so you wouldn't hold them to account." He examined the wound on Ben's head. "You've got quite a goose egg going."

Ben gingerly touched where'd he'd been hit and attempted a grin. "No wonder my brain feels scrambled."

"I think you're going to be all right, soldier," the nurse said with a smile of her own.

Tom examined Ben's pupils and reviewed the chart. "Your commanding officer wants you back on duty as soon as possible, but I'm not releasing you for another twelve hours at least. You need to get some rest, and once that happens, we'll take it from there, all right?"

Ben nodded and closed his eyes. "A little nap's fine by me, doc. A few hours and I'll be good as new."

Tom checked on a few more patients, making notes on each before heading back to an open table for his next surgical shift. He walked by Katherine's station, but she wasn't there. No doubt she was taking her own well-deserved break.

The next few hours went by in a blur. Tom barely had time to think about the intricacies of each surgery. A head, a hand, an arm, a leg; his focus was solely on preserving one life as quickly as possible so that he could move on to the next. Despite the pressure, his brain had never worked in such perfect cadence with his hands; so far he hadn't lost one patient.

He caught sight of Katherine now and again. At one point, he couldn't resist stopping by her station on the way back from a break. He leaned into her and whispered, "I'm glad you're here."

She nodded. "We're the fortunate ones."

And they were for a while. Then the luck of everyone in that vast hall changed—victim and healer alike.

And all because a mother wanted to cook a hearty meal for her rattled family.

In nearby Hayes Valley, a woman lit a fire in her kitchen stove to make breakfast for her husband and children, no doubt thanking her lucky stars that her home had survived the quake. Unfortunately, the tremor had blocked the flue of her chimney, and within minutes the trapped cinders had set fire to the walls of her house.

Already they were calling it the "Ham and Eggs" fire. And once it started, it began to devour every building in its path, merging with other, smaller fires to create an unstoppable inferno.

By noon, helped along by a stiff wind, the flying embers of that blaze had found the roof of the Mechanics' Pavilion.

CHAPTER TWENTY-SIX

"I saw him go off with Nurse Elkins to the back, where the critically ill patients were. He looked determined."

—Dr. Anson Cotter, Key Witness for the Prosecution

The city's chief surgeon, Dr. Charles Milbank, had been tasked by the Army to head the large medical team at the Mechanics' Pavilion. Tom knew him to be a highly skilled, dedicated physician who was nearing retirement. Today he looked ready to drop in his tracks from exhaustion. In addition to leading the effort to treat all those who needed help, he had been working feverishly on critically wounded victims. Judging by the growing numbers in the morgue, the success rate of Dr. Milbank and other physicians wasn't high. But who could blame them? They simply didn't have the equipment or the time necessary to save more lives.

In spite of his gaunt appearance, Dr. Milbank surprised Tom and the rest of the medical team by climbing on top of a table and shouting through a megaphone: "Attention. Attention all medical staff and patients. The Pavilion must begin evacuation procedures immediately. Doctors, please stabilize your patients, attach their records, and prepare them for transport via the Polk Street entrance following the direction of Army personnel. Conveyances will be waiting. I repeat: stabilize and prepare all patients for transport without delay."

Tom immediately sought out Katherine, who was assisting two tables away. When her eyes met his, she nodded slightly, seeming to agree with his unspoken plea—*don't let us get separated*—before resuming her work.

Tom did likewise, quickly closing a deep scalp wound.

He glanced at the scene before him. Hundreds of patients had filled the Pavilion, taking up any and all available space along the walls and aisles of the cavernous building, and the noise level was rising as they realized their new peril. Those who could walk, or even limp, surged toward every exit like cattle spooked and ready to stampede. Armed soldiers stood in their way, turning them back toward Polk Street. A burly man with a broken arm pushed down both an old woman with a bandaged head and the young boy caring for her. Others surged behind him. Tom was about to go after the thug, but a sergeant beat him to it, drawing his weapon.

"You get in line and stay in line, or I'm tying you to that post and you'll be the last one out of here," the soldier barked. He looked at the crowd, daring anyone else to move or speak. "The same goes for anybody else who thinks he's better than the person next to him. Just follow directions and we'll all get out of here as soon as possible."

For several tense moments it seemed like the barrel of a gun was all that stood between order and complete chaos.

Thankfully, the brute backed down, and the men, women and children who could move were herded out the proper doors. Soon there was room to begin transporting the patients who weren't ambulatory.

Tom was taking no chances. He walked over to Katherine and took her hand. "Stay close," he murmured.

Thus began a medical evacuation of massive proportions. Tom and Katherine were assigned a row and, armed with scant supplies, began a quick examination of each victim, making sure all bandages were clean, that bleeding had stopped, and the patient's pain was mitigated. Till had given each doctor a handful of morphine ampules, and Tom's only complaint about Katherine was her willingness to give it all out before they'd seen even a dozen patients.

"There's pain, and then there's *pain*," Tom said. "Let me handle it." To each man who looked to be suffering, he said, "I have only a few shots left for all these people, including women and children. Do you really need one?" Invariably the man would shake his head. Tom saved his stash for those who were too consumed by agony to answer.

As the two of them finished with each patient, Tom would call out "Next," and a pair of soldiers would carefully lift the individual onto a stretcher and carry them out. He glanced up once to spot Anson Cotter working with a nurse three rows down. He could barely tolerate the man, but he had to admit Cotter was good at his job; they were lucky to have him. Acknowledging each other briefly, they both returned to their work.

It seemed like it would take hours, but soon the combined staff hit a certain rhythm and the number of patients in the hall finally began to drop.

Progress, Tom thought. "Looks like we're going to make it," he murmured to Katherine.

He spoke too soon.

Just as they reached the end of their row, Nurse Elkins rushed up to Tom. She looked terrified and gestured for him to lean down so she could whisper to him.

"We need you in Critical Care right away," she said. "A man is waving a gun and threatening to shoot anyone who comes close. He says he's your brother and will see only you."

Tom paused in the act of pulling off his gloves. "That's impossible."

The look on the nurse's face told him otherwise. "Please," she begged. "He looks ready to kill."

CHAPTER TWENTY-SEVEN

Mid-April 1907

At his next scheduled meeting with his clerks, Jonathan turned out to be the tardy one. He arrived at his office just after the luncheon hour to find Oliver already standing at the blackboard writing down names. Days earlier, after Jonathan mildly suggested that the board be lowered, Cordelia had surprised him by not only giving him a smile of gratitude, but insisting that, given her counterpart's much greater height, the board stay where it was.

"I do not want special consideration of any kind, especially if it puts others out," she'd explained to Jonathan. "I am perfectly content to use my little soapbox, if it's all the same to you." She'd said the latter with a hint of devilment, and Jonathan couldn't help but grin back at her artful response. "Yes, that is quite all right with me."

Now, however, the mood in the room was less sanguine. Cordelia was shaking her head as she perused a slip of paper; she and Bean had obviously been conferring.

"I'm sensing something amiss," Jonathan said, removing his hat and hanging it up. "What have you found?"

Cordelia handed him the paper. Several names and their titles were listed.

Bean turned to address them, all business. "We know that Dr. Cotter, who leveled the accusations against Tom, was in the Mechanics' Pavilion the day of the earthquake. He was tending patients just like Tom was, and he has testified to seeing Tom head to the critical care section at the behest of Nurse Elkins. Those working with Cotter have affirmed his whereabouts with the exception of a time when they noted that he too headed toward Critical Care. He denies going farther than the outer curtain, although at this point we only have his word for it. If we assume he's telling the truth, however, that eliminates him as an eyewitness to the events that took place behind said curtain."

"That's the good news," Cordelia said glumly.

Bean tapped his copy of the paper. "You're right. It's *these* people who truly know what happened. These are the witnesses who can tell us definitively where Tom Justice was at the time of the murder." He pointed to the first name he'd written down on the board. "Dr. Charles Milbank, in charge of the critical care section of the Pavilion." He paused. "Dr. Milbank, I have recently discovered, suffered a fatal heart attack five months ago. There are also the two stretcher bearers, Privates McCrory and Sanders. McCrory was killed in action in Cuba and Sanders continues to serve overseas. According to military authorities, he is unable to return to the United States at this time."

Bean continued down the list.

"A guard by the name of Sergeant Roy Fenton. He took his own life only a month after the fire. He reportedly consumed a prodigious amount of alcohol along with several opiates."

A coldness swept through Jonathan. He glanced at Cordelia, who still wore her grim expression.

The lanky clerk wasn't finished. "Nurse Lena Elkins, currently working in Cuba with Dr. Carlos Finlay and the U.S. Army, is supposedly 'unavailable' for testimony, although I am pushing for at least a deposition. And an orderly by the name of Otis Carr seems to have fallen off the face of the earth. His family says they have no idea where he is."

No one spoke for a moment. Jonathan scrutinized the list on the board. "A heart attack, a suicide, a military casualty, two witnesses who are 'unavailable' to testify, and one who can't be found." He looked at his clerks. "What does this lead you to believe?"

"That we're missing a very large piece of the puzzle," Cordelia said.

Bean nodded. "And that some individuals, who could include members of the military, don't want us to find it."

Jonathan thought back to the times he had asked Tom Justice directly about the circumstances surrounding the crime. His client had danced around the answer in every instance. "I think Tom Justice knows more about what happened than he's admitted. The question is what."

CHAPTER TWENTY-EIGHT

"By the time we evacuated, we were all shell-shocked."

—Dr. Tilton Tillman, Assistant Surgeon at the
Mechanics' Pavilion

D r. Milbank and Tom were two of the last medical workers to leave the Pavilion. The older doctor drew him aside. "You know we cannot speak of what you saw, but I want you to remember that you saved a lot of lives today. Don't ever forget that. It's one of the few positives any of us can take away from this nightmare."

His words were meant to encourage, but his tone was forlorn. Did the man really believe what he was saying?

Try as he might, Tom couldn't see any silver lining in what he'd just experienced. There was no way to skirt the reality of what they'd done, and what they'd failed to do. He took a shuddering breath and let it out. He had to focus on something else.

Katherine caught up with him near the wagons and asked what had happened. She was cross that she hadn't been allowed to help him. He tried to brush it aside, but she wouldn't let it go.

"What do you mean, 'nothing'?" she said. "The nurse had been visibly upset when she asked for your help."

"So I helped her and there's no more to it," he'd insisted. "Come on, we'd better go." Katherine hadn't been mollified, but all Tom could think of was his own peace of mind.

You will get through this. You will.

He kept up the mantra as he and Katherine found seats in one of the remaining wagons. It was barely one in the afternoon, but the sky was already stained with the rancid murk of smoke and soot. His eyes watered and he told himself it was the malodorous air.

The streets were pot-holed and the ride was jarring. He used that excuse to wrap his arm around Katherine's waist to keep her steady. At least she hadn't pulled away from him; she had no way of knowing that right now she was the only thing keeping *him* upright.

They followed the other evacuees northwest toward the U.S. Army base called the Presidio. Tom had been there once for a meeting about the Chinatown plague and had marveled at the sheer magnitude of the place. Set on a windswept bluff overlooking the Pacific Ocean, the fort's mission was to protect the "Golden Gate"— the entrance to the enormous natural harbor that was San Francisco Bay. It was also the headquarters of the Army's Pacific Division, and just a few years before, it had easily supported thousands of troops who camped there in tents on their way to and from fighting what was now called the Spanish-American War.

The tents were back, only this time they were housing thousands of quake and fire victims who had lost their homes. The Presidio's lush parade grounds, well out of the fire zone, were once again a field of dusty white canvas. The Army was expert at sustaining a population in flux; by the end of the day Tom had no doubt it would be its own functioning town.

A sergeant registered Tom, Katherine, and the other medical workers as soon as they rolled through the gates. "We got a field hospital setting up in Golden Gate Park and you may get sent there eventually, but for now, we need you to follow up on the folks that's just come from the Pavilion, plus the others streaming in from other parts of the city." The NCO wrote down numbers on slips of paper and handed them out to each person. "This here's where you'll bunk at night. Each quadrant has a nickname, but don't lose the number, because all the tents look alike and it'll be a hell of a time getting access to this list once I turn it in." He pointed the group toward the nearby tent hospital where they'd be given their work assignments.

"Wait—who's giving the orders here?" a skeptical orderly asked. "Are we under martial law?"

The sergeant lowered his voice. "Truth be told, there's nothin' official says we are, but General Funston's the acting commander right now and he's a take-charge guy. As long as he's giving orders, you'd all do well to follow his lead."

Less than an hour later, Tom had been assigned to field duty while Katherine was sent to the official base hospital to assist their surgery staff. The idea of losing sight of her was unsettling, but for the best, he reasoned. He couldn't imagine what the future held for them now.

"I guess I'll see you around the camp, then," he said. "We'll probably run into each other, maybe at meal-time." God, it sounded like a dismissal.

Katherine looked puzzled. "I'm sure we will."

He'd already turned to go when she touched his arm. "Where are you staying?" she asked.

"Oh." Reluctantly he pulled out the housing assignment and showed it to her. "It says I'm in Forest Knolls."

He made a point not to ask about her circumstances, and after an awkward moment, she broke the tension with, "Quite a day, wouldn't you say?" She gifted him with a sad smile, a balm to the dark place inside of him. He felt the need to explain himself to the extent he could and reached for her hand.

"They said he had a gun, and I couldn't take the chance of you being anywhere near that. It would have killed me. I hope you understand."

"You seem to be in the habit of protecting me." She said it without heat.

He smiled faintly. "I can't help myself."

"Well, maybe someday I can return the favor."

He closed his eyes. Those last moments in the

Pavilion hadn't faded in the least; they remained stuck in his memory, clear and sharp as spikes. "I wish you could," he said, and squeezed her hand lightly before letting it go.

"I'll look for you later, then," she said.

They headed in opposite directions, and Tom was glad to report for duty. He needed to work and did so until the physician in charge ordered him back to his tent to rest.

Late that night his right hand began to tremble.

CHAPTER TWENTY-NINE

"He'd been through a lot and it was beginning to affect his work, so I assigned him lighter duty."

—Colonel Lionel Aldrich, Chief Medical Officer, Presidio

In the beginning, the tremor was so slight that he barely noticed it. A pinched nerve, he thought. Too many procedures, done too quickly under too much pressure. Tom coped well enough, discreetly massaging his hand when he could and hoping it would relax in time.

He'd been assigned to a non-surgical ward, which was fortunate, but the patients he saw were no less heartbreaking than those who needed a sawbones. For every quake-related injury there were now two or three victims of the subsequent fires. Those whose lungs were irreparably damaged from the heat of the smoke they'd inhaled. Those whose face or limbs or torso would be scarred for life. Those whose bodies had stopped melting long enough to get them to the hospital, but who were sure to leave it only after an agonizing death.

It was so disheartening that when patients came in complaining about a singed scalp or smoke-damaged hair, Tom barely refrained from advising them to get a fucking hat and make room for somebody else.

At the end of his first full day he grabbed a quick bite in the dining tent (there was no sign of Katherine) and headed straight to his sleeping quarters. He was the first to bunk down for the night and was grateful for the quiet, hoping sleep would overtake him quickly and his hand would stop its annoying flutter.

He should have known better. Neither his hand nor his mind would settle down, and all the images of the past two days, the scenes of horror and shock, desolation and death, even the harsh beauty of desperate love and unfettered grief—all fought for attention, all sought the center stage of his memory. And each was worthy of it, worthy of thought and tears and sadness, and he would have been glad to give time to all of them, but he was so damn tired, and had so little energy left.

Hours later, the other occupants of his tent, all medical workers, began to filter in. They were quiet, no doubt assuming he slept, but they needn't have bothered. Because sleep didn't come until several hours later, and even then it was fitful and broken.

And in the morning, his hand still shook.

He saw Katherine the following day in passing. He was ending his lunch break while she was starting hers. She asked how he was doing and he answered too quickly. "Fine. Busy. You know."

He kept his hand in his pocket.

She shared similar platitudes. The surgeries were constant, and they could use Tom's expertise, she said with a warm smile. She said she wished they worked together. Then she paused, as though waiting for him to say something more. Something about them.

He didn't oblige, saying merely, "Gotta run. See you soon," and left as quickly as he could.

He wouldn't bring her into his troubles. She would try to fix things, and this she couldn't fix.

By that afternoon, the tremor had gotten worse. While checking the broken wrist of a little girl, she'd asked him, in the guileless way children have, "Why's your hand shaking, mister? You all rattled inside?"

Fatigue, he figured it was. And, he admitted, some stress. He'd been existing on his reserves for some time now, and those reserves were running low.

By the fourth day, Tom was having trouble using both hands to bandage wounds, so he took it upon himself to get help. He went straight to the top.

"What can I do for you, Dr. Justice?" Colonel Lionel Aldrich had a baby face, short-cropped hair, a trim mustache, and an impeccably pressed uniform. He had moved his office from Presidio headquarters to the tent city, but he'd brought along his diploma from

Washington's new Army Medical School. It hung prominently on one of the tent poles, no doubt to remind skeptics that he was the man in charge.

Tom removed his hand from his pocket. It was trembling just enough to illustrate his dilemma. "I'm not sure what this is all about," he admitted.

"Let's take a look." The colonel examined Tom's hand and arm, feeling the muscles and the tendons. "Feeling any pain?" he asked.

"No, sir."

He then turned the palm over and noticed the old scar. "What's this?"

"Cut myself when I was ten. Healed just fine and never gave me a lick of trouble."

"But there's a newer cut next to it."

"Just some broken glass."

Colonel Aldrich nodded, dropped Tom's hand, and motioned for him to sit down. Then he leaned back in his chair. It was obvious he had something on his mind. "It was tough at the Pavilion, I heard."

"Yes it was." *More than you know*, Tom thought.

"When was the last time you got a good night's sleep?"

Tom had to grin at that. "Sleep? I'll sleep when I'm dead."

The colonel smiled back. The phrase was a common joke among medical students no matter where they attended school. "Tell you what," he said. "This may be nothing more than a case of sleep deprivation. I'm going to write you a prescription for laudanum. Get it filled at the pharmacy tent and take it this evening. Tell your bunkmates what you're doing, then let yourself sleep as long as your body tells you to. No heroics." He wrote out the prescription and handed it over. After a moment he wrote something on another slip of paper and handed that over as well. "If there's no change, I want you to contact my friend Dr. Wendell Sussman. He's over in the East Bay. A good man."

"Why him?" Tom asked.

"He specializes in nervous disorders. You might be suffering from some form of acute neurasthenia."

Tom let out a snort. "Not a chance." He got up and held up the prescription. "Thanks for this, at least."

"Remember—no heroics. Get the sleep you need and let me know how it goes."

"Thanks, doctor."

After the evening meal in the communal dining tent, Tom picked up the laudanum and retired to his bunk, took the narcotic, and waited for sleep to overtake him. In a matter of minutes, it did.

Twelve hours later, Tom woke up with a groggy head and a hand that still trembled. For the first time, he felt the stirrings of true panic.

CHAPTER THIRTY

"We spent only a brief time with him, but he was quite
helpful to the refugees in our little camp."

—Josephine Firestone, Director of Firestone Camp

Scowling, Tom grilled the soldier who'd been ordered to fetch him. "What's this all about?"

"I dunno, sir. All's I know is you're bein' sent over to some place in Pacific Heights—the real Pacific Heights, that is. Order says it's just for a day or two—an 'extended house call,' they told me."

The morning had not started out well, and by noon it had only gotten worse. Working in the field clinic, Tom couldn't pretend that nothing was wrong when his right hand was useless for at least half the procedures he needed to perform. It was impossible to stitch a shallow cut or reset a simple fracture. Even his injections caused more than one patient to yelp in pain.

Inside, Tom was fighting a sense of unreality, as if he inhabited someone else's body, a body he couldn't control.

Dr. Aldrich hadn't helped matters. Early that morning he'd passed Tom on his way to breakfast and looked pointedly down at the hand Tom was once again hiding in his pocket. They'd exchanged looks, Tom answering Dr. Aldrich's raised eyebrows with a small shake of his own head. The man had merely patted Tom on the shoulder and walked on, but Tom sensed pity in his demeanor.

Could the situation get any worse? The answer was yes. Because waiting by the wagon to take him to the new location was none other than Katherine. *My God, did she know? Had she felt pity for him and pulled some strings to take him out of an awkward situation?*

"What are you doing here?" His gruff tone matched his mood.

She looked as disconcerted as he felt. "I was told I was needed at a location in Pacific Heights." She busied herself adjusting her uniform's cape.

"What location?"

He watched her hesitate and swallow. "My parents' estate."

"What? Why in the hell would we be needed there?"

That response didn't sit well with her. "I am as much in the dark as you are about this! It was probably my mother's doing. I can see why she'd use her influence to get me to come, but you, I don't understand. I've never said anything to her about you or our...

friendship, and she only met you briefly at their New Year's gathering, do you remember?"

"And once while you were shopping. Of course I remember. But I find it hard to believe you had nothing to do with this. People like you are used to getting their way, aren't they?"

He knew the moment he'd said it that it was the absolute wrong thing to say. How *stupid* of him. He could practically see the cloak of disdain she drew around herself.

"People like me?" she asked. "Do you mean rich people? Privileged people? Perhaps you're right. We do get our way. But why on earth would getting my way involve you?" She didn't bother to hear his answer, just turned to climb aboard the wagon. He started to help her but stopped before she could reject him and cause even more embarrassment. Silently he heaved his medical bag in the back, climbed aboard and sat next to her. She followed the pattern of every piqued female that Tom had ever encountered and scooted as far as she could to the other side. God forbid that their bodies should touch.

The wagon master took the reins and they were off. As they rumbled out of the compound and south toward the privileged enclave of Pacific Heights, despair didn't begin to describe Tom's state of mind.

During the trip, neither of them spoke, and Tom found no solace in the passing landscape. Even after several days, destruction and desolation claimed every street, providing a surreal backdrop to the countless city dwellers who were attempting to get on with the business of living. A woman in a pretty blue walking dress with matching parasol stood on a corner, pausing, no doubt, to determine which pile of rubble would be easier to negotiate on her way across the street. Smartly attired in a suit and bowler hat, a gentleman reached a hand out to help her as if it were any other spring day and he a typical gallant.

By the time they reached the turnoff to the Firestone estate, Tom half imagined he was having a drug-induced dream.

The gate to the long drive leading up to the mansion was propped open.

"Oh my lord," Katherine murmured.

As they headed up the gentle slope, they saw row upon row of rudimentary lodgings. There were ready-made tents of all kinds, from simple pups to army-sized cabins. There were lean-tos and crude wooden structures, and even a series of what looked like large shipping cartons being used as gnome-sized houses. The shabbily constructed shelters took up nearly every inch of open space on the Firestone grounds.

People were everywhere, tending campfires, talking to one another, comparing horror stories, he imagined. Mothers watched their children dash crazily in and around the hodgepodge housing. The closer he and Katherine came to the main house, the more densely populated the camp seemed to be. Only a slapdash rope barrier kept the driveway and the expansive veranda clear.

"Your parents' home looks to be under siege," Tom said.

"I can't imagine my mother's reaction to all this. She must be livid." Katherine's voice held no antipathy, at least not toward Tom; she seemed more nonplussed at the spectacle playing out before her.

Tom noticed Katherine's mother waving wildly at them. "I don't know. She looks pretty jovial to me."

As soon as they'd hopped off the wagon, Mrs. Firestone gave Tom a beaming smile and swept her daughter into a hug. "Isn't it marvelous, darling? Welcome to Firestone Camp."

"We're so glad you could make it," Josephine said to Katherine after they'd dropped off their bags in the entry hall of the mansion. She put her arm through her daughter's and looked up at Tom. "And when I asked dear Lionel to add a physician to the mix, I never dreamed he'd send me a familiar face. You're Dr....?"

"Justice," Tom said.

"Yes, that's it. I believe we met around the holidays. Out shopping, and then you were Miss Cameron's escort for New Year's. I remember you filled out your tuxedo rather well."

"Mother. That is hardly—"

"Oh come now, Kit, this is no time to worry about offending someone's sensibilities. Isn't that right, doctor? May I call you Tom?"

"Yes, of course."

"Splendid, and do call me Josephine. Come, let's walk and I'll fill you in on what we're about."

Tom watched as Katherine processed the shock of seeing her mother, the well-known doyenne of San Francisco society, looking so pleased about having her home invaded. Not only was the lady not piqued, she appeared to be having the time of her life.

Mrs. Firestone proceeded to take them on a tour of the camp as if she'd founded it. Greeting one family after another, she was hailed in return with calls of "Halloo Miz Firestone!" and "Afternoon, ma'am. Nice day for a stroll."

"It's really quite remarkable how well our little camp runs given that it's less than a week old," she explained. "We supply water from our two wells, enough for drinking and cooking, at least. A lovely supply sergeant from the Army brings us basic food supplies and linens, and we distribute them as needed in an orderly fashion. And of course I have Bertrand making cookies and tarts and cream puffs all day long so that each afternoon we can pass out a bit of a treat to the little ones." She looked around and paused as if to soak it all in. "They have so little, after all." Her voice had lost its chirp.

"And health-wise, how are things?" Tom asked.

"Ah, that is where you and Kit come in. I've been told that living in these types of conditions can lead to illnesses of varying kinds, and I want to make sure we forestall such a calamity. We have set up handwashing stations throughout the camp, which they tell me helps to keep those nasty germs from spreading. But there are still residents with wounds from the quake and the fires that need to be treated."

They'd reached the estate's lower garden, which was much less formal than the area closer to the mansion. Sunflowers and wild lilacs and other flowers bloomed along meandering paths, some of which led to a fanciful Queen Anne-style gazebo, painted a rich red with white latticework trim. It was round, with half walls and views to all sides, and offered built-in benches topped with pretty cushions.

"I thought this might provide a good location for your little clinic. It's big enough to house a table or two, and we can string a curtain across for privacy, if you like. Plus there is plenty of storage underneath the seats."

Katherine sent her mother a look that was surprisingly kind and respectful. "I think this will work fine, Mother." She turned to Tom. "Don't you think?"

Tom walked around the small space. How was he going to keep his affliction from Katherine in this set-up? Chest heaving, he felt a mild sort of panic settling in. But what other options were there? He slapped on a smile, fake as a three-dollar bill. "Let's give it a whirl."

Josephine clapped her hands. "Wonderful! Just tell me what you need and I'm sure we can scrounge it up for you."

In short order the gazebo was furnished with tables, basic medical supplies, and a curtain to bisect the space. Tom suggested that in the interest of efficiency, Katherine should handle triage, and send Tom the patients she couldn't handle on her own.

One of the first to show up was Edward Firestone,

wearing a sling. Katherine explained that he'd dislocated his shoulder the morning of the quake.

"I told him I wouldn't open the clinic to others until he got some relief besides whiskey and ice," Josephine said. "Lord knows it's just going to get worse if he doesn't deal with it."

Katherine tsked. "She's right, Father. I told you to have it looked at days ago."

"May I?" Tom asked. At Edward's nod, Tom palpitated the shoulder, talking quietly the whole time. "You don't have much bruising, which is good. Have you felt tingling or numbness at all?"

"Some."

"And you've been icing it?"

"As often as I can get him to sit still," Josephine said.

Tom finished the exam and gestured to the table behind the curtain. "I don't feel any broken bones, so I think we may be able to realign it without too much trouble. I'm going to have you lie on your back so I can maneuver your arm back in place. Mrs. Firestone, could you please go back to the house and find your husband's favorite libation?" He glanced at Edward, who looked pale and was beginning to sweat. "He's going to need it. And Katherine? You should go with her."

"What? Why?"

"Please, Kitty Kat," Edward said. "Do as he says."

"Come along, darling." Josephine said, blowing a kiss to her husband before hustling Katherine toward the house. It was a good thing she did.

CHAPTER THIRTY-ONE

"I can't say a bad word about him. He got us help for our little girl that we never would have thought of. He bought us time."

—ELMER RANSOM, QUAKE VICTIM

"It's going to hurt like hell, isn't it?" Edward said.

"You know it is. No shame in screaming if you have to."

Tom gave Edward Firestone credit—for someone who'd lived a privileged life, the man had a lot of grit. After bracing his leg against the heavy base of the table, he began pulling firmly but smoothly on Firestone's arm, talking quietly to distract from the pain he was inflicting. At one point he asked the question he'd been pondering since they arrived. "Are you really all right with several hundred people taking over your home like this?"

Firestone panted as his swollen, twisted arm was stretched back into place. "N-not really. B-but my darling wife has her own v-version of the old bible verse. She...she says it's better to give than be taken from."

Tom chuckled and increased the pressure. "She's got a point."

"Ahhh," Firestone moaned. "Fuck, that hurts!"

"Damn, I'm sorry. Almost there." At that moment they both heard the *pop* Tom was waiting for. "There it is. The head's back in its socket. That should feel a lot better now."

Firestone let out a ragged breath and struggled to sit up. As Tom helped him, he looked at Tom's hand. "You've got a bit of a tremor there, son. Did I do that?"

Tom immediately stuck his hand back in his pocket. "No. I...uh, just a bit of stress, is all. I'd appreciate it if you wouldn't mention it, though. If you don't mind, that is."

Firestone rubbed his shoulder. "Your secret's safe with me."

Moments later Katherine and Josephine returned with a bottle of Glenfiddich and two glasses. Josephine poured a shot for her husband and offered another to Tom.

"No thank you, ma'am, but perhaps later tonight I'll indulge."

"Fair enough," she said. "By the way, we've made up a guest room for you. It's two doors down from Kit's old room. She can show you where it is when you're ready to retire. Oh, and Dr. Justice? Thank you for sparing me the pain."

"The pain?"

"The pain of watching Edward deal with *his* pain. Don't think I didn't know what you were doing, young man."

Tom smiled. He liked these people, very much. "I don't think I could put much past you, Mrs. Fire...Josephine."

The rest of the day, Tom and Katherine saw patients who lined up and waited patiently at the bottom of the gazebo's steps. They were lucky; most were there for scrapes and bruises or sleeplessness and headaches that were undoubtedly due to stress. So far, no contagions had broken out.

Tom let Katherine handle any injections, and even encouraged her to stitch up a relatively shallow cut. "I know you can do it, and this is the perfect time to practice," he'd said. She'd looked at him strangely, but agreed. As he predicted, her hand was steady and precise.

Late in the afternoon, a nearly hysterical young mother, small and too thin herself, came in with her newborn who was listless and suffering from diarrhea. The baby made little sucking sounds but was too weak to let out much of a cry, let alone a wail.

"I don't know what to do," the woman cried. "My milk dried up and I've been giving her regular milk, but she spits it out, so I tried apple juice but nothing's working."

"My guess is, your little girl—what is her name?"

"Amy."

"My guess is little Amy here isn't quite ready for what you've been giving her. You were smart to bring her in, because babies can get dehydrated very quickly. Our first goal is to get her suckling again, so if you've no objection, I'd like to find you a wet nurse, someone here in the camp who can help you out for a few days."

The mother started to blush. "Who would do such a thing for me?"

"You'd be surprised. You'd do the same for someone else, wouldn't you?" Tom called Katherine over to his side of the clinic. "Any chance you could send your mother on a mission for us? We need a woman who is currently nursing, and Mrs. Firestone probably knows everyone in the camp by now, so ..."

Katherine sent him a luminous smile. "Oh, she would love that mission!"

Her smile was so lovely, it made him want to move mountains for her. He did *not* want to feel that way. Not now. So he kept his expression neutral and added, "We need some white grape juice as well. Maybe her chef keeps some in stock. But make sure it's white, not purple."

Katherine nodded. "I'll see what I can do."

While she was relaying the instruction to Josephine, Tom tried to comfort the distraught mother. "It's not your fault you've stopped producing breast milk. It happens often, even if there aren't special circumstances like earthquakes to contend with. I'd say that would upset just about anybody's system, wouldn't you?"

The woman smiled shyly and nodded, more at ease now that her little Amy had fallen asleep.

Tom found an old paper wrapper from a package of linens and grabbed a pencil. He was about to start writing but realized his right-handed scribbles would be a bitch to read. Instead he handed both the paper and pencil to her. "Jot this down. You can make a basic cow's milk formula once Amy gets a little stronger. You'll need milk, water, honey, and cream. I'm sure Mrs. Firestone can help you find everything." He explained the percentage of each to use and touched Amy's forehead with his left hand, brushing back a wisp of hair. "It's especially important that Amy gets the honey because that will help her body retain water better. You can also use a little white grape juice dilated with water if she gets colicky or stopped up." Looking at the mother again, he smiled. "Of course, she'll probably grow up with a sweet tooth, but I'm sure you'll handle that when the time comes."

Tom also suggested some herbal remedies using fenugreek and fennel, in case the woman wanted to work on restarting her own lactation. A memory floated by of Tom getting all flustered listening to his grandma talk about that part of a woman's body, and how he told her to use the word "cleavage" instead.

"You know, boy, 'breast' ain't a dirty word. In fact, it's a downright pretty word, if you ask me. A lot softer and plumper than 'cleavage,' which is all hard and sharp like a sword. You may like the idea of a weapon today, but I guarantee once you get a mite older, you're gonna love the word 'breast' a whole lot more."

He had to smile. Nana Ruth had been one wise woman.

That evening, Tom begged off dinner with the family. They had gathered in the front parlor for drinks beforehand, which he'd learned was a longstanding habit.

"I need my beauty rest," he'd quipped on his way upstairs, and Josephine had giggled as he'd hoped she would. Edward, looking much improved, thanked Tom again for "setting him straight." Their eyes met, the older man's offering assurance that he would keep Tom's predicament to himself.

"I'll have a tray sent up to you, dear boy," Josephine said as he left the room. "You must keep your strength up for these trying times."

Katherine hadn't said a word; she seemed lost in her own thoughts, which was just as well.

The next morning Tom rose early and caught a bite to eat in the kitchen before heading back out to see patients. Bertrand, the Firestones' chef, was already at work baking pastries. At the moment, he was kneading dough on the wood-topped kitchen counter. Tom was tempted by a tiered plate of perfect looking molasses cookies and raspberry tarts sitting nearby.

"*Bien sûr*, help yourself," the large, rotund chef offered in heavily accented English. "Those are not up to Madame's standards but are perfectly edible for anyone else."

Tom grinned. "I take it the lady of the house runs a tight ship?"

"Like your *Capitaine* Ahab," the chef replied. He smiled, however; it was obvious he enjoyed the challenge of working for Mrs. Firestone.

Tom couldn't resist adding, "Seems like the daughter takes after the mother."

"Ah, Miss Kit," he said. "In some ways, *oui*, they are alike. But in others, the mademoiselle is much different." He began to roll out the dough with a wooden pin. "I have wondered if she was hurt at some point. She holds softness inside, like her mother, but she protects it with a beautiful yet rigid shell, *une coquille dure*. Like a chestnut, gleaming on the outside, but difficult to penetrate without a bit of warming."

Tom paused in the act of downing a tart while he reined in his imagination. "I see."

Chef Bertrand didn't seem to realize the double entendres he was using. "The monsieur who opens her will win a most valuable prize, *non?*"

It was time to leave before Tom had to seek out a very private spot. "Ah, yes, I'm sure that's true. Thank you for breakfast, Chef. I know the Firestones consider *you* a prize of the first order."

"Merci mille fois, monsieur. Bonne journée"

By the time Tom reached the gazebo, Katherine was already setting up supplies. They exchanged stiff greetings and Tom escaped to his ad hoc examination room. At least she wasn't hovering.

He caught himself stealing glances at her across the room like a love-struck swain. Hovering? Who was hovering?

It was too much. This had to be his last day with her; he would make sure of it.

Fate smiled on him at last and he was able to distract himself with a series of patients whose spirits as well as bodies seemed to be on the mend. A highlight came in mid-afternoon when little Amy's father stopped by. He was slight in stature, with thin brown hair combed carefully to the side. He smelled faintly of smoke.

"Just wanted to let you know it's working out good, doc." The young man held his hat respectfully in hand. "The lady Miz Firestone found is nursing Amy right alongside her own little boy. Says she's got plenty of milk and is glad to do it. Turns out her family tent is on the same side of the Big House as ours, so it's real convenient, too. We can't thank you enough."

He extended his hand, and Tom glanced at Katherine before extending his own to quickly complete the shake. Katherine looked at them briefly and turned away.

That evening at dinner, satisfied that he'd seen virtually all of those who truly needed medical attention, Tom announced that he'd be leaving first thing the next morning.

"Oh, must you go so soon?" Josephine asked. "I'm sure Sergeant Watkins could give you a ride back to the

Presidio once he brings supplies tomorrow afternoon. Isn't that right, Edward?"

Edward looked at Tom. "I'm sure the good doctor can find his own way back, darling."

"Ah. Yes. I've, uh, got to stop somewhere on the way. But thank you so much for your hospitality...all of you." He gazed at Katherine as he finished, but once again couldn't read her expression. Chef Bertrand's chestnut came to mind.

Luckily, their meal was a casual repast of vegetable soup and cucumber sandwiches, which Tom consumed without drawing undue attention before once again excusing himself early.

A bottle of scotch (no doubt compliments of Edward Firestone) waited on his nightstand. Around nine in the evening, despite taking a few shots, he still hadn't relaxed enough to fall asleep. Maybe a walk would help. He dressed quickly and headed downstairs to take a last stroll around the camp. On the way out, he noticed a light shining from underneath Katherine's door. Up reading? Was she as agitated by all that had happened as he was? He hoped not.

Outside, the air was cool, the sky nearly dark, and families were settling down for the night. Lanterns took over as campfires died, and sounds were reduced to quiet conversations, the occasional baby's cry, and the expected shush followed by a softly sung lullaby. Tom wondered how little Amy was faring and had his question answered as he came upon two women seated outside a tent, sharing a lap blanket between them. One was Amy's petite mother; the other was obviously the wet nurse Josephine had commandeered the previous day. The two ladies were conferring quietly while a baby—Amy, no doubt—suckled at the larger woman's breast.

"Dr. Justice," Amy's mother called out to him. "It's Beth Ransom. You saw my baby Amy yesterday? I'd like you to meet the woman who saved my little girl's life."

"Oh, I didn't do no such thing," the other woman said. She looked to be in her late thirties and was large in both body and heart, it seemed. She kept the baby at her breast but stuck out her hand. "Please to meet you, doc. I'm Sadie Wheeler."

"It's nice to meet you, Mrs. Wheeler. Thank you for lending a helping..." he stopped, feeling his face flush.

"Tit?" Sadie offered, and chuckled. "Sure and I've got enough milk to go around. Glad to do it." She stood up. "Here. Little Amy's about done for the night. Why don't you take her and give her a look-see before she goes to bed?"

Tom shook his head. "Uh, no, that's all right, I—"

"No, go ahead, please," Beth said. "I'd appreciate it."

Tom reluctantly took his hand out of his pocket. The two women glanced at each other when they noticed how it shook, but he muddled through, taking the weight of the baby primarily in his left hand and rocking her to mask the trembling. "She looks much more relaxed," he said to cover up the moment. "She's a beautiful little girl, ma'am."

"Yes, she is, isn't she?" a voice behind him said.

Tom turned around and faced the very last person he wanted to see.

CHAPTER THIRTY-TWO

*"Our city would do well to have a hundred more doctors
like him."*

—EDWARD FIRESTONE, BUSINESSMAN AND CIVIC LEADER

The lantern she carried cast Katherine in shadow,
making her appear ominous, yet tempting. He
had never seen her hair down; it cascaded halfway to
her waist. She wore a shawl against the chill; it outlined
her curves. Was it coincidence or had she followed
him? More important, had she seen his affliction?

"I'm the nurse who's been working here today," she
told the women. "I wanted to let you know the doctor
and I will be leaving tomorrow, but if you need any
help in the next few days, just let Mrs. Firestone know
and she'll get you what you need."

Tom handed the baby back to Beth Ransom, trying

to brazen out the moment. "Well, good luck to you, ladies. And goodnight."

He turned to leave, but Katherine fell into step beside him. "We need to talk," she said once they were out of earshot. "Will you come with me?"

Because she'd asked and not demanded, Tom assented. She was right, after all. They needed to set things straight before he left.

She led them away from the camp, toward a nearly invisible set of stairs built into the hill on the far side of the lower garden. Save for the pale arc of light in her hand, it was pitch black, but she appeared confident and he followed her down the steps and along a narrow path that followed the remnants of a small stream.

"Almost there," she murmured, and after a bit more walking they came upon the silhouette of what looked to be an enormous oak tree. Some of its branches were so large that several of them touched the ground before winding their way up again, creating a base that was perfect for sitting or climbing to the higher limbs. It reminded Tom of the oldest cottonwoods back home.

Katherine hopped onto a low branch and sat down. "This used to be my favorite refuge from being Katherine Madeline Mariah Firestone."

He remained standing on the ground, which put her slightly above him. How fitting, he thought. "You found that a tough assignment?"

"You've met my mother; no doubt you can imagine what it was like. It took me a long time to get out from under her shadow and find my own way."

"And now you have."

"And now I have. But that way led me to you."

Tom tensed. *Here we go. Perhaps I can stop it before it starts.* "No, we just happened to cross paths for a time, that's all."

"That's not all, and you know it. Less than a week ago we were connecting. I felt it. You felt it. I know you did. We have danced around it for so long, but I felt...I felt things were different. And now..."

"And now you see that I'm like all the rest."

Katherine jumped off the branch. Despite their height difference, she still appeared taller. More consequential. "You are not like all the rest. But you've changed." She pointed to the hand in his pocket. "Let me see it."

He froze.

"Let me see it," she said, tugging on his arm.

Slowly he drew his hand out, hoping against hope that it would be still.

In the meager light they could both see that it trembled.

"This happened five days ago, didn't it?"

"Yes."

"And you said nothing, thinking I wouldn't notice, thinking that you could just slink away. Was that your plan?"

He winced, resenting the inquisition and yet ashamed of the truth in her words. "Yes. So what?"

"So you could be overreacting. It's been less than a week. Maybe it's some kind of muscle spasm. Maybe you've been working too hard."

Tom let out a harsh bark of laughter. "Maybe I need sleep. Maybe I need to eat better. Maybe I need drugs. Maybe I need more sex. Who knows what the hell is going to fix it? All I know is, it isn't getting better."

She reached for him. "We can figure it out. There must be someone who can help you. We can—"

He stepped back. "No. *We* aren't going to do anything. I don't want you to be any part of this. Whatever *this* is."

The words came out wrong, as if shot from a gun. She recoiled. "There you go again," she said. "Deciding what's best for me."

"Not very modern, I know. But in this case, you know I'm right."

"I know nothing of the kind."

"Regardless. I'll be leaving in the morning."

"Where? Back to the Presidio?"

"To tie up loose ends, yes. Beyond that I have to find some answers." He held up his quivering hand. "I have to see what my new friend has in store for me."

Katherine waved her own hand dismissively, trying —and failing—to sound indifferent. "That's insignificant. You are so much more than your silly hand."

"It's a crucial part of who I am." He lightly touched her cheek, wondering how he could make her understand. "You should be with someone whole and healthy. Someone who doesn't feel like he's some kind of creature stuck in a body that doesn't obey him."

"What is the worst that can happen?" she said, taking his hand in both of hers, her voice desperately logical. "If you can no longer perform surgery, there are other forms of medicine. You were wonderful with that poor young mother yesterday, and see how grateful she was? You can consult. You can—"

He pulled his hand away. "Katherine. You're not listening to me. I will never be happy the way I am right now. And if I'm so caught up in my own misery, I will never be able to make *you* happy, to give you everything you deserve." He ran his good hand down the back of her head in one last selfish, proprietary gesture. "And you deserve everything. You surely do."

She looked down, and he could tell she was composing herself. When she faced him again her look was defiant. "I don't accept your premise."

"Well, you're going to have to, because you can't help me. And even if you could, I wouldn't want you to. Let's just leave it at that, all right? Now I really need to get some sleep."

They headed back to the house, leaving Katherine's childhood sanctuary behind. Had she thought it would magically make things right again? It seemed he was fated to disappoint her once again.

As they walked back through the refugee camp, even the muted conversations discernible earlier had trailed off into silence. It was so quiet, all Tom could hear was the soft crunch of their shoes on the path.

"We always seem to be finding our way through the dark," he said, once they were inside the mansion.

"Not always." She turned off the lamp and they walked upstairs together. Just before entering her room, she wished him goodnight, as if he were just another house guest. He supposed that's all he really was.

The Glenfiddich went down smooth. Tom lay on his bed for the next two hours with half a bottle left to savor, happily entering the phase of inebriation where his thoughts were still coherent but covered in a gauzy film that made them tolerable to contemplate.

He randomly considered careers that didn't require fine motor skills. Fishing, for instance. He'd always liked the ocean. He could be a lobsterman, maybe, or dive for abalone. Yes, but fishing required tying knots, didn't it? And depending on the fish, some of those hooks were pretty small.

Coaching. He could teach high school boys how to play football. That would be fun. But he threw right-handed. How in the hell would he be able to demonstrate a perfect spiral, or how to keep from fumbling a ball once they'd caught it?

There was always farming. He could shuck corn all the live long day. Sure he could.

Shit. He took another drink and almost didn't hear the soft knock on the door. Had he cursed out loud? He couldn't remember. Maybe it was the Firestones' butler telling him to pipe down.

"Come in," he uttered.

Katherine stood in the open doorway, silhouetted by the faint light of the sconces in the hall. The dressing gown she wore hugged the outline of her breasts and hips. She was being cruel to him again.

"I've come to see how you're doing," she said.

"What a good little nurse you are." He opened his arms wide. "As you can see, all is well." He waved his quivering hand wildly. "Except for a traitorous hand, life is glorious."

She shut the door and moved closer to the bed. The only light in the room came from a small electric lamp on the writing desk. Katherine was cast in shadow as she had been in the camp, still mysterious, and all the more forbidden. Her voice felt like a caress. "I'd like to give you something."

"A going-away present? Let me guess. Another pep talk? A piece of your mind? A kick in the ass?"

"No," she said. "Just me."

His pulse kicked up about ten notches. "Just you."

She came closer. "That's right. Just me. Tonight I want to be with you. It's as simple as that."

He chuckled without mirth. "It's never that simple."

She was next to the bed now. "Tonight it is." And then she slowly untied the belt to her gown and dropped it.

Underneath she was naked. Incredibly lovely. Better than any scotch or opiate or wet dream. He hardened immediately but fought it, shaking his head. "You don't know what the hell you're doing," he managed.

She leaned over to whisper in his ear. "You aren't the first. Does that matter?" Then she nuzzled him.

All he could do was slowly shake his head. Did she know what a gift it was to not saddle him with her virginity? She must. "You. You have to stop now, because—"

She climbed on the bed and straddled him. He knew she could feel him straining against his trousers, but it only encouraged her. She leaned forward and pressed herself against him. "Because you won't be able to stop yourself if I continue? I'm counting on that, Tom." She kissed him deeply. "I'm counting on that very much."

"Ah, Katherine," he sighed, and when he took her face in his hands and kissed her back, he knew beyond a doubt that all was lost.

The first time they made love, it was almost harsh. Katherine assumed the lead, passionately aggressive, as if fearful he would change his mind. At one point, summoning the last of his willpower, Tom took her by the arms and forced her to stop and look at him. "I have no protection," he said, his chest heaving.

She didn't hesitate, instead producing a rubber from the pocket of her gown. "I have only three," she whispered. "Will that be enough?"

"I doubt it," he murmured, "but we'll make do."

He put that hurdle out of his mind then, along with every other rational thought, and began to drink in the woman he had fantasized about for so long. Despite her confession, it was clear that Katherine had had little experience with sex, but what she lacked in technique she more than made up for with enthusiasm.

Tom let her lead until she had driven him to the brink, then laid her down and brought her satisfaction before pouring himself into her.

Afterward, neither of them said much. Tom couldn't bear to spoil the moment with reality. He suspected she felt the same. Instead they pretended time had stopped, leisurely exploring one another with their hands and their mouths, coming together again, and, this time, reaching their peaks together. As their heartbeats settled down, so did their bodies, and they fell asleep entwined as if they had shared the same bed for years. A few hours later, Tom awoke and reached for Katherine again. As she opened herself to him, he wondered if he'd drunk the entire bottle of scotch and was dreaming it all. But no, the bottle was still there, still half full. Katherine in his bed, lying beneath him, welcoming him, was no dream.

And throughout their coupling, he had forgotten all about his hand. Had it trembled like the rest of him?

Dawn was just beginning to light the sky beyond the bedroom's sheer curtains when Tom finished dressing. He sat on the edge of the bed gazing at Katherine, who lay on her stomach, still naked from their last tumble. Her face was turned away and her golden hair fell softly around her pale shoulders. He ran his hand softly down her back.

"You are more beautiful than I ever imagined, and I

imagined you just like this so many times," he murmured.

She turned onto her back and tucked the sheet around her, giving him a sad smile. "If you think me so beautiful, then stay with me."

His expression was equally melancholy. He held up his hand, which still shook. "I wouldn't make you live with this for all the tea in China."

"That's a prodigious amount of tea." She sat up and let the covers fall, revealing her breasts. "Think what you'll be missing."

He chuckled softly. "You are a very cruel woman, Miss Firestone. But so exquisite, in every way."

"Will you write to me?"

"No."

Do you...need any money?"

He frowned with a quick shake of the head; her look told him she regretted the question.

"One other thing," he said.

"What? Anything."

"Don't have me followed. Do you understand? You will not use your money and influence to control me. I am not some sort of family pet who's run away from home."

He could see the anger rise in her, along with the subtle admission that perhaps she would have done exactly that if he hadn't warned her not to. Still, she looked peeved. "Don't you think that's a bit extreme?" she asked.

"You're probably right. But promise me anyway."

She frowned. "All right. I promise I won't have you followed."

Tom gently touched her chin and lifted her gaze to his. "Thank you for that." He swallowed hard, realizing that of all the sacrifices he'd had to make, this one would be by far the hardest—this was a choice he might regret for the rest of his life. But he had to do it, whether Katherine believed it a good idea or not. For her sake, if nothing else.

"What would you like me to tell everyone?" she said after a moment, resignation in her voice.

He gestured to the writing desk in the corner. "I left your parents a note, and I'll inform Colonel Aldrich. He'll make sure someone good comes to take my place."

Tears welled up in her beautiful eyes. "No one can take your place, Tom," she whispered.

"They'll have to," he answered, his voice desolate. He leaned down to kiss her tenderly. "They'll have to."

And before he could second-guess the path he'd chosen, he quietly left the room.

CHAPTER THIRTY-THREE

*"I found no physiological reason for his tremor, so I reasoned
it was a case of neurasthenia."*

—DR. WENDELL SUSSMAN, PSYCHIATRIST

Tom needed money.

He caught an early ride back to the Presidio
and informed Colonel Aldrich of his plan to see Dr.
Sussman after all. The colonel wished him well, telling
him to do "whatever it took" to get back in shape.

That's exactly what Tom intended to do, but he
figured the travel, examination, and cure, whatever it
happened to be, wouldn't come cheap. Asking his
family for help wasn't an option; he'd barely been able
to tell them he was all right and not to worry; admitting what had happened with Eli was out of the question. And since all of its branch buildings had been
destroyed, the bank where he kept his savings was on

extended "holiday." That left only one other ready source of cash: Tang Lin.

On the edge of Chinatown, Tom stopped by the Presbyterian Mission House—or what was left of it. Before the quake, the five-story brick walls had been home to nearly fifty Chinese and Japanese girls, all rescued by Donaldina Cameron from lives of slavery, servitude, and prostitution. Now the girls and their living saint were gone, their refuge reduced to a heap of ash and rubble.

As he gazed at the ruins, he noticed he wasn't alone. A tong member, marked by the tall "highbinder" hat hiding his long queue, was poking around in the debris, a rice sack in one hand. Tom called out to him in Cantonese and the young man gave a start, turning around quickly and drawing his knife.

"It's only me. Dr. Tom. From the clinic." Tom stepped closer and the gang member stood up. Tom recognized him as one of Tang Lin's lackeys. Good. "Gan Deshi," he said. "I am glad to see you made it through the big shake up. What happened to the Angry Angel and her many girls?"

The highbinder seemed to relax slightly. "They walk to other church, then take boat to church school in the north."

Tom had to smile. If anybody could lead a passel of young girls on a perilous cross-town journey, much less one across the bay to points north, it would be Donaldina. "Good. And the members of your tong?"

"Li Park and Rong Shi die. And two more injured. But most make it through."

"Even Tang Lin?"

The acolyte straightened his shoulders. "Tang Lin always come through on top."

Tom looked around pointedly. The city as a whole was in terrible shape, but even by those standards, Chinatown had taken it on the chin. San Francisco's Chinese-hating factions had tried to destroy the community for years, but Mother Nature had done a much better job on her own. What was going to happen to all these people?

"Where are your headquarters now?" he asked. "I need to speak to Tang Lin about something very important."

"I take you there."

Gan Deshi hefted his sack—no doubt filled with silver and other looted valuables—and led them up Sacramento Street to Clay, and then to a side street off Washington. There, a rough-looking stone structure remained, its tin roof having somehow escaped the worst of the fires' wrath. Several tong members sat outside, throwing dice on a patch of ground that someone had swept clean. Gan Deshi spoke to one of the guards and went inside. Within a few minutes he returned and held open the scorched metal door.

Tom stepped inside to a cavernous room, the walls of which were obscured by stacked boxes marked with Chinese characters that Tom couldn't decipher. The middle of the space, however, was empty except for an oversized, ornately carved wooden desk with two fancy chairs facing it, each upholstered in a feminine rose pattern. The furniture looked comically out of place in the bare surroundings, but the man sitting behind the desk looked born to it. Tang Lin was checking what appeared to be a ledger, his fingers simultaneously working an abacus with lightning speed. He glanced up.

"Ah, Dr. Tom. Welcome to my new palace."

Tom shook the tong leader's hand and quickly shoved his own back in his pocket.

"Please to sit down," Tang said. "You are well?"

Tom nodded. Now that he was here, he didn't quite know how to begin. "And you?"

"I cannot complain. Because a certain doctor ensured that I kept my leg, I was able to escape the large shake-up and the fire." He patted his thigh and smiled. "This is a very handy piece of the body to have in such trying times." He paused a moment to close his ledger. "I trust you have been working hard to save other limbs these past days. I am honored by your visit, of course, but I sense you have a purpose in mind. What brings you here today?"

Other than his request for Katherine to stay away, Tom couldn't remember the last time he'd asked anyone for anything—perhaps it was back in college, when he'd been laid up and Jimmy Wong had stepped in to help. It was much harder to do than he'd imagined. "I...I find myself in need of a loan."

He was not prepared for the wide-eyed look of happiness his words brought to Tang's face. "You bring me a most auspicious gift," Tang said.

Tom flushed. Perhaps the man didn't understand what he was asking. "What do you mean?"

"To give a man the opportunity to repay a debt of honor—that is most sought after by those who have incurred the debt."

"I told you, you owe me nothing for saving your leg. I would have done it for anyone."

"Yes, but not any doctor would have done it for me. And as I was fortunate enough to be treated by you, so I am doubly fortunate that I can help you in return. What do you need?"

Tom held up his hand, much like he'd done with Colonel Aldrich. No sense beating around this particular bush. "I seem to have developed a bit of palsy since the quake, and I need to take the time to find out how to get rid of it."

Tang nodded his head. "Have you tried re-aligning your *hei*? Your energy flow may be disrupted. I could have my people track down Shing Tao. He—"

"Shing Tao had his clinic next to mine. We didn't always see eye to eye. I think he felt I was stealing his customers."

"That is not very forward-thinking of him."

"No, but it doesn't matter. I am going to try Western medicine first. I've been given a referral to a doctor in the town of Oakland." Tom grimaced. "Supposedly he specializes in 'nervous disorders.'"

"But you do not believe this is the problem?"

"The problem is that I don't know what the damn problem is."

Tang Lin smiled and tapped the side of his head. "The mind is the master of the body, you know. One must obey or be punished."

"Did Confucius say that?"

Tang's grin widened. "No, I did. But I think perhaps he would say something like that. It could be that you are fighting some thoughts and your mind is asserting itself in response." He leaned over to open a desk drawer and pull out a sack. "Will five hundred dollars be enough to begin with?"

Tom held up his hand, which continued to quiver. "Wait—that's way too much. I couldn't possibly pay that back any time soon."

Tang Lin clucked. "This is not a loan, Dr. Tom. This is a gift."

"I'll take two hundred if you can spare it, but only if I can sign a note promising to pay it back with interest."

"What good will such a note be to me? I will just tear it up after you leave."

"Then it's a good thing I know how to find you," Tom said. Because I *will* make good on it."

Tang and Tom took the measure of each other; Tom understood that each man's sense of honor was at stake.

At last Tang spoke. "I understand your need to repay this debt, and I hope you understand my need to give you something in return for the gift of mobility that you gave me. I propose the following: you may consider the principal a loan and I will consider the interest my gift to you. Is that satisfactory?"

"More than satisfactory." Tom brought his hand out of his pocket and stood up. It was a small relief not to have to hide it. He looked around the room while Tang

Lin counted out the bills. God only knew what kind of contraband those boxes contained. What was going to happen to the likes of Tang Lin and the tongs?

"I'm curious. What will you do now that Chinatown's been demolished? It's no secret that some in the government want you all to go away."

Tang looked up. "Oh, Chinatown is not going away. It is very much alive and well. We will rebuild. Right here. Much better than before. Only the tongs will change."

"Change how?"

"For the better. The old ways are no longer satisfactory. It is time to make way for the new."

"You seem confident, Tang. As if you know things."

Tang tapped his ear this time. "I am like that little dog—the badger hound, you call it? He keeps his ear to the ground and he can sense what is going to happen even before it does. Would you like to place a wager on it?"

Tom shook his head good-naturedly. "I would never bet against you, Tang. You are more like a cat than a dog. You have at least nine lives."

Tang handed Tom the money. "Use this to get well," he said.

"I'm not going to ask where it came from," Tom murmured as he put the bills inside his coat.

Tang smiled again. "That is a wise decision."

"But thank you. It is much appreciated."

Tang stood up and bowed. "We will meet again."

"You can count on it."

Before leaving Chinatown for the eastbound ferry,

Tom stopped by the Chinatown Free Clinic one more time. He'd saved more than one life there over the last few years, and helped countless others. Now it was nothing but a damp, sooty pile of charred wood and melted glass. Anything of value had been picked clean days ago. Jimmy Wong's dream of bringing Western medicine to his people had turned to ashes, literally. *I'm so glad he wasn't here to see it,* Tom thought.

But maybe Tang Lin was right. Maybe they would rebuild. If so, they would have to do it without Tom, because without two good hands he was "as useless as tits on a boar hog." Nana Ruth always knew just how to sum up a situation.

"I can find no underlying physiological basis for your tremor," Dr. Sussman announced three days later. "Physically, you are in excellent health."

Tom had undergone a battery of tests and had even volunteered to have an X-ray taken of his hand. Dr. Sussman had vetoed that idea because of the dangers inherent to the new diagnostic procedure. Reports of burns and hair loss had escalated and the previous year, X-ray researcher Elizabeth Fleischman had died from her exposure to excessive radiation. Nobody knew yet how much exposure was too much, and Dr. Sussman felt he could make a reasonable diagnosis without risking further damage to Tom's hand.

"Then what's causing it?" Tom asked, sensing he wasn't going to like the answer.

"It's hard to say," the physician hedged. "Tremors like yours can come and go. They can fade after weeks or last for years. But I believe yours is a case of 'psychogenic movement.' Essentially, you have an underlying psychological condition that is causing unwanted and involuntary muscle spasm."

Tom felt the age-old frustration of wanting to know *why*. "So, what does that mean?"

"Well, there are different types of disorders that could be causing your particular issue, but given what you've told me about being around so much trauma during the earthquake and fire, I would say it's most likely a 'conversion' disorder in which your body continues to react to the traumatic event you experienced."

"How does it do that?"

Dr. Sussman shrugged. "We do not have definitive answers to those questions yet. One plausible theory is that the brain is responding to the imagined threat by sending nerve impulses which in turn inject abnormal amounts of adrenaline into your bloodstream. This signals the limb—your right hand, in this case— to be anxious."

"In other words, some part of my brain is stuck in 'crisis mode' even though the crisis is over."

"That's the essence of the theory, yes."

As he had so many times before, Tom went over all that had happened the day of the quake. In the end, he had done his best, hadn't he? Hadn't he saved all he could save and let the rest go? What else could he have done? Or, in the case of Eli, what *should* he have done?

And what could he do about it now? "So how do I get my brain unstuck?"

"That is the question." Dr. Sussman reached for a book on the shelf behind his desk and handed it to Tom. "Are you familiar with George Beard's work in the field of neurasthenia? He postulates that we humans operate on a flow of bodily energy and that some individuals—you'll be happy to know that this often applies to the most gifted among us—may develop unwanted symptoms when they have a surfeit of energy, or when their energy is not being invested wisely. This can lead to the diagnosis of neurasthenia. But as I said, you are in the best of company."

Tom stiffened as the image of Jerry Dunkley, the snake oil salesman, filled his brain. "I'm not sure I'm following you."

Dr. Sussman walked to a bare wall near his desk and pulled down a chart titled "The Tree of Nervous Illness." On the bottom was a horizontal line denoting the ground, or a lack of symptoms. A vertical line ran up the middle like a tree trunk; starting at the bottom were branches labeled "Nervous Dyspepsia," "Sick-Headache," and "Nearsightedness," all the way up through "Hay Fever," "Hypochondria," and "Hysteria." Toward the upper reaches of the tree were branches labeled "Cerebral," Spinal," "Digestive," and "Sexual," all of which were clumped under the larger sub-heading of "Neurasthenia." Above those were only two more branches: "Epilepsy" and "Inebriety." Crowning the top of the tree was "Insanity."

"Think of it this way," Dr. Sussman said, obviously

warming to his subject. "You have an abundance of nervous energy that must be used in productive pursuits such as hard work and healthy sexual congress. Think of poor people—they don't have time to be nervous because all they do is work hard and procreate. Neurasthenics, on the other hand, are usually members of the middle and upper classes, with more education, more awareness, more sensitivity to the world around them. They may ruminate on matters —wondering "should I or "shouldn't I"—when those of the lower classes merely act instinctively. These individuals generally have more time on their hands to misuse their energy quota. Perhaps their overabundance of creativity or other talent leads them astray. In our parlance we would say they are not managing their energy investment wisely. They are squandering it in vices such as gambling, masturbation, illicit and unnatural sex, and so on." He pointed to the chart. "Continued misuse of their nervous energy can lead to a number of conditions, as you see here, all the way up to those considered the hallmarks of neurasthenia."

Am I crazy, or is this man crazy? Tom thought. Dr. Sussman must have read Tom's expression because he smiled indulgently. "I know it sounds a bit far-fetched, but the facts are born out every day. You would be amazed at how many exceptional individuals suffer from neurasthenia, and you may, I feel confident to say, count yourself among them."

Like hell I will. "So you're telling me that because my brain is hung up on a past trauma, my nervous energy is out of balance?"

Dr. Sussman pondered that possibility before answering. "Or, your inappropriate use of your nervous energy is impacting your brain's ability to effectively monitor the motion of your body, much like a drunkard cannot control the compulsion to drink."

"Well, which is it?"

Dr. Sussman shrugged again. "I cannot see inside your brain, I'm afraid."

Tom wanted to throw a chair across the room but refrained—who knew how high up the insanity tree that maneuver might land him. "So what do you suggest?" he bit out.

"The good news is that there is a promising cure for neurasthenia, one for which I think you are a perfect candidate."

Wait. If he suggests I wear one of those so-called 'health' belts... "It doesn't involve anything electrical, I hope."

Dr. Sussman chuckled. "The research isn't all we'd hoped it would be regarding the efficacy of electrical impulses to the various organs of the body. No, that's not what I had in mind."

Tom let out a prolonged breath. As outlandish as the entire theory sounded, he couldn't help but feel a dash of hope that there was something to get him from point A to a more positive point B. "I'm all ears," he said.

"Have you ever heard of the Muldoon Hygienic Institute in New York?"

"No. I've heard of Muldoon the wrestler. They called him 'The Solid Man' as I recall."

"It's one and the same. Mr. Muldoon has developed

a rigorous physical and dietary program for neuras-thenics that effectively redirects their energy into more productive pursuits. I think you would find the program most beneficial."

"What is it? A hospital?"

"No, no, it's a...well, frankly, some might liken it to a resort, although the activities that go on there are far from being merely recreational, I can assure you."

Tom thought of the hundred and forty dollars left in his pocket. That wouldn't go far, especially since he was clear across the country from the supposed cure. "Sounds like it's out of my price range."

Dr. Sussman flipped through some pages on his desk and pulled out a letter. "Not necessarily. I received this letter from Mr. Muldoon last week. He asks if I know of any physicians who would be willing to work there for the summer and possibly beyond. It seems the state of New York has begun requiring these kinds of therapeutic resorts to have licensed medical personnel on the premises." Dr. Sussman looked up; his voice held admiration. "Mr. Muldoon really is a victim of his own success. His was the first program to accept neurasthenics, and now there are several usurpers vying for the business. Fortunately for them, there is no end of potential customers. If you'd like, I can send him a telegram about you."

What the hell, Tom thought. *At least it's something to do instead of waiting for something to happen.* "Yes, I'd like that very much."

Three days later Tom found himself on the Overland Limited, only this time he wouldn't be stopping in North Platte to see his family.

This time he wouldn't meet a beautiful woman who even now, years later, invaded his thoughts every day.

This time he was traveling clear across the country to a place where fresh air and plenty of exercise were supposed to make his hand stop shaking. It sounded preposterous, but there it was.

What would Nana Ruth think of him now?

CHAPTER THIRTY-FOUR

Late April 1907

With the trial only weeks away, Jonathan was working late. His secretary, Althea, had gone home to her family hours before. It didn't matter that she had only been working for Jonathan a few months; Althea was a mother hen of the first order and regularly chided him for his "bachelor ways."

"You need a good woman to go home to," she'd said on her way out the door. "Nothing like a tasty home-cooked meal and a soft voice to take away the stress of the day."

Althea never mentioned that *she* was the bread-winner in her family, and that her husband, a disabled railroad worker, cooked most of their meals and watched their four children. But her point was well taken: Jonathan knew was it was like to have a good woman in his life, and he missed the feeling terribly.

He'd hoped Katherine Firestone might fill that void, but it didn't look promising.

His office was silent and rested in shadows, lit only by the amber glow of his desk lamp. He found the atmosphere calming, enabling him to think through what he'd accomplished and what still needed to be done. The most recent report from Oliver Bean citing the dearth of crucial witnesses had been particularly disturbing and warranted serious study. Jonathan was not one for conspiracy theories, but the lack of even one individual who could speak to events immediately prior to the murder was too odd to be merely coincidental. He began listing questions yet to be answered. What had led to the young guard's suicide? Were there any special circumstances surrounding Dr. Milbank's fatal heart attack? What, if anything, was Tom Justice hiding? And where had the orderly disappeared to?

In the midst of contemplating these issues, Jonathan heard steps approaching his outer office. Perhaps Althea or one of his clerks had forgotten something. But when several minutes lapsed and no one entered, he went to investigate. No one was in the hallway, but a small white envelope had been pushed under the door. A note inside read:

Something you ought to know about what happened at the Pavilion last April. Come to the Wharf Rat Tavern tomorrow night at 8. No police - we know who you are.

M. Carr
a concerned mother

Carr. That was the last name of the orderly Bean hadn't been able to locate. Evidently the man had gone underground, and his mother had something to say about it. Had he committed a crime? Or did he know someone who had? Tom perhaps?

This could be the puzzle piece they were missing. Jonathan couldn't wait to find out what it was.

"I insist on going with you," Cordelia declared across the table.

Jonathan huffed. "Absolutely not." He'd made the tactical error of calling a special meeting with his clerks the following morning. In case something went awry, he wanted them to know where to pick up the trail.

Cordelia pointed to the note in his hand. "You are going to meet a mother," she said, as if that explained everything. It didn't.

"And you're a mother, too, I suppose?" Jonathan's retort came off a bit rough, even to his ears, but really...

Cordelia glared at him, marshalling her small body as if preparing for battle. "No, but I plan to be, one day, which is something that neither of you two gentlemen can ever hope to achieve." She yanked on the ends of her short jacket. "Regardless, I can still more easily relate to the witness. I *am* a woman, in case you haven't noticed."

Oh, we've noticed, all right. Jonathan glanced at Bean for support, but his male clerk looked like he was hoping to skirt the ruckus by avoiding eye contact and fiddling with his notes. Jonathan took a breath to continue his counter-argument, but Cordelia beat him to it, showing more self-awareness than he'd expected.

"I know I abhor any suggestion that one sex might fare better than another in any endeavor, but I truly do think this is one of those rare exceptions. The woman obviously fears that her son is in trouble, and she will no doubt feel more at ease speaking with someone whom she thinks will empathize with her. Besides, we should take notes, and I do know Munson's shorthand."

Jonathan looked at her for several moments, weighing what he admitted was a typical male protective instinct against her reasoned case. With a sigh, he admitted defeat.

"You must dress the part," he warned her. "We cannot walk into a place called The Wharf Rat looking like representatives of the privileged class."

"I shall meet you there, dressed appropriately," Cordelia said.

"Now *that* is out of the question. I will either pick you up where you live or you will meet me here an hour beforehand. You will not go unaccompanied to such a place. That is final."

Cordelia pursed her lips, but she must have decided not to risk losing a battle because of a minor skirmish. "All right. I shall meet you here at seven p.m. this evening."

"What would you like me to do?" Oliver asked.

Jonathan handed him the list of questions that he'd developed. "Keep working on securing that deposition with Nurse Elkins, and try to arrange interviews with Dr. Milbank's widow and Sergeant Fenton's next of kin. I'd like to see if we can glean any insight into their states of mind prior to death. Perhaps there is no connection, but we must make sure we're not missing anything."

"Will do," Bean said, gathering his notes.

Pushing his uneasiness to the back of his mind, Jonathan turned back to Cordelia. "And I'll see you tonight. Don't be late."

The Wharf Rat was located near Pier 47, where the hearts of the city's fishermen beat the loudest. Fleets of commercial trawlers took off from it daily, plying the waters in search of bass, shrimp, herring, oysters, and salmon. Sweet Dungeness crab was also in season, but tapering off.

Jonathan and Cordelia took the F Line and hopped off the streetcar near what was known as "Fish Alley" before making their way to the tavern on Jefferson Street. The smell of brine and dead fish was pungent, more noticeable in the quiet and near darkness near the docks. It was not the kind of neighborhood a young single woman should be visiting in daylight, much less during the time when tired sailors and fishermen might be drunk and on the hunt for a pretty skirt.

And make no mistake—Cordelia Hammersmith dressed for the occasion was a very pretty skirt tonight. She'd dressed for the occasion by letting her long dark hair hang loose, held back with two tortoise shell combs in a style that made her look much younger than usual. Her dress, by its very plainness, drew attention to her slender but womanly figure. Fortunately it was at least partially obscured by a shawl and the tapestry bag she carried, which no doubt held her notebook and writing instrument.

Two working-class gents walked toward them in the gloom, but fortunately they did not appear intoxicated. Aside from an appraisal of Cordelia's charms, punctuated by a low whistle, they passed without interaction.

Setting his jaw, Jonathan stuck his hand in the pocket of his tweed walking jacket, which he wore over a pair of wool trousers usually devoted to puttering in the garden. The pocket contained a pistol, which he truly did not want to use.

He glanced at his clerk, who seemed oddly at ease with her surroundings, as if she'd left her starchier self at home. She hadn't reacted to the wolf whistle at all. "Are you familiar with this part of town?" he asked.

He could barely make out her smile. "Have I been to The Wharf Rat, you mean? Oh, dozens of times."

What? Was she—

"I am funning you," she said, sliding her arm through his. "While in school I once took a deposition at the Fruit Canner's Association nearby, but it was in the middle of the morning and I was accompanied by another attorney. We stopped at a place along the wharf for lunch, but that's the extent of my familiarity."

Jonathan discreetly let the air out of his lungs. "Well, I suppose we're both in for an adventure, then."

They passed a storefront for the Paladini Fish Company and saw the hanging sign for their destination two doors down. For a bar set in such rough-and-tumble surroundings, The Wharf Rat was surprisingly civilized. Clean sawdust covered the floor, and the long bar on one side was well-polished. The smell of ale was strong, but not overpowering. It was a spacious room, lit by electric lamps, and contained several tables filled with working men, and even some women who did not appear to be pursuing an age-old trade. The atmosphere was lively but not excessively noisy, and Jonathan realized The Wharf Rat could have fit right into the neighborhood pubs back home.

The bartender nodded to them and tilted his head. "There's a booth in the back," he said.

They found the table he'd indicated, and Jonathan, out of habit, sat with his back against the far wall. Cordelia sat across from him but seemed to enjoy taking in their surroundings. "What would you like to drink?" he asked.

"Just between us, a whiskey would be grand." At his raised eyebrows, she sighed. "Temperance can be so tedious, don't you think? Would you rather I have a sherry, or worse, a sarsaparilla?"

Jonathan would not go there. "By all means, a whiskey you shall have." He signaled a waitress.

Halfway through their libation (he'd ordered two of the same), an older woman, wiping her hands on her apron, approached their table. She looked to be in her late forties, with brown hair, streaked with gray and pulled back in a serviceable bun. Her eyes spoke of hard living but an unbroken spirit. "You're investigatin' that murder at the Pavilion." It was a statement.

Tom nodded. "I was asked to meet someone here. Mrs. Carr, I presume?" He made to get up, but she waved him back down. "Finish up and then head out the back," she said, and would have turned to go if Cordelia hadn't stopped her.

"Is it about your son?" Cordelia asked. "Is he all right?"

The women exchanged looks and Jonathan saw that his clerk had been accurate in her assessment of what would put the witness at ease.

"Yes, he's all right, and thank you for askin'." The woman emphasized her gratitude by reaching out and squeezing Cordelia's hand. "But you're here on account of the truth that needs to come out."

Jonathan and Cordelia took some time to finish their drinks before finding their way out the back door into the alley. Once again the hairs rose on the back of Jonathan's neck. This was not a safe situation.

The woman stepped out of the shadows. "This way."

Cordelia followed without hesitation. *It must be a female thing*, Jonathan thought. They headed down the alley, turned a corner, walked another block, and finally reached a nondescript doorway.

"In here," Mrs. Carr said, taking them up a flight of steps that led to a floor with several doors on either side. Mrs. Carr knocked on one of them. "Otis? They're here, son."

After a moment the door was unlatched and opened. Otis Carr was a hefty young man in his twenties, with a shock of unruly brown hair that looked like it hadn't been washed in a while. He peered down the hallway before ushering them in and asking them to have a seat.

Inside the small, poorly lit parlor was a ramshackle sofa just large enough for Jonathan and Cordelia to share. Otis pulled up a chair from the spindly table near the tiny kitchen and sat down. His mother laid her hand on his shoulder.

"This is Mr. Jonathan Perris and Miss Cordelia Hammersmith and they're here to help you. You just tell them what you know, and they'll know what to do with it." Then she left the apartment.

Now that his mother was no longer around to encourage him, Otis seemed to lose what little courage he'd summoned. He sat silently, twisting his large hands.

Jonathan took the lead. "Mr. Carr—"

"You can call me Otis."

"Otis, then. I'm not quite sure how, but your mother knows that we are representing Dr. Thomas Justice for the murder of Mr. Elijah Porter at the Mechanics' Pavilion."

"There's been more than one attorney lookin' for me, Mr. Perris," Otis said with the air of the hunted. "But we traced Mr. Bean back to you. We figured you'd want to know that Doc Justice didn't do what they're sayin' he did."

Cordelia whipped out her notebook and began to scribble. "How do you know that?" she asked.

Jonathan gave her a look to indicate he could handle the interview, thinking uncharitably that since Otis was a man, it was Jonathan's rightful place to do so. Cordelia looked at him and shrugged slightly, as if to say, *Well, get on with it, then.*

He turned back to Otis. "How do you know that?"

"Well, maybe that ain't the right way to put it. Maybe I should say, Doc Justice didn't do nothin' that the other doctor wasn't doin'. They was just following the Protocol."

Cordelia wrote so fast that she was able to pause mere seconds after he finished speaking. Jonathan glanced at her notebook, which seemed to consist of nothing more than squiggly lines.

"What do you mean by the Protocol?" he asked.

Otis lowered his voice, as if the walls had ears and he didn't want them listening in. "You gotta understand. There were hundreds in that hall. *Hundreds.* They was in all kinds of shape, and dozens of them so far gone it was only a matter of time before the good Lord took 'em. I was directin' traffic. As soon as one patient died off, I'd call the litter boys and they'd take the poor soul to the morgue, which was really just a blocked-off space in one corner of the hall. Then we'd get another one who was real bad off, and Dr. Milbank and Nurse Elkins would try their best to save him or her or whoever it was. But it was horrible what some of those people had: their skulls crushed in, their insides spilling out, or burns all over their bodies. It was plain as the nose on your face that most of those folks weren't going to make it through. But they tried. You need to know, they *tried*. And when they didn't make it, they just kept sendin' the bodies off to the morgue.

"It seemed like for every patient who didn't make it, two more was carried in to replace him, the other docs just hopin' Doc Milbank could fix 'em up. That old doc was runnin' ragged. So the deceased were stacking up, but the ones who weren't long for this world were stacking up, too. And then we get the word that all of us has got to leave on account of the Ham and Eggs fire comin' our way."

"So you began evacuating," Jonathan prompted.

"Sure we did, but the folks in Critical Care was in no shape to be moved, and we was lookin' at the numbers and knowin' time was running out, so Doc Milbank and some muckety-muck from the Army went off and hatched the Protocol."

"The Protocol," Cordelia repeated.

Otis paused and his eyes filled with tears. He wiped them with his stubby fingers. Cordelia leaned forward and squeezed his hand as his mother had squeezed hers. "It's all right, Otis. You can tell us."

Otis looked at her and nodded slightly, glad, it seemed, for the permission. "There were only so many wagons, see, not enough to take all the goners out along with those who would definitely survive. But we couldn't let them be burned alive, so ..."

Jonathan felt on the edge of a precipice. "So..."

Otis looked at him as if seeking absolution. He took

a deep breath. "So the doc gave them a dose of ether to put them out and the sergeant shot them in the head."

The room went silent as Jonathan and Cordelia absorbed what Otis was telling them.

"You mean...you mean they purposefully killed some patients?" Cordelia asked.

"Not some. A *lot*. Dozens, maybe. The ones who weren't going to make it. The poor souls who weren't gonna leave the Pavilion alive anyway." He seemed to get control of his emotions. "When the story came out about the evacuation, it was filled with good news, wasn't it? I remember a paper that said, 'Hundreds Rescued from Deadly Fire,' and that was true as far as it went. But you never heard about those who died once they left the hall, did you? Don't it stand to reason that some of the people they took out of there would have been hurt or sick enough to die even after they left?"

The young man was right. The evacuation of the Mechanics' Pavilion had been a feel-good story about saving so many people, which made Tom's alleged murder stand out as even more of an aberration. But according to Otis Carr, not everyone had been saved.

Jonathan was skeptical. "Why have you not come forward with this?"

Otis shook his head. "Those of us who was part of the Protocol were told by the top brass not to say a word about it, that even though we'd done the right thing, it wouldn't look good, that people might get the wrong idea. So we kept doing what we had to do, and didn't say a word about it to anybody. I thought it was all water under the bridge, but then this story comes out about Dr. Justice bein' a murderer and all. I heard they was lookin' for whoever was there that day and I got scared thinkin' they might put all of us behind bars for what we'd done."

Cordelia finished writing and looked up at Otis. "So you're saying for sure that Dr. Justice was part of this so-called Protocol?"

"Only at the end. One of the last to go was a man who pulled a gun and started askin' if we knew Tom Justice, and when Nurse Elkins said yes, he was working in the hall, the man said she'd better go get him or else he was going to shoot up the place. So she ran out and when she came back, I was told that my work was done, so I left."

Jonathan felt the letdown of someone who has scored rugby points and then had them called back. "So, you didn't actually see Dr. Justice perform this... Protocol on the man with the gun."

"No sir, but the man with the gun was brought to Critical Care just like all the others, and he was done in like all the others, too. So it's all the same thing in my book."

Touching Otis on the arm again, Cordelia asked, "What made you change your mind and get in contact with us?"

The young man looked sheepish. "It was my ma. I told her what had me spooked and she got all mad, sayin' no son of hers was going to take the fall for something he was ordered to do, especially when it was the right thing to do. She can get pretty feisty when she's riled up."

Cordelia smiled. "That's because she's your mother and she loves you."

After asking a few more questions for clarification (of which Cordelia had her share), Jonathan assured Otis that he would not reveal the man's whereabouts until he could guarantee that Otis would not be held liable in any way for what he'd done at the Pavilion. He felt confident that a discreet discussion with the current commander of the Presidio would accomplish that mission.

They said their goodbyes and headed toward the corner of Beach and Leavenworth. Cordelia had offered to hop back on the streetcar, but it ran less frequently at night, and Jonathan insisted on taking her home in a cab.

They said little as the driver made his way along the somnolent city streets, the gentle swaying of the carriage and the unhurried clop of the horse's hooves lulling Jonathan into a memory of simpler times. Times when life meant life and death meant death, and there were no gray areas in between.

They pulled up to the rooming house where Cordelia lived, and Jonathan bade the driver wait while he walked her to the front door.

She turned to him. "Thank you for letting me join you tonight; I hope I was of some use." Tapping her bag, she added, "I'll have my notes transcribed for our next meeting."

"We have a lot to think about," he said.

"And a lot to be grateful for. Goodnight, Mr. Perris."

Despite taking another shot of whiskey before

retiring, Jonathan found it difficult to fall asleep. Once he did, he dreamed of a giant cavern filled with hundreds of injured and dying men, women, and children, and a line of them forming, like zombies, to have him put them out of their misery. He woke in a sweat, and although it wasn't quite dawn, he dared not fall asleep again, because the lurid nightmare might resume.

CHAPTER THIRTY-FIVE

Two weeks before trial

Much can change in the course of a week. Through the Firestones, Jonathan set up a private meeting with Major General Adolphus Greely at the Presidio and told him about the orderly, Otis Carr. Upon hearing Jonathan's story, the commander realized quickly that no retreat could effectively counter an outcry against the "slaughter" (which was what the "damn yellow journalists" would call it) of vulnerable civilians by the Army. Instead, Greely shaped the battlefield of public opinion by orchestrating a series of leaks to a trusted, pro-military reporter for the *San Francisco Call* who wrote that the heart-wrenching 'Protocol' was unusual, yes, but necessary in order to relieve the suffering of countless victims of the great earthquake and fire. Those who participated in it should be lauded, not vilified, for their heroic actions—actions that took a terrible toll on those who performed them.

The latter point required no literary embellishment. In an interview arranged by Oliver Bean, Dr. Milbank's widow had told Cordelia, "What happened at the Pavilion changed my Charles forever. He came home from that experience a haunted man. And while he never talked specifically about it to me, I just know that he'd done something that went against every one of his instincts. As sure as I am sitting here talking to you, I know that's what led to his fatal heart attack."

Bean himself had elicited a similar reaction from Sergeant Fenton's sister. The soldier had lived with the young widow and her ten-year-old son, his nephew, while on leave; his death had taken quite an emotional toll on the small family.

"It was the saddest thing," Bean said. "Here was her little boy, all dressed up in a cape and walking around with a pipe in his mouth like Sherlock Holmes. Supposedly he and his uncle had shared a fondness for Arthur Conan Doyle's stories."

"That's *Sir* Arthur, if you please," Jonathan said.

Bean looked at him and continued. "In any event, I wrote down the sister's testimony." He scrabbled through his files, withdrew a sheet of paper, and began to read: "'I think Ray just saw too much death, that's my take on it,' she says. 'After the Army put him on leave, he spent every minute of it on the bottle. It just about killed Ned to see his uncle carrying on like that; Ray had been such a hero to my boy! Every day he'd get stinkin' drunk and by night-time, just before he'd pass out, he'd start relivin' his time in the Army. He'd been to China and Panama, you know, and it was like he was back on the battlefield, calling for more ammo and such. I did the best I could with him, but when he started in on the opium, I knew he was a goner.' She ended with a flood of tears, and I had a heck of a time trying to calm her down. And her boy was just standing there, soaking it all in. I wish I hadn't had to put them through that."

Dr. Milbank's and Ray Fenton's roles in the mercy killings were confirmed by military sources. The results were everything the Major General had hoped for: at first shocked, San Francisco's citizenry soon came to see the "The Pavilion Protocol" as a noble endeavor of the first order. Ray Fenton was singled out for his devotion to duty under extraordinary circumstances, and a special fund was set up for his sister and nephew. Otis Carr came out of hiding and enjoyed a mild flurry of celebrity.

In light of the revelations, Jonathan had tried to have the case against Tom dismissed, but the court was having none of it.

"Let the jury decide," Judge Rendell said, which meant Tom Justice was still scheduled to go on trial for murder.

Opening statements were growing closer by the day.

Back in his office, Jonathan met with his clerks for their now-daily briefing. "The emergence of the Protocol has given us many more pieces of the puzzle.

I'd like your thoughts on how you would proceed, given what we now know."

Bean twirled a pencil in his long fingers. "I'd say it takes the case in an entirely new direction. We could present it as a mercy killing, which the jury will be predisposed to agree with, given the official take."

"We could," Cordelia mused. "And we could quite possibly win an acquittal on those grounds." She flipped through the notes she'd taken during the interview with Otis Carr and found the page she'd been looking for. "Carr himself said that Tom wasn't really part of the operation and just stepped in at the end. And yet ..."

Jonathan caught her gaze. "And yet?"

"The bullet that killed Eli Porter wasn't fired from a military-issue weapon, so it could be argued that he wasn't killed as part of the Protocol."

"No, no, no." Bean grew animated, lightly slapping his slender hands on the table. "Porter was in Critical Care as *part* of the Protocol, wasn't he? If Tom committed the murder, even under the guise of the Protocol, why did he let the body be carried out of the Pavilion along with all of the survivors? The deceased remained behind in the morgue, remember? If he hadn't done that, Porter would have easily been considered just one more casualty."

"Perhaps he wasn't thinking clearly at the time," Cordelia argued. "None of the evidence paints Tom as a cold-blooded killer. He didn't go about tearing the wings off butterflies or setting puppy-dog tails on fire. Maybe he was too emotional, flew off the handle, and was overcome with remorse, or just maybe he didn't do any of it, which is why he'd have no reason to hide the body."

Jonathan sat back, rubbing his late-afternoon stubble. He did not like the feeling of being unshaven, and he did not like what he was feeling about this case. "Something just doesn't add up," he said.

His clerks both looked at him expectantly.

He got up and walked over to the time line pinned to the wall. At this point it was nearly complete. He tapped it. "Every professional associated with the Protocol, while they kept it secret, did not consider it criminal—personally problematic, some of them, and publicly unacceptable, all of them. But not *criminal*. Yes, Otis Carr went into hiding, but I think that was due more to ignorance than anything else. He wasn't sure if someone was going to accuse him of something he had no control over. Even at that, he stayed in the city, and ultimately brought the Protocol into the open through us. His motive—and Cordelia, you can reaffirm this with your notes—was that he didn't want Tom Justice to be convicted of a crime that as far as Otis was concerned, hadn't taken place. If he truly felt he had committed a crime, would he have done that? I don't believe so. Only one man out of all of them left the scene of the crime, as it were. Only one man left the city of his own volition, without leaving a forwarding address."

"Tom Justice," Bean murmured.

"That's right—Tom Justice." Jonathan sighed. "I just

wish we knew the reason why. Why in the name of all that's holy did he turn tail and run?"

The logical answer to Jonathan's question presented itself three days later, albeit not in the most auspicious way. Having caught a quick lunch at the Northstar Cafe on Powell Street, he was heading back to his office when Everett Bigelow walked in the door. Bigelow, one of the longest serving assistant district attorneys in San Francisco, personified law and order. He was a tall man and cut a commanding figure. His wavy, snow-white hair was combed back from a rather prominent forehead, but a thick bristle-brush mustache kept one's focus on his shrewd-looking countenance. For those and other reasons, he'd been tapped to handle the by now high-profile case of "The Murderous Medical Man." Bigelow was in the company of two other individuals, one of them a woman, and neither of whom Jonathan knew. He assumed they were Bigelow's assistants.

"Ah, Barrister Perris. Jolly fine day, isn't it, sir?" Although their interactions had so far been few, Bigelow had taken to using the English term for "trial attorney" when addressing Jonathan, and did so in a slightly sardonic way. His two cohorts appeared embarrassed.

Jonathan ignored the cut. "Good afternoon, Mr. Bigelow."

"I take it you'll be ready to do battle a week from Thursday, son?"

Jonathan looked him in the eye. "Indubitably." He glanced at the female; she was stifling a smile.

"Well, it's a shame about the Elkins deposition, I suppose."

Bigelow caught him off guard with that bit of news. Bean had been trying to secure it for weeks; was it not coming through in time?

"I'm not sure what you mean," Jonathan hedged.

"I mean what it does to your case. My guess is you thought you were sitting in the catbird seat with all that hullabaloo about the Pavilion Protocol. But Nurse Elkins, well, she put the kibosh on that defense, all right."

His mind beginning to race, Jonathan had but one thought: to get back to his office and read the bloody deposition that must have arrived while he was out. He made a show of checking his pocket watch. "I'm terribly sorry, but I must be off. I have an appointment I'm already late for."

"Sure you do," Bigelow said with a self-satisfied smile. "Cheerio, then."

Jonathan caught the first available streetcar back to Montgomery Street and practically bounded up the three flights of stairs to his office suite. Althea gave him a pitying look as he swept by. He opened the door to see both Oliver and Cordelia seated at the conference table, deep in conversation. The deposition was lying on the table in front of them.

"It's not good," Cordelia said.

Jonathan tossed his hat on the chair and turned the document around so that he could read it. After scanning several pages, he looked up, incredulous. "What? She can't be serious."

Bean shook his head. "I can't believe it either. Of all the people sent to the critical care section that day, Eli Porter was the one who didn't need to be there."

Jonathan reread a section. "He wasn't at death's door, she says."

"No," Cordelia said. "He could have been saved. *Should* have been saved. Neither she nor Dr. Milbank were present when it happened, but they left thinking Tom would merely subdue the man."

Jonathan frowned. "Subdue him?"

"Yes," said Bean. "Tom was supposed to keep Eli from shooting his gun off and harming those around him."

Jonathan sat back in his seat as the wretched truth stared him in the face. "Eli wasn't supposed to be part of the Protocol, but he was shot anyway—by his own gun, but *not* by his own hand."

"No wonder Tom skipped town," Bean said.

Jonathan looked from Cordelia to Bean and back again, but neither clerk had anything positive to say. "Bloody hell," he said.

CHAPTER THIRTY-SIX

"The farm's regimen did him a world of good. He was a helpful staff doc, too, although some of my guests didn't like hearing what he had to say."

—WILLIAM MULDOON, FOUNDER OF THE MULDOON
HYGIENIC INSTITUTE

"Pick up the pace, Mr. Choate, pick up the pace. You've got to make it up the hill in order to enjoy the reward of heading back down it."

Tom's new employer, William Muldoon, marched in place while his septuagenarian client huffed his way forward. Not quite six feet tall and weighing two hundred pounds, the world-renowned physical culture expert lived up to his nickname of the Solid Man with a build of rock-hard muscle. While Tom considered himself in good physical shape, Muldoon always set the pace on their morning runs. This one was no exception.

"I don't think I can make it," Joseph Choate wheezed. The ambassador's face was beet red. *His blood pressure must be skyrocketing*, Tom thought. *Maybe he ought to slow down a bit.*

"Certainly you can, sir. Your ego will not let you use the services of Dr. Justice. He is here for his own health too, you know. Besides, think of the delicious eggs and oatmeal waiting for you back at the lodge."

A taxing early-morning hike "to get the blood pumping" was a common prescription for clients attending the Muldoon Hygienic Institute. The "health farm," as Muldoon himself called it, was set on some of the prettiest countryside Tom had ever seen. Rolling hills and sunny meadows gave way to lush woodlands fed by crisp, clear-running streams. An easy train ride from Manhattan, Muldoon's retreat was fast becoming the place where athletes, politicians, and the wealthy paid a lot of money to be browbeaten into shape.

At fifty-four, Muldoon was a walking billboard for the benefits of an active life. He'd started his career as a policeman, but his love of physical competition ostensibly won out, because for ten years he'd held the title of World Heavyweight Greco Roman Wrestling Champion. Yet he was a realist, too.

"You can't live by brawn forever," he'd told Tom during their first meeting. "Someone is always ready and more than willing to take you down." So, he'd begun training athletes, including John L. Sullivan, and done well at that, too.

"Now this nervous energy business, that's where the real money is," he'd said in explaining his latest business venture. "The country's full of rich, busy men who don't know how to eat right or live right. They come to me, they do what I tell 'em, and they get back on track. We'll do the same for you. Simple as that."

Muldoon's technique *was* simple, but it wasn't easy. First, he took note of a client's overall physical condition, factoring in age and weight. Then he devised a custom plan, including exercise, diet, and even a sleep schedule, which each man had to follow. When Ambassador Choate first started the program, he'd naively reported for breakfast an hour early. Muldoon immediately sent him back to bed. "You don't get up until you get a knock on the door!" he'd barked.

Once Tom was hired, his employer put him through his paces both in the gym (located in a barn) and in the field. How fast could Tom sprint? How long could he run until his lungs started screaming? How much weight could he lift? The older man kept up with Tom every step of the way.

"Not bad," Muldoon said afterward. "You've got more muscle than most men your age, not counting those who make a living off the sweat of their backs. You ever play sports?"

Tom was still getting his wind back after three laps around the farm's running track. "A little bit of everything, but football mainly."

"Now that's a damn shame." Muldoon clapped Tom on the shoulder. "Football's the one sport I don't cotton to. Too violent. You got knocked around more than once, I'll bet."

That's putting it mildly, Tom thought. "Unlike boxing and wrestling, which is so civilized," he said.

Muldoon chuckled. "You got me there. But it makes my point. I've seen more than one old boxer come down with the palsy. And what do you have in common? You both got knocked in the head."

My God. Could the blow he took so many years ago be the cause of it all? Dr. Sussman hadn't given that theory much credence, but he was in love with the concept of poorly managed nervous energy. He had little knowledge of how a physically damaged brain might affect the rest of the body, even years after the initial event.

Tom couldn't decide which explanation he most feared. The idea of turning out like those down-and-out, rheumy-eyed fighters sent a shiver through him. But if it was all mental? That meant there was no way to turn that faucet off—the brain was just too complicated.

For the first time, Tom began to ask himself the dreaded question, the question Katherine was more than willing to consider.

What if my hand never stops shaking? What will I do then?

Tom wasn't convinced that "learning how to best invest your nervous energy" was a valid theory, but after two months at the health farm, he was convinced that just about anyone could benefit from Muldoon's program.

Tom's day began at seven in the morning with a cross-country run, followed by a hearty breakfast of the cook's touted oatmeal and eggs. During the post breakfast rest hour he would see patients in a building at the rear of the main lodge dubbed "The Firmary." (Muldoon had decreed that no one at the Institute should ever think of themselves as "infirm.")

Tom dealt with a variety of ailments, most of which he was able to treat using methods he'd learned from his Nana Ruth. ("Natural, son; keep it natural whenever you can," Muldoon said).

Today, his first patient was Roger Stenson, a bank president from New Jersey, who came in with a bad case of gout that caused both of his big toes to flare up. This caused no end of agony (and much cursing) when he was expected to take his prescribed afternoon hike. He said his regular doctor back in Trenton had told him gout was a sign of success ("Alexander the Great had it") and to simply bear with it. Muldoon—or "The Professor," as he was called by most of his clients— felt exercise was always the key, but Tom knew there was more to it.

"You've got to stay away from red meat and fried chicken," he admonished Stenson. "You need to change your diet."

The portly financier looked aghast. "But the Professor says protein builds muscle. Bertie Pilgrim gets steak nearly every day, too, and he doesn't have a problem. Why me and not him?"

"Because you retain uric acid, which causes the inflammation in your joints, and he doesn't," Tom explained. "And I've got some more bad news."

Stenson hesitated. "Do I really want to know?"

Tom shrugged. "You want fewer attacks? Then cut out turkey, gravy, liver, and probably two of your favorite drinks: coffee and beer. As my grandmother used to say, 'You take whatever road you want, but you'd best be prepared for who you'll meet.'"

"Your grandmother said that, did she?" Stenson grumbled.

"Yes sir. Among other things." Tom grinned at the memory.

Next up was twenty-seven-year-old Ralph Pulitzer, a classic example of the "neurasthenic" personality Dr. Sussman had talked about. Ralph's father, Joseph, was a successful newspaper publisher, and Ralph had big shoes to fill. He'd also gotten married the year before, and the stress was making itself known through excruciating migraine headaches.

"Drink more water!" Muldoon ordered. "Get more exercise and more sleep!" All of that was good advice, but when a migraine hit, Ralph needed something to stop the pain as soon as possible.

"Do you drink much coffee?" Tom asked.

"No, it makes me too jittery."

"How about salicylic acid? I think you might know it as 'aspirin.'"

"Ah, that new pain pill. I heard it'll rot your insides."

"It can. It depends on how much you take. Eating some food will help, although I know nausea is sometimes a factor with migraines. You can go a more natural route and use the feverfew plant, mixing it with willow bark or meadowsweet."

Pulitzer smirked. "You sound like a witch doctor. Where on earth would I get all that?"

"Mrs. Chambers, the cook, no doubt knows about them. If you ask her nicely, she'll probably whip up a tincture for you. As soon as you feel a headache coming on, put a teaspoon or so in a cup of water and drink it down. During a migraine your blood vessels expand, which causes the pain. The tea will help shrink them. The caffeine in coffee will, too, but that can also affect your stomach. Down the road you might also try the Chinese practice of acupuncture. A lot of people swear by it."

The scion gave Tom a look that said *you've got to be kidding*. "Thanks, doc, but taking the pill with food sounds a hell of a lot easier."

Tom saw him to the door and handed him a small bottle of the pills that many in the medical profession considered a wonder drug. "All right, then. Let me know how it works out."

New York senator Chauncey Depew stopped by Tom's office to see what could be done about his psoriasis, which had flared to the point where it was covering his lower extremities with red skin and dry, flaky scales—a marked contrast to the man's deep tan everywhere else. Depew was at the farm for a refresher course after being treated for neurasthenia a few years earlier. He'd just been through a tough re-election campaign, which he'd won, and at seventy-one he was still a relative newlywed, having remarried five years before. His wife, May, was thirty-two years younger.

"The rash is unsightly in the bedroom, if you know what I mean," he admitted. "Hard to get romantic if you're all bundled up, but hard to satisfy a woman if you're shedding all over her."

Tom shuddered slightly at the image. Given the challenges of the senator's work and private life, no wonder he was stressed. If he made it to his seventies, Tom did *not* want to be concerned with pleasing a woman nearly young enough to be his granddaughter. If he could have anybody, he'd have Katherine and they'd grow old together.

"Your skin is inflamed and regenerating much faster than it needs to," Tom told him. "I'm sure you've been told that sun is good for your condition, but it looks like you've gone overboard. Too much sun can cause its own problems."

Depew nodded. "Guilty as charged. I guess I figured if a little helps a little, a lot would help a lot."

Tom wrote a prescription as he spoke. "A lot of people think that way. If you can, try to limit your sun exposure to the affected area. And when you return home, try these variations in your bathwater. You want to keep the skin lubricated so that it remains soft."

Depew read off the list: "White vinegar, oatmeal, olive oil mixed with a glass of milk?" He frowned at Tom. "Oatmeal in the bath tub?"

"Yes sir. But not in combination with those other ingredients." He wrote down another recipe. "And if you have patches that are particularly troublesome, dissolve baking soda in water and apply it like a compress. Think of your skin as you would a woman; treat her gently and she'll respond."

The old man grinned. "I like the way you think, young man. You know the whys and the wherefores, but you're not afraid to bring in a bit of the old tried and true. It's good to stay in balance."

Balance. The thing that had eluded Tom for most of his life. But the senator was right: the practice of medicine called for it. Not every case could be solved with surgery, nor with a cup of willow bark tea. There was room for both, wasn't there? Tom feared the pace of scientific discovery was going to edge out the remedies handed down by his grandma. Pills like salicylic acid were so much easier to take. Maybe one day there would be a pill that makes eating or exercising obsolete. God, he hoped not.

He took a moment to examine his hand. It still quivered, but less so, or at least less often. In addition to horseback riding and other activities, Muldoon had Tom working with medicine balls in the afternoon. He and another client would quickly toss spheres of various sizes and weights back and forth, an exercise that required quick thinking and even quicker hands. Tom almost always had both. It seemed his "defect" had a mind of its own.

Tom saw his last patients during the afternoon rest period. On this particular day he saw Ben Yoakum, the chairman and president of the St. Louis, Brownsville and Mexico Railway, a spur that ran two hundred miles along the Texas border.

Muldoon had filled Tom in on Ben's career path. Each position had been more stressful than the last, and the man's lifelong asthma had gotten worse as a result. He was at the Institute to lose some weight, yes, but also to gain more stamina, both mental and physical. Muldoon felt that being outdoors would help toughen up his immune system against whatever was causing his lung problems. Yoakum was only forty-seven.

Tom checked the man's vital signs. His heartbeat was unusually fast. "Do you smoke, sir?"

"I have the occasional cheroot with business associates. Cuban, you know. Only the finest. My wife won't have it in the house. She thinks that's what brings on my attacks."

"When was the last time you had an attack?"

"About a week ago. It was bad, too. Had to use the damn adrenalin shot my doctor gave me." He patted his pocket. "I was glad to have it, believe me. I'll never be without it again."

"What brought it on—your smoking?"

Yoakum leaned in as if telling a secret. "I think it's our damn cats. My older daughter brought in a new stray last month."

"Pets are generally not advised for asthmatics."

"I know, but, well, we've got two daughters and asking them to give up their little furballs would be like asking them to give up candy. Not going to happen." He paused. "Truth be told, I kind of like the little things. They're a nice distraction."

The poor man was caught between a rock and a

hard place. Keep the pets, risk the attack; lose the cats, lose the stress relief. Tom felt the same way about his decision to leave Katherine. To stay and subject her to his defect was unacceptable, but was life better without her? Absolutely not.

"Tell you what," Tom said as he sat down at the room's small desk and started writing out instructions; fortunately his hand remained steady. "Call your wife and tell her the doctor said she needs to make both your bedroom and your office 'pet free.' All the furnishings should be washed in very hot water, and the floors cleaned. Don't use rugs if you can avoid them. Then have her and your daughters brush the kitties once a day and bath them at least once a week, even more often during the summer. Because it's not their fur that's causing your problems, it's what they get on it. And finally, do you drink coffee or tea?"

"Yes, sir. Don't tell me that's a trigger, too."

Tom smiled. "No, but when you feel your lungs begin to tighten, try drinking black tea. It has special stimulant properties like your adrenalin. Two or three cups should help open your airways."

Yoakum shook Tom's hand. "Thanks, doctor. You seem to know a lot about a lot of things. You ever thought about being a railway surgeon?"

"Uh, no. I'm...surgery's no longer my specialty."

"Oh, don't let the name fool you. Our docs are called surgeons because they deal with the outside of the body, not the inside. That's a throwback to the old days when surgeons and barbers plied the same trade. Our railway surgeons treat sprains, concussions, broken bones, things like that. Sometimes they even deliver babies. You generally don't cut into anybody on the railway."

"I'll keep it in mind," Tom said.

Over the several weeks that Yoakum stayed at the farm, Tom got to know him well. He was a good man, blessed with a big heart but cursed with a weak constitution, and Tom often worried that Muldoon pushed him too hard. Rigorous exercise wasn't the answer to every problem, but the Professor didn't include the word "moderate" in his vocabulary. Like Senator Depew, the health coach believed more was usually better.

Tom felt Ben Yoakum was an accident waiting to happen, not because of his lungs, but because of his heart. And his worst fears were realized the night of the fire.

It was a balmy evening in July, the kind of gentle summer night that reminded Tom of life back on the farm, a time of lazy competition among Tom and his friends: who'd catch the most lightning bugs, who'd spot the first star. The sweet smell of honeysuckle and freshly mown grass filled the air.

Mrs. Chambers had arranged a barbecue with Muldoon as head chef, turning steaks and chicken on the large grill in front of the main lodge. The men stood around, giving the Professor friendly advice or chatting amongst themselves. Some kidded Tom about being single; he refused to take the bait and focused on

Ben Yoakum, who was bending Tom's ear about the growth of the railway surgeon specialty.

"Not that many years ago, if you worked the railroad and got badly injured, that was practically a death sentence. Nowadays, many of our railroads have their own hospitals, plus hospital cars that we can send to wherever the employee got hurt. And we've got doctors on the payroll who travel the lines to make sure the workers are staying healthy."

"And the railroad pays for all that?" Tom asked.

"Partly. And part comes from the employees' wages. Not too many companies take such good care of their workers, but we're finding it pays off in the long run."

Yoakum was getting into detail about the kinds of policies followed by the railroad surgeons when the entire group heard the loud clanging of a bell from across the field.

"That means fire, boys," Muldoon called out. "Mrs. Chambers, finish off this meat. We're gonna be mighty hungry when we get back."

The Professor directed everyone to head over to the neighboring farm, where flames could already be seen billowing up from the barn. Yoakum struggled to keep up with Tom as they sprinted across the field.

"You don't have to go," Tom called out to him.

"Can't...stay behind," Yoakum panted. "Never h-hear the end of it."

By the time they all reached the farm, the two sisters who owned the property had already started a bucket brigade. Muldoon kept a fire wagon at the Institute, and soon drove up to help douse the flames. Tom fought a sharp sense of panic as memories of the post-quake fires engulfed him. *There's no time for that*, he warned himself. *People need you.* He looked around to see if everyone was all right.

Ben Yoakum wasn't. The man had stumbled out of the line and leaned over to catch his breath, then clutched his chest and keeled over. Tom rushed to him, pulling off his own shirt to serve as a pillow. "Ben! What's wrong? Is it your lungs? Can you breathe?"

In obvious pain, Yoakum feebly shook his head. "Not sure. Might be my chest. Tight." With that he fell unconscious.

Tom worked quickly, opening Yoakum's shirt and listening for a heartbeat. He heard nothing, but felt the epinephrine syringe in the man's pocket. Months before he'd read about the increased use of adrenalin to jump-start heart muscles in the case of myocardial infarction. Why not test it right now? Without hesitating, he opened the syringe and plunged it directly into the man's chest cavity, trusting it would find its mark.

"I owe you my life," Yoakum told Tom the next day. Tom's action had bought them enough time to get the ailing railroad executive to a local hospital, where he was now recovering from what had indeed been a heart attack. "If you hadn't known what to do..."

"I was lucky, that's all. And so were you."

"I mean it. I owe you. Any time you want a job on

the railroad, you've got one. We need quick thinkers like you."

Tom smiled and patted Yoakum on the shoulder. "I may hold you to it," he said.

Back at the Institute, Muldoon called Tom into his office. What he thought might be a dressing down for acting too hastily turned out to be a business proposition.

"You saved my bacon from some mighty bad publicity with Ben Yoakum," Muldoon said. "That shows me you got both the heart and the smarts. What would you say to joining up and opening a string of Muldoon Hygienic Institutes across the country? There's rich, flabby men like Ben Yoakum and Chauncey Depew in every state. We can slim their bodies and their wallets at the same time—and you know that's money well spent."

It *was* money well spent. Every patient who signed up for Muldoon's program went home healthier and had the tools to stay healthy if they wanted to. Still...

"How about I finish out the season and we'll see where we are."

"Fair enough," Muldoon said. "You just keep doin' what you're doin' and we'll go places, you and me."

Muldoon kept his health farm open through the middle of November, but it didn't take that long for Tom to realize it wasn't the place for him. He grew tired of hearing the same complaints from the same kinds of men: rich and flabby, yes, and high-strung self-centered, and ambitious, too. He learned which men cheated on their wives and which ones worried about performing at all. He prescribed the same treatments for headaches and bellyaches and sleepless nights and embarrassing rashes. Neurasthenia, he decided, really did exist. But it was an illness only the rich and successful could afford, and they'd continue to need treatment because of the lifestyles they chose to lead. Ralph Pulitzer wasn't going to feel any less stress in his life; the most he could hope for was temporary relief for his headaches. Ben Yoakum wasn't about to quit his job; he'd likely have another heart attack and probably die from it.

The average man or woman, on the other hand, was too busy living to have much in the way of nervous disorders. The problems they faced were physical: a broken leg, a tumor, a twisted bowel, the flu. And once those problems were dealt with, with those patients could go on about their lives.

It occurred to Tom that had he continued on the path originally laid out for him at Johns Hopkins, he would most have likely catered to the same clientele as Muldoon. However, a quirk of fate had led him to work with poor people, and now he found he missed the satisfaction of helping someone get well enough to resume their simple life. He couldn't have stayed aloof, as Dr. Halsted recommended; it just wasn't in his nature.

So where did that leave him? His hand still trembled, albeit less than before—or maybe he just didn't pay as much attention to it. Could he return to Katherine and find a position somewhere that didn't require a steady hand?

The season ended at last, and Tom turned in his resignation. "I'm meant to do other things," he explained to Muldoon. "Not sure yet what those things are, but I've got to keep looking."

"I thought as much," Muldoon said. "I've been in touch with Ben Yoakum."

Tom gave his employer a grin. "So have I."

CHAPTER THIRTY-SEVEN

"He's a deep-thinking, caring, talented young man. If I were thirty years younger, I'd go after him myself."

—Dr. Sofie Herzog, Railway Surgeon

Tom didn't believe in reincarnation or souls migrating or any such thing, but if he did, he would have sworn that his Nana Ruth had been reborn as Dr. Sofie Herzog. She was sixty years old by the time Tom joined her in Brazoria, Texas, as a railway surgeon on the St. Louis, Brownsville and Mexico Railway.

Ben Yoakum, who was back heading the railroad full-time, had mentioned Dr. Herzog when he offered Tom the job. "Check her out for me, will you? We didn't realize she was a woman when we hired her, but she told us in no uncertain terms that we could fire her only when she was no longer able to do her job. She sounds like quite the spitfire, but I'd like to know from the inside if she's doing a good job."

"Dr. Sofie," as she was known, was already a legend in South Texas. Tom learned she was Austrian and had been married to a well-known surgeon at the age of fourteen. Fifteen children later (he couldn't imagine it), she'd decided to join the medical profession herself. First a midwife, then a trained medical doctor, she'd moved to the wilds of Texas to be close to her offspring.

And Brazoria was wild, no two ways about it. Once a promising mill town, its star began to fade when the county seat moved eight miles to the north. Now it served the railroad and was the favorite haunt of cowboys who didn't mind settling their differences at the point of a gun.

Apparently the good doctor marched to nobody else's drummer. She had curly, salt-and-pepper hair that she wore short and topped with a man's hat. Since Brazoria had a muddy season, she'd taken to wearing split skirts so she could ride her horse astride and avoid the muck. The lady doc turned heads wherever she went, but her fame stemmed from more than just her eccentricity. By all accounts, she was a skilled healer, known especially for her unique method of extracting bullets from gunshot wounds. She even wore a necklace strung with the bullets of the patients she'd saved. *Nana Ruth would have loved you*, Tom thought.

For her part, Dr. Sofie wasted no time getting to the heart of who Tom was. After their first day of working together, she took him to the restaurant at the nearby Jefferson Hotel and bought him a drink. Perusing him over her glass of whiskey, she asked in her Austro-German accent, "Have you ever been married, young man?"

"No, ma'am."

"You should try it, a young buck like you. Let me tell you, it is a most wonderful thing, as long as you pick the right mate. I am a widow now, but I have my eyes open." She winked at him and he couldn't help but chuckle—at least until she turned serious. "You used to be a surgeon, but you've got a spot of the palsy now, is that correct?"

Tom bristled. "Who told you that?"

"No one. I notice your hands are lean and quick, a surgeon's hands, and you keep them clean and dry, the nails blunt, always ready."

He held up his right hand. It quivered slightly. "Ah, but then there's this."

"What is the cause of it? Do you know?"

A shrug. "I think it's in my head."

She took a sip of her drink. "That is both good and bad."

"How so?"

"Good in that you can hope for a full recovery at some point, bad in that it is difficult to get beyond it in the meantime. Difficult, but not impossible."

Interesting. He looked at his hand resting quietly on the table. "You sound like I could have some control over it."

"Yes, the potential exists. You can play tricks on it,

just as your hand plays tricks on you. You can get beyond it, much like shamans and Hindu priests do when they fire walk. Tell me, do you think it is physically possible to walk across hot embers without burning your feet?"

Tom smirked. "No."

"You are wrong. It is physically possible, depending on factors such as the internal temperature of the foot, the heat of the coals, the conductivity of the burning material, the quickness of the step, and so on. However, the mind gets in the way of such rational thinking. It says, 'If I walk over those coals, my feet will burn.' Most people cannot move past such a mindset and thus never attempt a fire walk. Only those who can get beyond the mistaken idea that they cannot walk across the coals will be able to achieve the walk. It is the same in your case."

"I don't see the connection."

"Based on my observations, your hand does not regularly tremble, nor is it influenced by a certain position or muscle use, all of which indicate your nerves are not physically damaged. I would say it is an electrical short within your nervous system, much like the occasional muscle twitch. But it has been going on for some time, yes?"

"Since last April. I was involved in the quake and fire in San Francisco."

Dr. Sofie nodded. "Then you must be grappling with something mentally, or emotionally. You may not even know what that is. Yet it is the barrier between you and the logic of having a hand that has no physical reason to tremble. My supposition is that you have defined yourself as a surgeon who is no longer able to function because of a palsied hand. It is the barrier of that definition that you must overcome."

"But how?" Tom couldn't mask his frustration. "I've considered every possibility, every treatment. Heat, cold, rest, exercise. Thinking about it. Trying not to think about it. Nothing has made a difference."

"Perhaps the key lies in focusing on what you have, not on what you have lost."

Tom thought of Katherine their last morning together, and how she'd been more than willing to see him as someone other than a surgeon. But he was meant to be a surgeon, dammit!

He lifted his glass. "I had a mentor once who stopped his shaking with a liquid somewhat like this."

Dr. Sofie tsked. "That is a facile and temporary antidote that loses efficacy over time. Only the mind is strong enough to overcome such things."

"Much easier said than done."

"Indeed. The next time I meet a Hindu priest I will ask him to share his secrets. Then I will pass them along to you."

Their exchange lightened after that and lasted late into the evening. At one point, Tom looked around and found they were the only ones left in the restaurant. He started to get up. "We should probably leave. They'll want to close up for the night."

"It is no problem," she said. "I own the place."

In the days and weeks that followed, Tom's respect for his colleague grew exponentially. Dr. Sofie had built her own clinic, in which she saw patients from both the railway and the town. She mixed her own medicines and made house calls at all hours of the night. It didn't matter what color her patients were or how much money they had; her only concern was getting them well. At the same time, she managed the hotel, ran the town library, and found time to speak at medical society conferences.

"Is there anything you can't do?" Tom asked after a particularly busy day giving railroad workers their annual physical exams, a practice Dr. Sofie had instituted when she took the job. It was half past eight in the evening and the woman looked as energetic as ever.

She thought for a moment. "I was never very good at playing the violin, so I switched to the viola. But that's all that comes to mind."

Despite his title, Tom wasn't required to perform surgery, and he found that he could now handle most non-surgical procedures, even those that required fine motor skills in both hands, like simple stitches. He still did not trust himself with a scalpel, however.

He found, too, that railway medicine was its own specialty, requiring a keen knowledge of emergency medical techniques. Something as minor as the unexpected coupling of an engine to a coal tender might throw a passenger or crew member off balance, causing them to bang their head or sustain a gash. Transporting such patients via rails could be risky, especially when injuries to the head or spine were involved. To mitigate the risk of further injury, each train on the line had been given emergency packs with medicines, sterile dressings, and the instruments needed for basic wound treatment and patient stabilization. Now, no matter where an accident happened, there were resources available to take care of victims until they could be transferred to a hospital.

But sometimes, a hospital was the *last* place the patient wanted or needed to be.

As Tom soon discovered, Dr. Sofie had that all figured out, too.

Answering questions about the earthquake and its aftermath would have killed him, so as much as it bothered him to do so, Tom avoided going home for Thanksgiving. The loneliness just about did him in. He missed his family, yes, but he missed Katherine more. He was beginning to ache for her.

At Dr. Sofie's insistence ("You will not find solace in a bottle"), he joined her family for the holiday. One of her sons-in-law, Randolph Prell, was a native of Brazoria, so it was a Texas-style feast with some Austrian highlights. Cheesy *käsespätzle* went down well with *hefeweizen*.

"You'll probably see my mama in action today," Randoph's wife Elfriede said during dinner. "You can just about set your watch by it."

What were they talking about? "I've already seen your mother in action," Tom said. "She is remarkable."

Randolph helped himself to another portion of the

spätzle as well as the roasted turkey. "Not like this, you haven't."

The Prells' residence was located downtown, just a few doors down from Dr. Sofie's clinic, which was itself a converted home. Later in the evening, as they sat down to teach Tom the old Bavarian card game of *Karnöffel*, shots rang out.

"It won't be long now," Elfriede said without concern.

"I'm afraid she is right." Dr. Sofie looked resigned. "Any kind of celebration seems to bring out the wild ones in our little town."

Before long there was a loud knock on the front door. Randolph answered it, but Dr. Sofie had already started to gather her things. "Come along, Dr. Justice. We shall see if we can add to my necklace."

What followed was an unbelievable blend of skill, logic, and ingenuity. As predicted, two young and scruffy ranch hands from competing spreads had come into town, drunk too much, and started to fight, first with words, then with their guns. One cowboy was hit in the abdomen, while the gunman, immediately contrite, ran to get the woman he knew could make things right.

"Lonnie Drake, you are a *dodl* of the first order," Dr. Sofie said, marching past him. "Next time it's going to be your hide that springs a leak."

The victim, Charlie Pike, was leaning against the door of the clinic, gasping and clutching his gut. Despite the holidays, the gunfire had drawn out several neighbors, whom Dr. Sofie drafted to carry the wounded wrangler through the front parlor's waiting area and into a back bedroom. They placed him carefully on the bed and Dr. Sofie gave Charlie a whiff of ether before examining the entry site of the wound. Afterward, she carefully washed and sterilized one index finger—only one—and gently probed the interior to get a sense of the bullet's trajectory. Tom watched in awe.

"You gonna take it out, doc?" Lonnie asked anxiously. "You gonna take it out?"

"No, young man, I am going to wait for it to come to me."

And that is precisely what happened.

"You're lucky Lonnie's such a bad shot," she amiably remarked to her patient, even though Charlie was already in twilight from the drug mixed with the alcohol he'd consumed. "There's just a little bleeding, which I shall deal with, and then we'll let you ponder your and his misdeeds for a while." After prepping him, she turned him on his side and raised his legs onto a bar that had been specially built for the frame of the bed. She looked up at Tom. "Now we wait."

Tom could hardly bear it. With two reliably steady hands he would have opened the man up immediately and probed for the bullet.

"I know what you are thinking," she said. "But let me ask you: assuming the bullet has not severed an artery or entered the heart, what is the number one cause of death in situations like this?"

"Sepsis," Tom said. So often infection laid waste to what had been an admirable piece of surgery.

"Precisely, which is why my technique has increased my survival rate tremendously." She gestured around the barely furnished room, which had walls painted a faded green and a scuffed wood floor. "As you can see, I do not operate under ideal conditions; this town is not known for its cleanliness and it is very difficult to secure and maintain a sterile environment. So I minimize contact with the body and use gravity to bring the bullet to me. You will see."

It took a day and a half of watchful care, but damn it if she wasn't absolutely right. Like a baby moving down a birth canal, the bullet slowly began to retrace its path. Eventually, with a satisfying *plink*, Dr. Sofie was able to pull the bullet out and plop it into a pan. She quickly re-washed the wounded area and stitched it up.

Lonnie, who had sobered up fairly quickly, was hovering in the outer room after waking from a fitful sleep on the cushioned bench near the front door. After bandaging the wound, Dr. Sofie called him in.

"It's up to you to watch him for another twelve hours; anything changes, you let me know. And Lonnie? If Charlie takes a bad turn I will hold you solely responsible."

"Yes ma'am," the chastened cowboy replied.

"And that's how it's done," Dr. Sofie remarked to Tom afterward. "Easy as linzer torte."

CHAPTER THIRTY-EIGHT

Nine days before trial

Time was growing short.

Sipping a whiskey, Jonathan sat alone in the library of his townhome, trying to distract himself by rereading Thomas Hardy's *Tess of the D'Urbervilles*, but putting the book aside after less than half a chapter. "Why should I read about such sorrow when I'm living it?" he muttered. All right, that was a bit of an exaggeration, but it was bloody irritating to be so close to trial and still not have a clear understanding of his client's innocence. He reached for his ever-present folder and leafed through his notes one more time. One question persisted: why had Tom Justice left town?

Jonathan resolved to speak with Katherine again. No doubt she would reiterate her claim that Tom was innocent, but perhaps she could give Jonathan some other insight to help prove it. He made the call requesting the interview and was nonplussed at the invitation she extended.

"Oh, I was thinking of calling you myself," she said. "Do come for a picnic. I'm free tomorrow at eleven o'clock. Meet me at my parents' home, won't you?"

Surely she understood it was not a social call. "I'm not certain—"

"Please, Jonathan." Her tone told him she knew precisely how high the stakes were.

The following morning, Jonathan rose early and put several hours in at the office. Then he brushed a piece of lint off his dark gray wool vest and donned its matching suit jacket before leaving, hat and coat in hand, for his lunch with Katherine. *This is not a personal visit,* he reminded himself, although he sorely wished it were.

From Montgomery Street it was a relatively short drive to the Firestone estate in Pacific Heights. He dreaded getting behind the wheel of his car, so he was glad the distance was short. But why had Katherine picked that location for their meeting? She hadn't lived with her parents for some time. Perhaps she felt the need to have her family there to support her in case he grilled her too severely. He grimaced at the thought; the last thing in the world he wanted was for her to suffer on account of him. Should things not work out with Tom, it would make his suit all the more difficult. Belatedly, he realized his concerns were more about his well-being than hers. What did that say about him?

He had visited the Firestone mansion several times over the past few months, and each time he was reminded of his childhood—not the reality of what it had been, but the chimera of what it could have been. The estates were similar, with substantial wood and stone edifices, set back from verdant rolling lawns, offering an oasis amidst life's rubble. He shook the memory away.

When he drove up, Katherine was waiting by herself on the expansive veranda fronting the house, wearing an elegant wool walking coat in hunter green that would have been the envy of any tailor on Savile Row. Though it was mannish in style, it looked spectacular on her long, lean frame. A matching hat covered her tawny hair, and she wore gloves against the chilly sea breeze. She held a picnic basket in one hand, which she handed to him with a smile before taking his arm and strolling toward the back of the estate's grounds. Clearly she wasn't worried about having the support of her family; it looked like they would be quite alone.

"You will love what Bertrand has prepared," she said. "I'm quite famished, myself."

They talked of inconsequential things as they headed toward the spot she had in mind. It was a large red gazebo with a linen-draped table and chairs set up inside. A small sideboard held a bottle of wine in a cooler along with a chafing dish that warmed a pot presumably filled with coffee or tea.

"Welcome to The Ruby," she said. "We've called it that since we were children. It's big, round, and red, like one of my mother's favorite brooches. I find it a comforting place...most of the time."

The luncheon was delicious, as he knew it would be. The Firestones' chef had prepared breast of chicken baked in pastry, along with cooled asparagus drizzled with a tart citrus sauce. The rolls were warm, and the *tarte tatin*, made with hothouse peaches instead of the usual apple, was exquisite.

"You're worried," Katherine said to him over tea (she'd remembered his fondness for Earl Grey). "Tell me why."

"It's not for the reason you might think," Jonathan said. "I have no concerns that politics might influence the path of justice. Tom will get a fair trial. But ..."

"You're worried that Tom is guilty, and that no matter what you say or do, the jury will see fit to punish him."

"The evidence does not lean in his favor. While I cannot go into the details, I can speak to an issue that has perplexed me from the start, and that is, why did Tom leave? He had to have known it would seem odd for him to do so. And yet he left his position—and presumably you—for parts unknown. Surely you can see how bad it looks."

Katherine finished her wine. Then she asked the strangest question. "What is it that defines you, Jonathan?"

He frowned, not sure what she meant. "I don't know. I've never been asked that before. I'd have to think about it."

She cocked her head to study him. "If I had to guess, I'd say you are a man of principle and reason, and most of the time you want to do what's right. You possess the skills of logic and oratory, and you have used them quite successfully to achieve your goals."

Jonathan felt as though the conversation was slipping away from him. "All right, for the sake of argument, let's say you're correct. What does that have to do with—"

"Now let's say your ability to reason is taken away from you"—she snapped her fingers —"like that. One day you wake up and you can no longer assemble a series of facts and come to a logical conclusion about them. That faculty is gone. Vanished. *And you don't know why.*"

"That would be horrific," Jonathan admitted. "Impossible to imagine."

She now took a sip of her tea. "Welcome to the world of Tom Justice."

"What are you saying?"

She gestured around the gazebo. "Less than a week after the quake and fire, this little structure served as an impromptu clinic for my mother's vaunted Firestone Camp. You weren't here to see it, but this entire estate was filled with refugees living in tents and lean-tos and any other sort of shelter they could cobble together. My mother used her influence to get me to come here and tend to those who were in need of medical care. Tom was selected by the chief medical officer at the Presidio to accompany me. Tom wasn't happy about it; in fact he accused me of having something to do with the assignment. I was confused by his change of attitude. Just days before, we had been, well, let's just say, getting along.

"We set up a clinic, and Tom tried his best to hide his suffering from all of us."

Jonathan searched his memory; he'd not heard about Tom sustaining any wounds or illness during the ordeal. "His suffering?"

She nodded. "A day or so after the earthquake, he developed a tremor in his right hand, and it grew worse. Can you imagine what it would be like for a surgeon—in Tom's case, a very talented surgeon—to find he could no longer do what he was born to do?"

Jonathan toyed with his teaspoon, then touched the linen napkin to his lips. Why hadn't he heard of this before? "I've talked with him several times and haven't noticed a thing."

"He would hide it from you, just like he tried to hide it from me. But I couldn't help but see what was wrong and confronted him about it."

"What did he do?"

She smiled wanly. "He lashed out at me, of course. Told me to butt out, that it was his problem to solve. Why do you think he did that?"

"Ego, perhaps? He didn't want you to see him in a weakened state. Men tend to be that way."

"Women, too," she said wryly. "But that's not why. Can you guess?"

Jonathan turned it over in his mind. He didn't want to admit it, but he knew. "Because he didn't want to burden you."

She looked at him with appreciation. "Precisely. In fact, I'll wager you would have done the same thing."

He wasn't sure about that. "What did you do?"

"I was prepared to do anything it took," she confided. "Tom and my relationship is complicated; our path has not been smooth. When he told me he was leaving, I wanted to hold him back." She chuckled softly. "Rather presumptuous of me to think I could have done anything about it at all, but I was much more self-righteous back then, convinced that I could fix anything."

"So he left."

"He left. But not—and this is what I want you to understand—not because he was running away. If you don't believe me, you can corroborate this with Colonel Aldrich, who knew he was leaving and had no problem with it. No. Tom was running *toward* something: a cure, or, short of that, at least an explanation. He would go anywhere, try anything, to return to the person he had been. Just as you would, were you in his place.

"No matter what happened at the Pavilion—and I so wish I could tell you precisely what went on—I know as sure as I am sitting here that he willfully killed no one. He is a healer. He was born to help people. The only time he'd ever consider harming another person would be if they threatened someone else. Especially someone he loved."

"Like you?"

She gazed at him; her eyes telling him the truth that he hadn't wanted to face. "Like me."

There was a brief, awkward silence as Jonathan contemplated the facts of the matter. He covered it by taking a sip of tea and gazing out at the garden. He could smell lilacs, idly wondering which varieties had been planted. But that was not important. Only one thing was important—the fading hope that affection between Tom and Katherine ran more strongly in her direction than his. He tested the water.

"Knowing he loved you, how on earth were you able to let him go?"

"It was difficult. I was still convinced of my own infallibility, you see. But when you...when you truly love someone, what else can you do but help them do what they need to do to be happy? And so I let him go."

It was as he suspected. "Yet eventually you did go after him."

She let out a rueful sigh. "Oh yes, that I did, and almost got my head bitten off in the process. It had been several months, and I thought I was getting along well enough. I had met you, and you are, oh, so very attractive, and I thought perhaps ..."

She reached out and squeezed Jonathan's arm affectionately, which made it worse, somehow, as if he'd lost a race by inches instead of miles. "What happened to change your mind about going to him?" he asked.

"A friend of both Tom and mine came to me with the news that there was a warrant out for Tom's arrest, that he was wanted for murder. Murder! The absurdity of that charge is crystal clear to all who really know him—all but those with their own agendas."

"Like Anson Cotter."

She held up her hand. "Please do not get me started on that poor excuse for a human being."

"So you wanted to warn Tom."

She sent him the beginning of a scowl. "You make it sound as if I wanted to help him evade the law. It wasn't that at all. It never crossed my mind that he had committed a criminal act, and I know it never crossed his either, or he wouldn't have left."

"You don't know that," Jonathan countered harshly.

She looked at him directly, never wavering. "I do know that. I know it from the inside out." She continued with her story. "Two things were immediately apparent to me: one was that Tom had to be warned so that he could come back to clear the matter up, and two, that I had to be the one to find him."

"Why you, for God's sake?"

"It had to do with a promise I'd made him. Unfortunately, the detective sent to bring him in was not that far behind me, and I had only just explained matters before Tom was arrested. And you know the story from there."

"Ah, but that's the problem. I don't know the story. Not the whole story. Katherine, something happened when Tom went behind that curtain. A man died. A man Tom was known not to care for. A man against whom many would say Tom held a grudge. I need to know what happened, no matter what it was, so that I can best represent his side to the jury."

She reached over and took Jonathan's hand in her own. "Then you must convince him that the only person he's harming by keeping the story to himself is him. Tell him ..." Here she paused to collect herself. She was trying hard not to cry. "Tell him that no matter what he did, I believe it was the right thing to do, because I know him. I trust him. And I love him."

An iron door, clanging shut in the deepest, darkest prison cell, wouldn't have filled Jonathan with more desolation.

They headed back to the mansion and once again made small talk as he got back into his car. Katherine then asked him to wait a moment, and, returning a few moments later, handed him a small envelope.

"Tom will not be happy I gave you this, which is why I've hesitated doing so until now. But you can tell him I wouldn't have done it unless I felt it was vital to the case. The letter was waiting for me when I returned from meeting Tom in Texas. You can tell by the postmark. It proves he wasn't running. Now please, prove that he's innocent."

Jonathan nodded and turned the car around. Halfway down the long drive, out of sight of the house, he pulled over, curiosity getting the better of him.

It was indeed a letter from Tom, a very personal letter, and it quite clearly indicated that he had no idea he was being hunted. By giving it to Jonathan, Katherine knew that it would be submitted into evidence and would eventually become public, which meant their relationship would be revealed. No Firestone would seek such publicity unless it was absolutely necessary.

Unless love trumped propriety.

Jonathan drove back to his office at a funereal pace, feeling the emptiness that invariably follows the ending of a relationship. But such desolation was hardly warranted, he argued; after all, they had never engaged in a full-fledged affair to begin with. Yet in some ways that made it worse, because they hadn't gone far enough to determine whether or not they were compatible in the long run. Jonathan suspected that time would have strengthened their bond, not weakened it, and that sharpened his disappointment to a fine point.

As much as such contemplations pained him, it was now quite clear what Jonathan had to do. He would use any and every trick he could think of, including sharing her heartfelt words, and Tom's written declaration, to get his client to divulge everything he knew. Katherine was convinced that the truth would set Tom free, legally and emotionally. And she was relying on Jonathan to make it happen. He could not disappoint her.

CHAPTER THIRTY-NINE

"He jumped right into the thick of it and did whatever
he could."

—BILL HODSON, MAYOR OF REFUGIO, TEXAS

Christmas came and went, the New Year dawned, and Tom began to consider, at last, a long-term strategy. His hand remained unpredictable: some days the tremor would disappear completely; he'd assist Dr. Sofie in procedures and at times even perform them on his own. He was his former self again, confident in his ability to cut, to repair, and to suture.

But a day or two later, the trembling would return, intense enough that he dare not try any technique requiring a steady hand.

For months he'd taken daily notes to see what might cause one condition or the other: what he ate or drank, how much work he'd done, the kind of physical exercise he'd put himself through, or the hours he'd slept—even whether he'd had dreams the night before. He found no correlation between any of it, but he did notice a trend: over time, the difference between a "good" and a "bad" day seemed to decrease in intensity. He began to accept his palsied hand, unpredictable though it was, with less rancor and more pragmatism. Days when he couldn't perform surgery were just as busy as those when he could, and every day was worth getting up for. He was "fillin' his life with livin'," and Nana Ruth would have approved.

Only one area of his life remained a constant vexation—his desire for Katherine.

At first he'd paid little heed to Dr. Sofie's suggestion to consider what he had rather than what he'd lost, but slowly it began to work its way into his consciousness. Assuming Katherine hadn't found someone else in the meantime (and who could blame her if she had?), maybe he could make a life with her despite his affliction.

After much grappling with the idea, Tom decided to write Katherine a letter; afterward he waited three days to see if he'd experienced a bout of temporary insanity. Still feeling the same need to contact her, he gathered his courage and posted it before he could change his mind. It read:

Dear Katherine,

I know I said I wouldn't write to you, so I suppose if you read this, it will show me to be a liar. Not an auspicious beginning! I've been searching for a resolution to my physical problem and have determined that there are no easy answers. There may never be. The truth is (if you can believe me), I have begun to think more and more about what you said, that I have more to offer the world (and you) than merely my surgical skills...that I can be of some good to others despite my diminished capabilities and quite possibly be content with that. The question I now ask myself is, can I be the man you deserve? I want to be, more than you will ever know. I think of you every day, and long for you every night. I want to be with you, plain and simple. If there is any hope that you might be open to trying again, will you please write to me at the above address? Say the word and I will return to you. If you have found another, I will understand, but would appreciate knowing that as well.

Yours,

Tom

A week went by, then two, without a word. A knot of misery formed inside his gut and began to grow. How could he have let her go? He was a fool. Worse than a fool. A weakling who couldn't face even a minimal dose of personal adversity. She was far better off without him.

But his other, perhaps better half, fought back. What are you waiting for? You love her. Go back to her. Fight for her.

It dawned on him that his vacillation regarding Katherine mirrored that which he felt regarding what had happened with Eli.

"Enough," he muttered. "It's time to think about something else."

That something else appeared in dramatic fashion in late January. A storm had begun early that morning and kept up a constant barrage, turning the dirt-packed streets of Brazoria into a swamp worthy of bayou backcountry. Sunday walking shoes and the hems of pretty skirts didn't stand a chance against the muck, and old Mr. Stuart had already been brought in by his son-in-law with a badly strained hip from slipping off his front porch. All Tom could give the man was some laudanum, a large measure of sympathy, and a prescription for taking it easy, which he knew the codger wouldn't follow.

Dr. Sofie was away at a meeting of the American Association of Railway Surgeons. It was mid-afternoon, and Tom was in the clinic sterilizing a set of instruments when word came down the line that the evening train bound for Houston by way of Brazoria had jumped some washed-out tracks just outside of Refugio. There were multiple casualties. A hospital car and engine were on their way from Houston and would stop by to pick up any available railroad surgeons before heading to the accident site. Tom was willing; for once he felt confident that he could help.

When the train arrived, he was relieved to see two other docs on board. One balding and lanky, the other portly and bushy-haired, both appeared to be in their sixties, no doubt nearing the end of their careers. Tom soon learned that being on call for railway accidents was a job the men liked to get paid for but didn't like to partake in. The rotund Dr. Sumner was at least relieved that Tom rather than Dr. Sofie had boarded the train.

"Ridiculous to have a lady railway surgeon," Sumner complained. "Never been done and I'm sure the workers don't like it any more than we do."

As the special train picked up speed, Tom thought it might be best to keep his mouth shut, but that lasted all of thirty seconds. "The workers actually prefer her," he said casually. "The ones who have seen her work know how competent she is."

Dr. Calhoun's thin lip curled. "I've heard she's afraid to cut folks open, so she lets bullets fester inside her patients. Doesn't sound very competent to me."

"She's not afraid to perform surgery but does so only when necessary. And I've seen her bullet removal technique. It works."

The men glanced at each other and didn't respond; obviously Tom wasn't giving them the red meat they wanted. The three of them sat silently for the rest of the trip. Rain splattered the window as he gazed into the blackness.

They were about fifteen minutes south of Refugio station when Tom caught his first glimpse of the accident site through the wet, inhospitable night. The engine had toppled, as had the coal car and the two passenger cars behind it. Lanterns fluttered like June bugs in a cemetery, and shouts competed with the hiss of escaping steam.

The hospital train was just rolling to a stop when Tom grabbed his medical bag, hopped off, and began running to the tangled wreckage. He passed four bodies already wrapped and lined up by the side of the track. The first passenger car, tilted crazily on its side, could only be accessed from a window on what was now the roof, and men—good Samaritans or local law enforcement, he couldn't make out which—

were in the midst of evacuating passengers who could walk.

A man who seemed to be in charge hurried over to Tom and stuck out his hand. "Bill Hodson. You from the railroad?"

Tom nodded. "How bad is it?"

"We're just about done moving the folks out who weren't hurt, but there's lots of injured still inside." He gestured to the wrapped bodies. "We lost four so far. No sure if there are any others."

"I'll take a look." Tom climbed up on the side of the car to peer into the black hole of the compartment. "I'm a doctor. Can anybody hear my voice?"

"Yes, yes, we're in here," came the reply.

He dropped into the abyss. As his eyes grew accustomed to the light, he could see the outlines of bodies sprawled on windows of the coach car, which were now running along the floor. Bolted bench seats divided the car into tall, narrow stalls occupied by injured passengers. Surprisingly, many victims appeared to have already been tended to.

"Has a local doc been here?" he asked.

"No," a teenage boy said, his head wrapped in what looked like a torn shirt. "Just a lady. She was a passenger like us. But she took control right away and said we should wait in here on account of the rain outside. She said help was on the way. You a doc?"

"Yes. What's your name, son?"

"Andy."

"Can you tell me who's in the worst shape, Andy?"

The young man shook his head. "Hard to say in the

dark. The worst of the cryin' has died down; don't know whether that's good or bad. But I know there was one older fellow in a bad way toward the back of the car. You probably ought to check on him first."

Tom took a cursory look at the gash in the boy's forehead. "You're going to need a few stitches," he said.

"Yeah, she said the same thing." He smiled grimly. "But if that's all I need I'll count myself damn lucky."

Tom worked his way to the back of the car and found the passenger Andy had mentioned. He was in his forties, it looked like, panting but conscious, his head in the lap of a young woman who was perhaps sixteen. A dim lamp cast their features in harsh relief while almost obscuring the piece of twisted metal protruding from the man's right calf. A bandage surrounded the wound, but it was soaked in blood. Not a good sign.

The girl was sniffling and tenderly brushing the man's graying hair back. "The lady told me not to move him or try to pull it out," she said tearfully. "She said he might lose too much blood."

"Is this your pa?" Tom asked.

She nodded. "Is he...is he going to be all right?"

"Don't put the poor man on the spot, Callie," her father said in a weak voice. "He's doin' the best he can." He turned his head to Tom and raised a shaky arm. "Silas Hall, not quite at your service."

Tom shook the man's hand and said to his daughter, "You did the right thing by waiting for us to come, sweetheart. We've brought a special train to help get your dad and others to a hospital and we're going to do everything we can to fix him up, all right?"

She nodded again and Tom squeezed her shoulder before getting up. He held up the girl's lamp to see Dr. Sumner clumsily hoisting himself into the car.

"Back here, Dr. Sumner."

He left the doctor to further examine the man's wound and worked his way back to the exit, checking on the injured along the way. There were deep lacerations, abrasions, concussions, and several sprained limbs. One very pregnant young woman was somewhat dizzy and her husband looked to have a broken arm.

Encouraged by those relatively minor injuries, most of which had already been seen to by the unnamed passenger, Tom climbed back out and headed to the second car. Once inside he found much the same thing, except that triage was still going on.

"You're such a brave girl, Ginny," he heard a woman murmur. "You're going to be just fine."

Tom couldn't believe it. He knew that voice.

CHAPTER FORTY

"He was more than happy to stay behind in Refugio. It's in the middle of nowhere; maybe that's why he liked it."

—DR. NORBERT SUMNER, RAILWAY SURGEON

Despite the dimness, Tom had no doubt that it was Katherine, kneeling at the back of the passenger car. She was tending a little girl who looked to be three years old at most, while a woman, presumably the child's mother, looked anxiously over her shoulder. Although he stood in shadow, Katherine must have sensed his presence, because she searched the dark.

"I told you help was coming," she said to the woman before calling out, "Are you a doctor?"

"I am," Tom said.

He could tell that she registered his voice as well, because she stood up and stared at him through the gloom. He worked his way over to her, fighting a maelstrom of joy mixed with ire. She was here...but dammit, why was she here? She could have been *killed*. He didn't address her, instead bending down to speak directly to the child.

"And who do I have the pleasure of meeting?" The little girl looked up at him with wide, shock-filled eyes, her breath hitching in little hiccups. Her arm had suffered a deep, six-inch gash that Katherine had just finished suturing.

"This is Ginny and she is a very brave girl," Katherine said softly. She brushed the child's tangled brown curls away from her cheek.

Tom caught the little girl's gaze and held it. "Ginny, you are very lucky to have met Nurse Firestone. She is one of the best."

He took some carbolic acid from his bag and dabbed a little on the wound. Ginny barely flinched, which told him how traumatized she was. He glanced at Katherine before taking out a roll of gauze and gently wrapping the child's arm. "So, you got my letter?"

"Letter? No, I—there was no letter."

He frowned. That meant she'd broken her word. Anger bubbled up inside of him. It was her damn need for control again. He couldn't stand it. His voice dropped and he murmured, "Then what in the hell are you doing here?"

Katherine knew better than he that it was not the time or place. She rose and wiped her hands on her dirty, blood-stained skirt. "Does it matter?" she said coldly. "You have work to do, Doctor."

By this time Dr. Calhoun had entered the car, and Katherine moved on to help him. She was right, of course. Tom did have work to do. He pushed his emotions to the back porch of his mind and concentrated on the patient in front of him.

And watched his hand tremble.

An hour later, all of the patients had been seen at least once and stabilized. Depending on the severity of their wounds, they would be transported as soon as possible to either the hospital car or the local hotel.

The most difficult challenge was removing Silas Hall through the window of the railcar without jarring the metal spike that was still embedded in his leg. A stretcher was brought in and Hall was strapped tightly to it. Tom had offered him some laudanum, but the man declined; he didn't want to be "loopy" in front of his daughter.

Katherine offered to take Callie to sit with the other able-bodied passengers. The girl hadn't wanted to leave her father, but after Katherine whispered something to her, she nodded and climbed out of the window without complaint. "I'll see you soon, Daddy," she called back in an attempt to sound brave.

"Yes you will, darlin'. Don't you worry."

After she left, three men stood on either side of the

stretcher and hoisted it up before awkwardly working their way back to the opening. Hall had made a feeble joke about not knowing his own pallbearers, but the laughter was cut short when the litter accidentally bumped against one of the seats, causing him to scream in agony.

When they reached the opening in the ceiling, they had to tilt Hall vertically to get him through. Once outside, six more men grabbed hold and carried him to the edge of the car before lowering him to the ground.

"Take him to the hospital car," Dr. Sumner said. "I'll be following right behind."

After the man was out of earshot, Sumner addressed Tom, Dr. Calhoun, and Katherine, who had returned. "Here's how I see it. The leg's got to go. We try pulling that spike out and no telling what we'll find. It may be blocking an artery, and by the time we get him plugged up he could bleed out. On the other hand, we do a normal transtibial amputation and leave him six inches, he's got enough for a prosthesis."

Tom was beside himself with frustration. "Can't we at least try? The metal might have missed the artery completely."

Dr. Calhoun waved his bony arm. "You'd take the chance on that? And let's say you're right. Are you going to sew him back together, layer by layer, nerve by nerve, just to save that mess of his? Because I'll tell you, neither of us"—he pointed to Dr. Sumner and himself— "has the skill for that kind of surgery. Meanwhile the rest of the patients need to get to a hospital, but we can't leave because Dr. Justice is still at it. And what if you lose him? What are you going to tell that little girl of his?"

Dr. Sumner concurred. "Whether you rebuild his leg or we amputate, he's still going to have a limp."

Katherine put her hand on Tom's arm. "I saw the wound, and I think the lower leg needs to go," she said softly. "This is not Tang Lin and you are not who you were."

You are not who you were. The words sliced into him, all the more painful because he knew without a doubt that she was right. This was what facing reality was all about. She was not afraid of it like he was. God, he needed her strength.

"Do you two know each other?" Dr. Sumner asked.

Katherine looked at Tom. "We used to work together. It was a while ago."

"Well, I vote to amputate," Dr. Calhoun said, "and if that's going to happen, I think we need to get it done now."

Tom looked at his three colleagues, who were waiting for his response. "All right," he finally said. "I would be happy to assist."

The accident the newspapers called "The Mission River Train Wreck" took four lives and one limb. Those who could travel were put up in local homes until their transportation could be arranged. Those who needed intense care were settled on the hospital train with Doctors Sumner and Calhoun and sent back to Houston. And those who weren't critical, but who still needed tending, remained behind at the hotel in Refugio, their bill paid for by the railroad, and their care supervised by Tom and a traveling nurse by the name of "Katherine Stone," her name changed to keep it out of the newspapers.

After a long morning of attending patients, Tom and Katherine retreated to their respective rooms to wash and change clothes before gravitating to the hotel's now-empty breakfast room. The waiter brought coffee and toast for Katherine, but Tom had no appetite. He ordered a whiskey.

Tom gazed at Katherine as she sat across from him. She wore a clean white apron over a pale yellow shirt-waist, which made her look lovely and fresh and innocent. Only her eyes gave away her tiredness. "Why in heaven's name were you on that train?" Tom's question held little of its former heat; his anger had dissipated along with his energy.

Her face was impassive. "Isn't it obvious? I was looking for you."

"But you promised. I'm surprised, is all. I didn't think you'd go back on it."

"I kept my word," she insisted. "You made me swear not to have you followed, and I didn't. You never said I couldn't follow you myself."

He mustered a weak smile. "Now you're splitting hairs."

"Perhaps," she said, "but it was necessary." She started to say something else but stopped herself and began again. "Mandy and my brother got married. It was lovely, but we missed you. How have you been?"

Tom swirled the contents of his glass like a fortune teller, as if he might find a suitable answer there. There was none. He looked up at her. "Not great, but you're a sight for sore eyes, and that's a fact."

Her eyes narrowed. "Stop it. You cannot say things like that and be fine with leaving me for no good reason."

"I had *every* reason." He held up his hand. "This... whatever it is, is *maddening*. I have tried everything. It's fine and then"—he shook it— "it's useless. I can't trust it." Frustrated, he emptied his glass.

"Then don't," she said. "Be someone who doesn't need that hand. I can love you without that hand. Why can't you?"

"You make it sound so simple, but it's not. It's like asking that poor fellow to give up his leg. As if he would ever willingly agree to such a thing."

"So, you just give up? You say, 'The hell with being happy if it means I have to do something different with my life'?"

Tom's right hand reached forward of its own volition and took hers. It was cool to the touch; he wanted to warm it with his breath. "No! God, no. I want to make it work. More than anything. But—"

At that moment the young father-to-be with the broken arm came bounding into the dining room. "Doc? My wife's going to have our baby now and we need your help."

Tom and Katherine glanced at each other. They

both knew it was likely premature labor brought on by the stress of the accident. Tom would try to stop it if he could. They headed upstairs where they could hear the wife's moans from the hallway.

"Carl—that's your name, isn't it?" Tom said to the father. "I need you to go downstairs and ask the clerk if there's a local midwife. If so, have her come right away and bring a tincture of red raspberry and cramp bark. She'll know what it's for. Can you remember that?"

"Red raspberry and cramp bark. Yes sir." The man, frazzled but determined, headed back down to the lobby.

Katherine immediately started the process of prepping the young woman for labor and, in the worst case, delivery. "Hello, Mrs. Lawson."

The young woman grimaced with another contraction. "M-Maggie. I go by Maggie."

"Maggie it is, then. Now, Doctor Justice is going to take a look and see how you're doing, all right?"

Tom examined Maggie and found she hadn't dilated much, nor had her water broken; that was the good news.

The bad news—she was breech.

"We're going to try and slow you down a bit, Maggie. Shouldn't be long now." He signaled for Katherine to meet him in the hallway. As he was about to explain the situation, the father returned with the midwife in tow, introducing her as "Miz Mabel Washington." The woman was eighty if she was a day, and her head bobbled worse than Tom's hand. But she'd come prepared.

"Ma'am, we need to stop the contractions if possible because Mrs. Lawson's baby is presenting breech."

"Breech, you say?" The lady was hard of hearing.

"That's right," Tom said, raising his voice. "We need to slow her contractions down right away."

The old woman smiled; she was missing her right eye tooth. With a surprisingly strong-looking hand she patted the bottle she carried. "This should put the brakes on a might. I mix it with a little St. John's wort. We got to move the babe back into place before the birthin' starts, though. Otherwise the mama's in for a world of hurt."

"Precisely, ma'am. If you would give her the tincture, we'll follow in a moment."

"Breech?" Katherine said as the woman headed inside. "Hadn't we better prepare for a cesarean?"

Tom shook his head. His hand was steady now, but there was no telling when it would begin to quiver. "I can't take the chance. Look, have you ever done an external cephalic version?"

"Flipping the baby inside the womb, you mean? No, I've never even seen it done."

"Well, if we can get Mrs. Lawson's contractions to subside, you may get an opportunity."

Tom and Katherine watched as the old but obviously experienced midwife worked the small miracle of easing Maggie's body out of delivery mode. After several hours of having her lie in a prone position, drinking glass after glass of water and tea and only letting her up to relieve herself, the contractions began to subside.

So far so good. "Excellent work, Mrs. Washington. Let's see if this holds, and if so, then tomorrow morning we'll try to move the baby into the proper position." He pulled out his wallet and handed the woman a ten-dollar bill.

Her eyes lit up. "Sure enough, doc. I'll be ready when you are."

After the midwife left, Tom turned to his patient. "How are you feeling, Mrs. Lawson?"

"Maggie. Pretty good now that the cramping's almost gone. What's in that tea, anyway?"

"A few things. Cramp bark is a muscle relaxant, so it slows down contractions, and raspberry leaves are good for strengthening the uterine muscles. The midwife put in some St. John's wort, too, which helps to calm things down." Already Maggie's eyes were drooping. A regular delivery was hard enough on a first-time mother; trying to deliver a breech birth naturally could spell big trouble, especially if operating wasn't an option. The thought of having to cut into that young woman with a shaky hand was too terrifying to contemplate.

Carl Lawson had been standing just outside the door for most of the afternoon and wringing his hands. He finally ventured in. "She gonna be okay, doc?"

Tom clasped him on the shoulder. "I know a lot of men find childbirth uncomfortable, but most mothers tell me they like it when their menfolk stick around to give them comfort. So now would be a good time to show your wife how much you love her and how proud you are of her."

Tom's pep talk had the desired effect. "I can do that," Carl said, turning back to his wife with purpose.

Katherine had left an hour or so earlier, and Tom intended to rest his eyes a bit before tracking her down. But the moment he lay on his bed, his lack of sleep caught up with him and he fell into a dreamless state.

He was gently awakened the next morning by Katherine, who was already dressed. Had he pulled the covers over himself? Had he even taken off his shoes? He didn't remember doing any of it.

"I've seen Mrs. Lawson already and she said she was able to get some sleep. Her husband and Mrs. Washington are with her now. I don't know how much of a window we have, but if we're going to attempt a version, now might be the time."

Tom agreed, and the two of them entered the room to find Carl Lawson holding his wife's hand while Mrs. Washington prepped for the procedure.

"You sure you got to do this?" Carl asked after Tom described the procedure. "I mean, she seems all right now."

"Her contractions have stopped but the baby's in the kind of position that will make a natural delivery very difficult," Tom explained. "If we can move your baby around, it will make delivery far less dangerous for both your wife and the child. You want that, don't you?"

Carl frowned. "Sure I do. What do you need from me?"

Tom took him aside. "Remember I told you

yesterday that women liked their men to be involved and to give them comfort? Well, this might not be one of those times." He grinned. "Your wife's going to feel a bit uncomfortable and she might take it out on you."

Carl held up his hands. "Enough said. Just call me if you need me." Dropping a kiss on his wife's forehead, he left the room.

"Now, Mrs. Lawson—Maggie—we're going to give your baby a gentle but firm nudge so that his or her head drops down into the birth canal. You're going to feel a lot of pressure, and you need to tell me if it's too much, all right?"

Maggie, who was lying on her back, nodded uncertainly.

"Don't you worry none, honey," Mrs. Washington said. "It may feel a bit tight, but it'll be well worth it when the baby's time comes."

Katherine had draped Maggie's front so that her stomach was exposed. Tom took some lotion Mrs. Washington had brought and covered the patient's stomach with it. She flinched from the cold.

"Don't hate me for what I'm about to do," Tom said, smiling.

He placed his hands on Maggie's distended belly and felt the baby's position. Its head was just beneath the woman's breasts, and he needed to flip it over so that it was head down. To do that he pushed behind the head while simultaneously pressing the baby's lower body in the opposite direction.

He increased the pressure.

"Oh, balls," Maggie panted. "This is not fun at all."

"I'm sorry," Tom said, but continued the maneuver. He could feel some movement, but the flip hadn't yet occurred.

Maggie continued to huff. "Oh, it's really beginning to hurt!"

"Just a little bit longer," he said, curling his hand into a fist and pressing even harder. This had to work. Had to. "Keep pressing here," he instructed Katherine, and placed her hands on the baby's lower half. "Toward the back." He then used both of his hands to continue coaxing the baby's head forward.

"Stubborn little cuss," Mrs. Washington said. She pressed a cool cloth against Maggie's forehead. "Wonder where he got that?" she teased.

Maggie let out a little cry, half laugh, half painful yelp.

"Almost there," Tom said. A few moments later he felt the baby flip into place. "There you go." He checked to see that the baby was in the vertex position. It was.

Not a moment later, Maggie cried out as a major contraction hit. Almost immediately her water broke.

"Not a moment too soon," Katherine said.

"You done good, doc," Mrs. Washington said. "Now let's get this here baby into the world."

Twelve hours later, they did.

Evan Carl Lawson weighed in at six pounds fourteen ounces, and both mother and child came through the birthing without mishap. Mrs. Washington left the hotel that evening with another ten dollars in her pocket and a charming grin on her face. Tom and Katherine, without even discussing it, headed to his room and collapsed on the bed.

Katherine turned to look at Tom. "You see? You didn't need your hand."

"This time," he said, holding it up. It trembled ever so slightly and he realized he hadn't given it a thought in hours.

"I think you need it now," she said, and placed it on her breast. "What do you want, Tom Justice?"

His response was immediate, ingrained, as if she'd asked for the sum of one plus one. "I want you. I've wanted you since I met you, and even more since I've known you. And God help me, I don't think that's ever going to change."

In response, she sat up and smiled, untying her apron before unbuttoning her shirtwaist. "I am very glad to hear it, because I have missed feeling you next to me."

And for the first time in a very long time, Tom took precisely what he wanted.

They made love with quiet moans and shuddering sighs, with light caresses that changed to frantic exploration, culminating in a deep joining that spoke of an even deeper love. Neither of them spoke about preventing a child, and both of them knew why.

They rose in time to make afternoon rounds of their patients, and when they retired for the night, they repeated their physical vows to one another without words.

It was just before dawn when Tom awoke, an idea niggling at him. He'd been spooning Katherine and he kissed her neck to gently wake her.

"Mmm," she said.

"Why did you come here?" he asked tenderly. "Why did you need to find me now?"

She turned over to face him, and he could tell that she had been holding something back.

"It isn't anything to do with your family, is it?"

She shook her head, and sweetly stroked his bristly cheek before sitting up. Her breasts were as beautiful as ever, but this time her intent was not to entice him. As she wrapped the covers around her, he felt a tightening in his gut, as if he were about to jump off a cliff.

"It was because of Tang Lin."

"Tang Lin? Is he all right?"

"Yes. Everyone is fine. But Tang Lin came to see me. He wanted help in in locating you. So he could warn you."

"Warn me? About what?"

"There are rumblings in the aftermath of the fire. People are blaming one other for mistakes that were made, and those in vulnerable positions are looking for something to distract the public. Tang Lin learned that a doctor had come to the district attorney alleging that a crime took place at the Mechanics' Pavilion. They're saying it was murder." She paused, took a deep breath. "And they're saying you're to blame. It's ridiculous, I know, but ..."

Tom's heart began pounding within his chest, clamoring to get out. Murder? It couldn't be. It—

"They're recalling everyone who was there to testify, and Tang says they have a warrant out for your arrest. It looks bad that you left the city, so I said I would find you and bring you back to clear it up."

To hell with them. The impulse to leave it all behind swept over him, but he beat it back—that was the absolute wrong thing to do, especially in light of the woman he had just made love with. However they twisted the story, he would not run. He would face whatever he had to, because he could not, *could* not imagine leaving Katherine of his own free will again.

He must have been staring at her because Katherine looked puzzled and faintly alarmed. "You know what they're talking about, don't you?"

He nodded slowly. "I do."

He watched as her mind put two and two together. She reached for his right hand. "And this has something to do with it."

"I think it does," he whispered.

She didn't say anything, just wrapped her arms tightly around him and held on.

Katherine grudgingly agreed to wait until the last injured passengers in their care were released before returning to San Francisco. Unfortunately, those plans were thwarted barely a week later.

They were finishing a late supper in the hotel dining room when two men approached their table. One of them was a uniformed police officer. The other, dressed in a dusty brown suit and holding an equally dusty bowler hat, spoke quietly so as not to attract the attention of the other diners.

"Dr. Thomas Aaron Justice? I am Mr. Beauregard Hanley and I have been authorized by the governors of both the state of California and the state of Texas to serve you with this arrest warrant and escort you to the city of San Francisco for prosecution."

Katherine shot venom at the man but didn't feign ignorance. "Couldn't this have waited until after dinner?"

"You are drinking coffee, ma'am. I'm assuming you already ate."

Tom wanted to hear it spoken directly. "If I may, what am I being charged with?"

Mr. Hanley handed him the warrant. "The willful murder of Mr. Elijah Eugene Porter."

Even though he'd had time to absorb the idea, Tom's heart still caught in his throat. "I am innocent," he said.

"That's up to the jury to decide. Now if you'll come with me, sir—"

"Wait," Katherine cried. "He has patients to attend!"

Tom rose from the table. "You will handle them just fine, Miss Stone," he said, willing her to play along. "Please contact my colleague, Dr. Herzog, in Brazoria, for your wages. You've been a great help to the company."

With that he left the room, flanked by the two lawmen and not daring to look back for fear he'd lose what little composure he had left.

CHAPTER FORTY-ONE

Six days before trial

Jonathan found his client Tom Justice standing at the small cracked mirror above the washstand in his cell. He was shirtless, exposing a well-defined, slightly furred chest and muscular arms. His lower face lathered with soap, he was taking a straight razor to his chin in expert strokes, dipping it in the wash bowl periodically before continuing to scrape away his heavy beard. *He is a handsome brute*, Jonathan thought with irritation. *Perhaps I should count myself lucky I was even in the running.*

The guard, Mr. Kirby, was standing outside the cell, chuckling. "Good thing I stropped that blade or you'd never get through that thicket," he teased the prisoner.

"You call this sharp? I'd call it dull as a day-old sermon. No wonder, dealing with your wiry brush every day."

Mr. Kirby grinned and glanced at Jonathan before lifting the ring of keys from his belt and opening the cell door. "He's all yours, counselor."

He has absolutely no concern that his prisoner will flee, Jonathan thought. *Either Kirby's an excellent judge of character or woefully naive. Which is it?* Jonathan still didn't know which was accurate, but today he was determined to find out once and for all.

He sat on the cot, his customary seat, and waited for Tom to finish his ablutions. After wiping his face, Tom handed the razor through the bars back to the guard.

"Thank you for that, Mr. Kirby."

"Right you are, doc." Kirby said, then cricked his massive neck and sauntered back down the hall.

Tom turned back to Jonathan, who handed him a notebook and a fountain pen with a new ink cartridge. "If you would be so kind, I need you to take some dictation for me."

Tom frowned slightly. "What?"

"I need you to write something in this book using your best penmanship."

"What for?"

"I'll let you know momentarily. Please humor me."

Tom shrugged and sat down on the lone chair, placing the notebook on the table. "What would you like me to write?"

"Oh, anything. How about, 'I am innocent of the murder of Eli Porter and here are the reasons why.' That sort of thing."

Tom nodded in mock solemnity. "How about I

explain the technique for applying a tourniquet instead?"

"That will do."

Tom quickly wrote a paragraph and handed it over. Jonathan glanced at it and put it back in his satchel. "As the trial is set to begin in six days, I want to tell you where we stand."

"That sounds good."

"These are the facts: we know that Eli Porter was killed with a bullet from a Colt single-action revolver that was not a military-issue weapon currently used by Army personnel. We know that he did not shoot himself with the weapon. We know that on the day in question you were called to subdue Mr. Porter because after he'd been brought to the critical care section, he had pulled out a gun with which he was threatening to harm people. We know you were called to do so because Mr. Porter had referred to you as his 'brother,' even though you are in fact first cousins with a, shall we say, *complex* relationship. And we know that the sergeant working in the critical care section that day carried the body of Mr. Porter out of the building before it could be destroyed by the fire. All of that is true, yes?"

Tom tipped his head. "It is."

"But here is where it gets complicated. No thanks to you, we have learned about the so-called Pavilion Protocol, which essentially allowed for euthanizing critically injured patients."

"I was asked not to—"

"It doesn't matter now," Jonathan said, hardening

his voice. "What matters is that it has come to light through credible testimony that Eli Porter wasn't part of the Protocol because he was *not* critically injured. Is that true as well, doctor?"

Tom let out a long breath. "Yes."

"All right. Now on to what we don't know. We don't know precisely what happened when you went behind that curtain; the only known witness, Sergeant Ray Fenton, committed suicide, which greatly impedes his ability to testify." He waited for Tom's reaction and saw both sadness and empathy. When he didn't respond, Jonathan continued. "We don't know why Eli's body was removed, and until recently, we had no idea why you left town only a few days after the murder."

"What do you mean 'until recently'?"

Jonathan drew out the letter and showed it to Tom without letting him touch it.

"Let me see it," Tom said. His face had contorted in anger.

"Why? You already know what it says."

"How did you get it?" he bit out.

Jonathan was beginning to boil over as well. "How do you think I got it? The woman you sent it to gave it to me in order to prove you didn't run."

"You can't use it," Tom said, desperation clouding his voice.

"I can and I will. I *must*. Because right now, the benefit of the doubt is not resting on your side of the ledger. You had motive, you had means, and you had opportunity. And even if you aren't smart enough to realize the peril you are in, the woman who loves you *is.* She knows you need all the help you can get, and if her name has to be dragged through the public mud to help your case, then she is willing to suffer through it. My God, man, do you know how special that is—how special *she* is?"

"Goddammit, of course I know!"

"Then don't let her sacrifice her good name for nothing." Jonathan paused to let it sink in. "It's a funny thing about a jury. The members are usually quite logical. They weigh the evidence and determine what makes sense to them. If the prosecution can tell a story that encompasses all of the facts and paints a picture of your guilt, that is more than tempting to them. It's not enough for the defense to say, 'Well, this, and that, and the other puzzle piece fits *my* story, but I have no answers for those other odd bits of information, so just forget about them and take my word that he is innocent.' No, it doesn't work that way."

Tom's head was in his hands, but when Jonathan finished speaking, he looked up, his eyes bleak. "What can I do?"

"You can tell me what went on behind that curtain, moment by moment—what you saw, what you thought, what you felt, what you did— so that I can make all the puzzle pieces fit. You can bloody well tell me *everything* and let me sort it out."

You've a right to change your mind about what's right and what's wrong in this world, and what's important and what's

not. Some things may be worth keepin' bottled up inside, but if they begin gnawin' at you, then maybe you ought to reconsider what to do with 'em.

Nana Ruth's words from so long ago flowed through Tom's brain. He'd kept what had happened to Eli to himself, in part because he'd made a promise to others, but in part because the answers weren't clear, even to him. His body had paid the price for his ambivalence. Maybe it was time to face it. All of it. And accept whatever came next.

He looked at his hand, which held steady.

"Katherine explained about your tremor, but I don't see it," Perris said. "Do you still have it?"

Tom looked up. "Not at the moment."

"Maybe that's a sign."

"Maybe it is." And Tom began to talk.

"Miss Hammersmith, Mr. Bean, I very much need your help."

It was early the next morning, a Saturday, and Jonathan had called an emergency meeting. His two law clerks now sat at his conference table, alert and ready to undertake any measures he deemed necessary to make the case for Tom Justice. No matter what happened in the days ahead, he really couldn't have asked for better professional colleagues.

"I am relieved to report that I now have the elements necessary to mount a spirited defense, however there are a couple of loose ends we must address." Jonathan handed Oliver the letter Tom had written to Katherine, along with the sheet of paper with Tom's handwriting. "Mr. Bean, I have arranged for you to deliver these documents to an English professor at your alma mater in Berkeley by the name of Dr. Taylor Burnside. He works on the side as a forensic document examiner and is by all accounts highly respected in that field. I would like you to have him examine these two documents and write up his opinion, which will undoubtedly be that they were written by the same person. I know for a fact that Tom wrote both documents, so his task should not be difficult. Wait for his report, please, and let him know he will be handsomely compensated. Contact me if there are any difficulties."

"With pleasure, sir," Bean said, grabbing his coat and hat from the hall tree before darting out the door.

"And what can I do for you?" Cordelia asked.

She was dressed fetchingly, and she looked at him with wide, intelligent eyes. A prurient image flashed through Jonathan's mind and within a few seconds, he experienced surprise, fascination, and shame. The thought was quickly squashed.

"Miss Hammersmith, I am hoping that you can be of help in approaching a female witness who may, if my hunch is right, be able to corroborate a bit of critical testimony." He examined his pocket watch. "We are not due at our destination for another hour or so. Let me buy you breakfast and I will explain what we are looking for."

Cordelia rose and began to put on her own coat. "I will pay for my own meal, thank you."

Jonathan smiled inwardly. Leave it to The Hammer. "As you wish."

After sausage and eggs at a nearby cafe (Jonathan was disappointed they'd run out of kippers, but made do), they caught a hansom cab and headed toward the Richmond District in the western part of the city. The widow Sarah Fenton Spencer lived with her son Ned on Cabrillo Street near Thirtieth Avenue in a little green bungalow with white shutters and a matching picket fence. A young boy, presumably Ned, played outside with a spotted black-and-white puppy. The boy once again wore the cape Bean had mentioned when he spoke of his initial interview with Sergeant Fenton's sister.

"Let me guess the puppy's name," Jonathan said by way of greeting.

"It's Sherlock!" Ned declared in the manner of all little boys who cannot wait to tell what they know.

"We're here to see your mama," Cordelia said, her voice friendly and maternal. "Is she home?"

Ned led them into the house. "Ma! Another man and lady to see you!" Mrs. Spencer paused in the act of shaking out the doilies that covered the arms of her sofa. She seemed to be in much better spirits than Bean had reported, quite possibly because of her improved financial circumstances.

"You're Mr. Perris, then?" she asked.

Jonathan, who had sent word by messenger of his visit, nodded. "And this is my associate, Miss Cordelia

Hammersmith. Thank you for taking the time to help us clear up a few matters, Mrs. Spencer. As you can imagine, the truth is very important to our client."

"Certainly. Please sit down and I'll fetch some coffee."

Both Jonathan and Cordelia chose the sofa, and as they waited, Jonathan thought about how best to approach the topic of Ray Fenton's final days. They must have been filled with pain and anger at what had befallen him, but had he said anything of import to the case?

Several minutes later, Mrs. Spencer brought out a tray carrying two earthenware mugs filled with black coffee and a small plate of butter cookies graced with dollops of jam. Jonathan and Cordelia each took one.

"I know this might be painful," Jonathan began, "but if you could, I'd like you to recall what your brother talked about when he had, shall we say, 'overindulged.'"

Mrs. Spencer sighed. "I don't recall precisely what he said. But I know it had something to do with fighting the wars, as if he was sad he'd done so much killing. He mentioned having two of something, two more than he needed. But then he mentioned bullets, not having enough of them, and wanting peace, of all things. I couldn't make heads or tails out of it."

"I know what he said, Mama."

Jonathan, Cordelia, and Mrs. Spencer turned as one. The boy was standing at the entrance to the parlor. He'd been listening.

"What do you mean, son?" Jonathan asked.

"I know what Uncle Ray said those last few nights. I wrote it down."

Jonathan and Cordelia looked at each other, eyebrows raised.

"You wrote it down?" Cordelia asked.

"Yes. I-I thought it might be code. Uncle Ray and I was working on a secret code." The boy's face started to crumble; tears beginning a journey down his ruddy cheeks. "But I don't think it was a code. Leastways I can't figure it out."

"Perhaps I can," Jonathan said slowly. "Do you still have the paper?"

"Yes," he said and turned abruptly toward the back of the house.

"You have an unusually observant son," Cordelia said to Mrs. Spencer.

The woman shook her head. "I had no idea he was writing things down like that. But it stands to reason—he sure does love those detective stories. I made that cape for his birthday last summer, and he still wears it nearly every day. And you saw what he named his new puppy. He and Ray used to talk about how they were going to be crime stoppers once Ray got out of the Army." She sniffed, dabbed at her eyes with a small lace handkerchief she'd pulled out of a pocket in her skirt. "I guess that won't happen now."

Cordelia, true to form, leaned forward to comfort the woman. "But your son may still pursue that line of work. It's an honorable field—takes a special sort to get it right."

At that point Ned came back in with a small notebook. He squeezed in between Jonathan and Cordelia and opened it. "Here." He pointed to an entry with a slightly grubby finger. "I wrote down the date: May 20, 1906. And Uncle Ray, when he was nearly asleep, kept mumbling, so I listened real hard and wrote down what he said. He said:

'Had to—too many—one to go—need a bulet! —make peese— no more—no more.'"

He closed the notebook. "That's what he said."

Jonathan took a deep breath and let it out. "Ned, this is a masterful piece of detective work. Your Uncle Ray would be very proud of you. Would you mind if I borrowed your notebook for a while? I promise to return it, but right now, it could help the doctor who worked with your uncle."

Little Ned's eyes grew wide. "You mean it's like a piece of evidence?"

Cordelia grinned and hugged the little boy. "That's exactly what it is. Sherlock Holmes has nothing on you!"

Back at the office, Jonathan explained to Cordelia how he planned to present the case to the jury. His clerk listened attentively, making suggestions that largely improved his approach. Around mid-afternoon he received a message that Oliver Bean had the analysis —its conclusions were as Jonathan expected—and would return on the evening ferry. Shortly thereafter he shooed Cordelia out to salvage the rest of her day.

She was invested in the case nearly as much as he, it seemed, and left only after much protest.

Now Jonathan sat alone with his notebook and a set of fountain pens with sharpened nibs. Armed with nothing but his logic and his reasoning and his gift for oratory, he began to build an argument that just might save Tom Justice from the gallows.

CHAPTER FORTY-TWO

Night before trial

"You got some visitors, doc," Mr. Kirby said. "We figured you could use some company the night before the big show."

Tom had been trying to read his well-thumbed copy of *The Lancet*—anything to take his mind off the next day's proceedings. Mr. Kirby stepped aside and Tom saw his mother and father standing outside his cell. She wore a dark-blue dress with a white collar; he wore a brown striped suit. It was their Sunday best, he knew. They had traveled from Nebraska to support him, to be there for him, no matter what happened. They claimed him without reservation, and his eyes welled up with a fierce mixture of shame and love.

"May I hug my son, Mr. Kirby?" his mother asked.

"Yes, ma'am, you surely may." The guard opened the cell door and took several discreet steps back.

Meg Justice murmured "Tommy" and gathered Tom close in an embrace that nearly unmanned him with its tenderness. Tom's father followed suit, and it was several moments before any of them could speak.

"This...I want you to know—"

"That you are innocent? Of course you are." His mother's tone, as always, was measured and calm. "We know it, your brothers know it, even your Aunt Trudy knows it."

My God, he hadn't even considered the impact on Eli's mother. She must be broken. "Are you sure?"

His mother nodded. "She couldn't face the trial, but she has faith in you. We all do."

Mr. Kirby brought an extra chair from down the hall so the three of them could sit and talk about other things. The farm was expanding thanks to adjacent tracts bought by Tom's younger brothers, both of whom were courting local gals. There would probably be at least one wedding in the fall. Tom's father ribbed him about once again missing the hard work of planting, and shared their biggest news: Old Nicodemus wasn't so old, after all. He'd gotten to Maribelle and she was due to deliver a colt by late summer.

The mild banter washed over Tom like a fresh spring shower. For those few moments he felt no grief, no remorse, no uncertainty; only affection and a longing for a simpler time.

All too soon Mr. Kirby reluctantly signaled the end of the visit; it hadn't officially been sanctioned by the court.

"Where are you staying?" Tom asked, realizing that

on top of everything else, he was causing them to spend their hard-earned dollars on a frivolous visit to the Golden City.

"The Firestones insisted we stay with them," his mother said. "Josephine is a lovely woman and she has already set up a time for me to speak with Mr. Durand about his peach tart recipe."

"I doubt his could hold a candle to yours, dearest," Tom's father said with affection. "You win every spring fair hands down."

His mother stood up, signaling her emotions only through the way she fussed with her reticule. "We'll see about that. In the meantime, we should let Tom rest up. He's got a big day tomorrow."

A big day. That was putting it mildly. Tom fought the lump in his throat as he said goodbye.

Just as his mother was about to disappear around the corner, he called her back. "Ma," he said, reaching for her hand through the bars in a way that made him feel ten years old. "You and Nana Ruth were always telling me things. Things about Eli."

"I know," she said.

"I just want you to know that I listened."

His mother's eyes filled then, and she paused before giving his hand a squeeze. "Dear boy," she whispered before turning once more down the hall.

"I'll see you," he called.

"Every day," she answered.

The building that housed the Superior Court of San Francisco had been destroyed in the earthquake, so the trial of Tom Justice took place in one of the larger meeting rooms of the Temple Beth Israel on Geary Street near Van Ness. It was an old, tired building, and the congregation had been on the verge of moving to a larger synagogue when the earthquake struck. The new temple was now rubble, but the original stood unfazed, serving its congregation and the needs of the public as well.

It seemed unreal to Tom that the process deciding his fate should be comprised of so much tedium. For the past several days, he'd sat next to Jonathan Perris and watched his life unfold through the perceptions of others. He'd listened as a parade of witnesses for both the prosecution and the defense offered testimony, and as sworn depositions and pieces of evidence were entered into the court record. He tried to put himself in the jury box: what would he think if all he knew was what had been presented? He'd probably be confused as hell.

The Assistant District Attorney, Mr. Everett Bigelow, was very good at his job, presenting his version of events as though it were a foregone conclusion that evil, in the form of Tom Justice, would not escape the long arm of the law. Despite everything that had happened, Tom still couldn't fathom why there were those who wanted to bring him down.

"I'm sorry to say you've been chosen as the sacrificial lamb," Jonathan explained during one of their last meetings. By now they were comfortable with each other, talking in the cell as if it were Tom's parlor. On this occasion, Mr. Kirby had even brought them cups of strong black tea, joking that it was Guinness in disguise. It was a warm afternoon, almost pleasant, given the normally chilly atmosphere, and Mr. Kirby's keys, heard far down the hall, seemed to jingle a happy tune. Odd to be having a political discussion in such surroundings, but there it was.

"What do you mean, a sacrificial lamb?" Tom asked.

"Just this. The earthquake and fire exposed a plethora of social and economic woes stemming from citywide graft and corruption. Everyone knows who the perpetrators are, but they're having a devil of a time calling them to task because there are so many connections that if one goes down, where would it all end? That is why Katherine wanted to hire an outsider to be your advocate." Jonathan took a sip of the somewhat bitter brew. "Yet the public is angry, as they should be, so someone needs to be held responsible. That's where you come in."

"But that is what puzzles me," Tom said. "Even if I'd done what they say I've done, it has nothing to do with the corruption you're talking about."

"Of course not, but like magicians, they are hoping to redirect the public's anger using smoke and mirrors. By acting self-righteous while convicting a murderer who flaunted human decency—that would be you—the District Attorney can let the truly morally bankrupt slide on by. It's sickening."

Tom got the feeling that Jonathan had been down this road before, but he didn't ask for details. What did it matter, anyway? The wheels of justice had been set in motion, and he would see the results soon enough. He realized with a sense of irony that he would miss "Barrister Perris." It was obvious the man held a torch for Katherine, yet he'd been nothing but professional throughout the entire process. If Tom was convicted, it would be through no fault of Jonathan's.

And if the worst happened, where would that leave Katherine? She had spent time with Perris while Tom was away; she obviously cared for him. Perhaps in time she could return the man's affection. They were both worthy individuals.

"About Katherine," Tom said, wanting somehow to come to an understanding about it. "If things shouldn't go well—"

Jonathan held up his hand. "Stop right there. You are going to spew some rubbish about how it's quite all right for Katherine and me to get together if you come to a sticky end. Surely you must know your woman enough by now to understand that she would cosh you on the head for such machinations."

Tom laughed. "You're right, I suppose."

Jonathan gathered his belongings. "I am most definitely right, more's the pity. Now try to relax, Dr. Justice, because we have a case to win."

Now, several days into the ordeal, it was time for both sides to sum it all up.

May the jury see through the smoke and mirrors, Tom thought. *May the better story prevail.*

CHAPTER FORTY-THREE

The day of summation

Unlike most dreary, fog-filled mornings in the Golden City, the day of summation dawned unusually clear and warm. As Tom watched the same twelve men trudged obediently into the improvised jury box, he wondered how many of them were anxious for it to be over. How many were confused? How many were hoping that either the prosecution or the defense would make such a compelling case that it would be easy to render a verdict?

Everett Bigelow stepped confidently up to the jurors, looking like an avenging angel in all but robes and wings. The room was quiet as he began to speak.

"Gentlemen of the jury, you've heard testimony from those who've known Tom Justice throughout his life and you've no doubt formed some kind of picture of him in your minds. Let me put some flesh on those bones, as it were, based on what we've all learned about this poor excuse for a man.

"We've learned that Tom was a big brute of a kid, the oldest of three boys, very athletic and very competitive. He hated to lose—and that's very important.

"He was also odd. Some might have called him 'cunning.' He would rather study about this and that than work around the farm. He was more than willing to take advantage of a young classmate just to satisfy his own lust. And as soon as he could leave his country roots, he did so. He left his family as fast as the train could carry him, not caring one whit about how they'd carry on without his help. Why, he rarely visited them during his stint in medical school. As far as Tom Justice was concerned, they were all a bunch of hicks.

"Now, Elijah Eugene Porter had a much harder life. He wasn't as big as his cousin, and being an only child, he was no doubt lonely. His father was a patriot and was often away fighting for our country. In fact, Eli's father was killed doing that very thing, God rest his soul.

"Eli just wanted to be friends with his cousin Tom, even wanted to strike up the old childhood friendship once more after college. But Tom didn't have time for him. Nor did he have time for his own college sweetheart, the lovely Carina, who felt so neglected that she gravitated toward Eli and fell in love with him. He was everything that Tom was not.

"But this didn't sit well with Tom. No, gentlemen, it did not. He was like a dog with a bone. Even though he didn't want Carina, it stuck in his craw that Eli had won her. Remember how competitive Tom is.

"Years go by, and Eli and his lovely bride are happy as clams. Eli works in the banking field and is promoted to an important position in San Francisco— in a brand new bank, no less! He's also got a son to carry on the family name. He has it all, gentlemen.

"But Tom? Tom hasn't been able to attract any decent woman. He's stuck working in a lousy clinic for heathens in Chinatown. His career is going nowhere, and he sees how his cousin has left him in the dust. He watches Eli with Carina and his jealousy grows. It burns inside him like a sick, green monster just waiting to bust out.

"The quake happens. It's a chaotic time. The fires burn out of control, destroying much of the city, and Fate gives Tom an opportunity for revenge.

"When Tom meets up with Eli at the Mechanics' Pavilion, Eli is completely at Tom's mercy. His spine has been crushed, and his son is dead. His beautiful wife has succumbed to her injuries as well. Tom is asked to come in and participate in the Pavilion Protocol, which we've learned was a two-step mercy killing for those who were too near death to evacuate. Tom's job is to administer a sedative that will put the patient out; a soldier will then fire the killing shot to spare the patient the horror of burning alive.

"Tom knows that Eli isn't anywhere near death, that he can easily be rescued. Eli begs Tom to save him, but Tom convinces the nearby medical staff that Eli is out of his head because of his grave injuries. Callously,

Tom administers a very strong dose of the sedative and the soldier, not trained in medical practices, assumes that Eli is close to death just like all the others. He administers the coup de grâce and the deed is done. Tom Justice has had his revenge, and no doubt assumed he'd get away with his heinous crime.

"But he miscalculated, gentlemen. He didn't figure on you twelve upstanding citizens standing up and saying 'Enough! We won't have murderers in our midst who disguise their revenge as mercy killing. We won't have it!'

"Members of the jury, you know what to do. Return a verdict of guilty to Thomas Aaron Justice for the willful murder of Elijah Eugene Porter."

Jonathan Perris approached the jury box slowly, shaking his head in disbelief as he walked.

"Gentlemen. I mean no disrespect to Mr. Bigelow, but I think we have a case in which an elderly person is hard of hearing but decides not to take advantage of an ear trumpet, or one of those new electric hearing devices, out of vanity, perhaps. Because the testimony I have heard bears no resemblance to what the good man just laid out before you. The man on trial, Tom Justice, isn't perfect by any means—he'd be the first to tell you that—but he is in no way the monster Mr. Bigelow has described.

"The testimony from those who know Tom point to a young man who, early on, knew he was meant to be a healer. He knew he had to work hard to become a doctor, and that required certain sacrifices of time and yes, relationships. But he succeeded, and it was only his sense of gratitude to his friend Jimmy Wong that inspired him to follow a different course than the one he'd originally intended.

"A man, if he's lucky, makes choices his whole life long: where he's going to live, how he's going to make a living, who he's going to marry. Sometimes those choices are easy, but sometimes they're quite difficult.

"I've gotten to know Tom Justice and I can tell you he's made hard choices and has had to live with the consequences of all of them. But they were the right choices, and that makes all the difference.

"Picture, if you will, a slightly different scenario on April eighteenth of last year..."

CHAPTER FORTY-FOUR

April 18, 1906
12:35 p.m.

"I t can't be my brother," Tom said to Nurse Elkins as they hurried to Critical Care. "I have two of them and I know they're both in Nebraska."

"He says you're his brother, that's all I know. Maybe he's delusional. He's definitely dangerous."

As they drew near, Tom could hear the man's agitated voice, and it sounded familiar. Dammit, it did. *God, please don't let it be him. Or her. Please.*

But God wasn't in a generous mood. Tom knew in his soul that the man calling himself Tom's brother was in fact his cousin Eli.

"He's my cousin," he whispered before taking a deep breath and moving the curtain aside. He noticed with a start that no other beds were occupied.

"Ah. You finally made it." Eli waved the pistol in his

hand. "I knew this would bring you." He was propped up in a bed, his upper torso wrapped in bandages. His face looked ravaged, as if he'd fought a war full of bloody, hand-to-hand combat in order to get where he was. And his eyes...his eyes were wild and gleaming like an opium addict suffering withdrawal. But it wasn't that, Tom knew. It was the look of someone who no longer gave a damn about his place in the world. And there could be only one reason for that.

"Where's Carina and Eli John?" Tom asked.

An armed soldier was standing near the bed along with the nurse and Dr. Milbank. All three of them looked rattled. Eli pointed the gun at them. "Leave us," he commanded.

Dr. Milbank looked at Tom. "Are you sure? Maybe we should—"

"I said leave us!" Eli pointed the gun at the older physician, the nurse, and the soldier in turn.

"It's all right," Tom said. "I can handle it."

As she left, Nurse Elkins put her hand on Tom's arm. "We're running out of time."

Tom nodded. Once they'd stepped to the other side of the partition, Eli beckoned him to come closer and lowered his voice. "You want to know who killed Carina and little Eli? They did."

"What? Killed them? How?"

"Like the others. The old doctor put them to sleep, and the sergeant—pop, pop through a pillow."

"That's absurd," Tom said. "Why—"

"Because we're the walking dead, brother, don't you know? All of us here. We're not going to make it anyway, and there's no time to ship our bodies out before the fire gets here. Gotta make room for the living."

Eli started to cry, the tears rolling freely down his cheeks. Tom tried to steady his own breathing, to move past the shock of Eli's ludicrous charge. Because it wasn't true, was it? It couldn't be.

"What happened, Eli?"

Eli wiped his face with his sleeve. "I fucked up is what happened, just like when we were kids. We were in bed, and when the first tremor came, little Eli John ran into our room. I should have gotten us out of there, but I didn't. I thought the worst was over, so we were all huddling together and a beam came down right on top of us." He shook his head slowly, as if even now he couldn't understand how it had all gone so wrong. "It crushed their heads, but they were still breathing, and it hit my back and I couldn't move my legs, but I started screaming and someone pulled us out and brought us here."

"But the gun..."

"Always near me. Like my pop always said. Had to protect what was mine." He bashed the pistol against his forehead; it left a gash that started to bleed. "*God.* But now I'm stuck and you gotta help me, Tom."

"Of course I'll help you. We'll get you out of here. We'll—"

"No! That's what *they* want to do. The doc says I'll never walk again, 'but other than that you'll be fine,' he said." Eli grabbed Tom with his free hand. "Fine? *Fine?* She was seven months along, Tom. We were sure it was a girl. We were going to call her Lillyanne. Eli John was going to be a big brother. We were ..." He stopped, shook himself as if to regain control, and focused his eyes on Tom. "She loved you, you know. But I won her fair and square, didn't I? Didn't I?"

Tom covered his cousin's hand with his own. "You did, Eli, and she loved you right back. I know she did." Tom could feel the tears rolling down his own cheeks now, thinking of Carina and what he hadn't been able to give her, grateful to Eli for what he had. And most of all, imagining what would never be again. "What can I do to help you, Eli?"

"Help me go to her."

"What are you talking about? You said she's gone."

"Yes, she's gone, and my little boy, too. So I want to be with them."

"I'm not following you."

"It's simple. You put me out and let them pull the trigger. They say they'll take me out of here and I'll recover, but I'll never recover from this...never. Would you?" He leaned back and put the gun to his own temple. "If you don't, I swear I'll shoot the place up 'til there's one bullet left and then I'll fucking do it myself."

He stared until Tom was forced to look away. God, what should he do?

From the other side of the curtain Tom heard the soldier say, "We got to handle this right now, sir. We're wasting time." His voice sounded quick and shaky, on the verge of panic.

Tom turned back to Eli.

"You owe me," Eli said.

"I owe you."

"Yes. For Sergeant. For what you could have done but didn't."

In a flash Tom was ten years old again and wondering if he'd done the right thing. *You save who you can save and you let the others go*, Nana Ruth said.

Fuck. All right. He'd sedate Eli, remove the gun, then transport him out. Eli would hate Tom's guts when he woke up, but at least he'd be alive. Maybe in time, he'd forgive him. That was the right thing to do, wasn't it? It would have to be.

"All right," Tom said.

"And you promise. Blood brothers, remember?"

"I promise."

Eli gazed at him then, with trust and all the love he had left, and Tom could see exactly what should happen. The table next to the bed held a bottle of ether and a rag that had clearly been used before. Tom doused it in the sweet-smelling drug and placed it over Eli's nose and mouth. "I'll see you later, cousin," he said quietly.

And Eli smiled. "I won this one, too."

When he had fallen unconscious, Tom took the pistol from his cousin's hand and put it carefully on the table next to the bed. Then he pulled the curtain aside and said, "He's out."

Nurse Elkins and Dr. Milbank had left; only the young sergeant remained. "You'd best go to the wagons with the others, sir," he said, wiping his brow and stepping back inside. By the time Tom realized what the soldier was going to do, he heard a muffled *pop*. "Wait!" Tom cried, but it was too late.

The soldier had put a pillow over Eli's sleeping face and used Eli's gun to put a bullet in his brain. The soldier looked at Tom sheepishly and held up the revolver. "I ran out of my own." Gingerly putting the gun back on the table, he added, almost to himself, "Just too many. Thank God we're at the end. I can't do no more."

"Wait ..." Tom could only repeat the feckless, feeble word, not knowing exactly what he should do next, paralyzed by what had just happened.

"You've got to get out *now*, sir," the soldier insisted. "I'll get rid of the body with the others."

Get rid of the body? No. No! Tom shook his head to clear it. "No, you'll take his body out of the building along with everybody else."

The sergeant looked at him as if he'd grown two heads. "He's gone now, sir. There's no need..."

And the rage over what he'd just witnessed—no, what he'd just taken part in— tripped into a clear, concise burst of anger. "No need? No fucking *need*? There's a need, all right. There's a need for me to see this man carried out of this building. I mean fucking right now!" He leaned over to pick up Eli's body and the soldier tried to stop him, but Tom flung the man's arm away and hefted his cousin into his arms. He could feel tears streaming down his cheeks. "God," he said.

The young soldier must have had a heart somewhere under that uniform because he stood with arms outstretched. "Sir," he said. "Lemme take him. I promise he'll go outside with the others. You can watch me. But we have to go."

Tom stared at him for a long moment and finally handed Eli over.

"Follow me, sir," the soldier said, and headed toward the Polk Street exit where he placed Eli's body in one of the last patient wagons to leave the Pavilion.

Tom watched it roll away in a daze, barely noticing Katherine come up and tap him on the shoulder.

"Tom, are you all right?" She was frowning. He must not look all right. "What happened back there?"

"Nothing," he said.

"What do you mean, nothing? The nurse had been visibly upset when she asked for your help."

"So I helped her and there's no more to it," he'd insisted. "Come on, we'd better go."

"Gentlemen," Jonathan continued, "I ask you to put yourself in the critical care ward of the Mechanics' Pavilion on that fateful day. Sergeant Fenton's words— nearly a deathbed confession, if you will—indicate that he fired the fatal shot that killed Eli Porter, under enormous stress himself, mistakenly thinking the victim was part of the Protocol, and using the victim's own gun because he had run out of military-issue bullets.

"Put yourselves now in the shoes of Tom Justice. A kind act has gone horribly wrong, and you, who are used to fixing things, are helpless to do anything about it. Powerless. It begins to weigh on you, and you can't even talk to anyone about it because you've promised not to, and you are a man who keeps his promises.

"But the emotion roiling inside of you has to go somewhere, and it escapes in the form of a tremor—a trembling hand that renders your skill and training as a surgeon completely useless. God can be cruel sometimes, can't he? Tell me, what would you do if that happened to you? I suspect you'd do what I'd do in those circumstances: I'd search high and low for answers, for a remedy, for some rational explanation that would help me get my life back.

"Tom Justice didn't run from what he'd done, because he did nothing wrong. His insistence that his cousin's body be spared incineration proves he did not consider the man's death a crime.

"Tom Justice didn't leave town to avoid consequences. His referral from Colonel Aldrich and his letter to Miss Firestone prove that well beyond a reasonable doubt.

"No. Tom Justice set off in search of understanding the horrific, untenable choice he'd had to make." Here Jonathan paused to look directly into the eyes of each juror. "And I believe each of you would have done the same. For those reasons, I believe you have no choice but to render a verdict of 'innocent' for Thomas Aaron Justice."

Had it been enough? Jonathan asked himself the same question each time he reached this stage of a trial. In this case, he had one more arrow in his quiver— unpredictable though it might be. Would it help or hurt

Tom's chances? Jonathan honestly didn't know, but his client was adamant about using it, so he felt honorbound to do so. He turned toward the judge.

"Your Honor, I had originally intended not to do this, but my client has asked it of me, and if the prosecution has no objections, I would like to call Thomas Aaron Justice to the stand."

Tom knew it was killing Jonathan to have him testify; most lawyers, he'd learned, will do almost anything to avoid putting their clients in the clutches of the prosecution.

"It's too risky," he'd told Tom during the midmorning break. "You never know what's going to happen up there while you're under oath, and you'll be subject to a cross-examination that we haven't prepared you for."

But Tom's gut told him that Jonathan's recitation of the events at the Pavilion might not be enough. The jury deserved to hear what had happened in Tom's own words. Or maybe Tom just wanted to get it off his chest.

"I need to do it, Jonathan," he'd said. It was the first time he'd called his lawyer by his first name.

"All right, then. Let's get this over with."

Sitting on the witness stand, swearing on a Bible that he'd tell the truth, the whole truth, and nothing but the truth, Tom prepared to do just that.

"Can you tell us, Dr. Justice, what happened at the

Mechanics' Pavilion on the afternoon of April eighteenth, 1906?" Jonathan asked. "Please be as specific as
your memory allows."

"Your summation covered the basic facts of the
situation: I was called to Critical Care by Nurse Elkins
because a man, who turned out to be my cousin Eli,
was yelling for me and waving a gun. As you related, he
indicated to me that he wanted to die alongside his
wife and son."

"And what was your reaction to that?"

"I was heartbroken that he had lost his family. I was
devastated that a woman I'd loved was gone. On top of
all the death and destruction I'd seen that day, it
seemed like too much to take in. I was stunned, but I
can tell you, at that moment, I was still thinking, 'The
right thing to do is subdue Eli, remove the gun he's
waving around, and then have him evacuated.' Because
the truth was, he *wasn't* close to death, not in a physical
sense, at least. He would never walk again, he would
never see his wife and child again, but he could live
a life."

Jonathan sent Tom a smile of encouragement,
which was probably going to be short-lived, based on
what he was about to say.

"However, while I was thinking that on *one* level,
I'm not sure that's what I really believed deep down
inside. I'm not certain, but I think that part of me
wanted to do whatever I could to ease his pain, even if
it meant helping him to die."

There was silence in the courtroom. Everyone

seemed to be poised, wondering if what they'd just heard was a confession. Maybe that's what it was.

"As Mr. Perris said, I've learned that some of the choices we have to make in life are monumentally hard. No, make that impossible. Like deciding which child to save because you can only save one of them. No matter what decision we make, it takes a toll, forcing us to let go of whatever hopes and dreams we might have had before we made the choice. Even if the path we take is the right one, it can still be full of pain."

He caught Katherine's gaze and held it. "I didn't realize it at the time, but now I know what it is to love openly, deeply, and completely, as Eli did. And I can tell you, I'd be just like him. I wouldn't want to go on without that love in my life."

He turned back to the jurors. "So, would I have consciously set my cousin up to be killed by another? The answer is no. Of course not. But did part of me wait a split second too long *on purpose* before telling the sergeant not to shoot? I don't know. Did some part of me want to give my cousin the relief he so desperately wanted? I hope to God part of me did. I hope I had, and still have that in me.

"As doctors, we pledge to do no harm. And I'm not convinced that forcing my cousin to live would have met that pledge. No matter what happens here today, I will always ponder that."

Tom sat back in his chair. He'd said what he wanted to say, and felt drained, as if all the poison he'd been keeping inside had been drawn out and his wound lay open to the healing light of day. His right hand rested.

Jonathan, realizing Tom had finished, let out a deep breath. "Your witness."

Mr. Bigelow stepped in front of the jury. To his credit, he didn't seem to enjoy doing what he was about to do. He kept it short and to the point. "So, are we to understand from your testimony that some part of you wanted to kill Mr. Eli Porter, even if it was to give him relief, as you put it?"

"Yes."

"No further questions, your honor."

Judge Rendell seemed subdued as well. "You may step down, sir."

Despite his speech about the difficulty in making choices, Tom found it infuriating that he had absolutely no control over the decision that would impact his life more than any other. After the jury left to deliberate, he could do nothing except return to the locked office he'd been assigned near the courtroom and ruminate on what might happen. Jonathan had put his hand on Tom's shoulder, exhorted him not to worry, and left, citing an important errand. As the guard assigned to Tom, Mr. Kirby sat on one side of the room, an unused office, reading the afternoon paper by the light of the window. Tom gazed outside. Would he ever walk the streets of the city again? He turned to Mr. Kirby; learning the latest news had to be better than brooding over his fate. "What's happening in the world?" he asked.

"Nothing. Nothing at all." Mr. Kirby carefully closed the paper, a sure sign that something was amiss. "Let me see it," Tom said.

Mr. Kirby shook his big head. "Trust me, you don't want to."

Tom extended his hand, and with a disgusted sigh, Mr. Kirby handed it over.

The headline provided the distraction Tom needed:

LOVE LETTER TO SOCIALITE PROVES MURDEROUS DOC PLANNED RETURN TO CRIME SCENE

Below the headline was a photograph of Katherine, caught unaware by a photographer as she entered Beth Israel Synagogue. Although Jonathan had spared her the witness stand, she had braved public censure and, like his parents, faithfully attended the trial every day. He wanted to howl.

"I told you it weren't a good idea to read it," Mr. Kirby said. "They'll print any bloody shite just to sell a few more papers. You can't believe anything you read nowadays."

There was a knock on the door, and the guard opened it to reveal Katherine herself. She stood alone, dressed in deep purple like a member of San Francisco royalty. Her hair was pinned into a tidy bun at the base of her pale neck, and Tom longed to reach over and let it free. She held a small piece of paper in one hand and her reticule in the other.

"Speak of the Devil," Mr. Kirby murmured.

"I've been given permission by the judge to spend a few minutes with the prisoner," she said, handing him the paper. "I hope you don't mind, Mr. Kirby."

He scanned the slip and tugged his forelock, a reflex from the old country. "Not at all, miss."

When the door shut, Tom had no words, but took Katherine in his arms and held her, feeling her warmth, inhaling the scent of lilac that belonged only to her. He wanted to stay there forever, simply absorbing her, but after a few moments, he pulled back so that he could see her eyes. They were glistening.

"I am so sorry for everything," he finally said. "I didn't want you to get dragged into this. But here you are, and you and your family have been so kind, to me"— his voice cracked—"and to my parents. I can't tell you how much—"

She put her fingers on his lips. "Do you love me?"

He smiled. She was so direct, this woman. He ran his right hand down the side of her cheek. "You know I do."

She took his hand and entwined their fingers, injecting some bravado into her words. "Well, I can't think of anything more important right now than that."

But there *was* something more important, and he had to say it. "Katherine, if the verdict should come back—"

"No. I will accept nothing less than your acquittal," she proclaimed.

That was the Katherine Firestone he'd fallen in love with. Stubborn. Brave. Fiercely loyal and loving.

She touched the front of his chest. "I have plans for

you, you see. You're going to make an honest woman out of me, and...and ..." Her eyes filled with tears and she stopped, then blinked and whispered, "Marry me now."

Heart pounding, throat closing, Tom was unable to respond. How stupid he'd been to worry about subjecting her to a trembling hand. That was nothing. Nothing! But this? To yoke her to a convicted murderer? He absolutely could not do that. Without him, she would have time. Time to make a decent choice. Someone good. Someone like Jonathan. He slowly shook his head.

She stepped back, smiling gamely and reaching into her reticule for a dainty handkerchief. "I figured as much, you stubborn man. We will just have to prevail, that's all."

He took her face in his hands and kissed her with all the desperation and love churning inside of him. "You will always prevail, Miss Katherine Madeline Mariah Firestone. You are magnificent."

After she left, Mr. Kirby returned and tried his best to cheer Tom up.

"I knew in my gut you weren't the type to do such a thing. The jury'll see it the same way. Just you wait."

Tom sent him half a smile. "All right, Mr. Kirby. I guess I'll wait."

An hour later, the wait was over.

What is taking them so bloody long? Jonathan tried not to

pace the private reception room the Firestones had commandeered at the Flood Building at Powell and Market. One of the few downtown office buildings to survive the previous year's disaster, the twelve-story marble edifice was beautiful, but cold—an imperious grand dame.

In truth, it hadn't been very long at all since deliberations had begun—hardly enough time for the jury to settle in and conduct an initial poll. But for those who had come to the Flood Building to await the verdict, time had crawled to a near standstill.

The Firestones, to their credit, tried their best to warm up the proceedings. Josephine, looking peaked but stalwart, glided serenely from guest to guest, making small talk and encouraging them to keep up their spirits with something to eat or drink. Judging by the repast on the sideboard, Bertrand had been instructed to feed an army.

Few took Mrs. Firestone up on her offer. Who has an appetite when the stakes are so high? Tom's mother and father were talking quietly with Dr. Sofie Herzog, and a group of Tom's colleagues from Saint Francis Hospital shared war stories over cups of coffee. Will Firestone, carrying his newborn, talked with his father, his wife Amanda, and Donaldina Cameron. Cordelia and Oliver conferred in the corner.

Katherine was absent. Her mother (who knew Judge Rendell's wife) had finagled a pass so that Katherine and Tom could spend a bit of time together before the verdict. Had he been in Tom's predicament, he would have wanted the same.

The Hammer marched over to him, Bean trailing behind. "The verdict is obvious," she fumed. "Why are they dawdling?"

Jonathan sent Bean a crooked smile before answering. It would never do to tell her he was feeling the same way. He was the experienced one, after all.

"It could mean a lot of things," he said. "They could be arguing a point, or sharing their feelings about the case, or even just killing time so that it appears as if they deliberated carefully and did their job."

"Well, whatever it is they're doing, they've done enough of it," she said. "I think—"

There was a knock on the door. A runner had arrived to tell them it was time to return to the courtroom. Slightly over two hours had passed.

Jonathan watched as Tom sought first his parents and then Katherine. Tom kept his eyes on her and she on him, as if to say, *Whatever happens, we are together.*

Once everyone was in place and Judge Rendell had called the proceedings to order, he asked the jury foreman to stand. "Has the jury reached a verdict?"

"We have, Your Honor." The foreman handed a paper to the court clerk, who turned it over to the judge. Rendell read it silently and returned it to the clerk, who read it aloud.

"In the matter of the state of California versus Thomas Aaron Justice, the jury finds the defendant... not guilty."

Because it was a murder case, the judge asked the jurors to be polled individually, and each member said the same two words. Afterward the judge addressed Tom. "In so far as the state has failed to prove its case against you, Dr. Justice, you are hereby cleared of the charges set forth in this proceeding. You, sir, are free to go. Gentlemen of the jury, thank you for your service. You are hereby dismissed." To put a period on it, he banged his gavel. "Court is adjourned," he added, and slammed the gavel once more for good measure.

Everyone in the courtroom seemed to pause. There were no loud cheers, nor were there raucous boos. It seemed as if everyone knew there were no winners here. After a moment someone started to clap, and many joined in, an acknowledgment that the best had been made of a terrible situation.

Jonathan stood and shook Tom's hand, then, in an uncharacteristic display of emotion, hugged both of his law clerks, who'd been sitting just behind him. As he let go of Oliver Bean, he glanced farther back and saw Anson Cotter, scowling. Jonathan couldn't suppress a chuckle.

Tom strode past them toward Katherine. She met him halfway and he swept her into his arms, kissing her passionately, public be damned. Jonathan looked at Cordelia, who was watching the display along with everyone else. She caught Jonathan's eye and shrugged, as if to say, *One cannot win them all*. He smiled and shrugged in return.

Tom was soon besieged by well-wishers, and

Jonathan saw Katherine step aside to let family and friends share their happiness.

A throng of reporters waited outside the temporary courthouse, firing questions. "Dr. Justice! How does it feel to be exonerated?" "Dr. Justice, what do you think about the Pavilion Protocol?" "What are your plans now that you've been found not guilty?"

Jonathan took on the role of palace guard as he ushered Katherine and Tom down the steps. Katherine's parents had gone ahead, but the rest of the family trailed behind.

None of them saw the gray-haired man in dirty overalls until he was within a few feet of them.

None of them realized he had a pistol until he shouted, "Murderer! You're all murderers! You took my son and daughter and let them burn!"

And Jonathan was a split-second too late to see that the man was aiming for Tom, that Katherine knew it, and that she'd stepped between them.

The bullet meant for Tom Justice entered her chest instead.

CHAPTER FORTY-FIVE

"We cannot use my technique on her, Tom."

They'd stanched the bleeding and transported Katherine to the nearby mansion of Dr. Redmond Payne. He, along with Walter Coffey, had been one of the founders of Saint Francis Hospital, and had donated his home as a temporary clinic until the new structure was built, even transforming an upstairs parlor into a fully equipped operating room.

Once there, the Firestones had acceded to Tom's frantic demand to let Dr. Sofie examine their daughter. Katherine now lay on a table, unconscious and breathing shallowly. After listening to her lungs and heart, Dr. Sofie had scrubbed up and gently traced the bullet's path with her finger as far as she was able. She wiped the blood off her hand and looked up at Tom, shaking her head.

He wasn't buying it. "What do you mean, you can't? You've done it dozens of times. We can rig up a table.

We can do this." Tom was pacing the room, glancing at Katherine's family lined up against the wall: Will and Mandy and Edward, all looking stunned. Josephine, steely and determined. *My god, Katherine had taken a bullet meant for him.* He could barely wrap his mind around it—he felt manic, as if his world were moving as fast as a train, as if he were running for his life in some sort of garish race.

"There's too much damage," Dr. Sofie said calmly. "By the look of its trajectory and what I hear in her chest, I think the bullet nicked her diaphragm and possibly her heart on its way to her lung. My guess is it's lodged in her upper left lobe. She needs a lobectomy as well as some internal repair. She must be opened up, and you must do it. You, Tom. I'll help you, but you need to do it."

"What? No. No! I can't. I haven't—I'm not—"

"Qualified? You damn well are." Dr. Sofie looked at Katherine's mother, as if willing her to understand and to lend support. Then she ordered Tom to hold up his hand. He just stared at her, so she repeated her command. Quietly. Firmly.

Breathing heavily, Tom did so. Despite his anxiety, his right hand showed no tremor. None.

"You see? You have the skill and the dexterity to do what needs to be done."

"There are other surgeons. They can—"

"They can try, and if they fail, and Katherine dies, you will have to live, knowing that you didn't do *everything* that you could do."

"But if *I* fail," he whispered.

Josephine Firestone stepped up to Tom. Physically she looked small and vulnerable, but power emanated from her. "If Katherine were awake, she'd say you were the best there is." She squeezed his arm. "We could have anyone operate on her, but we want the best."

The best. Nana Ruth's admonition so many years ago came flooding back to him. *There's gonna be times you don't have every lick of information, so you got to act on what you do know and do your best.* If it were anybody else, Tom would step up without hesitation and perform the surgery because he knew he could. He had performed similar procedures before with great success.

But this was Katherine. So much more was at stake —not just her life, but his own. He'd told the truth in the courtroom: life without her was unthinkable.

Yet Dr. Sofie was right: how could he let anyone else do it and risk knowing he'd failed her?

Now you got yourself an opportunity to make things better. Tom could take a chance with someone else or go with the person he knew could do what needed to be done.

It was time to make the choice and pay whatever price needed to be paid. He paused and looked at the sea of expectant faces. Then he turned to Dr. Sofie. "Let's prep for surgery."

Dr. Payne was willing to serve as anesthetist for the

procedure, in order to keep Dr. Sofie free to assist Tom.

"Be careful," Tom couldn't help but warn him. "Her breathing is already compromised."

"You can count on me, son." Dr. Payne began to administer the proper combination of ether and chloroform through the face mask he'd placed over Katherine's nose and mouth.

Having scrubbed within an inch of his life and donned a surgical mask, Tom took a deep breath and paused. What he saw while looking at her exposed chest caused him to falter. He looked at Dr. Sofie with alarm. "My God, I think she's—"

Dr. Sofie's reply was measured. "I know. By the looks of her, I'd say about ten to twelve weeks along, give or take. You would know better than me. But you can't think about that now. You've got other concerns. She's a patient like any other and you are going to perform surgery to repair a wound. That is all."

He swallowed hard. No turning back now. She— they—were counting on him.

It's far more important for a woman you care about to be alive than to be intact. Now he felt the absolute truth of Dr. Halsted's words.

He looked at Dr. Sofie one more time and nodded. Then he made the first cut, eight inches long.

Blood spurted and caught him by surprise. Dr. Sofie wiped it away and waited. A long moment passed and something inside of Tom clicked. He wasn't a surgeon. He was a healer with surgical skills—skills that were needed right now. Right this minute.

He began.

"Breaking the sternum," he murmured. He cracked the bone and retracted both sides; the bullet had indeed nicked the diaphragm. Miraculously, the heart had been torn only slightly as the slug sped past to the left upper lobe, which was shattered beyond repair. As he removed it, he could feel the shape of the bullet lodged inside. He extracted it from the pulpy mass to make sure it was intact. "I will make you a ring out of that one," Dr. Sofie said.

Tom ligated all the leaking blood vessels, examined the area for further damage, and began the process of backing out, repairing the torn muscles of the heart and the diaphragm with the tiniest of stitches and then proceeding downward following the path of the bullet. Satisfied that he had caught all affected areas, he checked once more for bleeding before setting the sternum and closing up both the entry wound and his initial incision. She had needed blood, but that had worked out, too.

Everyone was quiet as he stepped back.

"Masterfully done," Dr. Payne said. He decreased the ether and eventually took the mask away from Katherine's face. Tom went to her and leaned over to stroke her hair and kiss her. "You're my strong girl," he whispered. "You're coming back to me."

Dr. Sofie finished dressing the wound, stepped back and pulled off her surgical gloves. "Now we wait," she said.

Afterward, you say a little prayer hopin' things turned out the way God meant them to. That's the way it works.

"No," Tom said. "Now I pray."

The fever set in twelve hours later. It was almost guaranteed in cases like Katherine's, but that didn't make it any less worrisome. Tom knew that infection was the enemy, and despite all that he and Dr. Sofie had done to prevent it, he could see that some inflammation was taking place. Katherine didn't regain consciousness, but grew hot, restless. She mumbled about Tom and the baby and kept telling them to wait for her. She began to thrash, threatening to break her stitches. It was obvious she was in pain, and it was killing him to watch her.

Late on the second evening following the surgery, Tom and Dr. Sofie removed the bandages to check on Katherine's progress, only to reveal red streaks emanating from her incision. His heart lodged in his throat. "We need to do something," he said.

The irascible lady doctor was subdued. She knew all too well what Katherine faced; it was why she'd avoided such surgeries except when absolutely necessary. "What do you propose?"

"When I was young," Tom said, "I cut myself badly and my grandmother lathered my wound generously with honey. I've heard garlic works well in tandem with it."

Dr. Sofie nodded. She, more than anyone else, would understand his need to try something, anything. "Then by all means, let's make a salve."

They made their way to the kitchen of the makeshift hospital and located the ingredients. For several minutes both were distracted by creating the strange paste.

"Someday there will be a pill and none of this will be needed," she said.

"Maybe. But until then..."

"Until then we try everything."

They brought the paste back to Katherine's bedside. Thankfully she was resting. Tom removed the dressing once more and gently, ever so gently, spread the mixture over the incision before covering it up again. Katherine stirred fitfully as he worked but didn't awaken.

They talked in the hall. "I don't know what else to do," he said, overcome with the kind of weariness he hadn't felt in years. "She risked her life for me. I would settle for shaky hands the rest of my life if it would only bring her back."

"You have done everything you could," Dr. Sofie assured him. "And that is what you needed to do. I am proud to know you, Dr. Tom Justice. Now go say good-night to Katherine and try to get some sleep."

Tom pulled a wooden chair as close as possible to Katherine's bed and sat facing her, his right hand holding hers. Hers was slender and pale, the blue veins showing through—a sign of life, he told himself. His own hand rested tranquilly. It had done all he'd asked of it, all it had been trained to do. Dr. Sofie was right: there would be no second-guessing, no "should haves" or "could haves."

He thought of what the future might hold. Amazingly, Dr. Halsted had contacted him the day before to congratulate him and reiterate his desire to talk to Tom about coming back to Johns Hopkins. And there was Chinatown. Despite the odds stacked against them, the leaders of that community had prevailed and a new neighborhood was rising, better than before.

But an idea had been rambling around in Tom's head for some time now, an idea that said: why not combine the best of everything in a new kind of clinic? Muldoon had been on the right track with his "back to nature" approach. So much of what Tom had learned from his grandmother was useful, and often, that's all that many patients needed. But prescribing the "tried and true" didn't mean one had to discount all that modern medicine, especially surgery, had to offer.

He fell asleep that way, dreaming of a happier time, a fanciful meld of memory and hope. He and Eli were running through a field of sunflowers on a hazy summer day, approaching a cliff that he knew without question he could fly across. He was ready to leap into nothingness when he felt a gentle tug bringing him back down to earth.

She was gazing at him with those radiant blue eyes set in alabaster. She looked weary, as if she'd just arrived from a long, arduous journey. She didn't apologize for not telling him beforehand; she simply got to the heart of the matter. "Am I still going to be a mother?"

"Yes," he said.

She frowned. "This time around, I mean?"

He interlaced their fingers, stalling for time. "You haven't miscarried. But sweetheart, you lost a lot of blood. There may be complications down the road."

"Whatever happens, she will be fine."

He quirked his lips. "She?"

Katherine's eyes were already beginning to droop. "Of course. You're going to have two opinionated females to deal with now."

"Does this mean you're going to make an honest man out of me?"

He didn't think she'd heard him, but after a moment, her eyes still closed, she murmured, "You'll have to wait and see."

So he waited.

Sometimes the days that change your life forever play no tricks on you at all. They are direct and honest and sear themselves upon your heart with no pretense or subterfuge.

Sometimes the decisions you make are simple, too. Easy as peach pie. As vital and as nourishing as taking your next deep breath.

Tom waited as Katherine slept and healed, nurturing the daughter or son inside of her until she grew large enough for the world to know they were creating new life. Then, on a lovely summer day, near a field filled with sunflowers and lilacs, he stood with her in front of family and friends and a man of the cloth, and promised to love her until death parted them, and even beyond that.

And she did the same.

THANK YOU

Thank you so much for reading *The Price of Compassion*. Readers like you are powerful, and you would be doing me a great favor by posting an objective review on Amazon, Goodreads, or other platforms based on the e-reader you use. In today's publishing world, those reviews are "golden" to authors like me.

Sharing your thoughts with others (including me!) on social media would be wonderful as well. You'll find me on **Twitter, Facebook, and Pinterest.** And don't forget to stop by my website (abmichaels.com) to learn more about my work. There you can join my Readers Group and receive a welcome gift along with monthly updates and special content.

OTHER TITLES BY A.B. MICHAELS

The Price of Compassion is Book Four of "The Golden City," a series of historical novels set in nineteenth and early twentieth century San Francisco during the "Gilded Age." It was a time of great upheaval and boundless enthusiasm, when scientific discoveries began to erode centuries of tradition; when wealthy individuals walked the same streets as reviled immigrants, and natural disasters leveled the playing field. From gold miners and artists to shipping barons and railway surgeons, you'll meet unforgettable characters, both fictional and historical, who must negotiate the raucous world in which they live. Other novels in the series include **The Art of Love, The Depth of Beauty, The Promise,** and *Josephine's Daughter (2019)*. Summaries of those novels are listed below.

The contemporary romantic suspense series "**Sinner's Grove**" follows a number of descendants from The Golden City as they work to re-open the famous artists' retreat north of San Francisco known as "The Grove." Brief excerpts from the first two novels in that series, **Sinner's Grove** and **The Lair**, can be found below.

Each of the novels is a stand-alone read.

Thanks again for reading—see you soon.

THE ART OF LOVE
(Book One of "The Golden City" series)

At the end of the Gilded Age, the "Golden City" of San Francisco offers everything a man could want — except the answers August Wolff desperately needs to find.

After digging a fortune in gold from the frozen fields of the Klondike, Gus head south, hoping to start over and put the baffling disappearance of his wife and daughter behind him. The turn of the century brings him even more success, but the distractions of a city some call the new Sodom and Gomorrah can't fill the gaping hole in his life.

Amelia Starling is a wildly talented artist caught in the straightjacket of Old New York society. Making a heart-breaking decision, she moves to San Francisco to further her career, all while living with the pain of a sacrifice no woman should ever have to make.

Brought together by the city's flourishing art scene, Gus and Lia forge a rare connection. But the past, shrouded in mystery, prevents the two of them from moving forward as one. Unwilling to face society's scorn, Lia leaves the city and vows to begin again in Europe.

Gus can't bear to let her go, but unless he can set his ghosts to rest, he and Lia have no chance for happiness at all.

THE DEPTH OF BEAUTY
(Book Two of "The Golden City" series)

In San Francisco's Chinatown circa 1903, slavery, polygamy and rampant prostitution are thriving – just blocks away from the Golden City's elite.

Wealthy and well-connected, Will Firestone enters the mysterious enclave with an eye toward expanding his shipping business. What he finds there will astonish him. With the help of an exotic young widow and a gifted teenage orphan, he embarks on a journey of self-discovery, where lust, love and tragedy will change his life forever.

The Depth of Beauty was nominated for a RITA award in 2017 in the category of general fiction.

THE PROMISE
(Book Three of "The Golden City" series)

April 18, 1906. A massive earthquake has decimated much of San Francisco, leaving thousands without food, water or shelter. Patrolling the streets to help those in need, Army corporal Ben Tilson meets a young woman named Charlotte who touches his heart, making him think of a future with her in it. In the heat of the moment he makes a promise to her family that even he realizes will be almost impossible to keep.

Because on the heels of the earthquake, a much worse disaster looms: a fire that threatens to consume everything and everyone in its path.

It will take everything Ben's got to make it back to the woman he's fallen for—and even that may not be enough.

JOSEPHINE'S DAUGHTER
(Book Five of "The Golden City" series)
(Available 2019)

In the late nineteenth century, wealthy and head-strong Kit Firestone chafes under the strictures of The Golden City's high society, especially the interference of her charming but overbearing mother, Josephine. Kit's secret rebellion leads to potentially catastrophic results and keeps her from finding happiness.

When her brother nearly dies from a dangerous infection, Kit defied convention and becomes a working nurse. Through her troubled romance with a young doctor and a series of dramatic events, including a natural disaster and her mother's own critical illness, Kit begins to understand who her mother truly is and what their relationship is all about. She may not get the chance to appreciate their bond, however, because through no fault of her own, a madman has Kit in his crosshairs.

Set amidst the backdrop of the Gilded Age and beyond, Josephine's Daughter explores many of the social and medical issues facing women of that era— issues that resonate today. Independence, reproductive rights, birth control, childbirth and parenting are all put to the test in *Josephine's Daughter*.

SINNER'S GROVE
(Book One of the "Sinner's Grove" series)

A startling discovery when she was fourteen left San Francisco artist Jenna Bergstrom estranged from her family; unforeseen tragedy only sharpened her loneliness. But now her ailing grandfather needs her expertise to re-open the family's once-famous artists' retreat on the California coast. The problem? She'll have to face architect Brit Maguire, the ex-love of her life.

Seven years ago, Maguire spent a magical time with the woman of his dreams, only to have her disappear from his life completely. Now she's back, helping with the biggest historic renovation of Brit's career. No matter how deep his feelings still run, Brit can't afford the distraction of Jenna Bergstrom, because something is going terribly wrong with the project at Sinner's Grove.

An excerpt from *Sinner's Grove:*

"What the hell?!" Brit turned around when a second explosion followed on the heels of the first. He immediately wrapped his arms protectively around Jenna.

"My God, was that a bomb?" she cried. She couldn't

believe what was happening. She quickly dropped her leg and straightened her dress, fear turning her passion into panic.

"I don't know," Brit said grimly. "Let's find out."

They ran out of the building, passing several workers and a few investors rushing in different directions with terror-stricken faces. The street lights had not gone out, and Jenna saw her brother across the lawn.

"Jason! Do you know what happened?"

"It looks like the equipment barn blew up!" he called as he ran in that direction. "I just called 911."

"Anybody hurt?" Brit yelled.

"Don't know yet!"

Brit took Jenna by the shoulders. "Go back to the Great House. I'll check it out."

"Not in your life," she shot back. "I'm staying with you."

Brit set his jaw and started running toward the maintenance area. Thankful she'd worn flats to the presentation, Jenna easily kept up with him. As they crested the hill, Brit stopped short and stuck out his arm to keep Jenna from running past him.

"Too dangerous!" he yelled.

She grabbed onto his arm to stop her momentum. *Oh my God— this is hell on earth.* The front two-thirds of the huge barn was a fireball shooting flames a hundred feet into the sky. And the heat was so intense, she felt as if even her blood was boiling. Smoke was everywhere, sucking the oxygen from the air. Men were shouting and running back and forth, trying to be heard over the roar of the inferno. *Please keep Jason and Da away from this*, Jenna prayed, her breathing harsh and labored.

"How's it looking, Jack?" Brit called out to the man he'd pegged to help manage the crew.

"Not good." Jack, looking disgusted, tossed a hose on the ground where it joined several others coiled haphazardly in the gloom like somnolent snakes. "Whoever did this cut the hoses. We can't get any pressure, so we're down to a bucket brigade until the fire trucks get here."

"Everybody accounted for?"

"I think so, but it's pretty crazy right now. Maybe we oughta do a head count."

Brit looked around in frustration. In the distance sirens could be heard. "Good idea," he said. "Maybe—"

"Mr. Maguire! Mr. Maguire!" Parker Bishop and Kyle Summers ran up to the group.

"What's wrong?" Jenna cried.

"I think...I think—" Parker seemed to be particularly anxious.

"Spit it out, man," Brit barked.

Jenna glared at Brit. "Give him a chance to calm down!"

"We think...we think maybe that guy Lester's still in the building!" Kyle said.

"How do you know?" Brit asked sharply.

"We were on litter patrol down around the lower bungalows. Parker said he saw him go inside."

"How could you see in the dark?" Jenna asked.

"I think it was him, but I don't know for sure," Parker hedged.

"The light wasn't that good, but we saw *somebody* go inside and close the slider. You can tell when that big sucker closes," Kyle explained. "I didn't think much of it and kept working."

"Me too," Parker said.

"No, you were on the phone, dude, remember?"

Parker nodded. "Yeah, that's right. My dad called. And then, *Kablam*! So we started running back here."

Brit didn't waste a second. "Anybody seen Lester?" he yelled to the members of the makeshift fire crew.

A chorus of "no's" came back.

"Jack, you got a master key on you?" he called out.

The man shook his head.

"Get one!" Brit yelled. He then headed toward the back of the barn.

"Where do you think you're going?" Jenna cried, grabbing his arm.

"If he's in there, there's a chance he's in the back and can't get out," Brit said. "He may not be able to get to the side door. We've got to get it open and help him out."

"But you're not going in after him, right?"

Brit paused and looked at Jenna, running his fingertip down the side of her cheek. "Don't worry." With that he took off, glancing back once before he turned the corner of the building.

Speechless, Jenna watched his retreating figure as if in slow motion. She noticed vaguely that Kyle and

Parker had walked up on either side of her. Kyle put his arm around her shoulders.

"It's all right," he said soothingly. "We're here."

Jenna turned and looked up at the large, muscular young man. He had the same glittery look he'd had the last day of school. Then she looked at Parker. He was staring at Kyle and his eyes burned fiercely, just as they had that same day. Fear, slippery and cold, slid over her.

"We need to help Brit," she said neutrally, hoping her voice wouldn't betray the anxiety threatening to overtake her.

By the time she worked her way safely around to the side of the burning barn, several burly workmen were in the process of battering the side door with what looked like a large fence post. The door was already starting to buckle from the heat. When it finally gave way, smoke billowed out and Jenna watched in horror as Brit tore off his jacket, tie and shirt, soaking the latter in a nearby bucket and wrapping it around his nose and mouth.

"Don't go in there—please!" Jenna cried.

Brit looked at her briefly, his eyes communicating what words could not. Then he disappeared inside the carnage. Moments later another deafening explosion ripped apart the air.

"Nooooo!" Jenna screamed. Tears streaming down her face, arms wrapped around herself to keep from falling apart, Jenna stared in shock at the burning, crumbling building, her only words a mantra-like "please God, please God, please God."

She felt someone—Parker, perhaps—urge her back from the heat of the fire, but she couldn't seem to move. Her entire focus was on the jagged hole into which Brit had run. She couldn't believe he was gone. Wouldn't believe it. He was going to walk out again. Any second now. Any second. Any second.

THE LAIR
(Book Two of the "Sinner's Grove" series)

After her father dies in a boating incident, innkeeper Daniela Dunn must travel from Northern California's Sinner's Grove back to Verona, Italy and her childhood home, an estate called the Panther's Lair. It's a mansion full of frightful memories and deeply buried secrets, where appearances are deceiving and the price of honesty is death. As Dani is drawn further into her family's intrigues, she has an unlikely ally in handsome Marin County investigator Gabriele de la Torre. He says he's come along merely to support her, but his actions show he has an agenda all his own.

Gabe de la Torre needs to settle old family debts before starting fresh with the woman he feels could be The One. But once Dani finds out whom he's beholden to, all bets might be off. When a mystery woman reveals that Dani's father may have been murdered, the stakes rise dramatically and Gabe realizes they're now players in a dangerous game. Protecting Dani becomes his top priority, even as she strives to figure out whom she can trust: her relatives, Gabe, or even herself.

An excerpt from *The Lair*:

"Nothing like a wide awake drunk," Gabe muttered an hour later. They'd gotten back to La Tana and as usual Fausta had grudgingly let them in. "Hey, you can always give us a key," he'd joked, but his aunt had simply turned around and gone back to her room.

Once in their suite, Dani had been asleep on her feet, which were a little unsteady at best, so he'd pointed her in the direction of her bedroom and reluctantly bid her good night.

God she was beautiful. So elegant, so feminine, even though she didn't put on airs *at all*. He'd spent the entire evening fighting the impulse to touch her everywhere, even in places that demanded privacy at the very least. He'd known instinctively that she'd get along great with Marco and Gina, and she hadn't disappointed him. Man, she was driving him crazy. He heaved a sigh. Both tired and wired, he couldn't tell which was more to blame, the alcohol or the stress of keeping his desire in check.

He reflexively reached into the small refrigerator for a beer before he realized he was already half pickled, so he opted for water instead. Unscrewing the cap, he drank half the bottle while pulling his shirt out of his slacks. To keep his libido in check he decided to focus on something decidedly unsexy. Reaching for the jacket he'd tossed on the back of the sofa, he pulled out the report that Marco had given him earlier that evening.

"I think we're on to something," Marco had told him quietly. "We found a match."

He was just beginning to scan the document when the bedroom door opened and Dani appeared. Her hair was tousled and she walked a bit uncertainly, as if she were slogging through mud in high heels, even though she was barefoot. She wore an ivory-colored cover-up of some kind and she looked nervous. "I'm ready," she said.

He looked at her quizzically. "Ready for what, bella?"

"For us...you know." He didn't have a chance to reply before she tottered up to him and threw her slender arms around his neck, locking her lips with his.

After his initial shock, Gabe took a moment to enjoy the feel of Dani's curves against him. Jesus, after all that booze his body still reacted immediately, hardening in response to her softness. She felt so damn good—like falling into the most luxurious bed when you've been sleeping on the floor all your life. He smiled inwardly at her inexperienced but earnest attempt at seduction and cursed his inner cop—the prig who wouldn't let him take advantage of her while she was intoxicated. Reluctantly he took her by the upper arms and peeled her away from his body. "Uh, sweetheart, I don't think this is a good thing to be doing..."

"What?" she asked softly but defensively. "Don't I measure up to your other women friends? Don't I? Just a little?" She stepped back and before he could stop her she dropped the cover-up, revealing a perfect—and perfectly naked—female form encased in a 5 foot two inch frame. She was biting her full lower lip, practically screaming for his approval.

An image flashed before him of Dani pregnant. She was ripe and luscious—the epitome of Woman. Instead of cooling him off, the thought of her big with child —*his* child—only made him hotter and made what he had to do all the more difficult. He looked at her a long time, so long that he could see uncertainty, followed by embarrassment, overtake her. He reached down and picked up the wrap, putting it around her shoulders.

"I...I'm sorry," she mumbled. "I thought ..." She turned to go, but Gabe took her shoulders and turned her back toward him.

"If you think for one second that I don't want to bury myself in you right now, you are sadly mistaken," he said roughly. "When you and I make love, I am going to be all over you. You are going to feel me everywhere and know when I've taken you higher than you've ever been before." He tore himself away and covered her back up. "And the next morning, you're going to remember everything I did to you and want me to do it all over again. Count on it. Now go to bed."

"But—"

"Please," he said firmly, turning her around and practically pushing her back into the bedroom. It took several minutes after her door shut for Gabe's upper brain to start functioning again. "Keep your eye on the prize," he repeated like a mantra. "Keep your eye on the prize." The prize, in this case, was a Dani who felt no regrets about whatever physical gymnastics they might partake in together. He'd waited this long for the timing to be right; he could wait a little longer, even though it was damn near going to kill him.

THE JADE HUNTERS
(*Book Three of the "Sinner's Grove" series*)
(*Available 2019*)

Award-winning jewelry designer Regina Firestone is proud to exhibit her famous grandmother's multi-million dollar "bauble" collection at the grand re-opening of The Grove Center for American Art. The fact that she's considering modeling the jewels in the nude like her grandmother did infuriates photographer Walker Banks, an owner of The Grove who's in charge of the exhibit. Their spat takes a back seat, however, when Reggie discovers that one of the most compelling pieces in the collection is not at all what it seems. Tracking down the truth will take the couple into the dark heart of a quest that's lasted more than a century – one in which destroying human lives—including Reggie's and Walker's—means nothing in the pursuit of a twisted sense of justice.

ABOUT THE AUTHOR

A native of California, A.B. Michaels holds masters' degrees in history (UCLA) and broadcasting (San Francisco State University). After working for many years as a promotional writer and editor, she decided it was time to focus on writing the kind of fiction she likes to read.

A.B. and her husband currently live in Boise, Idaho. On any given day you might see them on the golf course or bocce court, or walking their four-legged "sons" along the Boise River. More than likely, however, you'll find her hard at work on her next book.

https://abmichaels.com

CPSIA information can be obtained
at www.ICGtesting.com
Printed in the USA
LVHW052307200319
611369LV00001B/106/P